I0611249

Books by John Patrick

Non-Fiction
A Charmed Life: Vince Cobretti
Lowe Down: Tim Lowe
The Best of the Superstars 1990
The Best of the Superstars 1991
The Best of the Superstars 1992
The Best of the Superstars 1993
The Best of the Superstars 1994
The Best of the Superstars 1995
The Best of the Superstars 1996
The Best of the Superstars 1997
The Best of the Superstars 1998
The Best of the Superstars 1999
The Best of the Superstars 2000
The Best of the Superstars 2001
The Best of the Superstars 2002
What Went Wrong?
When Boys Are Bad
& Sex Goes Wrong
Legends: The World's Sexiest
Men, Vols. 1 & 2
Legends (Third Edition)
Tarnished Angels (Ed.)

Fiction
Billy & David: A Deadly Minuet
The Bigger They Are...
The Younger They Are...
The Harder They Are...
Angel: The Complete Trilogy
Angel II: Stacy's Story
Angel: The Complete Quintet
A Natural Beauty (Editor)
The Kid (with Joe Leslie)
HUGE (Editor)
Strip: He Danced Alone
The Boys of Spring
Big Boys/Little Lies (Editor)
Boy Toy
Seduced (Editor)
Insatiable/Unforgettable (Editor)

Heartthrobs
Runaways/Kid Stuff (Editor)
Dangerous Boys/Rent Boys (Editor)
Barely Legal (Editor)
Country Boys/City Boys (Editor)
My Three Boys (Editor)
Mad About the Boys (Editor)
Lover Boys (Editor)
In the BOY ZONE (Editor)
Boys of the Night (Editor)
Secret Passions (Editor)
Beautiful Boys (Editor)
Juniors (Editor)
Come Again (Editor)
Smooth 'N' Sassy (Editor)
Intimate Strangers (Editor)
Naughty By Nature (Editor)
Dreamboys (Editor)
Raw Recruits (Editor)
Play Hard, Score Big (Editor)
Sweet Temptations (Editor)
Pleasures of the Flesh (Editor)
Juniors 2 (Editor)
Fresh 'N' Frisky (Editor)
Taboo! (Editor)
Heatwave (Editor)
Boys on the Prowl (Editor)
Huge 2 (Editor)
Fever! (Editor)
Any Boy Can (Editor)
Virgins No More (Editor)
Seduced 2 (Co-Editor)
Wild 'N' Willing (Co-Editor)

Worldwide Praise for the Erotica of John Patrick and STARbooks!

"John Patrick is a modern master of the genre! ...This writing is what being brave is all about. It brings up the kinds of things that are usually kept so private that you think you're the only one who experiences them."
– Gay Times, London

"Barely Legal' is a great potpourri ... and the cover boy is gorgeous!"
– Ian Young, Torso magazine

"Collections of stories have become increasingly popular in the past couple of years: leading the way is the prolific and consistently entertaining John Patrick who, under the STARbooks imprint, has edited fifteen or more collections of erotica written another dozen books himself and published several handfuls more by other authors. ... Burly (500-plus pages) anthologies of erotic writing, the perfect bedside companions..."
– Richard Labonte, Q Magazine

"A huge collection of highly erotic, short and steamy one-handed tales. Perfect bedtime reading, though you probably won't get much sleep! Prepare to be shocked! Highly recommended!"
– Vulcan magazine

"Tantalizing tales of porn stars, hustlers, and other lost boys...John Patrick set the pace with 'Angel!"
– The Weekly News, Miami

"...Some readers may find some of the scenes too explicit; others will enjoy the sudden, graphic sensations each page brings. Each of these romans clef is written with sustained intensity. 'Angel' offers a strange, often poetic vision of sexual obsession. I recommend it to you."
– Nouveau Midwest

"Angel' is mouthwatering and enticing..."
– Rouge Magazine, London

"Superstars' is a fast read...if you'd like a nice round of fireworks before the Fourth, read this aloud at your next church picnic..."
– Welcomat, Philadelphia

"Yes, it's another of those bumper collections of steamy tales from STARbooks. The rate at which John Patrick turns out these compilations you'd be forgiven for thinking it's not exactly quality prose. Wrong. These stories are well-crafted, but not over-written, and have a profound effect in the pants department."
– Vulcan magazine, London

"For those who share Mr. Patrick's appreciation for cute young men, 'Legends' is a delightfully readable book...I am a fan of John Patrick's...His writing is clear and straight-forward and should be better known in the gay community."
– Ian Young, Torso Magazine

"...'Billy & David' is frank, intelligent, disarming. Few books approach the government's failure to respond to crisis in such a realistic, powerful manner."
– RG Magazine, Montreal, Canada

"...Touching and gallant in its concern for the sexually addicted, 'Angel' becomes a wonderfully seductive investigation of the mysterious disparity between lust and passion, obsession and desire."
– Lambda Book Report

"John Patrick has one of the best jobs a gay male writer could have. In his fiction, he tells tales of rampant sexuality. His non-fiction involves first person explorations of adult male video stars. Talk about choice assignments!"
– Southern Exposure

"The title for 'Boys of Spring' is taken from a poem by Dylan Thomas, so you can count on high caliber imagery throughout."
– Walter Vatter, Editor, A Different Light Review

My Three Boys

Erotic Tales
About Group Sex

Edited By
JOHN PATRICK

Herndon, VA

Entire Contents Copyrighted © 2011

STARbooks Press, Herndon, VA.

All rights reserved. Every effort has been made to credit copyrighted material.
The author and the publisher regret any omissions and will correct them in
future editions. Note: While the words 'boy,' 'girl,' 'young man,' 'youngster,'
'gal,' 'kid,' 'student,' 'guy,' 'son,' 'youth,' 'fella,' and other such terms are
occasionally used in text, this work is generally about persons who are at least
18 years of age, unless otherwise noted.

First Edition Published in the U.S. in September, 1995
Library of Congress Card Catalogue No. 95-068063

Many thanks to graphic artist John Nail for the cover design. Mr. Nail may be
reached at: tojonail@bellsouth.net.

ISBN 13: 978-1-934187-92-0

Contents

INTRODUCTION:
COME TO THE CANDYSTORE
John Patrick

When asked if he had ever had a sexual experience with another guy, actor Nick Poletti, who plays the gay seducer in "Pool Days," one of the shorts that make up the film "Boys Life," stutters, collapsing into incoherence: "I don't know if you'd really call it... Well, it was a sexual experience, and there was another man there, where we'd have, like, a threesome... with friends, you know, like a girl and two guys... I remember one time of couples, two couples... a foursome. And, me Mr. Sexual Experience, and everything. God, it was like a 'Candystore!'"

Nick doesn't say when this was exactly, but we do know there were many "candystores" in the '70s and '80s. But sometimes you had to travel far and wide to find the best.

"From June to September, the Greek island of Mykonos is a paradise for the young, the empty-headed, and the beautiful," veteran tour director Hanns Ebensten reports. "Anyone over the age of thirty-five is unpleasantly conspicuous and apt to find it difficult to attract the waiters' attention at the cafes along the harbor front. A German tour company which sends large groups to Mykonos every week during the summer restricts participants to those between the age of 18 and 32, pale boys and girls who join others from many European countries, Australia, South Africa, Israel, and North America to become gloriously sun-tanned and spend the nights in discotheques and copulation. From eleven o'clock at night, when the cruise passengers have returned to their ships and the souvenir shops have closed, until 3 or 4 a.m. the dark, narrow, twisting alleys of Chora, the island's little capital and only town, are crowded with prowling men who stalk each other like panthers in heat."

The wise made their connections earlier in the day, Hanns says, on the small beach outside the Hotel Leto, where back-packers defy the authorities and camp during the day and sleep at night. He recalls during one visit he and his travel companion saw a naked young man

1

sitting in the yoga position on his towel, facing the road with tourists passing to and from the bus station, and studiously picking the lice out of his pubic hair.

"Well, I guess it pays to advertise, and he sure is well endowed," said Hanns' travel companion, enthralled by the sight. "Indeed," Hanns says, "the impecunious young men and women on that beach are often not in the least adverse to being approached and engaged in conversation by the Hotel Leto guests and will cheerfully accompany them to their rooms to enjoy the luxury of a hot shower or to share a bed for a cozy night. Some take the initiative and, having ascertained a lonely man's room number and finding the beach too uncomfortable, creep late at night through the hotel garden and appear outside a bedroom window, gesturing to be invited in. One year, a bold member of my group entertained two bearded Swiss giants in his room, where they stayed for three nights and when he returned to Athens, they parted with mutual demonstrations of regret."

Fortunately, horny men speak an international tongue, Bill Strubbe says, as they loiter in that questionable place, taking a lingering look or a second take, asking for a light. "The thrust between spread thighs, the smack of hand on bare flesh, the muffled moans of delight are all proof that the language of lust needs no translation. It can be important, however, to discern the distinctive choreography of the local mating rites. In the Middle East, you'll likely have to settle as a bossy bottom in a land of terminal tops; with those furtive Brits, take the oblique approach over tea and crumpets before suggesting the nasty, for that's what they still think it is.

"For the daring and creative, sex can be had just about anyplace. Among my most memorable – if not the most comfortable – of trysting spots are: behind the curtain in the throne room of the Winter Palace in St. Petersburg; in the middle of the Golden Gate Bridge with 600,000 people pressing on all sides; on the second level of King Herod's cliff palace on Masada; in the employees' loo at Harrod's Department store in London; in an ice-encrusted tent on the steppes of Central Asia, and with a Cuban cop outside the American embassy. (Moving tanks and airplane rest rooms are highly overrated, and terribly gauche to boot, but if you could pull it off in the cockpit...)

"My all-time favorite cruising ground is the green oasis in the center of Jerusalem, Gan Hatzmaot (Independence Park) where a cross-section of Israel's male population can be had: soldiers in uniform, university students, religious Jews in full Hasidic garb, mustached Arabs, Scandinavian kibbutz volunteers, and businessmen looking for a quickie. There's something wonderfully romantic, subversive and politically correct about humping with a Palestinian on an ancient stone mausoleum drenched in moonlight while two Hasidic Jews and a German tourist look on."

A reader of Boyd McDonald's books recalls his fun times in Paris: "My all-time favorite was the baths, the Milan, near the Gare St. Lazare. Alas, it is now gone and the clientele has fled to other places. My best afternoon there was several years ago in one of their open cubicles (no privacy, which is fine by me).

"There I was lying on a padded bench. Along came three guys. One proceeded to suck, lick and bite my nipples; the second sucked away on my prick; and the third rimmed me. After a bit someone replaced me and I then circled behind this trio and fucked each one from behind. That was great.

"It was one hot place with a lot of public action. It had a sauna which was somewhat more luxe than the rest of the establishment. Better behavior apparently was expected there. I enticed one guy into a cubicle to eat my meat and as I was getting ready to fuck him, the attendant came up and said such disgusting conduct was not permitted there. Group sex at the Milan took place almost everywhere except there.

"My partner at what was to be my last visit to the Milan was completely shaved, with the biggest, pinkest nipples I have ever chewed on. He couldn't get enough. He wore what looked like a jeweled, tasseled cock ring, a good deal flashier than my rubber one. With a sizable audience we pinched, slapped, stroked, and otherwise felt each other all over. Then he went down on me and I shot a wad in no time."

A favorite Paris haunt of show business types was The Trap, the sleaziest, slimiest, most wonderful gay bar in the City of Light, described by the late Otis Stuart in his best-selling biography of Rudolf Nureyev, Perpetual Motion: "A gateway to another era, it's the kind of hole-in-the-wall dive that doesn't need a sign over its flat gray door, just a line of iced blue neon spelling out 'Bar.' Those who want what Le Trap has to offer have always known where to find it, wherever they are. They also know to make other plans until midnight, when the Trap opens. One minute past midnight and the place is swarming with gay men in their choicest whoredrobes, most of it tight, tighter in key areas for an assist to the right spot-check (the lighting is not the brightest), cuir at every turn. Once you've knocked on the door, been snarled at by the doorman, and finally pushed your way to the bar, you might think you were in any gay cruise joint anywhere in the world. Pinball machines. A garish jukebox. Just a touch too much red light.

"And that's when you register the stairs. Once upon a time, back in the early '80s, when sex was still a verb, the stairs leading to the second floor of the Trap were a little harder to find. They were flush against the back wall of the bar, and might easily have been just a service route for the bar staff, were it not for the constant flow of men up and down. The service upstairs wasn't for the staff (generally). It was for the patrons, by the patrons. The famous Trap staircase was, in fact, a ticket to a world in which only time stood still. Everything else was as mobile as a shower room. By the mid-eighties, the Trap's stairway to paradise had been shifted to the center of the room. The new visibility served only to stiffen the resolve.

"It's a hell of a place to see an international superstar offstage for the first time, late one wintry Paris night in 1985.

"'Look over there.'"

"'Where?'"

"'Down near the end of the bar. The guy with the leather cap.'"

"'Which one?'"

"'The one who's laughing. Who does that look like to you?'"

"Oh, my God."

"'Nureyev.'"

"On a so-so, middle-of-the-week night, leaning comfortably against the bar, clearly in good humor, making no attempt at all to draw attention to himself, as if he had to. With one last swallow of his drink, Nureyev tips his hat to the jokester he's been enjoying and mounts the stairs. First at a trickle, then en masse the entire room follows. What came next, and more than once too, was a sylvan blond youth grinning from ear to ear, once he could straighten his back again, and among the most fervently attentive audiences of Nureyev's career. A paparazzi crush without the cameras."

Stuart also quotes a compatriot on the party circuit in New York during those heady days saying, "Rudolf liked big. Big in everything. I don't think he was very inventive in what he did. He just liked a lot." He also let the world look on, in the proper setting. Stuart

4

quotes the late gay activist Michael Callen fondly remembering an ecstatic evening at a New York bathhouse watching Nureyev "take on four huge black men, one right after the other."

Chocolate, and lots of it, it seems, never goes out of style. Consider the revelations of James Hannah, who writes about being invited to the latest craze of the Gay Nineties: the sex party: "I'm auditioning for a sex party: It sounds like a joke from some play about New York excess. The men who organize this seven-year-old monthly orgy publish their phone number in a local queer rag. It's one of those elite organizations you're tempted to join (a) to find out if you measure up, so to speak, and (b) for the pleasure of confessing your sin later.

"Kwame, the paranoid brother who sits in the right hemisphere of my brain and says things like 'Church's Fried Chicken was invented by the KKK to kill Black people!' tells me that the screening process will automatically disqualify men of color and that I should join a club that would have me as a member. I decide to ignore Kwame's advice. Too easy. An organizer who returns my first, furtive phone call instructs me to show up on Sunday at 6 p.m.

"When I call back to change the time, he reveals a bit more.

"'You can come for your audition at five,' says R.

"'Should I prepare a monologue?'

"'No, just work out those pecs.' It's only after hanging up that I realize R sounds like a brother. Kwame has a conniption.

"On Sunday, I nervously find my way to an elevator bank in a West Side high-rise hotel. Only one other person looks like he might be going my way. When I get to my floor, I'm enveloped in quiet: little signs guide me to my destination, a room at the end of a long, colonial-style hallway that puts me in mind of the final moments of 2001: A Space Odyssey. A sign on the door says 'Come on in.' Inside sits R, a regally chunky brother, indeed as African American as he'd sounded by phone. From a door behind a makeshift reception desk, a man naked except for his boots and a Freedom Rings necklace, makes an energetic entrance. 'He passed,' says the nudie to R, pointing toward the bedroom he's just exited and handing me a questionnaire.

"'Well,' says Kwame, 'the SAT it ain't.'

"Attached to a bedpost is a sign reading 'You must strip to your underwear or less.' I fill out a questionnaire and, at a blank marked endowment, scribble a modest $5000 before the naked man, who I soon discover is my auditioner, comes to lead me to another room where the incandescent bulbs have been replaced by dim red ones that cast a seedy candy apple glow.

"Now clothed, the auditioner asks whether I've been to safe-sex events before and what I like to do. There are parties centered around 'specific scenes,' he explains, before requesting that I strip.

"When I ask how he expects to make a good judgment in this light, he says, 'Sometimes we do it military style, but this makes people less nervous.'

"I drop trou as politely as possible for this medical examination-meat inspection and feel like I'm back in junior high, where the combination of innocence and libido made everyone polymorphously perverse. Except me, as I recall. It occurs to me that this may be why I'm here. 'Turn around, please,' says my examiner, making a few notes on his clipboard before telling me they're having a party that night. Gee whiz, they're gonna let me into the sex tree house!

"When I return at 9:45, the downstairs lobby is serene. There's certainly no indication that on a high floor of this building the scene I'll discover after checking my clothes and taking a quick shower is going on. Only the security guard, who accidentally barged into the last party, knows the deal. In the room where I'd auditioned, a group of about 40 men, most in the 25 to 35 age range, have crowded. The attendees aren't particularly beautiful, observes Kwame, just white. No one's grotesquely out of shape or grotesquely grotesque, but an aesthetic utopia it is not. Weeding out the 'trolls' hasn't worked; it's just raised the level of attractiveness at which one becomes a troll. I recognize someone I know from college. I recognize people I see out all the time. Kwame notes that what few brothers there are ain't giving each other the time of day.

"Body heat raises the temperature exponentially as guys pair off with a stroke of the abs or a gentle butt grab, or else pull out their willies and stare at a trio jammed into a corner in a jerk-and-suck tableau. This is no clam-plate orgy: even in an atmosphere with the potential for total abandon, guys tend to focus on one or two people at a time, then hangers-on get involved. I'm too bashful to become a focal point, like the gentleman surrendering to a gang-bang over there, and too proud to settle for just a feel, so I spend most of my time shuttling between rooms, cruising. Damn! Even in the context of group sex I have monogamous tendencies. I'm not completely alone: one guy I eventually try out has to wait for his boyfriend to leave to feel comfortable fooling around.

"The promoters have provided plenty of condoms, lube, and not enough paper towels, but there's little anal sex – let alone unprotected anal sex – going on. Although GMHC 'monitors' don't patrol here, not many guys do more than spank the monkey and fellate. A short hallway darkens to a murk that no amount of squinting can penetrate: from the end, I hear passionate moans and groans ('Oh yeah, fuck me!'). For all I can tell, there's just one person in there slapping his own ass. The sex party is so tense and serious it's all I can do to keep from making faces. A phone rings. 'I told you never to call me here,' I hear myself say. I ask myself why this can't be a relaxed affair, a classic orgy, grapes and wine, and why talking breaks the spell so quickly. I vow that I'm not coming back.

"And yet, when a month later the second invitation arrives, I'm drawn back, as if this were some secret order within the secret order of homosexuality, a way to get the adrenaline high the closet used to provide.

"At the second party, I see that the need for exclusivity has escalated to the point where clothes check boys take phone numbers and inform certain people about even 'smaller' events. Extrapolating from this concept, I arrive at the idea of a monogamous sex club and then a j.o. party for one. Despite his militancy, Kwame relaxes a bit, seeing that the slightly higher percentage of POC have eyes – well, more than eyes – or one another and are moving multiculturally about the room. Has R. instituted some kind of diversity-training-self-love program, I wonder? Not exactly. But his assistant, a tall, light skinned man with a mouth on him keeps hissing to men of color, 'Bring more chocolate. We need more chocolate here.'"

Peter Macallaster, writing in Savage Male magazine, tells about his memorable times acting as a host for a sex parties put on by a group called The Men's Exchange: "It was after dinner on a Sunday evening, and pedestrian traffic in the lobby was light. A number of tourists straggled in, along with some businessmen and airline flight personnel – and between and amongst these people arrived The Men's Exchange partygoers, sometimes alone, sometimes in bunches, always unmistakable. Some of them I knew from previous parties, some had interviewed with me, a small handful were personal friends – and the rest I could identify just because they were, well, hot! I couldn't keep track of exactly how many guests showed up – that was someone else's duty, anyway – but by the time the party's doors officially closed, I must have greeted at least 150 men. I waited half an hour longer, in case there were any late arrivals, and then joined the party myself.

"Once past the suite's entrance foyer and clothes checking area, soft lighting permeated. Judging from the heavy breathing and writhing bodies – standing, sitting, and lying down – the onanistic activity was just reaching its height. I wandered into one of the bedrooms and approached one of the beds to see what might be going on there. A bystander looked me over and then reached out to touch my chest. I reached out to touch his, and we smiled at each other.

"'Hi,' we both said, quietly.

The man was tall and had a nice, hairy chest and well-developed arms. He leaned towards me and kissed me tentatively on the lips. For some men, kissing is too personal an activity to engage in with a stranger, and I appreciated his consideration in not assuming I would automatically want to kiss him back. But I did kiss him back, and I would have embraced him too, only all of a sudden I felt someone else's mouth at my crotch, blowing warm air through the fabric of my underpants onto my genitals. It felt good, and I pulled my underpants off.

"For the next 30 minutes or so, I was involved in this threesome, and we were joined from time to time by other men – at one point I counted six of us altogether – but eventually I wound up alone with the man who had first reached out to me. Finally, he lay across the bed and I knelt next to his shoulder as we masturbated ourselves into simultaneous orgasms, his semen spurting up onto his belly and mine splashing down across his chest."

After washing up, Peter proceeded with the man, who introduced himself as Glenn, to an area where refreshments were available. "I helped myself to a glass of seltzer, and Glenn chose lemonade. Relaxing on a couch, we rested our backs against opposite arm rests and gave each other a foot massage. Other party-goers drifted in and out of the room, some sitting down for awhile to relax and converse quietly, others just resting momentarily before returning to the 'playing' areas. It was interesting to note that several couples I knew were in attendance, putting some extra 'oomph' into their relationship.

"A few of my friends came over to shake my hand or kiss me, and one of them sat next to the couch, resting his head against my thigh. 'Whew,' he sighed, 'this sure beats going to some dumb old bar. But now I need a full body massage!'

"Eventually the men started to gather up their belongings, get dressed and leave. Some exchanged phone numbers, and seeing this pleased me very much. Since nobody's Aunt Ida was holding mixers where men could meet other men, it was up to us to fill Aunt Ida's shoes. Apparently we were doing a pretty good job of it."

So good, in fact, that Peter continued to work for the Exchange, becoming an interviewer. His first interviewee was Henry, whom he quickly bedded. Henry stayed on to help Peter interview the second applicant, Mark.

"We had just enough time to clean up and throw our clothes back on before the doorbell rang," Peter relates. "I opened the door, and in walked one of the most stunning men I'd ever seen. Mark was a six-footer with shoulder-length blond hair. This is a style which few men can carry off very well – a fact I'd realized on my last trip to California, where it is much more popular than in the Northeast – but on Mark the effect was beautiful. The features of his face were, to put it simply, exquisite: finely-formed yet manly, with almond-shaped eyes framed by long lashes and a wide mouth the outside corners of which were slightly upturned even when not smiling, like a dolphin's. Because Mark was wearing a heavy jacket, it was difficult to speculate on what his body might be like, but I felt almost ready to accept him on the spot.

"It turned out that Henry and Mark knew each other, intimately, I gathered, and Mark told Henry it was okay for him to stay through his interview.

"When it came time for Mark to disrobe, I was not disappointed. He was muscular and proportioned like an artist's model. Covering much of his spectacular body was fine, almost down-like hair – surely the softest looking body hair I'd ever seen on a man.

"Despite his comeliness, however, Mark appeared to be anything but conceited; on the contrary, he was soft-spoken and refreshingly unpretentious. Undoubtedly he knew he was good-looking after all, he thought enough of himself to apply to The Men's Exchange, and, in his early 30s, he was old enough to have gathered sufficient feedback from the world at large to understand that he wasn't chopped liver. Yet it appeared quite possible he was unaware of the extraordinary potency of his sex appeal.

"As with Henry before him, I told Mark he was 'in.' And, like Henry, Mark was in no hurry to put his clothes back on either.

"'Okay if I touch?' I asked.

"'Yeah!' He sounded as though he wanted it but was too bashful to admit it.

"Within five minutes, Mark and I were fully undressed, sprawled across my bed. Henry undressed too, but, having only just ejaculated a short while earlier, he stayed mostly on the sidelines as Mark and I made love. At several junctures, I did make a point of including Henry to some degree – being careful, at the same time, not to pressure him to 'perform' when I knew there was likely to be a limit to what he could do with us right then.

"Finally I stood up next to the bed, and, gently grasping Mark around the hips, drew him across the mattress to the edge. I lifted his legs into the air, and – eager to show me what I wanted to see – he tilted his pelvis upward. The puckered hole between his buttock cheeks contracted momentarily, as though to wink at me, and I leaned over and kissed it softly. Then, applying some lubricant to one finger. I stroked it and slowly worked my way inside, gently massaging the muscles. Mark was clean as a whistle within, and, as his muscles relaxed and opened up for me, a tiny bit of air escaped – as though his entrails were sighing and welcoming me.

"Slipping on a condom, and then more lubricant, I slowly entered his warm, smooth anus. Then while thrusting slowly with my hips, I leaned between his spread legs, and kissed him on the lips. Which was sweeter – the softness and wetness of his mouth as he kissed me back or the firm pressure he applied to my cock with his sphincter – I couldn't decide. Then I pulled back from the kiss so I could engage his hindquarters with deeper thrusts. Mark clasped his own penis and rubbed it energetically. I increased my velocity, and then, all of a sudden, spurts of semen spewed forth from Mark's penis onto his abdomen.

"'BZZZT!' It was the intercom again, sounding as if on cue.

"Reluctantly, I withdrew from Mark and went to answer it.

"'Doug's here to see you!' The third applicant of the night had arrived.

"'Send him up!'"

For advice on how best to handle group scenes – and sex in general – it is helpful to turn to the pros. "There were a number of lessons I learned," a former hustler told the late John Preston. "One was to avoid a certain type of man who exuded a peculiar intensity – a certain monomania, you might say. It's hard to fully describe. This type was always very banal in appearance and conversation but would seem intensely fixated on some aspect of sex. These guys were weird and made me uncomfortable. After all, one had always heard tales of monsters. Jeffrey Dahmer was far from the first. In line with that, I avoided S/M scenes, did not accept drinks or food when on the customer's premises unless I really trusted the guy. I always scoped out my escape route first thing.

"Another precaution is one which I believe is quite a common saying in the field – it was told to me by a theater manager first, but I have since come across it a number of times. If you come into a room and find two guys waiting for you, be very careful. If you find three waiting, and they're smiling, get the hell out of there as fast as you can. I never had that experience, but I knew a few guys who did, in fact, walk innocently into what turned out to be heavy scenes from which they were lucky to get away. However, these occasions are rare. Of course it takes only one such occasion to work a serious mischief, so one really must be on guard."

Preston said that there were times when a group is an acceptable risk. For instance, his friend Boomer once was hired through a trusted friend to be the boy toy for a group of Japanese businessmen who were visiting Chicago: "I went to the Four Seasons Hotel, where they were staying. I had a wonderful time. There were seven of them, all waiting for me. They hadn't wanted my friend because he wasn't as muscular as I am. They would have preferred a blond, but I have such a big dick they settled for the substitution.

"I like group scenes and I have a major fetish for Asian guys. I got a good workout that night. Two of the guys were really hot, in a fuckable kind of way, but none of these fellows wanted to get fucked. It was, I guess, just a major body-worship thing. I got lots and lots of tongues licking my body which was fabulous I have to admit. They all ended up licking my cock and balls. Having that many guys crowded around your crotch is one of the most erotic things..."

When it comes to sex, sometimes even being a third-hand observer can be fun. Consider the adventure of Ralph, the manservant in Tony Peake's story "The Good Butler." Ralph had taken to going to the baths to swim and he became smitten with a young man. One day, Ralph was showering and the young man came into the room. He stepped under the shower next to Ralph's and slipped off his trunks: "Ralph waited for his breathing to return to normal. Then, not daring to catch the young man's eye, he retrieved his soap from its container and began very carefully to lather himself a second time.

"'Do you mind if I borrow some shampoo?'

"Ralph looked up and found himself confronted by that remembered, knowing smile.

"'Of course. Here.' And fumbling behind him on the windowsill, he handed the young man his shampoo.

"The young man poured a generous dollop of shampoo into the palm of his hand and returned the bottle to Ralph... The young man closed his eyes and began to lather his hair. His body was angled towards Ralph, and as he worked at his hair, his eyes still closed, Ralph was able to devour its every detail. He felt himself starting to harden and turned away.

"...Cock in hand, the young man was lathering between his legs. He looked up and saw the direction of Ralph's gaze, then looked down and saw the extent of Ralph's excitement. His eyes went hard, and twisting sideways, he muttered something under his breath.

"For a moment Ralph couldn't think what to do next; then, his panic subsiding, he decided it would only compound matters if he didn't acknowledge the mutter.

"'I'm sorry,' he said, then, faintly, 'I didn't hear.'

"The young man swung round. 'I said it's a good thing you've got a towel. You're going to need it.' And with those hard, ungiving eyes, he held Ralph's gaze until Ralph, near to fainting, snatched up the aforementioned article, and shielding himself behind it, fled from the showers."

For the next three days Ralph didn't go to the baths at all. He was simply too frightened; too frightened and too hurt. Never in his life had he made such a fool of himself. He finally decided to risk being foolish once more and went back to baths. He began to undress. He'd only got as far, however, as slipping off his shoes, when another young man came swinging into the room, a young man every bit as heart-stopping as the first. For a moment, despite himself, Ralph gasped — and then was tempted to gawk. But he'd learned his lesson, and even when the young man commented on what a nice day it was, Ralph kept his head averted. He couldn't, of course, help a quick sideways glance as the young man peeled down his jeans, but no sooner had he seen what he wanted to see than he looked away again, and scooping up his soap and shampoo, made for the pool.

"There, pacing himself carefully, and emptying his mind of thought, he managed to swim as many as twenty lengths, and one for luck, before getting out and making for the shower. To his amazement (for he'd still been ostentatiously naked when Ralph had left the changing room) the young man was there before him, under the shower by the window. Ralph opted for the shower in the opposite comer, balanced his soap on the tap and began, with particular absorption, to wash himself.

"It was some moments before he looked up again to discover that the young man was staring at him.

"'Knackering, huh?' The young man's eyes were decidedly mischievous, and that wasn't all: his hand was making another kind of mischief with what hung between his legs.

"Ralph turned quickly away and reached for his soap.

"A second later, and much to his relief, he heard the door open, though when he glanced up to see who it was, he found to his horror that he was looking straight into the taunting eyes of the very man he'd been avoiding. His first instinct was to bolt, but something – he didn't know what – made him nod back, hold back and watch with growing amazement as, stepping casually under the shower midway between Ralph and the first young man, the newcomer slipped off his trunks, and taking out his soap, began with slow, luxurious strokes to apply it to his cock. Unable now to tear his eyes away, Ralph watched mesmerized as both young men began to soap themselves until their cocks came wholly erect. Then, shooting a look half of defiance, half of disdain at Ralph, the young man nearest to him leant over and reached for the other man's cock. It didn't take the pair of them more than a minute to come. Then, as if nothing more untoward had happened than an exchange of shampoo or a request for the time, both men returned to their separate ablutions. Ralph looked down at his own, pathetically eager member, and powerless to prevent himself, came on the spot in a series of short, sharp spurts.

"...That night, at the club, Ralph confided in John and Henry.

"'I mean,' he said, 'isn't it bizarre? What is he playing at?'

"'What young men like to play at,' said John. 'Each other.'

"'But why lead me on like that? He flirts with me, then he cuts me dead, then he comes in front of me.'

"'Narcissism, dear,' said Henry. 'Young men like that get a kick out of being admired. I should know. I've done enough admiring in my time to satisfy whole armies of them.'"

And armies of guys is what this anthology is all about.

THE MORE THE MERRIER COMPLICITY
John Patrick

I. Brandon & Dick

Carl was pushing Brandon as they left the gym after watching the basketball game. "Enough of this shit," Brandon said, picking up his pace.

Dick looked at Brandon. "Christ," he said softly.

Brandon tried not to meet anyone's eye. But Carl ran up to him and blocked his way, standing so close their chests were touching. Dick said, "Fuck off, Carl."

"Aw Dick," Carl said. "It's a fair fight." He bumped Brandon.

But Tom said, "Shut up, you little shit," and grabbed his brother by the shoulder. "That boy pussy ain't worth fightin'."

Now Patrick had taken out cigarettes, and Dick was saying, "Gimme." Patrick offered the pack around.

"Hey," said Carl, grabbing one, his eyes bright.

Brandon saw with amazement that Carl had forgotten all about fighting – he hadn't even been mad, just wanted to start something. "Let's go around back," Carl said. "If my old man drives by he'll cut my balls off."

Patrick passed around his lighter. Then they all walked, Brandon in the rear, behind the school building, out of sight of the road.

They all settled down in the darkness, on the steps to the rear entrance to the gym, and everyone but Brandon was smoking. Brandon found a spot near Dick. The air was getting chilly, but the steps were still warm.

"She starts shakin'," Patrick was saying.

"I'll give her something to shake," said Carl.

Brandon could tell they were talking about Barbara, the school's whore. He didn't know her, but she was famous – she'd do anything, she couldn't control herself. When you kissed her she began to shake. Patrick always talked about her two younger boys, repeating what he'd heard, and by now she seemed like someone he had fucked.

"She starts shakin'," Patrick said. "I haven't even done anything, and she's goin' ape."

"I'll give her an ape," said Carl.

"I'm kissin' her," said Patrick, "and she's shakin' and like rubbin' her tits against me. Then she takes my hand and sticks it up under her sweater."

"Jesus," said Carl, rubbing his crotch. "What're they like?"

"They're like that." Patrick pantomimed the palming of two basketballs. "I can't hardly get my hands around them."

He reached up, groping at the height Barbara's breasts would be if she were standing in front of them. Carl rubbed his crotch harder.

His brother said, "Carl, don't be so disgusting, you little prick," and grabbed for Carl's hand.

"Rape, rape!" Carl squealed.

Listening there in dark, Brandon angled his legs so only Dick could see he had an erection. Talk of sex, any kind of sex, always got him going.

"I slide my hand down," Patrick said, "and she's wet. She's like a fuckin' furnace! She's creamin' for me."

"So?" asked Dick. "You screw her?"

"You know it."

"My ass."

"Go ahead, ask her." Patrick sulked for long a moment, then continued, "Yeah, she's creamin' for me. And she's shakin' like all over. And she grabs my leg. And I've got this huge rod on."

"Jesus," said Carl, staring at Patrick's crotch. "You've got one now just thinkin' about it."

Patrick stroked the bulge in his pants. "Yeah, I've got this rod on. And she says 'Oh, Patrick, you're so hard.' And she starts to rub it. Jesus!" Patrick slipped a hand down the front of his pants to relieve the tension. Carl did the same. His brother raised a fist, and Carl hurriedly withdrew his hand.

"Then she says, 'Oh, Patrick, my pants are wet.'"

"Jesus!" Carl groaned.

"And she takes 'em off. So I open her up and slip it in."

"My ass," said Dick.

"What's it like?" asked Carl softly.

16

Patrick took a long drag at his cigarette. "Nosy little prick, aren't you?"

"I'd give her a nosy little prick," said Carl. "Right in the old twateroo."

"Jesus, Carl," his brother said, shaking his head.

Brandon had breathed in all the smoke and he was beginning to feel light-headed. He wanted to leave, but would wait for Dick. He always waited for Dick.

The cigarettes were burned down, and one by one they ground them out. Patrick handed the pack around again.

"C'mon, Brandon," Carl said, shoving the pack in his face. "Be a man."

Brandon's father had stained, sick-looking fingers, panted when he climbed stairs, sometimes coughed until he was purple, and said it was smoking that had ruined him. Brandon hated even the idea of smoking.

Dick handed him a cigarette. "Put it in your mouth and sort of draw through it," he said. "Easy, or it'll burn." He reached for Patrick's lighter.

Brandon was surprised at how slight the cigarette was. It had no substance at all, he could hardly feel it in his hand. But when he put it in his mouth it seemed huge, like the first time he had taken Dick's cock in his mouth, and he almost gagged. "You're drowning it," said Dick, and showed him how to hold it between his lips by the very tip. Then he struck the lighter. "Just draw easy." As the flame touched the cigarette, Brandon tightened his lips around its base and breathed in.

But Brandon wasn't prepared for the heat. He'd thought he wouldn't like the taste, but never imagined he'd be swallowing fire. He staggered up, unable to breathe, the cigarette dropping from his lips, his eyes watering so he couldn't see. He took a few steps, still couldn't breathe, and sank to the pavement.

"Fuckin' pussy," Carl snarled.

To Brandon, it felt like a heart attack. Then the night air was searing his lungs and throat, each breath making him cough uncontrollably.

"Bran, are you okay?" Dick asked.

"Fuckin' kid drags up half the cigarette," said Patrick.

When he could, Brandon got up and walked away. He sat down by himself against the wall of the school, where the others' voices reached him unintelligibly. All he could see was the glow of their cigarettes, which might have been yards or miles in the distance.

The night was getting cold. He held his throat and shivered, waiting until he was well enough to go home without his parents seeing he'd been smoking. He would never touch a cigarette as long as he lived. And no matter how his mother licked her painted lips and curled her fingers, no girl would tell him, "Brandon, you're so hard."

Now the glowing sparks were rising. They started to float away from him.

He heard Dick call, "Bran?"

He didn't answer. A minute more and the points of light were gone and Dick was sitting next to him, rubbing his shoulder. "You okay?"

"Sure."

"You want to stay at my place tonight?'

"Sure."

Dick was an enigma to Brandon. He was always one of the guys when he was with them, but when it was just the two of them, he was as gay as Brandon. He had, after all, taught Brandon everything he knew about guys making it together. It had begun innocently enough. Dick was two years older but they had been friends from the day Brandon's family moved into the house down the block. What began as you show me yours, I'll show you mine" session ended with Dick demonstrating how good a blowjob could feel.

Now, once a week or so, Brandon would sleep over at Dick's and they would have sex long into the night.

The next day, they again would have to act like everybody else, keeping their secret. Brandon said he understood but he didn't. He'd been called a "pussy" and a "cunt" by Carl enough times that he actually believed it.

"I'm a male pussy," Brandon said as Dick began to fuck him. "Just a male pussy."

"Better'n any girl pussy I've ever had," Dick moaned, and Brandon knew he meant it. As far as Brandon knew, Dick hadn't fucked a girl since he took Brandon under his wing. Not once.

"Oh, fuck me, Dickie, fuck me!"

Dick put his hand over his friend's mouth. "Quiet, you'll wake the dead!"

II. Brandon, Kent & Jeffrey

Three Years Later

Brandon's principal had suspended him for setting fires in wastebaskets. Then his mother, in mourning for over a year since her husband died of throat cancer, started in; she could no longer deal with Brandon and his desperate need for attention. So Brandon left New Rochelle and hitchhiked to Shirley's and Kent's house in Connecticut. For as long as he could remember, he had been secretly in love with his older cousin Kent, though it was a secret that Brandon somehow sensed Kent knew. He could never forget one hug Kent had given him when he was in junior high school. Kent was a "toucher," his mother said, a "lovable guy." Brandon couldn't have agreed more. The fact that Kent was now married didn't seem like much of an obstacle to Brandon. He knew how Dick played it straight everywhere but in bed with Brandon.

"Now I've got nothing," Brandon told Kent, and, when he heard his voice whining like a child's, he felt like smashing himself in the face. He knew when he was forty, he would not be a man the way Kent was. Everything about Kent fascinated Brandon – his broad shoulders, his serve on the tennis court, his red Mercedes convertible, the thick black hairs that sprouted out of the collar of his polo shirt, and, most all, his bear hugs.

Kent smiled. "You've got time," he said.

"Now I'll find out what real suffering means. That's what my mother told me."

"She'll get over it," said Shirley. "You're staying with us awhile." Shirley had short hair and triangle-shaped earrings; only the earrings interested Brandon, they caught the light like mirrors. "You need to relax. Kent's already said he'd take you into Manhattan."

"Yes, you'd like that I know," Kent said. He threw another log on the fire. Watching it sear and smoke, Brandon felt the burning desire for another man he hadn't experienced since Dick went off to college.

Later that night, when Brandon got out of bed, the coals of the fire still glowed in the darkened living room, and the bricks before the fireplace were warm to his bare feet. Behind the married couple's door there was silence.

The living room's sliding glass doors looked out on a dense woods. Dusted with snow, the motionless branches seemed turned to stone. He lay down on the carpet, his bathrobe parted, and his hand stroked his cock. Brandon stared at the ceiling, and dreamed of Kent. Of having Kent between his thighs, shoving his cock into him the way Dick had done for nearly four years. God, how he missed Dick. And not a single letter. Not a single call. Nothing.

Kent had slept badly and opened his eyes several times, thinking he had heard something. Finally he got up and made his way to the living room. He stopped short, his eyes focused on Brandon, stroking himself in front of the windows. He could see Brandon was fully-grown, his cock was enormous. He longed to step into the room, go to him, but there was plenty of time for that.

Kent knew he drove too fast for the icy road conditions but driving slowly made him feel as nervous as a prison escapee. To see the landscape, of which he knew every bush and utility pole, sliding past gradually was monotonous, as monotonous as his marriage had become. Lately he had taken to leaving the house earlier and earlier, whenever he woke up, sometimes before dawn.

When he reached Manhattan he pulled into the basement garage of his lover's apartment building. For several months he had had no office. He had told Shirley he was looking for a new one, and that in the meantime he was working in board rooms. But all he really needed was a telephone, and there was one next to his lover's bed. Kent was the manager of thirty portfolios, belonging mostly to friends of Shirley's father. Once he had worked at them full-time, but they seemed to do just as well if he paid them no attention. Once a day he phoned for quotes, and once a week he spent the afternoon calling his clients. The rest of the time he was free to fuck his young lover, Jeffrey, and, god knows, the aspiring young actor needed plenty of fucking.

Kent let himself in and went directly to the cozy bedroom. Jeffrey was still sleeping. Kent tiptoed into the room and undressed. When he got into bed Jeffrey nestled against him sleepily and began to caress him.

But Kent was distracted, the arrival of Brandon on his mind. Jeffrey began to press hard against him. "I think we should talk a bit first," Kent said, but he gave in, let Jeffrey go down on him. Kent's fingers were twined in the boy's blond curls, pushing his face down. When Kent was fully aroused, Jeffrey backed onto him and guided the big cock into his ass. He jerked himself off as he impaled himself on the cock.

Panting and exhausted, they remained locked until the acute sensitivity of his glans subsided enough for Kent to withdraw. He gave Jeffrey's sweet ass a final, lingering caress, reluctant to leave it. But Jeffrey padded quickly to the bathroom and started running a shower.

"So what did you want to talk about?" Jeffrey asked, coming out of the bathroom moments later, toweling his mass of tangled curls.

"My little cousin Brandon has come to visit us for awhile. He's been suspended from school and is pretty low. Anyhow, I want to bring him into town."

"So?"

Kent looked Jeffrey straight in the eyes. "I want to fuck him."

"Oh," Jeffrey sighed, his brilliant blue eyes suddenly downcast.

Kent rolled over, his face to the wall. "I guess I've always wanted to fuck him. Now I have the chance. But I don't want to do it without you knowing about it."

Jeffrey went back into the bathroom, began brushing his teeth.

Finally Kent got up and went to him, hugging him. "I love you ..."

"And you want to fuck your cousin."

"I could've just gone to a hotel and gotten it over with, but there's so much dishonesty already ..."

"Right. I'm supposed to put up with your going home to your wife every night and now I'm supposed to leave so you can fuck your cousin in our bed."

Kent pulled away. "I'm sorry I mentioned it."

"No, no," Jeffrey said, gesturing wildly. "You bring him here, but I want to be part of it. That's the way it's been with all the ones I've wanted to fuck. You've been here, right in that bed."

"Only if I wanted to be. I remember ..."

Jeffrey brought his finger to Kent's lips. "That was your loss."

Kent took the younger man into his arms and kissed him. "I love you, Jeffrey. Nothing will ever change that." Dried sperm tugged at the inside of his thigh as he stepped toward the shower.

Shirley sat alone in the kitchen. It was dark now and she had stopped crying, but she still leaned forward on the table, cradling her head in her arms. Just before noon, she had been standing outside Brandon's door when it opened suddenly and he stumbled out to go to the bathroom, his giant erection preceding him. She fled back to her bedroom and locked herself in. Shirley was sure he understood what she had been about to do, and he had seemed silent and distant all day. She was sure he understood her need, her terrible desire for a man, even one as young as Brandon. She and Kent seldom had sex anymore. She suspected he was having an affair but couldn't prove it. Brandon's mood only brightened when Kent finally arrived and talk turned to their day in Manhattan, just the two of them. Or so Kent said as they finished their dinner, a meal so spicy it made Brandon's eyes water.

The next day, Kent and Brandon drove away from the house around nine. They listened to talk shows on the radio all the way into Manhattan. It began to snow heavily. Traffic became hopelessly snarled. Kent began talking. He told Brandon the city was divided into those coming up and those coming down, those in crowded restaurants and those on the street, those with three locks on their doors and those rising in elevators from lobbies with silver mirrors and doormen.

"And, speaking of those coming up, there's something you should know," Kent said casually as they finally started moving again. "I have a lover."

"What?"

"Yes. And I want you to meet him."

"Him?" Brandon gasped.

"Yes, him."

Now Brandon was trembling with excitement. This was more than he could ever have hoped for.

"His name is Jeffrey and he's an actor. Right now he's in a play down in the Village. We'll go tonight to see him."

Brandon could not look at Kent. Speechless, he looked out the window at the snowflakes that had started to fall. He managed to chirp, "Okay."

On the radio, they said it was going to snow all day and all night. "Everything will come to a standstill," Kent said. "We might as well plan on staying overnight."

"Okay," Brandon said, still staring out the window, but now he had moved his hand to cover his erection.

A policeman in the middle of the street blew his whistle and waved on the line of streaming cars. Kent cursed him as he passed.

Whistles and sirens, clanging and shouting, ominous rumbles underground: Brandon thought it was all quite a spectacle, arranged just for him, to welcome him to The Big Apple. They finally arrived at the apartment shortly after one. The radiators were ticking and pinging, warm and dry. Kent called out to Jeffrey but there was no answer. He took Brandon through the living room into the kitchen and they began making bacon, lettuce and tomato sandwiches. As they ate, Brandon confessed his affair with Dickie, of his complicity in maintaining the secrecy of their intense passion for each other.

"Maybe someday," Kent said finally, "men who love men will have nothing to fear, but if we want to get along, we have to go along." Kent told him how much he envied men like Jeffrey who worked in the arts where one's sexual persuasion was not a problem. Brandon said that was what he wanted, to fit in somewhere so he wouldn't have to lie.

Kent stopped the discussion by taking Brandon's hands and holding them. He brought the boy's fingers, sticky with mayo, to his lips one by one and licked them clean. Finally they stood and Kent hugged the boy to him, crushing him, feeling his excitement.

Kent helped Brandon jerk off his jeans and shorts. The boy's semi-hard penis flopped into his waiting hand. Brandon gasped when Kent's warm, wet mouth engulfed the head of it. Kent gently manipulated the boy's balls while his tongue lapped exquisitely at the underside of his glans. Kent let the cock slide farther and farther into his mouth. It hit the back of his palate and he swallowed hard; he gagged a bit as it went down, the cock was quite large, and soon Brandon's balls were bouncing against his chin. Brandon closed his eyes and threw his head back, thrilling to the man's expertise. He dimly heard someone enter the room. He looked to his right and saw the man, bundled in a yellow terrycloth robe, standing transfixed, watching Kent suck Brandon's cock. Finally he said, "Man, what a cock!"

Kent pulled the cock from his mouth and said, "Brandon, this is Jeffrey."

Brandon immediately liked Jeffrey, who was as short as he was and good-looking in an open, boyish sort of way.

"Mmmm," Jeffrey moaned, coming over to Brandon. He straddled his leg and kissed him, tongue probing. He clasped his naked ass, so excitingly unfamiliar. Jeffrey's heat burned through his robe as he rubbed himself vigorously against the boy's leg.

Lowering his head, he stuck one of Brandon's nipples into his mouth. As he sucked, feeling it grow and stiffen, he glimpsed his lover sucking Brandon's cock while Kent stared up at him. Jeffrey kept on massaging his hairless pecs, squeezing each nipple, tugging and twirling, clenching his teeth. Brandon sighed; he had never had anyone working over him, let alone two.

Jeffrey spread Brandon's legs wider apart, hungrily inspecting the inviting asshole, burying his face in it, reveling in the smell and taste, craving it. He began pleasuring the boy with his tongue, but his concentration kept slipping, drawn to Brandon's cock sliding into his lover's mouth. Kent nipped gently, softly sucked. Brandon squealed and began bucking rapidly against his teeth. Cum filled Kent's mouth, wet his face. He swallowed. Brandon's lithe body suddenly tensed and quivered, out of control. He yelled, then abruptly relaxed.

They moved to the bedroom.

Jeffrey got on all fours on the bed and eagerly lifted his head to look behind him as Kent began to enter him.

Brandon's face became flushed and contorted as he watched Kent slowly squeezing his big cock into his lover, then sliding back. On one partial withdrawal, Brandon ran his finger up and down Jeffrey's damp, nearly hairless crack, lingered on the crinkled anus, feeling the powerful buttocks clenching in effort. Loosely encircling Kent's cock with his other hand he let it slip slickly between his fingers, feeling it going in and out of Jeffrey's body. Then Brandon fingered Kent's warm hole, pressing in lightly to assist each forward thrust.

Then Brandon lay on his side, his face a foot from the intense coupling. Jeffrey's head jerked up off the pillow, eyes springing open. When Kent's cock was all the way in, he yelled at the top of his voice, "Oh my god!"

Kent grabbed his lover's buttocks, pulling him snugly against him. Jeffrey thrashed his head, gasping rapturously, completely skewered now, impossibly full, utterly ravished. "Oh goddamn! That's too...uh!...yes!" Kent's strong arms bulging, he suddenly held himself still and rigid, plugged tightly into Jeffrey, rocking slightly from side to side. "Do it! Fuck me!" Jeffrey cried, his hand reaching out to grab Brandon's semi-hard cock. Brandon lifted himself up and Jeffrey began sucking him to hardness.

At last, Kent withdrew an amazing length of gleaming flesh and began long searching strokes, in and out, unhurried, generating utmost bliss. At the end of each of the deepest penetrations, he gave a little twist as his ball sac settled down over Jeffrey's ass crack. Muscles rippling, Kent shuddered and grunted, "Ah, yes!"

As Kent pulled out of his lover, Jeffrey's supple mouth clamped over Brandon's pulsing erection for the last time. Withdrawing it, he begged, "Fuck me with this, please, Brandon."

It was a moment Brandon had dreamed about for so long, yet he could not believe it was actually happening. One of the most attractive men he'd ever laid eyes on was lying before him with his legs spread wide apart, his ass oozing the cum of his lover, begging him to fuck him.

Kent lay beside them, his eyes feasting on the sight of Brandon's erection entering his lover. Brandon started to fuck Jeffrey like a rabbit, with fast, hard little strokes. Jeffrey held on to the mattress so he wouldn't wind up against the wall. After a few minutes of this, Brandon came, with a moan that soared into a high-pitched, chilling yell. Slowly, he pulled his cock from Jeffrey's ass, then stood up on the bed, straddling his body with his muscular legs.

Jeffrey's screw of Brandon was the exact opposite. He wanted to watch Brandon fuck himself with his prick, savoring the look on Brandon's face as he arched forward and lowered himself onto the shaft till he was sitting on Jeffrey's hips. His eyes never left that beautiful face, those fawn-like eyes and that mischievous mouth. For a few moments, they held hands. But mostly Brandon humped, slowly, taking it deep.

It went on and on. Jeffrey didn't come, he just lay there letting Brandon enjoy himself. The fuck lasted half an hour, and when Jeffrey finally came, it was a peaceful, serene, nearly religious experience. Brandon squeezed his asshole around Jeffrey's erection, making it even more exciting and sweet. Then he came forward, and with Jeffrey still hard in him he shot another load onto Jeffrey's belly.

Panting and replete, Brandon gave Jeffrey's ass a final, lingering caress, reluctant to leave it.

Just then, Kent came in from the bathroom bringing damp towels. Kent wiped each of them clean and they lay together, limp and relaxed for a few moments. Brandon closed his eyes. The next thing he felt was Kent sliding his hardening cock from his forehead to his mouth, his pubic bush tickling his nose and cheeks. He opened his eyes. They were in the 69 position. He grabbed hold of the velvety brown shaft and kissed the pinkish cockhead before chewing on it. At the same time, his own cock was getting a tonguing and a series of suction-like chews. Kent plunged the shaft as far as it would go in

Brandon's mouth and he shifted to his side. As soon as he felt his loins shivering, he widened his throat and pushed in his cock as far as it would go. Kent came in several jerky spasms – without letting go of Brandon's cock. Then it was Jeffrey's turn. He took over at Brandon's cock, and they just lay there, adjusting themselves comfortably, sucking and licking. Occasionally Kent would blow his cool breath on the erect shafts as he played with their balls.

"Come up here," Jeffrey murmured, and he sat the perfectly proportioned youth on his face. His tongue jumped up to the well-fucked but now clean ass, and pried his cheeks apart slightly, then widely, and his lips chewing the soft flesh. As it yielded to his tongue, he pushed past the opening into the asshole.

He heard Brandon sigh. Kent was playing with Brandon's cock, nibbling on it as Jeffrey sucked the other end. Brandon wasn't fully aware of Kent's subtle hand job, so great was his ecstasy, but he did come.

When his short spurting was over, his head fell back in temporary exhaustion. But he soon bounced off Jeffrey's face, then licked up his own jism from his abdomen, his hands on Jeffrey's thighs.

Jeffrey looked up, the actor expecting the audience's reaction. Kent smiled and mouthed, "Bravo!"

Kent gave him a big hug and Brandon went to the bathroom. Four gray towels hung on one wall. Above them was a grow light sunk in the ceiling that glowed lavender. Pink-budded plants cascaded from a shelf above the towels. There was an 8 x 10 photograph hung next to the sink, of Jeffrey standing beside a pool in a white Speedo, his pelvis thrust forward, thumbs pointing at his crotch. It was signed, "To Kent, all my love."

New York City was shut down that night; Jeffrey said he wanted to make the most of his unexpected night off. They raided the refrigerator, drank all the wine in the apartment, and watched television. Eventually, Jeffrey went to bed, leaving Kent and Brandon on the couch. Kent hugged the boy, and as he wet his lips in anticipation, he ground his crotch into Brandon's. Then he explored his mouth with his tongue and Brandon's tongue found his and they started to duel.

Kent's hands were moving all over Brandon's back, slowly, naturally finding their way to his ass. Their mouths parted, and Kent started nibbling on his neck. He moaned into Brandon's ear and

Brandon urged him on. He began licking his way down to his smooth shoulder. He tasted and smelled sweet. A baby-fine layer of hair began near his belly button and continued down.

Brandon's legs slung over his shoulders, Kent rimmed the boy for a good while. Then he stood. Brandon was again amazed by how great Kent's cock looked. He was large and hard. A long dribble of juice had seeped from the tip and nearly reached his knee. Brandon grabbed his shaft and began to lick his balls. They were surprisingly big, too, and covered in dark fuzz. He nibbled and licked each crevice, each strand of pubic hair while he rubbed his soft hands all over Kent's cock until he made him stop. His balls had lifted up, and Brandon knew he was close to coming.

Brandon knew he couldn't have stopped him even if he'd wanted to. Kent's hands began touching his ass and legs. Brandon nearly fainted from the quickness of Kent's actions as he reached down and pumped Brandon's cock into his mouth. Brandon grabbed his hair and could easily have popped a load into him but he didn't; he wanted to come while Kent was fucking him. Kent pulled Brandon's dick from his mouth with an audible pop and Brandon leaned back on the couch. He lay there, just fingering his asshole and licking his lips at Kent. Kent's big cock was sticking straight up and he dropped to his knees and lifted Brandon's legs up higher, saw his puckered pink hole and began to shove his sex into him. Brandon was tight, but Kent could tell that the friction was exciting to both of them. Brandon literally pushed himself against Kent and wrapped his legs around his back. Kent began pumping and soon he was in as deep as he could go, his crotch hairs rubbing against the boy's butt. Kent fell on top of him. Their sweaty chests were sticking together as they kissed long and hard. Kent began to fuck very hard, and Brandon grunted with each thrust, but smiled at Kent. Kent's sweat was running off his forehead and falling onto the boy's face. Kent licked it up, then reached down and began jerking Brandon's erection. The boy came quickly now, heaving with the intensity of it, and Kent moved his sticky hand to Brandon's mouth, letting him lick his hand, tasting his own sperm.

Still pumping, Kent pushed the boy's legs toward his head so he could look down and see his incredible jack hammering in and out of the boy's now incredibly sloppy hole. He even pulled myself out completely at one point to let Brandon savor the sight of the slick invader, then reentered. Brandon was stunned at how experienced both of his hosts were at fucking and the pleasure they gave themselves and each other.

Finally a few slow, very deep thrusts sent Kent over the edge and soon his spunk was surging into Brandon's ass. Brandon bit his lip and, even after he thought Kent was through, the older man continued, shoving his now semi-flaccid cock into the clenched rectum and kissing Brandon all over his face.

Brandon said he could not sleep in bed with them so they fixed him a bed on the couch in the living room. The night was long and never silent. Through sirens in the streets and strange noises in the building, he slept soundly. In the morning, Brandon's ass and cock felt sore and weak. Standing in the shower, he let the dried cum and musky scent of his two lovers wash down the drain.

"God, what a night," he thought, lifting his ass into the hot spray, trying to wash the pain away.

He dried himself with one of the towels that was lying in a tangle on the floor, inhaling the scent of the English soap they used. Then he put it back where he had found it.

As Brandon brushed his teeth, Jeffrey came into the bathroom. He was naked. He kissed Brandon on the shoulder and made his way to the shower. Brandon thought Jeffrey was unimaginably beautiful in the warm morning light that was streaming in through the sooty window. As Jeffrey stepped into the tub and pulled the curtain, he said, "You okay?"

"Never better," Brandon said.

"We haven't had sex like that in a long time, I'll tell you that much. I can't thank you enough for coming."

Brandon giggled. Coming? He'd come so often he'd lost count.

"Thank you for having me," Brandon said.

Brandon watched him lean his head back and get wet. When Jeffrey took the soap and run it down his body, Brandon craved his body all over again. He stepped over to the tub and took hold of his cock and savored the heft of it. He dropped down and tried to take it all. He gagged, then apologized for not being able to please him by taking all of it in his mouth. Jeffrey looked up, then down, and told him he pleased him better than any of his previous lovers except Kent and to quit it.

Brandon obeyed, for a moment. But when he saw the effect his sucking had on Jeffrey's cock, he joined Jeffrey in the tub and turned around to encourage Jeffrey with the gyrations of his ass. Jeffrey took the soap and filled his hands with suds. He began washing Brandon, his hands sliding around his ass, his cock and balls. The streams of water hit Jeffrey's erection as it slid into Brandon. Holding on to the soap dish with one hand to avoid falling down, Brandon jacked himself off with the other, contracting his ass as Jeffrey went deep inside him. The pressure was excruciating for both of them and Jeffrey moaned his pleasure as he fucked the boy. Finally, his knees buckling, he came inside Brandon.

Brandon found Kent in the kitchen making French toast.

"I'm awfully hungry," Brandon said.

"I know teenagers are always hungry. I made all this for you." His hand swept across the table. "Real French toast with real French bread."

Kent's greedy expression from the night before had not changed. It appeared to Brandon that while he might have French toast, Kent really wanted only to devour him for breakfast. He picked up a knife and began to spread butter over the thick golden slices of bread. Then he raised the small pitcher and watched as the syrup poured out.

He cut the first slice and then his right hand brought the fork up to his mouth and he slid the sodden bread in.

Kent leaned against the stove and smiled. "It's a pleasure to watch you eat. In fact, it's a pleasure to watch you do everything."

Mouth stuffed, Brandon could only nod.

To this day what Brandon remembers most about being suspended from school that winter is that it snowed so hard in Manhattan that he and Kent had to stay overnight.

And now, every time he says "snow," his lips move so that they seem to kiss the air.

A RIDE HOME
John Patrick

Douglas Duncan was a cute rich boy who played on the tennis team. He was the first boy I knew who owned white tie and tails. He was also the first to push my hand into his crotch. It began when he gave me a ride home from school in his daddy's big Chrysler. After a minute or two, Doug was pleading, "You could give me some relief."

"Not here," I said. We were, after all, parked along the roadside in the golden light of late afternoon. I told him to take me home. Mom was working overtime at the factory and we had plenty of time, but Doug was in a hurry, or perhaps a bit anxious. He stood by the back door while I dropped to my knees, undid his pants and drew his hard, throbbing cock from his underwear. I heaved a long sigh and a shiver ran down my spine. It was the moment I had been waiting years for and I wasn't disappointed. It was a lovely cock, cut, about eight inches long with a big mushroom head. I bent forward and took the head of his cock between my lips. I sucked gently for a moment, nibbled on the head, then slid my tongue up and down the shaft before I took it fully in my mouth. As I sucked, he let out a strangled cry, "God, where'd you learn to do that?" I think he knew, just never wanted to admit it. I never told him his best buddy, Joe Barnett, had taught me what to do years before. But I think Joe finally told him because when Joe moved away, Doug suddenly got very friendly.

I slid forward again and when his cock was deep in my mouth, I began to swallow, letting my throat milk his cock. When I sensed he was close, I began fondling his balls. Doug's orgasm was so intense I had trouble keeping his cock in my mouth, and I did want to swallow all of his cum.

A week later, Doug gave me another ride home. This time I sat on the toilet and sucked him off, then washed him off when we were finished. He let himself out and I stayed in there and jacked off holding the washcloth to my nose.

Poor Doug was in such a hurry to leave, still fearful we would be discovered, that he just pulled up his pants and ran to the Chrysler.

After that, Doug would give me a ride home whenever he had to borrow his daddy's car. Soon he was making up excuses to borrow it just so he could take me home and get his blowjob. I had him hooked.

One day, near the end of the school term, he told me to meet him in the parking lot after my last exam. He had been very moody lately, first making a date and then cancelling. I knew he was dating Betsy Woods and maybe what we were doing was beginning to get to him. Anyway, on the way home, Doug took a long detour to a bad part of town and slowed the car as we approached a bar and package store named The Pit. He wanted a six-pack.

"You're not old enough," I said as I tried to keep him from turning in.

"They don't care who they sell to in these places," he said and pulled onto the littered dirt apron in front of the place. Red neon tubes outlined round windows. The tubes buzzed like angry insects.

When Doug entered the joint, I heard hillbilly music swirl out along with heavy smoke. As I sat waiting, I thought of what it must smell like inside, all those dirty, sweaty bodies, the odors of the beer and bourbon, and the cheap orange-blossom perfume used by the whores who worked there.

Finally Doug came out carrying a paper sack. Just then, three boys a little older than we were stepped from the side of The Pit. They wore tight black T-shirts, jeans, and filthy boots. They positioned themselves between Doug and the Chrysler.

Doug tried to back off and come around to my side of the car but they blocked him. No matter which direction he moved, they shifted to stay in front of him. The glow of the neon tubes reddened their faces devilishly.

"Lost, ain't you?" the largest boy asked, adjusting a beaded Indian headband.

"I'm not looking for trouble," Doug said.

"Thing about trouble is it can come lookin' for you," the boy said and lifted his fingers to the sack Doug carried. "Kid like you shouldn't be foolin' with no stuff like this."

"He's sweet 'nuff to be wearin' a dress," a second boy said, thin and ugly, pale hair stringing straight to his shoulders.

Doug tried to protect the sack, but the Indian-headband boy snatched it away. Bottles fell and rolled across the pavement. Slowly I slid to the driver's seat.

"I paid for them," Doug said as if that would make any difference.

"Shit, we're just upholdin' the law," the third boy said. Short and heavily muscled, he wore a black bandanna around his neck. "You got proof of age?"

The boys stooped to gather the bottles. Doug brought out his wallet. I thought he meant to show them his fake ID, but he offered money. He always had plenty.

"Take it and let me go," he said.

They took the bills as well as his wallet. They emptied the wallet and tossed it back at him. The muscled boy opened a beer by biting off the cap and spitting it out. He licked at foaming suds. Doug again tried to approach the Chrysler. The boys grinned and blocked him. He made a wide circle to the driver's side of the car, but they still cut him off.

"Guess what's here waitin' in the car," the boy with pale hair said, pointing at me.

"Maybe your little boyfriend'd like to give us a ride," the Indian-headband boy said.

Doug lunged toward the car. They tripped and jumped him. He struggled, but they held him down. I screamed. They pulled at his seersucker pants. I kept screaming. Because of the thumping music, nobody inside the bar heard.

I tried to start the car. The Indian-headband boy sprang at me. "Yeah," he yelled, "we're all goin' for a ride in this fancy car."

The sun had gone down by the time they told me to turn off the main road and take a dirt road into a shadowed valley. "We can't stop here, this is Old Man Elkins' place," I said.

"He's probably havin' his dinner," the Indian-headband boy said. "Besides, this won't take long."

While Doug silently sat between two of them in the back seat staring at his shoes, our captors finished off the six-pack and were a bit high as they ordered us out of the car. Laughing and joking, they quickly had Doug's underpants off. Doug was sobbing now and that made them start slapping him around. I ran over to them and began swinging at them as hard as I could with my fists. "Leave him alone," I screamed. "Do what you want with me, but leave him alone."

"Hey, the little twerp really loves his boyfriend," the heavily muscled one said, grabbing me and shoving me to my knees. His jeans

I jumped up and ran over to them, slamming at Bubba with my fists. He pushed me hard and, screaming, I toppled over into the brush. I had never screamed so much in one afternoon in my life.

Doug started bawling like a baby as Bubba began sticking his spit-and-cum-coated cock into his ass. "No, no," he pleaded, but Bubba was not to be denied.

I ran back to them, only to have the ugly one push at me while he held Doug down as Bubba fucked him. I fell to the ground again and had a bird's eye view of Bubba sticking that huge one into Doug. It was an incredible sight. Bubba would pull back roughly and drive back in again and again. The car was rocking as the slamming continued. I'd never seen anything like it; my sex had been limited to giving blowjobs. Now I was getting turned on like never before. As much as I wanted to help Doug, I was mesmerized by the sight of this crude assault on Doug's dignity.

It seemed like Bubba was taking his time, enjoying the raping of this cute rich boy, and the other two were getting anxious.

"Hey, let us have some," the ugly one said.

"Now!" Bubba yelled, rearing back for one last plunge, but he misjudged and his cock came completely out of Doug's ass. "Yeah, I'm comin'! I'm comin'!"

It was an awesome sight from my place on the ground as Bubba's sperm wildly flew all over Doug's backside and splattered on the bumper of the Chrysler.

Doug started struggling again once the ugly one began to stick his cock into him, but Bubba and the other boy went over and held Doug down. Doug cried out in pain as the ugly one's cock slipped right in deep where Bubba had been.

Suddenly a shot rang out, then another, then another. "Get off my land, you fuckin' perverts!" Old Man Elkins shouted, firing again.

The three boys from the Pit let go of Doug and ran off down the side road towards town, pulling their pants up as best they could. Elkins chased after them, firing his rifle in the air to scare them and laughing. I got behind the wheel of the Chrysler and started the engine. Stunned, Doug tumbled into the seat beside me and we roared off. I switched on the headlights so we wouldn't run down Elkins and I honked at him as we passed him. He fired a couple of shots at us, but straight up in the air. He didn't want to hurt anyone, just get us off his land.

Doug sobbed and patted his handkerchief against his bleeding face. I stopped the Chrysler at a gas station in town to doctor him. I took him into the restroom and wiped away blood and got his clothes back on. I guessed he was in shock; he didn't say a word. He drove then but wouldn't look at me. In the flaring headlights of oncoming traffic I could see the tears were again streaming down his pretty face.

I couldn't console him, and he never again offered me a ride home, though I didn't breathe a word about the incident. After that, when I saw Doug, he greeted me politely, yet averted his eyes. I guess I reminded him too much of that night.

SEX SIESTA
James Medley

I was sailing out of San Juan alone, on a short vacation from the rum company where I worked in the export department. As my little sailboat skimmed through the gentle swell caused by a soft tropical breeze, the shimmering sea reflected a cloudless aqua sky. I was about a hundred yards off shore when my tiller suddenly snapped and I lost control. I could see the village of Manzanillo, but I didn't know its name at the time. I hastily lowered my sail and paddled toward the primitive cluster of tumbledown shacks. Since there were several small boats similar to mine anchored in the shallow harbor, someone, I thought, would have the tools to repair a broken tiller. But as I neared the shoreline, I saw the beach and tiny cabins lining the crude dock were deserted.

I bobbed around a bit before I managed to get my boat alongside the rough pilings of the pier. I moored it with a heavy hemp rope just at the edge of the shoreline and jumped into the shallow water. I was barefoot and shirtless, wearing only a pair of baggy white pants with the cuffs rolled up.

I waded ashore and walked up the beach toward the small business district. Still, I saw no sign of habitation.

I found a market with a rusted tin roof supported by unbarked timbers and barren stalls running its considerable length. Still, no signs of life. I entered the open front and made my way into the dim interior. As I stepped further toward the dark recess at the rear, I smelled something faintly familiar, a musky, spunky smell. Suddenly, I froze. My heart pounded like a drum. Just ahead of me in the gloomy near-dark, I could see a sleeping boy, lying on his back in one of the empty stalls, on a wooden table, his legs spread apart. He was sleeping on the wooden boards on which I presumed produce was normally displayed. But the reason for my excitement was that, even in the dim light, I could see today something else displayed: he wore nothing but a pair of cutoffs and his huge brown dick had slipped out one leg.

I breathed deeply. This kind of youth was what had started the trouble between my lover Carlos and me. I had originally come here on a vacation with Carlos, and while he was busy with his family, I set about to see the sights. And what beautiful sights I found them to be! I had many wonderful liaisons until I got caught with my cock up the ass of a comely boy when Carlos came back to the hotel early one day. Fed up with me, he went back to the States, but I chose to remain in San Juan. I had simply fallen in love with the old-world beauty of the city – to say nothing of the youths.

Now I stood in wonderment at unquestionably the most beautiful boy I'd seen yet in Puerto Rico. He stirred fretfully in his sleep, obviously dreaming by the tight little smile which played about his fleshy lips. He drew one leg further to his hairless chest, his smallish hand cupped to his groin. He shifted half to his side and, still sleeping, began to languidly shaft his over-large dick. My breathing grew ragged as I watched him manipulate himself. I crept closer.

Looking around me, half-fearful of being observed, I sneaked to within three feet of the unconscious youth. He had the lithe, sleek look of adolescence about his body. His black hair had fallen in long straight strands over one of his closed eyelids. My eyes skimmed over his well-muscled legs, which were lightly tufted with the same dark down. I took in the dense brush of his pubic hair just at the gap in his cutoffs.

But his cock was what my eyes feasted upon. Standing out on his blood-engorged penis were virtual rivers of bluish veins which crossed and recrossed the huge swollen underside tube of his uncut dick. Lube oozed from the tightly flesh-sheathed head. Thick darker skin clutched his knob, curtaining all of the pebbled crown but the cum hole, which glistened a dusky crimson. Even semi-erect, the boy's cock was obscenely out of proportion with the rest of him. He wasn't truly masturbating as such, more like tenderly caressing it.

My legs trembled as I stood rooted to the spot and gazed at him with lust-filled eyes. My cock jutted against my belly, threatening to sneak above the waist band, and leaked pre-cum all over my blond pubic hair. It was an immediate, intense erection which was almost painful in its severity.

I tip-toed closer. The place seemed suddenly moist and oppressively warm, electrically charged, reeking with sex. I tentatively dropped to my knees when I was no more than inches from the boy's thick-headed meat, my eyes fervently glued to his sex. I could feel his body heat on my face, could smell his lube mixed with sweat.

Was he awake? I feared that he would suddenly be startled awake and slug me senseless, but he moaned softly and made another slight shift to his side, bringing that wondrous cock closer to my lips. I stared at the beautiful youth's face, his eyes closed tightly. I breathed hot air onto his distended shaft. There was no response. I looked out; there were still no other signs of life. I brushed the pulsing underside of his cock with the tip of my tongue. He moaned. Extending my tongue to its fullest length, I licked the velvety flesh, tasted the delectable pre-cum, and glided my lips over the shaft. He spread his legs wider and sighed. I licked the little ridge of skin which ran from the base of his cock to his sweet nether mouth. The boy's silken flanks responded to my touch by protruding further toward me until he now arched to the side. I grasped the cock and I worked my mouth over it, inches at a time, slowly, tenderly, more, a bit more, until I had six inches down my throat. I felt every vein throbbing against the inside walls of my mouth as I sought to take each inch of him. I pushed his cutoffs up and got the head lodged at the back of my throat, then lunged hard onto it, gagging as I got all his cock inside. As I sucked and slurped up and down, he moaned once again and started humping his loins into my face.

I felt his small hands take my feasting face between his palms and glide it up and down, firmly yet tenderly, pressing my cock-filled cheeks with increasing urgency all the way to his drawn up balls. These I cupped in my hand and pulled his cream bag to my chin, nuzzled his firm and yielding gonads to each side and pressed the heated genital flesh to my lower face, reveling in the deliriously wonderful feel of him.

My cock had now managed to slip from my pants, saluting my navel a good two inches out of the baggy waist band. I hunched my hips and felt the tingling friction from my constraining belt and felt like I could come any minute, sucking him and grinding my dick into the torque of the material. I knew I was going to come any minute when I felt, rather than saw, his hand drop over the side of the ledge and seek my crotch.

His touch was soft and warm as he rubbed his palm tenderly over my fully-exposed knob. Then his hand fumbled at my belt, undid it, then the copper button, the fly until he had my cock out and the full length in his fist. My pants slipped to my feet and fondled my balls as I continued to feast on his glorious prick. He clutched and relaxed, clutched and relaxed, driving me to new heights of ecstasy.

"Gustaria mamar me grande pinga!" he gasped from above. Suck my cock!

With his dick all the way in me to his balls I gagged. Soon I felt him getting ready to shoot and I sucked with increasing fury, gobbling and slobbering, then I held him still and fast, wanting to prolong the explosion, savoring the essence of him. I could feel his ejaculation cresting at the base, rolling in his balls, rushing up from deep within. He moaned as his spasms intensified. I swallowed and kept swallowing, while his hand fisted my cock more rapidly, dragging me to the edge. I felt my own orgasm begin. He squeezed out my jism onto the ground.

Licking the last of the boy's cum from the cockhead, I heard a cough. My heart began pounding. I turned to see a man leaning against one of the large columns. He had his hands on his crotch and a broad smile on his wide, florid face. He looked to be in his middle thirties and, though not what I would call handsome, he had a craggy sort of outdoor sensuality. He was dressed in a loose fitting guyabera shirt over wrinkled white cotton trousers and I could see his boner straining against the thin fabric.

"I see you found our little Manny at siesta," the man said in perfect English.

My heart stilled a bit as he fondled his cock, then outlined its considerable length through his pants. I muttered, "Yeah."

"Little Manny loves to get fucked too. Isn't that right, Manny?"

"Si," the boy sighed.

"And I know he can get off again," the man said. "How 'bout it, Manny?"

The boy impishly grinned. "Yes. Here or at your place? "

"My place. Folks around here will be waking from their siestas pretty soon." Looking at me, he asked if I wanted to join the party.

Nodding enthusiastically, I got up and hauled up my pants. Manny struggled to get his still-tumescent cock back up the leg of his cutoffs, then jumped eagerly off the bench.

On the way to his house, the man introduced himself as Lars, and told me he was a geologist in town on an assignment

Manny had obviously been to the house many times, for as soon as we entered he immediately dashed for the bedroom. When Lars and I reached the Spartan room, Manny had already stripped naked and was lying on his belly in the middle of the double bed. His cute little butt shone like burnished copper in the afternoon sun, the model for the perfect boy-butt, dimpled and smooth spheres of twin ass-globes, taut and well-toned – just made for fucking. He lay there looking over his shoulder at Lars and me, clenching his butt-muscles and hunching his slender loins against the bedspread.

Lars dragged down his pants and his cock swung to attention with a wet slap against his flat, hairy belly. I slipped out of my pants, my cock dripping pre-cum as we fell to each side of the boy. Manny kissed us in turn and Lars said to me, "Get him ready for me, will you? Eat his ass out."

I climbed aboard Manny's thin and trembling torso and stretched myself full length atop him. Every inch of our pressed flesh felt deliciously hot as I squeezed my fat cock between his butt-cheeks, then rode my dick up and down till he was juicy with fuck-oil.

Lars crawled to the boy's face, knelt before him and spread his hairy legs apart. "Suck me, Manny," he growled.

Manny sucked on that incredible nine-incher like a pro, licking and slurping his way down the bloated shaft.

I rode my cock between his butt-cheeks till he was slimed up, then ate my way down his back and nibbled at his shoulder blades. I trailed my tongue down his spine to end up at his ass. I licked concentric circles to his puckered hole and washed him with my spit. As I began tongue-fucking him, he hunched his ass back onto my face, wriggling and moaning as Lars fucked his mouth. I palmed his ass crack apart and thrust my tongue deeper still.

"Get under 'im and suck 'im off again," Lars grunted as he pulled his cock out.

"I wanna suck some more," Manny said.

At that, I got the boy's juicy cock in my mouth and he took mine in his. Lars got behind Manny and ate his ass awhile before saddling up on the two of us.

I felt Manny's big veins pulsate more strongly in my mouth as Lars squeezed his prick into the boy's rump. I felt his weight and his slow, initial pumping as he worked his dick into the kid. It was like having Manny's cock fucking my mouth as Lars went into a rhythmical, slow grind in Manny's hole.

Manny was taking my meat all the way to my balls, and spreading my legs wide apart with his hands as he ate away at my cock. I gorged on his cock while Lars's heavy slamming forced him deeper down my throat than I'd ever taken a cock. I couldn't hold out much longer and started gyrating my hips to the kid's face, working my cock all around the inside of his mouth. Manny squeezed on my balls so hard, it was like he was trying to squash the cum out of them.

I got my arms around both their straining haunches and shoved one finger up Lars's butthole. Two fingers in and Lars started grunting again: "Oh yeah! Oh yeah!"

I kneaded his sweaty balls and he fucked Manny with hard, heavy, deep strokes. As Manny ate my prick more frantically, his cock stiffened, swelling in my mouth.

"Here it comes! Take it, boy! Take it!" Lars wailed, driving his cock harder and deeper into Manny, who sent a gusher of cum down my gullet. I shuddered and finally came. We all milked the last drops of spunk and fell into a sweaty tangle, totally spent.

After we caught our breath, we dressed and headed back to town. It was crowded now that siesta was over and Lars introduced me to a fisherman who repaired my sailboat.

Back on the water again, I did a little teaching: "That's right," I said, "just lean to the side and let the boom swing leeward. Good. Are you sure you're going to like San Juan, Manny?"

And I wasn't speaking to myself.

HALF THE TEAM
Andrew Richardson

It was another long Sunday at University; I suppose I should have used the day to catch up on all that homework and get my essays written. But this was rarely the case because, in the winter months, all the hunky boys from the school rugby team were out on the field in hard training. How lucky for me that the rugby pitch was right outside my window: I had a perfect view of all those boys in tight shorts – fabric stretched around their firm asses and fitting snugly over their tackle.

And I had the perfect excuse to watch them all afternoon – a gorgeous but sadly straight best friend of mine was the team. If I wasn't attending a match as a rowdy supporter, then Paul knew I would be watching the team just to check out their progress. He had no idea that my enthusiasm as a spectator had ulterior motives and furnished my filthy mind with enough jerk-off dreams for a week – till the following Sunday! What I would have given to be a bar of soap in their showers after a match.

I knew this day was going to be a treat: there was a home match planned with a team from a nearby college. I'd already made my apologies to Paul that I wouldn't be at the game supporting – I knew that seeing two teams in rugby kits would be too much for me, and I'd be busy tossing off in my room all afternoon. Paul had been a little disappointed when I told him, since his girlfriend was off campus that weekend and was also unable to attend.

The visiting guys trotted past my window, their boots sounding like clogs and littering the path with dried mud from previous games. But it was the thighs I was watching – thick, muscular and powerful thighs; stretching down from hard, flat torsos and well-defined chests. Broad shoulders and solid arms to grab the opponent with and steady scrums. I could feel myself getting horny already, my belly tingling as if all the spunk was already churning around in there.

It was a surprisingly warm November day when the ground should have been frozen and the players breathing white breath over each other. We were being grimly warned by the weathermen that a cold spell would come along shortly – but that day could have been spring and the pitch wasn't half as bad as it could have been. The game got started with all the beautiful fellas frantically running around and giving me some brilliant views of muscle in action.

A scrum – heads down, arms interlocking and those magnificent asses poking up into the air. I imagined I was inspecting each of the players – shoving a hand down his shorts feeling a moist and eager asshole and, further, a tumescent cock and balls slack with heat and energy. I often wondered how many of the guys would actually fancy a bit of cock if they got the chance. My cock was so hot I was nearly coming within five minutes. But I knew the best bit would be later, when the game ended and our hall common room became the home team's post-match mess. Since it was the hall nearest the field, all the boys would simply flake out for an hour or so afterwards, and have a beer before they got cleaned up and went to the bar for the evening. Since I was Paul's mate and lived in the hall, it was generally assumed that I'd join in the drinking session afterwards. And eye-up all the men.

Paul stomped down the corridor in a glorious good mood. His admittedly fabulous run in the closing minute of the game was the winning point and meant the team was through to the next University Friendly's match. Paul was grinning and knew that, as always, I had our stash of beer in the refrigerator cooling – this time ready for the celebrations.

The away team went to the official changing rooms and would be offered a hospitality drink at the bar later. Meanwhile, the home team ploughed into the common room and filled it with their combined heat, sweat and good spirit. As they recovered their breath the beers were opened and the shirts came off.

Paul and I went into the large common room where more beer had appeared and was flowing freely. Some of the guys were relaxing back, and reveling in their win. The tough, muscular chests were beautiful, and I subtly had to shift my raging hard-on so that it wasn't obvious through my jeans. One chap, Greg, did not realize in his reclined state, with his muscular legs sprawled apart, that his ball sac was sagging out of his shorts. Or maybe he did realize and was enjoying my gaze. Either way, I could hardly look elsewhere and longed to get my face between his hairy thighs and onto that slack scrotum. And the beer was hardly making me discreet.

I was looking at his groin and felt wild inside. He was chatting to someone and carelessly stroking his thighs with his beer-free hand. I couldn't stop thinking of just licking his ball sac and taking each of his testicles into my mouth – seeing his cock fill out and strain against the black fabric of his shorts. As my gaze travelled over Greg's well filled bulge, he briefly looked directly at me then took his balls into his hand, squeezed them, and let his thumb creep over the fabric to pull his waistband down a little. All the other lads were busy making a row as Greg offered me a plain view of his pubic hair and heavy balls. He suddenly sat up and joined in with the conversation – leaving me a little stunned and all the more determined that I might one day get a suck on a real rugby player's prick.

As the other guys were having a good time, Paul went to fill his bath and soak off all the ground-in dirt. I knew that he usually had a shower before the bath, just to wash away the thick mud that he inevitably got covered in and once I had caught him nipping from the shower room into the bath cubicle and was agog at the huge, flaccid cock swaying between his legs. As he strode towards me, he rubbed his thick member and loosened his balls – then merrily wandered into the bath cubicle where his dumb girlfriend was usually waiting – leaving me to have a furious toss, thinking about the cock I'd just seen being fully erect and in my mouth, ass, face, hands.

The boys began to split from the common room and tidy the place up a bit. Some hung around, including Greg, who by now was already buzzing with beer; apart from anything else he had initiated some of the post-match beer games where 'the loser' had to drink the pool of beer out of another man's belly button. The loser? How could they consider licking a lighted- furred stomach a loss? That's all I ever want to do when I was in the room with them. As well as all the rest....

I went to my room to fetch them the last few cans of beer certain that Greg at least wanted more than to slurp beer, then laughed at my fantasy accusations of him being a closet queen.

I decided that I'd also throw one to Paul over the high partition to the bath cubicle – knowing that I had probably missed my chance to glimpse him in the shower.

Just as I'd got the cans, Paul shouted to me from the bathroom. "Rich, Rich. You there?"

"Yeah," I muttered.

"Rich. You there or what?"

"Yes I said. What's up?"

"Oh. Could you...?"

I walked into the bathroom and called over the partition where the thick steam was spilling over. "Could I what?"

"Get me a beer. Any left?"

"Sure thing. I'll lob one over the top. Here, get ready to catch it."

"No," Paul said, "the door's not locked, come in a pass it to me. I've got soap in my eye."

I couldn't believe my luck – I might get to see a bit more of what his girlfriend had seen all those times before. What I had never imagined was what Paul had actually got planned for me in that bathroom.

He was sitting in the tub splashing around and washing soap suds off his face, his short, blond hair wet and dripping. The remains of some mud dribbled from his neck and down his back. I passed Paul the can and fought my stiffening cock as I set the other cans down. He was chattering away about the match and then simply asked me to scrub his back for him. Quite without bashfulness, he passed me a sponge with soap and leaned forward for me to do the honors. Paul was chattering on while I gazed at his strong shoulders and broad back, his soft skin and the few bubbles on his neck. I pressed the sponge onto his shoulders and watched the soapy water fall out, trickling into his deep set armpits and down his torso into the hot tub. Where his muscular thighs left the water, the murky depths offered no view of his member – but as my hands slipped off the sponge I was grateful just to feel the heat of his skin and imagine that I was stroking his fleshy ass.

As I rubbed and sponged Paul's back, my hands slid deeper into the water behind him. I scooped the water up to bring it down over his back and determined that this way I could at least get a quick feel of his crack. Paul was really turning me on with his quiet sighs as I carried on washing his now perfectly clear back. "Oh, that feels good Rich," he said. "God, I could sit here all night."Me too, I thought.

"Ooh, yeah, that feels really nice..."

At this point, I genuinely thought Paul was just playing with the water – his right arm slowly moving back and forth – he drifted off and was quiet, the way water sometimes mesmerizes you.

I never stopped washing his back even when it was perfectly clean. It just felt wrong to stop, and he didn't seem to want me to stop.

In the watery quiet, I was amazed at actually how hard my cock was and that although he was a straight friend, I just wanted to flip it out and spurt onto his back. It seemed that Paul was having precisely the same thoughts about me at this point: he laid back in the water and proudly guided his enormously erect penis into the air.

"Do you think you could take care of this for me as well Rich?" He seemed almost worried to ask, a slight quiver in his voice – but the twinkle in his blue eyes told me how confident he was that of course I could fucking take care of it.

I stared at his massive cock – a full nine-inch weapon heaving in the steamy air, and, sitting beneath it, a pair of balls the size of eggs.

"Come on," he gently stroked his member, and needn't have encouraged me, but I was stunned, "I've seen you eyeing this up before. Not to mention half the lads in the team..." Paul was slowly stroking his cock as it lay upon his wet stomach, and peeled the soft foreskin back over his bulging head. He had noticed my own throbbing meat pressing down my thigh, and his prick swelled to a glow. He was gripped it with white knuckles – keeping the length of foreskin peeled back as his other hand swiped over his raw bellend.

My stomach was in knots, but I shoved my hand forward and clasped his cock hard where his hand had been, gripping it and stretching my fingers around its girth – feeling the purple veins pulsating. The number of times I had imagined this, and tried to picture the erect secrets of Paul's constantly fat packet.

"Oh, yeah," he moaned, as I stroked away. I looked right into his dark eyes. "Oh, I've wanted this for so long Rich. God, every time I fuck my girl I imagine it's you between my legs." His now free hands were feeling my face – this was getting fucking intense!

"I'm gonna suck you dry," I promised and got a hand between his hairy thighs, under his raised body to find his ring. As I slid a couple of fingers along Paul's deep and tensed crack, I began licking his nipples. They were big but soft and a deep pink color. Then I went down his softly furred belly, over his belly-button, and to the huge cock leaning towards me. He smiled blissfully as I opened my mouth and took the head of his wet cock into it. It was even more sensational than I had ever imagined; enormous, hard, but velvety soft. His broad piss hole, the bright red tip, all in my mouth and no longer in my dreams. I began to spiral my tongue around the glans. My anus was pulsating.

He was panting, and expertly unfastened my jeans to grope at my lengthy erection and squeeze my balls. Paul shoved his hand in-between my legs and thumbed my throbbing hole. He slid down in the water a little to relax his buttocks. I found my fingers were slipping easily beyond his sphincter into his own soft passage and I left sucking his cock long enough to say, "You're really ready for it aren't you?" Then I got the slab of meat again and devoured the head – pressing it into my mouth and letting his force glide it down my throat. As he drew out, I got two fingers right into his hole: Paul gasped and I tasted the small amount of pre-cum emerge from his piss hole.

He smiled. "Oh, yeah, I love to finger myself in the shower. I crouch down and, ooh, get half my fucking hand up there. Oh, I want you to fuck me. Uh, oh, I've even shoved half a shampoo bottle up there, wishing it was your prick."

I was astonished. He wanted me to fuck him?

As Paul lifted himself out of the bath, I stripped and slung my clothes down onto the wet floor. His balls hung low and his cock swayed heavily from the pubic base. I got behind him, took hold of his full balls between his legs, and rolled them in my palm.

He bent over, held the side of the bath and, offering me the sight of his virgin rosebud said, "Lick me."

I quickly got my face between his cheeks and aimed straight for his dark slit. Paul's cock stood rigid against his stomach. I was rubbing his hairy thighs, nuzzling his crack and had his big rocks slapping against my chin as he gently tossed himself off. As his hole loosened even more, I began to rub my cock against the backs of his legs. I found my tongue was exploring deeper and deeper into his rectum, and I was getting onto a writhing rhythm which Paul was obviously loving. He was gasping for me to fuck him good and hard – so I stood up, spat on my rigid cock and held his fleshy buttocks apart.

He held onto the side of the bath – my aim was good, and with the slightest pressure, Paul relaxed to let my full shaft glide right up to the hilt. My pubes pressed onto his crack, my balls collided with his. His deep moans and grunts were a sure sign that he was loving it. And I was on the edge of orgasm myself as I felt his warm, moist, smooth innards allow my cock to plough through.

Paul stood up and we locked into a vice-grip. My arms set around his well formed chest, occasionally gripping his springy cock; and his arms stroking my legs, my pelvis working in and out of his backside. My breath heaving out onto his neck. I couldn't believe I was this close to him. More, inside him – fucking him, feeling his body, his back on my chest, looking at his square jaw, kissing his ears and hearing nothing but our pleasurable gasps. Nothing, that was, until it was obvious some people had stumbled into the bathroom and were shouting out for their beer.

Paul and I could do nothing in time, and the three lads left waiting for their beer fell into our cubicle, to witness our gay fuck in all its naked glory. Their mouths fell open. But swiftly, and to our utter astonishment, the half cut lads looked at each other and seemed to agree that they liked what they saw. Walking over the wet floor and my clothes, they came right in and closed the door behind them. Surprise, or sheer disbelief prevented anyone from saying much, but I could tell Greg was eager to have his meat sucked by a guy, and he was the first to strip naked and join in. After the initial shock, I composed myself and realized the vice grip Paul's shocked ass had on my cock was exquisite. I gracefully used Paul's cock as a wand to motion Greg over to us. Greg simply opened his mouth wide to take Paul's dick, as if he'd been doing it for years. Then again, for all I knew, maybe he had! Paul held Greg's head and guided his face over the massive cock, easing himself along the salivating tongue.

As Greg gave head, Bruce got down to savor Greg's own big balls and lick his cock. I knew I wanted to get a good slurp on those genitals as well – and now was sure I'd get a chance to. The third lad, Phil, was interested in watching my cock go in and out of Paul's ass, and stripped off to sit between our legs, tonguing our scrotums as I slowly continued to fuck Paul. Phil's head was between my legs and as he lapped our balls, my thighs rubbed his hair and face.

The bath water stilled and steam was rising as things in the group were warming up. Soon I was crouching down to let Phil fuck me while Greg lay out before me alongside the bath, letting me get my face on his cock and balls. The very same ones I had been gazing at half an hour before, longing to lick and feel in my mouth. Just before I parted my lips, I turned and saw Phil close his eyes, his face melt with pleasure and slide his cock inside me. It felt like an iron bar going into me – and I groaned out loud as Phil clutched my waist and Greg pushed his cock into my face.

Greg's sagging sack was loose and hot – filled up and ready to spurt semen all over us. While I got busy on Greg's prick, Paul decided to explore Bruce's rigid length.

"Oh, yes," Greg moaned, lying back as Paul was about to sit on his face, introducing him to the delights of rimming a smooth, juicy rectum. Having had my prick up his ass, Paul was desperate for his hole to be serviced by anything – mouth or cock or fingers. As Greg got his mouth glued to asshole, Paul was pulling and rubbing his own pert nipples, stroking the muscles of his brutally sexy chest, grinding his hole on Greg's face.

My guts were throbbing and quivering as Phil got his member deeper and deeper inside my ass. Bruce was busy licking Phil's crack and reaching around to toss my cock off in a frantic blur. As Greg's tongue flicked between Paul's wrinkled, gaping hole and his balls, I could feel Phil increase his rhythm. His muscular legs shifted closer as he rammed his cock harder and harder into my glory hole. I leaned forward and got a suck on Paul's cock, then down again to Greg's slightly shorter but fatter cock.

Greg's foreskin was drawn right back down his shaft and as I worked my lips on the head, it went from a glistening red to full and throbbing purple. Paul began to toss himself off as Greg got a couple of fingers up the crack where his tongue was. Phil was holding onto my shoulders and was violently shoving himself back and forth – his cock right up my ass, then pulling nearly all the way out. A second for my hole to recover, and then ramming himself up again. I was loving every second of it.

Bruce shifted around from Phil's now rampantly moving ass to be behind Paul – and give Greg a close up look of cock entering man-hole. Paul, grateful for another thick member sliding up his passage, raised his ass, parted his knees and got his cock onto Greg's face. He winked at me as Bruce first rubbed his cock over Paul's ass cheeks, then glided it forward into the slick depths.

As Phil fucked me – positioned between Greg's tree-trunk legs, who was sucking Paul's mighty meat – I watched Bruce's spread of pubic hair ram onto Paul's crack. Bruce had a hairy chest which was now glistening with sweat and steam. His hands were pulling and slapping at Paul's ass cheeks and rubbing his legs. The rhythm became frenzied – five cocks, five fuck holes and five mouths all busy working towards the goal of a spurting climax. Phil was fucking me like an animal, sporadically masturbating my cock like a whip. I got guzzling Greg's stiff prick like a starved beast and sniffing his pubic hair as his shaft went past my throat and down my neck. As I looked up his ripped stomach to his smooth chest, I saw his tongue lashing over Paul's member, which was glistening with moisture oozing from his lubricated backside which Bruce continued to pump.

Paul leant down to get a gobble on Greg's cock while I licked his balls. Briefly, our lips met and we lashed tongues out around the erection − our kiss travelled up to the head of Greg's cock where it lasted a moment longer and confirmed this wouldn't be a one-off for us at least.

The grunting was getting louder and the moans deeper. Bruce was gasping and gasping as his cock demanded faster and faster thrusts. He was holding onto Paul's waist and I watched as he pulled right out of the ass, close his eyes and let go a spurt of semen right up along Paul's back. He pointed his cock down, his orgasm lashing out onto Paul's ball sac and cock base. His cock rubbed over Paul's ass and thighs and covered its path with slimy ejaculate. Greg was immediately licking the white streaks of Bruce's cum and I felt his cock suddenly swell one final time − the moment before an exquisite climax. He cried out and jerked his pelvis up. I quickly stuck a finger as far up his crack as it would go, just before it seized tight and he blew his load of salty cum into my mouth and all over my face.

As I gripped his cock and felt the pulsating shots of sperm travelling up Greg's shaft, Phil was bucking and riding my asshole, grunting and ramming his orgasm deep into my guts. Finally, Paul and I reached forward over Greg and as I felt Phil's cock slip out of my spunk-filled anus, we grabbed each other, kissed again and both shot our orgasms over each other's cocks. My thick spurts landed over Paul's hard member, and his cum exploded on our chests.

As we came down a little from the high of our sex, Paul made us all swear to keep what had just happened our "special secret." I was the first to agree. After all, having half the team was better than nothing.

HITCHING TO L.A.
Greg Bowden

It was a cold, foggy morning when I started out and I was pretty chilled through by the time I got out to the highway and stuck out my thumb. But I was lucky and almost immediately a shiny blue Chevy pulled over and an elderly couple offered me a ride. They said they were on their way to Reno for the slot machines and would be glad of my company. They seemed a little disappointed when I said I was trying to get to L.A. but they told me to get in anyway. I rode with them all the way over to the Interstate and then they went out of their way to drop me at the big truck stop just outside Sacramento. The old man said he was sure I'd find someone to give me a ride from there, maybe a trucker who'd take me all the way down to Los Angeles. The woman gave me a sandwich and an apple from their lunch basket and patted my hand, telling me to be careful. I told them I hoped they hit all the jackpots in Reno.

The sun was out in Sacramento and I was beginning to sweat under my heavy shirt and jeans. I looked around and finally found the rest room squeezed in between the convenience store and the restaurant; I went in to change into the gym shorts and T-shirt I had stashed in my backpack.

There was only one guy in the rest room, standing at the urinal and paying no attention to anything, so I slung down my backpack and pulled off my shirt. The guy at the urinal finished, zipped up and left without so much as a glance in my direction.

Another man came in about the time I got my boots off and was shucking out of my jeans. He went over to the urinal, pulled out his dick and then stood back a little, letting me watch him piss. He had a nice dick, long and thick with a dark, flaring head. I wondered how much bigger it would be when it got hard.

By this time I was naked except for my jockeys and the guy was looking me over pretty good so I thought what the hell and pulled off the underwear, too. It looked to me like his dick was beginning to grow as I took my time hunting around in my backpack for my gym shorts. When my back was to him I kind of flexed my buns and then bent over a little, not enough for him to see my hole but enough so's he'd know where it was.

When I looked at him again his dick was well on the way to a hard-on. He started to say something to me but a couple of guys came in just then and one of them asked him how it was going. He must have known them because he stuffed his dick back in his pants real quick so they wouldn't see it was getting hard. They ignored me so I pulled on my shorts, laced up my boots and went outside. I hung around a few minutes to see what would happen but they all three came out together and went off towards the coffee shop without so much as a glance in my direction. Seeing them go in the restaurant made me realize I was hungry so I went over to a shady spot by the diesel pumps and ate my sandwich and apple.

"We're goin' to L.A. if you're lookin' for a ride that direction." It was the man from the rest room, standing about three inches behind me.

"Yes, sir. L.A.'s where I'm headed. I would appreciate a ride very much."

"Well, come on then. Al, that's my partner, Al's hot to get goin'." He grabbed my backpack with one hand and stuck the other out to me. "The name's Roy."

We shook. "Dan."

"Well, come on, Dan. Let's get with it."

I followed him through the fuel islands to a bright green eighteen wheeler. There was the name of some furniture store stenciled on the trailer but I saw Al & Roy Trucking painted on the door to the cab.

"Al, this here's Dan. Needs a ride to L.A." I went to climb into the cab but Roy put his hand flat against my ass and just pushed me up, onto the seat. Then he got in and tossed my backpack onto the pad behind the seat.

Al was a big man, very muscular and with an unruly tuft of black hair spilling out over his tight tank top. "Howdy, Dan." He looked at Roy. "Well, come on, let's get going." Roy slammed the door, Al gunned the engine and we pulled out of the truck stop.

I watched Al maneuver the big rig down the road and onto the Interstate. He was a good-looking man with a very promising bulge at his crotch.

"How come you're hitching?" Roy asked.

"Usual reason. Not much money and I want to get to L.A.."

"Well, we'll get you there." He looked me up and down. "You sure do look a lot cooler than I feel. Good move, getting out of those jeans back there. It is hot!" He tried to pull his shirt off but seemed to get caught in it and knocked Al's coffee cup out of its holder onto the seat, practically in my crotch. I jumped up so I wouldn't get scalded.

"Shit, Roy, now look what you done. There's coffee all over the damn seat. And all over Dan here, too." He ran his hand lightly over my ass.

"Jeez, I'm sorry, Al. Here, Dan, move over here so's I can wipe it up." He pulled me to him, sitting me on his lap.

"Just leave it be, Roy. No sense in staining your shirt, too. The seat'll dry. You don't mind, do you Dan? Just for a while?" "No, I'm okay," I said. "How about you, Roy? Am I too heavy?"

"Not if you'll just shift a bit." He took hold of me just below my arm pits and lifted me up, sliding himself a little further under me. "There, that's better."

I could feel the hard ridge of his fly buttons pressing into the crack of my ass. That, along with the feel of his breath on my neck made my dick begin to stir in my shorts. I squirmed a little.

"Those metal buttons digging into you?" Al asked. "Roy, pull that fly back so Dan there ain't sittin' right on it."

Roy pushed me up and I heard the sound of popping fly buttons. He adjusted himself for a moment and then said okay. I sat back on another firm ridge but this one was warm and flexed under me. My dick rose up and made an obvious tent in my shorts.

"Hey, I got a better idea," Roy said. "First, we get rid of these." He tugged at my shorts and I lifted up a little, letting him push them down. "Then," he reached into the door pocket, "some of this." He pushed me up again and spread a cool slickness on my ass. Then he pulled me back down until his hardness was pressing into me. I took a deep breath. "Easy, Dan. Take it slow," he said. Suddenly my ass ring relaxed and the head of his dick slipped into me. He held me there for a couple of seconds, letting me get used to the heat and feel of him. Then he slowly let me down until I was sitting on him and his throbbing dick was buried completely inside me.

"You okay, Dan-boy?"

I took his hand and wrapped it around my hard dick. "That answer your question?"

He stroked his hand along my dick a couple of times and then reached up and pulled my shirt off. His hands played over my chest and he made me groan when he lightly rolled one of my nipples between his thumb and forefinger. "You like that too, don't you?" He ran his hands down, across my belly and then back to my chest. "You got great pecs, Dan-boy, you know that?" He was pinching both my nipples now and driving me wild.

I tried to move on him, raising myself up and then dropping back down on his dick but he wouldn't let me.

"You leave that to the truck, Dan-boy. Just settle down and the truck'll do it all for us." He ran his hand slowly over my belly. "Feel it?"

I relaxed against Roy's body and kind of let myself go. Sure enough, it was there, a deep rumbling vibration way down in my gut. At first it seemed to come from Roy's dick buried deep inside me but then I felt it in my balls and my own hard dick. It was like a million feathers falling over me and in me, charging every part of me with some sort of electricity.

"Yea, you feel it." Roy was touching my nipples again, sending charges of pleasure through me, charges which seemed to go directly to his dick because I could feel it pulse inside me, a second vibration layered over the first. He seemed to grow, filling me and focusing the power of the truck deep inside my ass.

As we rumbled down the highway I kind of gave myself up to that pole of hard flesh pushed up inside me. It was almost like dozing off except that I was wide awake, aware of Roy's hands on my belly, his fingers on my nipples. And that huge dick filling me as full as I'd ever been.

I became aware of a new sound, a new sensation. Roy was moaning and kissing me on the neck. I knew it was about to be over.

"Oh, Dan-boy. Here it comes." I felt him let go inside me, a sudden sensation of heat and motion. His dick throbbed in my ass and filled me with his liquid fire. His pleasure washed over me and then I realized it was mine, too. My dick became a fountain, spraying its own white fire onto the windshield.

When we finally caught our breath, Al looked at us and laughed. "You guys really got into that, didn't you? Well, Dano," he said, reaching out and pinching one of my tits, "I hope you also like it just a little rougher."

I saw that he had taken his dick out. It didn't look like it was even firm yet but it was already bigger than Roy's. I reached over to touch it but he pushed my hand away. "Not yet, not while I'm driving. I just let it out to cool a little."

Roy's dick began to soften and I felt it shrink a little in my ass. He pulled me further into his lap so it couldn't slip out and the feel of it stirring around inside me kept my own dick at half mast.

We passed another truck and the driver honked and waved to us. "I wonder what the other truck drivers think about all this," I said. "I mean, they must know what's going on when they see me sitting up in your lap like this."

"Well, it's one of two things, Dan-boy. Either they don't notice or they don't care."

"Or they're jealous, like he was," Al chimed in.

An hour or so later we came to one of those highway rest stops and Al pulled off the Interstate. "Time for a piss break," he said, "and for you, Roy, to wash your dick. You probably need a little relief too, huh Dano?"

I lifted myself off Roy and his dick, which was full hard again, slipped out of me. He wiped it with a towel while I pulled my shorts up. As we walked into the rest room Al gave my buns a quick pat and said, "you better go in a stall and sit for a spell. Let some of Roy drain out of you."

Roy pointed out the far end stall. "Use that one. It's always the cleanest one here. We'll wait around so you take as long as you need."

The stall was clean, so clean there wasn't even much wall writing to read. The door latch didn't work either. Al had been right though, I did need to sit for a while after having Roy's dick up my ass for the last hour and a half or so.

I hadn't been in there long before I heard someone come into the rest room, walk up to the stall door and pause for a second. Then I heard the sound of a zipper and suddenly this guy just walked into the stall, his cock and balls hanging out of his pants. I was too surprised to say anything as he pushed the door shut behind him, wedging it with a match book. Then he stood silently in front of me, his dick slowly rising. He flexed it, showing me how hard it was and then took a step closer so that it was swaying right in front of my face.

It was a good looking dick, too, shorter than average but thick and neatly clipped, leaving the skin nice and tight. The cock-head was smooth, dark pink, with a flaring ridge and an oversized pee slit, slick with honey. I leaned forward and tasted the honey, just barely touching the slit with my tongue. The guy caught his breath and his cock bounced off my nose. I brushed my lips across the head and then let him ease it into my mouth. He moaned when I brushed my tongue over that little bundle of nerves just under the head but he didn't stop. He pushed in until my nose was rubbing around in his wiry hair and his balls were settled in against my chin. He stayed that way for a while, letting me get used to the feel of his thick shaft filling my mouth.

It seemed a perfect fit, that dick and my mouth so I let him do whatever he wanted. I played with his balls and patted his buns but all he really seemed to want was to keep his dick plugged into my mouth while my tongue scrubbed it down.

After a while he took hold of my head and began to move, giving me a long, slow face fuck. When his movements became faster my tongue wrestled with his dick, trying to wrap itself around that flared head. I sucked in my cheeks and let him feel them against his shaft.

His breathing became real ragged and he locked my head in his groin, thrusting faster and faster until he let out a little yell and filled my mouth with warm, salty cum. He held me that way for a little, catching his breath and letting his dick go soft on my tongue.

"Jee-sus," he said as his dick finally slipped out of my mouth. "You give one hell of a blow job, that's all I can say." He tucked himself away, zipped up his pants, opened the door and walked out.

My dick was up and ready to go but I decided I'd better get out of there and back to the truck before Al and Roy drove off without me.

Back at the truck Roy was sitting in the driver's seat.

"Where's Al?"

"Back there, checking something in the trailer."

Another truck pulled out of the parking lot and sounded its horn. The guy I'd just blown in the rest room was driving. Roy waved at him and sounded his own horn.

"Friend of yours?" I asked.

"He is now. Probably for life." He laughed.

I looked at Roy quizzically and he laughed, handing me a fifty-dollar bill. "I just steered him to a fifty-dollar blow job and he thought it was the biggest bargain of his life."

"What the hell does that mean?"

"Hey, you said money was short. We just told the guy where you were and stood watch for him. Told him to pay whatever he thought it was worth. He thought it was worth a thousand but fifty was all he had." Roy shrugged. "Hey, it's hard to find a really good blow job when you're out on the road. What can I tell you?"

I thought about it for a second and then laughed. The one time in my life I sucked cock for money I didn't even know I was doing it.

"Here's Al. Let's get going." We began to roll towards the highway.

As soon as we were back on the Interstate Al pushed his hand into my shorts and started playing with my cock and tugging on my balls. By the bulge swelling up in his jeans I could tell he liked what he was doing; he knew I did, too, since the head of my dick was beginning to push out over the top of my shorts.

"Here," he said pulling at my shorts, "let's get you out of these silly things. I like to see the dick I'm playing with."

As soon as he had me naked he began to slap my dick lightly with his palm, making the thing snap up against my belly. Then he grabbed my nipples and pinched them, hard.

"Come on, Dano, let's see what you can do." He shrugged out of his tank top and then pulled me on top of him, burying my face in the thick, wiry hair covering his chest. His big hands held my head and pushed it down on his tit. I licked, tasting the salt dried in his hair.

"A little harder, Dano." He forced my mouth tighter against him and I sucked in his nipple and rubbed it against my teeth with my tongue. "Harder." He increased his hold on me so I bit down on his nipple. "Oh, yeah, Dano. Yeah, that's it." I felt the bulge at his crotch expand.

Al shoved a hand down between us and ripped open his jeans. "Better get down there quick, before it's too big to swallow." He pushed me down between his legs until my face was in his crotch. I reached up and took hold of his dick which was firm but not yet really hard; already it was a monster. I pushed my mouth down on it and ran my tongue around under the hood, feeling for the flair of the head. The taste was of musk and salt and it made my dick snap up harder than ever. I slid my mouth down on him, pushing his skin with me, uncovering his cock-head as it worked itself back towards my throat.

"Oh, that's it, Dano. That's it." He pushed my head farther down on his dick and then grabbed my tit, squeezing and twisting the nipple. I took hold of my own cock but he slapped my hand away. "Not yet, Dano. We're just starting and you sure don't want to unload that thing yet." I let go of myself and played with his balls instead, pulling on the long hairs and lightly pinching the sac. That really set him to groaning. He kept pinching and squeezing my nipples until they were hard, super-sensitive points.

After a while I felt the truck slow and finally swerve off the road and come to a stop. Roy reached over and ruffled my hair. "Can't drive and watch this, too. Damn, you two are hot."

Al pulled me up from between his legs. "Come on, Dano, let's us get up where Roy can see." He pushed me up onto the mattress on the platform behind the seat. Then he slipped out of his jeans and followed me up. Roy turned around and leaned against the dash, his hard cock already out of his pants and in his hand.

Al stretched out on his back and pulled me onto his chest, indicating I should go back to work on his tits. When I did he reached back and began rubbing and patting my buns. I felt his huge dick grow between us until it felt like a club pressing into my belly.

"Okay, Dano. Up and over." Al pushed me off and rolled himself over, onto my back. He sat on my legs, massaging my buns for a while before he spread some cool, slick lube over my ass. Then I felt the head of his monstrous dick, pressing against my hole, trying to force its way in. I tried to relax but God damn, he was so big I didn't think I could ever take him.

"Relax, Dan-boy," Roy said quietly. "Just relax and let him in." I felt Al's big hand on my ass, rubbing it lightly. The tip of his cock-head was forcing its way in and my ass began to loosen up but I still didn't think I was ever going to get that huge bat of a dick up my ass.

Al pushed harder against me and then suddenly hauled off and gave my ass a stinging slap. I sucked in my breath and bucked back; the head of his dick slipped neatly inside me.

"So that's what it takes, huh Dano?" He slapped my ass again, hard, and another inch of dick slipped into me. "You like that? I like it too." Another hard slap and another couple inches of dick pushed up my ass. "Oh, Dano," he said, slapping my ass again, "there's nothing better than a good, rough fuck, is there?" One more time the flat of his hand made stinging contact with my ass and he shoved the rest of his dick into me. He stopped for a minute, gently caressing my stinging buns and letting me feel that monster of a dick buried deep in my ass. The fullness was like nothing I'd ever felt. Then he moved, settling against me and I felt his balls brush against mine. He pulled back an inch or two, testing my openness. "Still kind of tight, aren't we, Dano?" He delivered another stinging slap to my ass and pulled that thing back until only the head was inside me. It felt like he'd pulled my guts out along with his dick but he put it all back in order by lunging back into me, shoving his dick even further into me than before.

"You like this, don't you Dano? Getting fucked." He began to rock his dick back and forth , pulling out just an inch or two, then pushing back in.

"Oh God, Al," I said, "don't tease me with that thing. Come on, man. Fuck!" I pushed back against him, wanting to feel that dick of his slamming in and out of my ass.

"You heard the man, didn't you," Al said to Roy who was watching us, slowly pulling on his own dick. "The man said he wanted to get fucked. Shall I accommodate him, Roy?"

"Sure, Al. Go ahead. Fuck the shit out of him."

Al pulled back, sliding about half of his dick out of me, then he slowly pushed it all back in, filling my guts again. He did it again only faster this time, then again, faster still. Finally he was yanking his whole dick out of me and then driving it back in with all the force he could muster. As he pounded that dick in and out of me I felt the fire in my balls get hotter and hotter until I knew they were going to explode out my cock.

"He's gonna to come, Al. I can see it in his face," Roy said, working his dick faster.

"Ah, shit, then so am I, Roy. So am I." He pounded my ass, trying to drive that dick of his clear through me and out my mouth. I lost all control then and started shooting the biggest load of my life. It just went on and on and on. That triggered Al and I felt him hosing down my ass, filling me with white hot cum. His thrusts in my ass gradually slowed until he finally collapsed on my back, his dick still hard but quiet in me.

"Dan-boy? You want to help me out?" It was Roy, leaning up into the compartment, his rigid dick throbbing just a little.

"Sure he will, Roy," Al said, shifting us so my lips just brushed Roy's dick. "Won't you, Dano?" He pressed on the back of my head pushing my mouth onto Roy's hard cock. It only took a minute or so. I ran my tongue under the head of Roy's dick a couple of times, he thrust forward once and then came, filling my mouth with bittersweet cum. I drained him and then lay quietly, feeling his dick begin to soften in my mouth. Finally Roy let his cock slip out of my mouth and he sat back in the driver's seat. "Guess we better get going. You guys gonna to stay up there for a while?"

Al rolled me onto my side. "What do you think, Dano? A little nap?" He flexed his dick in my ass and pulled me tight into his crotch.

"I tell you what, Roy, I'll keep him loose while you drive for another hour or two and then he can sit on your lap while I get us home. Fair deal?"

"Fair deal, Al." Roy pulled the big rig back onto the highway and drove while Al gave me the longest, slowest fuck of my young life.

THE ADULTERERS
John Patrick

The flavor of our sex was made the better by the adultery. Luke was cheating on his older lover, I was cheating on my wife. It was the pure act of doing something so wrong that everything else I had ever done paled in comparison. We were in his lover's house again, his lover's things all about us, and he was fucking me, bringing his hips to mine with a deliberate languor. I was forcing him to keep this slow, sure rhythm, making him bring his pleasure up into my body. I was somehow detached, thinking how helpless I was at this moment, unable to resist the power of his incredibly big cock. It was the most sublime moment of our love-making and I wanted to draw it out as long as possible. We couldn't wait to get to the bedroom; we were fucking in the kitchen, with me bent at the waist, guiding him in. I had prepared myself before I ever got there. Now I straightened up, reached behind me to put my fingers on his ass and press him deeper into me.

I was hoping that his lover would sometime barge in on us, thinking our crime really wouldn't be complete unless he knew about it. To have him see how my face became contorted with every contraction of my ass with every bend of Luke's sex, he would have known that I possessed his lover in the same way he had, and that his lover's cock, his hands, and his lips were leaving marks on my body, indeed my life, that would last forever.

When I didn't see Luke, I remembered the perfection of being fucked by someone else's lover. It probably had happened many more times than I ever realized because most of the time I was travelling and, meeting a stranger, I didn't know if he had a lover or not. I didn't ask and he didn't tell. When I did know, I became intoxicated with the complexity, drunk with the shame and fun of being bad, intoxicated with the idea of leaving lives we said we hated, lives that oppressed us.

"Let me meet him," I asked Luke one day. "I want to see this horrible life you want to leave."

I thought he would reject the idea, but he thought it was "groovy." My cock pulsed with excitement.

"There's no turning back now," I said, bringing my lips again to his groin.

I agreed to attend a party his lover, Ben, was giving. I arrived electric with the knowledge of how our fucking had somehow altered their lives. When I walked into his house, it was as if I was seeing it for the first time, filled with the objects Ben had collected in years of travelling. His world was material, ours was carnal: all we needed was a bed. But seeing how Luke discussed the paintings and the books and the furniture with the other guests, I realized he was not strong enough to pull himself away from all the excess.

While he was obsessed, I was oppressed by all these things, these objects. The place reeked of a life of material things, a life without passion. I wanted to leave but I stayed, talking with the decorator who had pocketed a fortune doing the place.

Finally all the other guests fled to the bars, leaving the three of us alone.

"I'm ready," Luke announced, dropping next to me on the thick cushions of the sofa, bringing my hand to his groin.

"You're drunk," I replied, pulling my hand away.

"He usually is," Ben said sharply, feeling no pain himself. "That's the only way he can stand me." He had the look of a polite man and I was a little sorry we had been punishing him for his small cock. At least, Luke had said it was small. "But everybody's small compared to this," I had countered, holding up Luke's cock.

I looked across the room at Ben, sitting in the armchair, calmly sipping a cognac. I would never have had anything to do with him if I had met him alone. He was not unattractive, just not young and thin and cute like his lover. Still, he was ten years younger than I and had a certain charm. His eyes told me he would welcome a change of pace. Ben went to their bedroom first and when we arrived, after several minutes of heated necking, Ben was lying on his stomach on the bed. He was naked and began undulating his hips the moment he saw us. Luke switched out the hall light, plunging the room into darkness. I stepped over to the bed and Ben ran his hand up my thigh, bringing it to rest on my groin. "Fuck me, somebody, please fuck me. Fuck me!"

Chuckling, Luke stripped and climbed on the bed, his nearly ten-inch- long, incredibly thick erection leading the way to Ben's puckered hole. Ben had made himself ready and Luke slowly began feeding his cock into Ben.

I let Ben undo my belt and slide down the zipper of my chinos. I dropped to my knees on the mattress and my cock hung tantalizingly in his face. It was not fully hard but getting close. Ben took it between his lips. I glanced at Luke; he was watching us intently as his cock hardened inside Ben and he began slamming it into his lover, showing no mercy.

"I want to taste your cock," Ben said, leaning forward. I smiled and cupped one hand around the back of his head, urging him down. He bent to it, hungry for me, sliding his lips around the plump head, wet with pre-cum. My fingers kneaded the back of his neck and he moaned softly as he took more of me, my knob sliding into his throat, his lips stretched around the eight inches of my thick shaft. Luke began fucking in time with Ben's sucking. Ben's saliva dripped into my pubes and coated my ball sac. He was ravenous for me, loving the taste and feel of my dick in his mouth and throat. Occasionally he would squeeze my shaft with his hands to milk more of my pre-cum out onto his lips.

After several minutes, I put my hands on the sides of his face and gently pushed him away from my cock. Luke pulled out, making a place for me. I knelt behind Ben and a moment later I was in him, a few inches at a time, until I had it all in. Suddenly I felt Luke's lips on my ass cheeks, kissing and nipping them while one of his hands slipped between my thighs and spread them a little farther apart, his fingers tugging and squeezing my balls. Then his lips pulled away and he moved closer; I sighed with anticipation when his dick pressed lengthwise into my wet crack. Gripping my hips with both hands, he moved his hard cock slowly back and forth in the crevice, his thumbs holding my cheeks apart. I blinked. I wasn't sure if I could concentrate on fucking Ben while Luke was impaling me. He pulled back a little and I felt his fat knob press against my sphincter. As I tried to keep up a steady rhythm fucking Ben, Luke pushed his mushroom head inside me and I groaned with pleasure, leaning over and clutching Ben's body tightly.

"Oh, yeah," Ben said. "Both of you fuck me."

Luke pushed another couple of inches of his shaft in and I squirmed. He moved his hands from my hips to my back, alternately caressing and massaging. "Can you take it all?" he whispered.

I grunted. Another few inches slid into me, and he increased his tempo to match mine. His hands slid across my belly and squeezed my cock as I plowed into his lover. Ben's fingers dug savagely into the mattress as our fucking continued. He tossed his head from side-to-side, lost in the passion of the moment. Hammering away at his ass for ten minutes, sweat streamed down my chest, and I started to slip over the edge.

When Ben realized I was coming, he began jerking his cock frantically. I sighed as my orgasm began and Luke held me tightly. Driven by our passion, he unloaded into me first. When I finally came, he had dropped to the mattress and stuffed his head between my thighs so that he could suck on my balls.

We rested on the bed, a tangle of sweating bodies. I was still hard, and so was Luke; our cockheads bobbed together, still slippery with cum, ready for more.

Threesomes can be difficult – someone always seems to feel left out. I suddenly felt that, as Ben began preparing Luke's asshole. In seconds, Ben was starting to put it in. Luke was guiding him because he always thought he was too quick, always hurting him. Ben was doing beautifully I thought, stroking softly, kissing Luke everywhere. When his penis was halfway in, he pushed Luke to the mattress and as his cock slid in completely, I brought my hand to Luke's ass cheeks, parting them. Ben said, "I think I can handle it from here."

It broke my mood, as if I was being dismissed. Luke had his head turned away from me and was lifting his butt to meet his longtime lover's thrusts. After cleaning myself, I left.

# # # # #

It had begun innocently enough. I kept seeing Luke at the post office when I went to pick up my mail around the same time every day. He seemed to be a happy person, always smiling, pleasant to everyone he dealt with at the post office. As the weeks passed, when I saw him alone I would return his smile, sometimes make a joke. Finally I screwed up my courage and asked him for a date. I stood close enough to read the little plastic name badge he wore: "Luke Spencer."

"I'd like that," he said, flashing his dazzling smile.

"How 'bout Friday?"

He had plans. We settled on the following Tuesday. I told him we'd finalize the details later. Later to him must have meant the next day because, after returning from making some calls, there was a message left on my answering machine: "Missed you at the post office.... What time and where?"

I called him back at the number he gave me but got no answer. I called the main number listed in the directory. The operator switched me to him. "I tried the number but it just rings and rings," I scolded.

"Oh, dear," he said, "we'll have to fix that."

Then I mentioned a seafood restaurant I was fond of. He said he knew of it but I detected hesitation in his voice.

"You don't like seafood?"

"Well ..."

I didn't let him finish. I quickly suggested a couple of other places downtown. He mentioned an oriental place. We settled on the Main Street Cafe, famous for their gourmet burgers. We agreed to meet at six. "I won't go home," he said.

"Oh, where do you live?"

"On Lido."

On Lido Beach? What on earth was a messenger boy for the government doing living on Lido Beach? I had lived on Lido for years, when it wasn't as pricey as it is today, so the only thing I could figure was he had a sugar daddy. And he doesn't seem to like seafood and his phone at the office doesn't work. What was I letting myself in for? No, this was not going well at all.

How surprised I was, then, that he met me precisely at six, greeting me with his usual happy smile, looking very clean-cut and stylish in black slacks and long-sleeve green shirt. After we were seated at our table, he let me pick the wine and then told me he did like seafood, it's just that he'd had a couple of bad dinners at the place I had first mentioned. Well, things were looking up. And maybe he got his phone fixed. I was anxious to know how he could afford to live on Lido but I decided to work up to it.

I wasn't looking for trouble, I hadn't been planning on committing adultery. I was content, I thought, to look and not touch. Yet here I was, entranced by him. I liked his slender fingers, and the way he moved, shifting his weight or rolling the stiffness out of his neck and shoulders as unselfconsciously as an animal.

I gazed for a time at his intriguing, less-than-classical profile, then shifted my stare, let it fall in a caress on his shoulders. I remembered the many times at the post office while he was standing in line before me, I would ogle his back, letting my gaze slid to the ass, which so nicely filled his tight, faded jeans. After the waiter poured our wine, I told Luke I found him very attractive, especially his smile. "Why are you so happy?" I asked.

"I guess I have nothing to be sad about, really. I was just thinking about that today. I have so much and so many people have so little."

He told me an abbreviated version of his life history, which always fascinates me. He was half-black and had been adopted at birth by a white couple who already had four daughters. His new father was multi-degreed and highly respected in his field. Luke grew up in an upper-middle class suburb of Boston and nothing was denied him. But, by high school, he had several strikes against him. The school was busing black kids in from the ghetto and he didn't fit in with them anymore than he fit in with the white students. One day, two hulking black football players cornered him in the hall and demanded to know if he was black or white. "You say you're black, show us your dick. Show us your big black dick." They held him down, undid his belt and exposed him, then dropped him in a heap. "You ain't black," one sneered. Humiliated, Luke ran home and cried himself to sleep that night. He made up his mind: he had to escape. Rather than run away, he investigated a foreign student program. His father agreed to pay for it and Luke spent his junior year studying in France. That made all the difference. There he was not white, not black, not straight, not gay, just an American.

He returned to Boston and finished high school with honors, then decided to attend a small arts school in Florida, where one of his sisters lived, rather than a large university, thinking he could more easily become part of a clique of gay classmates. But he found he wasn't particularly attracted to any of the students. The ones who turned him on were the professors, one in particular.

"I invited him out," Luke told me.

"Just like that?"

"Yeah, and I've been with him ever since."

A wave of affection swept over me. Yes, we might well get on together... We suited each other. I want nothing to do with innocents; give me a boy who has had experience, who knows what it means to please another man. And now sitting across from me was this exotic-looking boy, revealing strong white teeth between his full-bodied lips, dark cow eyes with enormous lashes, a flawless cafe au lait complexion. He appeared to be a boy of sixteen, yet he was a man of twenty-two. He was supposedly quite respectable, yet he was living with a lover twenty years his senior – a professor at his college. At once I began to desire him.

People say a lot of things against lust. They say it's disappointing – that it makes one sad – that it prevents one from working – that it prevents one from being an entirely moral person. But what they don't say is that it's never-ending. In the middle of the act of fucking I think to myself: "Oh, this is great." And yes, the boy of the moment gives me pleasure and happiness, and I feel desire and affection, but when it's over, I go on pursuing. It's as if I had never had anyone at all. And that first night with Luke, I was starved.

He was starved as well, apparently, for as we stood at our cars parked on Main Street saying goodnight, I hugged him and he hugged me back, bringing his lips to mine. I was astounded. Here I was making a public spectacle of myself on Main Street and not the least bothered by it. We kissed for several moments until I broke away and said, "Let's get in the car."

"No, I have to be getting home."

"Just for a minute."

There was no argument. In the car, our passion grew. We clutched each other tightly as we kissed. I took a break, caressed his face. "I've been wanting to do this all night."

"Me too," he sighed.

We kissed some more. Then he pulled from my embrace. "What you must think of me," he said sadly, "being with someone ..."

I shook my head. "We've been looking at each for months. This had to happen." I groped his crotch. At first, I couldn't believe what I was feeling. There seemed to be no end to his cock, only semi-hard.

I chuckled, gazed down at his crotch. "I thought those guys said you weren't black..."

"I was very young then. Besides, I have what's known as a surprise package."

"I'll say," I sighed. I started to tug at the zipper of his trousers.

He brought his hand to mine, stopping me. "I have to go."

"Lunch tomorrow?"

He smiled, then nodded. "I'll think of something. Maybe I'll get sick around noon and have to leave."

# # # # #

The next day, Luke did meet me for lunch, behind the locked door of my office. I told my secretary I was not to be disturbed. After some heavy petting, I brought my hand to his crotch. He stood up and let me open his pants. Up close, quiveringly alive, uncut and unreasonably huge, Luke's cock glistened. I have been with a few black men in my time and am usually impressed, not so much by the quantity of it but by the quality of their fucking. I had become a fan, of sorts, and indulged whenever I could, usually when I travelled to New York.

But Luke was something else. He was the youngest black I had ever been with and I now knew he had the longest, thickest cock I had ever encountered, a monstrous rod of polished ebony. Massive and upward-curving, it both fascinated and horrified me. It was a cock I'd dreamed about, a sculptured masterpiece. Like my own cock, when fully erect, the foreskin disappeared completely. My heart pounding, my mouth was open in awe and anticipation. I kissed the tip of it, gingerly at first, then with longer, sucking movements. Little by little, I took the head into my mouth, and after working it for awhile, Luke took over, taking hold of my head and pushing forward. His cock was soon pressing at the soft skin at the back of my mouth, and I gagged.

"Just relax," he said.

I tried. I sucked the pulsing flesh into me, choking, gagging again, tears forming. He sensed my discomfort and tried pulling away, but I grabbed his hips and kept sucking. He groaned as my throat contracted. My entire body was shuddering as another inch or two of hard cock went down my gullet. Luke slowly moved back and forth, establishing a rhythm. My throat expanded as he fucked. He came, groaning, tugging at my hair, then dragged his cock out of my mouth, but I desperately tried to hold him, running my tongue over the head while I breathed around it. I jacked myself off as I lapped up his cum.

Before that fateful lunch, there was no thought that this was anything more than a harmless flirtation. Now all that had changed: we began our affair. We had to. All values were changed. From the moment I saw that cock, my lust for it was all. It would be stupid if we could not have these moments of happiness. And the strength I would draw from him would be great enough to enable me to again deal with my life, a life that had become sad and hopeless. And for his part, before he could find no place for me in his life, now I had one. I would be his secret lover.

70

For our second meeting, I rented a hotel room just down the street from where he lived with his lover on Lido Beach. The moment we were alone in the room, I wrapped him in my arms. His kisses were as invigorating as the first time: deep, warm, passionate. His hands roamed my body, found my erection. I let him undress me and suck me for awhile, exquisitely preparing me for the main event. He undressed and came over and stood next to the bed. I reached up and put my hand around the monster. I wanted it up my ass this time. I rolled over and lay face down, a pillow under my hips. I felt the bed sink when Luke got between my legs. I tried to relax as he held me down, greased me, then pushed the head of his cock into me. A flash of lightning lit up the room, followed by a vast, long drawn-out roar, stifling my groan as he entered me. As I writhed with the pain, the surf slammed insistently against the beach outside our window. Luke backed off a bit, brought his fingers to my asshole, played with me. He tried again. Then again. Finally I was pushing back at him, the shaft gently sliding deep into my tight ass. He rocked the cheeks of my ass while he relentlessly plumbed my depths. I lay still and took it. He lifted me to my hands and knees and brought his hand around to play with my dick. My ass clenched his cock tightly as he developed a languid rhythm. He was in no hurry today but I couldn't help it – I came, my jism flooding the pillow beneath me. I collapsed under him but kept squirming as he planted his hands on either side of my head and began pistoning in and out of me. "Give it to me," I pleaded.

And he did. The thrusts became more frantic and he flung himself upon me, kissing me violently as his cum filled me. After the last shudders of his orgasm, he collapsed on top of me, panting. His dick was spent but remained sizeable, still lodged in me. Slowly he pulled it from me and rolled off of me. He smiled and gave me a quick kiss. "I've got to get back to work."

"I know," I said.

After we showered, we stood briefly at the window, watching the storm.

"I have to go to New York next week. Oh, how I love New York," I sighed, dreaming of all the cute boys waiting to be corrupted there.

"I'd love any city if I was there with you," he said.

"Maybe we can go together sometime."

"Promise?"

"Of course."

I had already fallen into the habit of thinking of the future in relation to Luke. And continually, now, Luke sought physical contact, something quite new to me. He had put his arm round my waist and laid his head on my chest. He kissed my hand. I smiled, then kissed his forehead. He chuckled.

"Why do you laugh?" I asked.

"It's fun seeing you so happy." His hand slid down and gripped my cock, now rising again. "This happy!"

He had given me a fresh strength, unused for perhaps ten years. I wanted this stranger to be mine forever. How normal, how natural it was, this life we had begun together. It was as if I had never lived in any other way. How quickly my past had closed up behind me. And it seemed the more aware I became of it the more our love grew, as a torrent swells gradually more and more. As he leaned against me and stroked my cock to full attention again, his hands slid over my waist, down my hips.

I had no time to object. He went to his knees before me, his head bent. He laid his cheek against my erection, and my breath caught in my throat. I was all hard, searching desire, a question in need of an answer, and I found it in his lips, tentative, sweet, in his delicious murmuring moan, in the teasing tug of his mouth slipping over and back, back and forth.

When I could bear it no longer, I withdrew from him, slid down his body, knelt with him, stifled his protest with a kiss, tasted myself on his tongue. I pulled away, breathless. "I am not used to this, to being wanted so much."

His response was a sigh, a lingering kiss, a hand that crept round my back and pulled me closer. I cupped his ass in both hands, lifting him slightly so that I could slide between his thighs, my erection pulsing against the soft damp heat there. I slid back and forth, and he gripped his thighs tight around it, his dark, intense eyes softening, hazing, as the sensation flowed from me to him, and all through him. His head fell back; I kissed his throat, traced with my tongue the clear sweep of his jaw.

"Please," he whispered against my mouth, and I laid him down on the rough carpet, covering him with my body. He wrapped his legs around me and guided my cock into his asshole. He closed his eyes, waiting, waiting, until finally I was all the way in him and we began to move together in harmony again.

"I wonder if any of the other men here fantasize about their wives making love to strangers like you do," Marie said, between bites of her chicken salad.

I had taken her to lunch at the Brass Rail, a leafy greenhouse-style restaurant she liked because they hung her paintings on the walls.

I smiled, glancing quickly around to see if anyone was listening. I leaned over the table. "You should know better than to believe anything I say when we're making love."

She fixed her eyes on me. "Anything?"

I looked away, sorry I had said it.

Her face was serious and slightly puffy, short black hair tousled, dark eyes moist. "I love you."

I didn't answer right away.

She insisted. "The question is, do you love me?"

The question – its timing, the plea in it – suddenly irritated me. Not her usual style. It wasn't something to be asked for, like a panhandler asking for a quarter. "Sure, you know I do."

Her quiet, watchful eyes widened and a touch of pink brushed her cheeks. "You've met someone again."

I poured the rest of the bottle of white wine in her glass.

"Well?"

"No...I mean, yes. Of course, I meet someone every day."

"You know what I mean."

"No I don't, dear."

"I do. I'm not enough for you. You're back to those boys again. But this one, he must be special. Another special one. Like the last one, what was his name?"

"Don."

"Oh, yes, Don. Dandy Don the Dancer." Then, with a hint of challenge, she asked, "Can I meet this one?"

"Absolutely not."

But there was no refusing Marie. She always got her way, one way or another. It was a subtle blackmail. She had accused me of marrying her for her money and it was true, I had. But she was also a talented, open-minded artist as well as a Coca-Cola bottling company heiress. She said she understood my being bisexual because she was one, too. As long as it didn't affect our marriage, we agreed to indulge ourselves as we wished. She had her friends, and I never questioned her. It was as "open" a marriage as I could tolerate.

Don, the dancing fool, was the last one of my lovers she wanted to meet; he left town rather than face her. Then there was the underage prostitute that I kept stashed in a motel room across town. He left town, too, but losing him didn't affect me. It had been a torrid three weeks of fucking that I will never forget, but there was no future in it. But Luke represented something new to both of us – a clear threat to the sanctity of our marriage, such as it was. Even after being with Ben and Luke, I still held out the possibility I could lure Luke away, keep him somewhere for my exclusive use.

I called Luke at work and invited him to "a party" at my house. I told him Marie would be there. "Groovy," came the response. Luke arrived quite late. Ben was with him. Later, Luke took me aside and told me Ben was giving him a hard time about being in my house, with my wife present. They fought and Ben left in a huff. Luke asked if I would take him home. "Maybe you should stay here tonight," I suggested with a wink.

Luke looked across the room at Marie and then back at me. "You sure?"

"She's never had a black man," I said.

When we were at last alone, I went to kitchen and got some joints out of the freezer. When I returned to the living room, Luke was taking a large conch shell from the end table. Marie was asking him about his work. She watched him a moment, putting the conch to his ear and listening eagerly. The shiny pink convolutions of the shell always reminded Marie of a vagina and she had quite a collection. Luke's eyes widened. "These things are so neat."

Marie smiled at him and took a toke of the strong reefer. "You don't hear the ocean. That's blood pulsing in your inner ear."

"Is that right?" He put the conch back on its stand.

He sat alone on the couch, facing Marie and I as we sat on the couch opposite.

Feeling sexier with each puff, Marie smiled at Luke. She began slowly opening and closing her legs. She wore no panties. Grinning lewdly at Luke's rapidly expanding crotch, she asked him about his "boyfriend."

"He's okay. He just had a little too much to drink tonight." Luke couldn't think of anything more to say, just stared and swelled.

Finally Marie went over to Luke, started taking off her blouse. She straddled his leg and kissed him, tongue probing. Luke pushed up her skirt and clasped her naked ass.

Marie reached down, kneaded the bulge at his crotch.

As Luke began kissing her back, I grew achingly hard.

Lifting a freckled breast to his face, she stuck the nipple into his mouth. As Luke sucked, feeling it grow and stiffen, he glimpsed me getting up and joining them.

Marie helped Luke jerk off his jeans and shorts. Marie looked as dumbfounded as I had when I first saw Luke's cock. Timorously, she cupped the pendulous nut bag. It drooped over the sides of her wrist. The trembling, delicate fingers of her other hand fluttered along the veiny swollen monster. It swelled even longer and thicker, rising fully erect and vibrant, stiff and massive in her small hand. Marie licked her lips nervously, eyes wide and fascinated. She slipped the foreskin back and forth, covering and uncovering the great, fleshy knob, shiny and dimpled like an apple.

"Go ahead and suck it," I said.

Marie released his sac and the weighty testicles sagged. She grasped the shaft with both hands and struggled to work her mouth around it.

She pulled back, licking her lips, staring in wonder at the magnificent dick jutting from her hands. "God," she gushed. He gasped when her warm, wet mouth engulfed it. She gently manipulated his scrotum while her tongue lapped at the underside of his glans, alternately sucking it against her hard palate. Luke closed his eyes and threw his head back. I moved closer, my cock dangling in his face. I took his head in my hands and turned it. He opened his mouth and I slid the head in.

I was soon grunting along with Marie's lascivious smacking sounds. Despite the pot, I was already getting close. My cock surged as Marie suddenly fingered my anus. I had to squeeze Luke's head tightly to hold back. "Wait! I'm gonna . . ."

Luke's warm mouth suddenly released me into the cool air.

Luke lifted his head, dazed by lust and pot and wine.

"Fuck me," I pleaded.

I was soon on my back, naked, one leg high along the top of the sofa, one foot on the floor. Luke entered me, slowly, gently. Marie stood next to us, her eyes wide as I managed to take it all. Marie's hands twisted in Luke's hair as his head moved between her widely spread legs. He clutched a breast in each hand. Marie's head arched back, tendons standing out in the slender neck, her face flushed a bright red. Black hair mussed, lips smeared and swollen, eyes bleary, she was obviously high and aroused. Luke massaged her voluptuous breasts, squeezing each nipple, tugging and twirling, clenching his teeth. Enraptured, a wanton expression on her face, Marie gazed spellbound at the black cock pummeling my ass.

I came even before Luke managed to get a good rhythm going.

He pulled out of me, anxious to put it into Marie.

Marie sat next to my feet on the sofa and lifted her legs. Afraid and admiring at the same time, she fondled its thick girth as though it were a jeweled, dangerous dagger. Luke sighed in recognition as she palmed one dangling nut, gently squeezing it while she continued working the foreskin back and forth.

Then she obediently leaned forward and began rolling her tongue over and under and around the sculpted, flared-back glans.

Luke grunted. "Ah, yes. Lick it baby, lick it. It likes you. That's it."

On his knees in front of the sofa, he slid fully into Marie easily on the first try. She squirmed, locked her mouth onto his, wrapping her legs about his waist, pumping.

"Oh no!" Marie cried. "Easy... go easy, please "

"Don't worry, honey," Luke reassured. "I won't hurt you. Umm...yeah, relax, let me do the work."

The couch rocked.

"Uh!... my god! ...please go slow! Oh, just let me adjust... Uh! ...yeah ..."

"Ah yes! No hurry... Yes... Tight hot pussy!"

I jerked myself as I leaned over and kissed Marie, then dropped my head to her shoulder to watch Luke fuck. This seemed to relax her.

Luke was happier. "Better...um!...oh, baby, that's better...oh, easy."

Luke's muscular back writhed, extended arms straining to hold his weight off Marie while forcing her legs wide apart. The view was shockingly erotic. He's a master at this, I realized. He could fuck anything. He was all black in bed. His buttocks rippled, pressing carefully in and out. Right before my eyes, the mighty shaft was impaled only halfway into Marie's furry nest.

Marie's body began hunching in short, quick jerks. I thought, "The bitch is finally getting what she deserves!" But the anxious tone of her voice gradually changed to one of intense pleasure. "Fuck me! Oh, God!"

Slowly Luke squeezed it in, pinning her down to stop her elated thrusts. He kept sinking it in deeper, inch by salacious inch. After each partial withdrawal, more of the invading dick shone with Marie's lubricant. A lot of it was still dry.

I went over to them and loosely encircled the hot column with my hand, letting it slip slickly between my fingers, feeling it going in and out of Marie's body, an odd, thrilling sensation. Luke kissed me. I kissed him back. "Fuck her, stud," I said. "Fuck her like she's never been fucked."

"Uh...uh!...it's so...yes," moaned Marie. "Like that. Oh, yeah, fuck me! God, that's good!"

Luke suddenly shoved it all the way home and Marie's head jerked up off the back of the couch. She yelled at the top of her voice: "Oh my god!" She thrashed her head, gasping rapturously, impossibly full now, utterly ravished by sensations she'd never known. "Oh goddamn! That's too...uh!...yes!"

Muscular arms bulging, Luke suddenly held himself still and rigid, plugged tightly into the rhapsodic Marie, rocking slightly from side to side. I stood over them, jacking off at the incredible sight before me. Marie was no longer my wife, nor was she a lesbian. She was a slut of the first order, being savaged by a black man, every white woman's greatest fantasy.

At last, Luke withdrew almost completely, then began long searching strokes, in and out, unhurried, masterful, generating utmost bliss. Muscles rippling, he grunted. "Um!...that's it. Yeah!"

Marie's feet drummed spasmodically against his back. Her bottom bounced compulsively upward, impaling herself repeatedly on the stiff dick, smacking into Luke, taking it all, thrilling to it. "Uh!...uh!...so...don't stop...God don't ever stop! Fill my cunt!"

I ejaculated tremendously, feeling as though my spine was jerked out with it. My cum landed across Luke's sweaty back.

Luke smiled at me and suddenly tensed; soon he too was shuddering. "Oh shit!"

I stood over them, still jerking my cock, which had lost little of its hardness.

Marie yelled fiercely, "Give it to me, stud! Oh, God, I'm coming!"

Luke waited until Marie's convulsions had slowed and then slipped out. "She's all yours, man." I took his half-hard cock, sopping wet, in my hand and played with it while I got between Marie's outstretched thighs. As I began sliding my cock into Marie's hot pussy, Luke moved closer and brought his cock to my lips. I sucked him and fucked her for less than five minutes before I came again. Then it was Luke's turn again. I left them there on the couch, fucking, and went to bed.

# # # # #

Rubbing the stubble on my chin, I peered wearily through smarting eyes into the cone of light splitting the darkness. I had left New York early. I hadn't been able to reach Marie for three days. She was fine, sleeping soundly when I left early Monday. A well-earned sleep, I thought. She took Luke home and returned to the house at around three and came to bed. I pretended to be asleep when she crawled in next to me. There would be plenty of time to talk about what had just occurred. She had to be exhausted and sore. What stud Luke was! I got hard just thinking about it.

At last I pulled into the driveway and got out, leaning on the car to do a few deep knee bends. The house was dark at eight o'clock. I unlocked the door, somehow feeling like a burglar, and entered, clicking on lights. I called out to Marie. There was no answer. I slowly made my way to the bedroom wing. The door to Marie's bedroom was slightly ajar. A pale moonlight spilled into the room, allowing enough illumination so I could see clearly and I easily recognized the young black who was fucking my wife. This had become one of those peculiar affairs between the wife who has been betrayed and the object of her husband's lust. I was sure this ridiculous liaison, born of shock and jealousy, was unworthy of Marie and would soon end. Still, tears came to eyes as I turned and raced out of the house and got into my car. I needed a stiff drink and a stiff cock to spend the night with – and I knew Ben would be happy to provide both.

THE BOYS IN THE WINDOW
John Patrick

It began as a flash of flesh, a glimpse of cock.

Even though it was raining and the window was wet, the first time I saw the figure I knew it was a boy. I moved closer. A bare shoulder, a sinuous hip. When the figure turned, a bit of light pubic hair, a glimpse of cock. And then he was gone.

I had just moved to the Colony Club and my apartment was across the courtyard, Building C to the boy's B, my 4 to the boy's 3, on the second floor, and the thought of him there, in the window, for some odd reason, left me with an incandescent glow. I stood at the window hoping to see the boy again, not looking for another free show, just to prove I hadn't been dreaming. The rain stopped. Darkness fell. A light switched on, but the boy didn't re-appear in the window.

The next day when I returned from work, I went to the window and looked out, across the courtyard. Occasionally, I swore I saw something, but there were no more flashes of flesh, glimpses of cock.

When I went to bed that night I felt uneasy, as if I had done something wrong, and that there was a potential in me to be something I had never thought much about: a voyeur. In fact, I had really never given sex a whole lot of thought. When I was very young, I wondered why most boys seemed preoccupied with it. I married right out of high school and Ann was a gentle woman who, I thought, cared as little about sex as I did. There was little passion in our relationship; we never experimented beyond the missionary position and she seemed satisfied with having sex once a week or so. But after a couple of years of a dull marriage, I found myself looking at other men, single men, obviously free, happy. I was missing something. Then one day I was driving home from a business meeting and stopped at a rest stop on the interstate. There was only one person in the john, a young man, with a yellow windbreaker. He stood at the sink, combing his hair. As I pissed, he walked over and stood next to me. He undid the buttons of his jeans and pulled out his cock. I could sense he was staring at me, at my cock as I pissed. I looked at his face. He was staring down. I shook my cock and his hand fell to it.

When I went to the rest stop again, a man warned me about the police; he told me about the bookstore. There, I was again warned about the police. I decided such sex was too dangerous to even contemplate. Then Ann met another man at work. We parted amicably.

Now there was a naked boy in the window. On Saturday, when I returned from grocery shopping, I finally saw him again, only this time he was with a man, a man much older than himself. I could now see plainly that the boy was fair, with a slim, nearly hairless body. He sat on the bed and unzipped the older man's trousers. His sucking of the man lasted only seconds. An hour later, another man, even older than the first, visited the bedroom. An ugly, hairy man. The boy only had to touch the man's penis and it became hard in loose trousers. As he had done with the first man, he took this man's cock in his mouth. The speed with which the boy brought the men off was remarkable. He reminded me of the talented young man who gave me my first blowjob at the rest stop.

But it was the man who came that night that excited me. The two of them lay together, the dark man taking the younger, fair one in his arms. He held him gently for a time, then started rocking him, comforting him, soothing the tender skin. Slowly they sought each other's lips. They teased, probed, tantalized each other and I stroked my erection to climax. Then I moved closer to the window, so close I was pressing against it. The dark one drew the fair one to him and, as his hands lifted the loose shorts and moved under them, I could almost feel the younger one opening up to his lover. After they had stripped each other of their clothes, the dark man lowered himself across the boy full length and they moved in unison, hips and thighs undulating, and they sucked at each other greedily. I slowly rubbed my cock again, my mouth hungry to taste my neighbor's. Consumed, I imagined myself kissing their nipples, spreading their thighs and sucking and sucking and sucking...

\# \# \# \# \#

"You're the guy in the window." The boy's voice betrayed no animosity.

"No," I said. I wanted to hang up the phone but could not.

"Oh, yes, I know it's you. The man that lived there before you, he became a nuisance, but you, I can tell you'd be fun."

"Me? Fun?"

"Yeah, the shy ones are always the most fun. At least I think so."

"How did you get my number?"

"I know someone at the phone company. You'd be surprised at all the things I can find out."

I hung up.

An hour later, the phone rang again.

"Come to the window."

"No."

"Yeah, come to the window."

I put the phone down and stepped over to the window. The boy lay on the bed; he was naked, stroking himself, holding his cordless phone with his other hand.

I went back to the phone. "So?"

"Yeah," the boy moaned, "you're the stud I've been waiting for."

"Me, a stud?"

"I think so. But I want to make sure. I want to see what you look like naked."

"No." I hung up the phone.

When the phone rang again, I ignored it.

The next day, the boy was on the phone again, going on as if he had never been interrupted. "What's so perfect about this is that we can give in, enjoy each other, and have nothing to be ashamed of."

As the boy went on, talking dirtier and dirtier, my cock began throbbing, reaching out. I crouched in the darkness, entirely alone, invisible, yet exposed.

"Yeah, I've gotta see your dick. Your big dick."

"No," I said, hanging up.

I imagined the boy was basically good but circumstances had forced him to become a prostitute. Then one day he had forgotten to draw the curtains and the man who had rented the apartment before me had seen him with a client. The boy began to enjoy the theater of it so much, he even entertained his dark lover in the spare bedroom. I mused that the man who was spying had passed away from cardiac arrest, watching this sexy youth, his clients and his lover in the window. At night I lay still, listening, thinking, somehow, that if I listened intently enough I could hear the secrets the room held, the secrets of the man who had been there before me, wondering what he had done to become a nuisance to the boy. My eyes searched the carpet for signs of the semen the man must have spilled there, watching the boy and his tricks. I knew that when I came watching the boys in the window, those were the most violent orgasms I'd ever experienced.

I bought a cordless phone. I had always wanted one and found one on sale. And I bought binoculars. But a week passed without a call, without a show.

Then, on Saturday, there were six men in a row, starting at noon. The boy even entertained two at once, in the best show of the day. I watched through my new binoculars. The two men, in their mid-thirties, appeared to be lovers. They kissed each other on the lips but did not kiss the whore. He lay on the bed and sucked them, alternately, then stuffed both cocks in his mouth at once.

They indicated for the boy to stand and pulled his shirt tail out of his jeans. He took off his shirt while their thumbs worked at the buttons on his 501s. The pair pushed his jeans down over his hips and they fell around his ankles. He stepped out of the jeans, and stretched out on the bed, raising his arms over his head.

The two lovers knelt beside him and ran their hands over his soft body. They kissed his nipples and stroked his cock.

The boy opened his legs, like I'd seen him do before, inviting an invasion. The taller lover stretched out on top of the boy and moved in a gentle fucking motion. The boy rested one leg over his back and braced the other on the mattress. The tall man moved down the whore's belly and ate his cock and balls slowly, as if he was lingering over an exquisite meal. The boy's body began to rock gently. I could see him rise up and the man put three fingers snugly inside his ass.

While he was being finger-fucked, the boy was rocking like a baby. The other man put his cock in his face and the boy began sucking it.

The taller lover replaced his fingers with his cock. The shorter lover moved down hesitantly, to where he could no longer avoid the cock furiously pumping in and out of the boy. Soon he was licking the prick as it made its journey in and out.

At one point, the shorter one took the whole of the taller's cock down his throat, sucking eagerly, his fingers kneading his lover's large balls. The taller man pumped in and out of the shorter one's mouth just the same as if it were the whore's ass.

The whore sidled his way around so he could take the shorter one's cock in his mouth again. He stroked and squeezed the head, finally taking the pulsing meat into his mouth. I lay back and began stroking my cock feverishly, enjoying the show.

Feelings of lust coursed through me, along with a little bit of jealousy. I came when I saw both men shooting. As their hard-ons withered and they returned to reality, the whore reached down and took a cock in each hand, stroking and kneading them until they were again erect. Eventually he sat up and pushed their cocks closer together, rubbing the head of one up and down the other's shaft. He knelt and licked each of them, then took both inside his mouth, though he could only fit an inch or two. They all appeared to be breathing heavily.

Now it was the shorter one's turn to fuck. The whore gently guided the cock inside of him. I could see he was moaning, spreading his ass cheeks as the shorter lover sank it in inch by yielding inch. The shorter man began to fuck the whore, slowly at first, then faster, until the boy was on all fours, pushing against the shorter one's dick, and it appeared he was begging for more.

The taller one slid beneath the whore and began sucking the boy's cock as his lover thrust in and out of the asshole without missing a beat. The whore bent down and began sucking the taller one's cock again. They went on like that for several minutes and I thought I'd die of pleasure right then and there. Then the taller one squirmed free and mounted his lover, sticking his cock deep in the man. It was an incredible finish: the whore jacking off as he was fucked by the shorter one, who came while being fucked by his lover, who was the last to come. Incredibly, I came again.

Hoping for another show like that, I couldn't drag myself from the window, my new phone close at hand. Even though I was as exhausted as the boy must have been, I brought dinner into the den for fear of missing the dark lover's visit. But the room remained empty all night. And the phone never rang.

Sunday, only two men came calling, late in the afternoon, one leaving shortly before the other arrived. The boy gave them blowjobs. Then darkness. Again, the phone didn't ring.

By Wednesday, I was desperate. Finally, late that night, the phone rang and I scrambled to answer it.

"I want to see your dick."

"Oh, no," I groaned.

"Please."

"Oh, all right," I found himself saying. I stood before the window, removing my clothing. I could see the boy was nude, lying on the bed, abusing himself.

I picked up the phone. "There."

"I like it. But you've been a bad man."

"I have?" I caressed the new phone.

"Yes, you watched me all weekend."

"But I ..."

"Oh, but it's okay. You're a stud. Spread your legs."

I did as I was told. The boy stood and came to his own window. He stroked his cock, posing in the window. It was a lovely cock, I decided, one that I would suck. Yes, I really would. If I were over there, I'd suck it. As I came, violently, I cried, "Oh, babe, my sweet baby..."

I let the phone fall to the floor.

"What?" the boy asked when I had the phone back in my hand.

"What?"

"You called me your sweet baby. That's what you called me."

"Yes. That's what I call my wife."

The boy chortled. "Your wife? Where the fuck is she?"

"Oh, I mean, my ex-wife. We're divorced."

"And I bet you're horny, just like all the married guys that come here. Does it bother you that so many come here?"

"Oh, no. I rather enjoy them. You probably hate them, but I enjoy them, especially seeing how happy you make them."

"I don't hate them. I use them."

Still short of breath, I asked, "Whatever happened to the dark one? The one who used to come at night."

"His wife found out. Always happens to me."

I continued to move my fingers, sliding them up and down my cock, now swollen again. And when I came, he did as well.

"Oh, yes," the boy sighed, "I'd like you over here. It makes me excited. If you were here, that'd even be better, don't ya think?"

Spent, I hung up.

Friday came and the boy was calling me again. "I'm watching," he said.

"Yes, I can see you."

"I wish you were here."

"No." I could feel how hard his cock would be, how sweet and wet his kisses would be, how he would make me come again and again. The boy was easily the most exciting person I had ever known.

"I want you to come over."

"Oh, no, I couldn't."

"Oh, c'mon. It'd be fun."

"No, I couldn't go there." I closed my eyes and imagined myself there, whipping the boy for being a prostitute, a whore. "Goddamn you!" I would cry. And the dark man, the boy's real lover, would be there and he would help me tie the boy up. The dark man would go first, shoving his ghastly little prick in the boy's mouth while I teased the boy's cock until he cried that he wanted to come and, after several minutes, we would let him. Then we would switch places and I would let him suck on my cock while the dark man fucked him, holding back, enjoying himself at the boy's expense, stabbing him, hurting him.

"Then I'll come over there," the boy said into the phone. "Yes, tomorrow. For drinks."

"No."

"Yes."

"No. Please, no."

The following day, I watched as the boy crossed the courtyard, his teased blond hair lifting proudly from his plain, faintly handsome face. His dangling gold earring seemed to wink at me. He was about five feet, six inches tall and as he tip-tapped in his shiny black boots across the tile and brick expanse of the courtyard, making his way to the foyer, I imagined the clouds of cheap scent that wafted behind him.

The boy rang the bell to my apartment and I imagined the amusement that was written all over his face would slowly melt when he realized I was not going to answer, not going to let him in.

A few minutes later, the phone rang. I ignored it. An hour later, it rang again. This time I picked it up.

"What's wrong?" the boy asked.

"Nothing."

"What did I do?"

"Nothing, it's just that I – well, I just can't ..." My hand moved to my cock and as I stroked it, tears came to my eyes.

"Story of my life," the boy said, his voice broadening out into the kind of laugh you hear at the end of a late, good party.

A WEEKEND IN THE COUNTRY
Greg Bowden

To this day I'm not sure just what there was about the stud that caught my attention but something sure did. I first saw him sitting in the coffee shop where I usually pick up my morning coffee on the way to work. He was obviously a construction worker – those of us who spend our days in the towers of commerce rarely wear jeans and flannel shirts to work – a nice-looking guy with a great body, sporting a reddish mustache and dark hair, cut short, but not exactly a man who would stand out in a crowd. I really didn't think all that much about him, except perhaps that in some way he was interesting.

I saw him in the coffee shop every day for the next few weeks and I took to nodding and smiling at him when I went in for my morning caffeine fix. After a couple of days he began to nod back and sometimes even added a smile or wink of recognition. One morning he was sitting with another guy and when I nodded the other guy looked up and kind of half nodded at me too.

By the end of the second week we had graduated to a mumbled "G'mornin'" as I passed through with my coffee. When his buddy was there he would look up and sometimes toss me a quick smile too. It wasn't long before I began to look forward to this little morning ritual.

Ever since the building boom began a year or two ago one of my frequent lunchtime routines has been to wander around the Financial District and watch the new buildings go up. Well, to be strictly accurate, what I watch are the guys who are putting the new buildings up. Anyway, one day I looked down into the hole where the Surety Life building used to be and found my morning greeter driving a bulldozer around on the sub-basement level, getting it ready for the pile drivers.

Once I found him I spent all my lunch hours standing behind a safety fence, watching him work. It wasn't long before he became aware of me standing at that fence and it didn't take much more time to put me together with the morning coffee shop greeting.

I was afraid that seeing me standing there watching him every day might put him off but it didn't. He still smiled or winked when he saw me in the coffee shop and, as the days went by, he began to play to me as I stood and watched him drive his dozer around. He would glance up and smile when he saw me arrive and often nodded to me as I left. One day when no one else was standing around watching the construction he glanced up at me and then hopped off the dozer and stood behind it. I could only see him from the waist up but it was obvious that he was taking a leak, looking up at me and grinning the whole time. When he was finished he stepped back and made a little show of buttoning up his fly. He didn't show me anything but he still made my dick stir in my pants.

A few days later when I stopped at lunchtime the bulldozer was gone and the pile drivers were being set up in the hole. I'd seen my man in the coffee shop that morning as usual so I figured he had to be around somewhere, maybe on a new job already. When I turned to go someone behind me put a hand on my shoulder and said, "Looking for me?"

He caught me totally by surprise. "You're not working," I stammered.

"No. This job's finished as far as we're concerned."

I regained my balance and said, "Then what are you doing here? Checking your work?"

He laughed. "No, the Devil created foremen to do that. I just came around to see if you were here. You've been such a loyal sidewalk supervisor I thought maybe I could return the favor and buy you a drink or something after work. What d'you say?"

"Uh, well, I don't get off until after five and..."

"No problem. Tell you what, why don't you meet me over at the union hall whenever you get off and we'll go from there. Just tell the guy at the front desk you're looking for George, okay?" Before I could say anything he handed me a card with the union hall address on it and disappeared into the lunchtime crowd on the street.

I went back to my office and spent a very unproductive afternoon wondering why an attractive but apparently straight bulldozer operator wanted to take me out for a drink and what I was getting myself into. I wasn't even sure I was going to keep the appointment until I found myself standing in front of the union hall at a little after five.

Inside a bored looking guy at a desk seemed to be expecting me. "Yea, George said to send you back to the locker room. You lookin' for work or somethin'?" He looked me up and down with an expression that said construction workers in three-piece suits rarely got jobs.

"No, just looking for George," I said.

"Well, you can't miss him. He's the only guy back there. Hell, he's the only guy in the whole fuckin' place 'cept me. I'd take you back only I'm not supposed to leave the desk. Just go through there," he pointed at a door off to his left, "and down the hall. There's signs." He dismissed me and went back to his Popular Mechanics.

When I found it the locker room was silent except for the sound of a shower running. While I was wondering what I was supposed to do next I heard the shower shut off and then George appeared, a towel tied around his waist. Without those heavy shirts and baggy jeans he always wore he was quite impressive. He was a big man, a little on the stocky side and very solid looking. His chest was wide and flat, his dark nipples pushing out through a dusting of wiry reddish hair which tapered down to a narrow line which then disappeared under his towel.

"Hey, here you are," he exclaimed. "I still gotta shave so why don't you grab a shower if you want. Towels are there by the door and you can put your clothes on that bench over there, by my stuff." He indicated an open locker, clapped me on the back and went into the lavatory. I was a little nervous but I thought oh, what the hell. The shower room in the construction workers union hall – it'll make great fantasy material. I stripped out of my clothes and headed for the showers.

As I passed the lavatory I could see George standing at the mirror. He'd discarded the towel and showed an ass that was just as impressive as the rest of him. "I left you some soap in the shower," he called to me. "Don't take too long."

Under the hot water I tried to imagine what it would be like to shower there when the place was filled with naked construction guys. True to form my dick began to rise at the thought but I was afraid George might look in and catch me that way so I gritted my teeth and flipped on the cold water. That brought me back to a more presentable state right quick. I let myself have a fast hot rinse and then got out. I dried off, wrapped the towel around me and went back into the locker room.

George was digging around in his locker when I joined him. "Nothing like a hot shower, is there?" he said, turning to look at me.

Another surprise. A big one. From a thick bush of auburn hair at George's crotch hung the biggest, thickest, most beautiful dick I had ever seen in my life, nearly as thick as my wrist and perfectly proportioned. He hadn't been clipped but the soft, supple looking foreskin couldn't hide the deep flare where the head joined the shaft. The whole thing glistened like damp velvet and looked like it would be smooth to the touch.

"You're staring," George said quietly.

I tried to recover but didn't make a very good job of it; I just couldn't seem to pull my eyes away from his crotch. Finally I blurted out, "That has to be the most beautiful dick I have ever seen on anyone."

He chuckled. "Well thank you. I'm glad you think so. Go ahead, look at it all you like." He flexed and it jumped a little.

"It looks so smooth..." I said. "Does the skin pull clear back? I mean, does it go all the way behind the head? It looks so..." I knew I was babbling but I couldn't seem to stop that, either.

George chuckled again. "Sure, it'll skin all the way back. See for yourself." He thrust his hips forward, pushing that thing closer to me. When I hesitated he said, "Go on. Skin it back if you want. It's okay. Really."

I watched as my hands took on a life of their own and reached out to that huge instrument. It was warm to the touch and velvety smooth, just the way it looked.

I couldn't believe what I was doing but I couldn't seem to stop myself. I slowly pulled the skin back along the length of the shaft until the cock-head slipped out into the light. It was a dark pink, much darker than the skin that had covered it, and smooth as polished glass. I slipped the skin forward again and it was like I was sliding it along an oiled surface. When I'd covered the head again I looked up at him. "Does the head stay covered when you're up? I mean, when you get hard does it push out of the skin or..."

He laughed again. "Keep that up and you're going to find out soon enough. You're about to make me as hard as you are."

I glanced down at myself. My towel had fallen off and there was my dick, sticking up 45 degrees into the air. I didn't care. At that moment I didn't care about anything but the feel of that dick in my hands...

"You mean this?" I asked, stroking along the shaft of his dick. I pulled the skin all the way back to the base and then forward again until the head was back in its warm covering. I felt him begin to harden, the shaft growing thicker and becoming rigid, the head swelling in my palm. I hadn't really thought his dick would get much bigger. The few big cocks I'd had any experience with didn't; they just became rigid but George's seemed to grow quite a lot – until it finally stood out proudly, maybe the biggest dick in the world.

"About five more strokes and you're going to have to finish that, you know," he said with a little catch in his voice.

Of course I was. I counted out loud: "One... Two... Three... Four..."

"There's a massage table over there in the corner. I like it better when I'm lying down."

He stretched out on the table with that great cock of his laying out along his belly, reaching well past his navel. I didn't know what, exactly, he expected me to do but I did know there was no way I could suck that monster off. I probably could have gotten the head in my mouth but even that would have been difficult so I went back to jacking him off. He sighed and let me do it my way.

I got to playing with his balls while I jacked him off and found that he loved having the skin there pinched ever so lightly. I did that until he began to moan and his balls pulled up in the sack. I knew he was close so I slowed down, keeping him right on the edge of his orgasm for as long as I could. I was also feeling some strange sensations in my own dick but I couldn't dwell on them; I was concentrating on keeping my bulldozer driver just one stroke from coming.

Finally it got to be too much for him; he bucked and moaned and his dick tried to throw itself out of my grasp as it shot a load of cum over his head and onto the wall behind him. I felt a sudden rush in my own dick and gasped as I came along with him, my own cum spraying the underside of the table.

We didn't move for a few moments, catching our breath. When I finally released his cock he got off the table and wiped the cum off his chest with his towel. "Wonderful," he said. "Now come on, let's get dressed and talk."

As we dressed he played around, showing off his dick, waving it around and "accidentally" letting it brush against me. I loved it and he could tell. He didn't actually put the thing away until he was completely dressed but when he did he tucked it in between his legs, pinning it there with his jockey shorts. When I raised an eyebrow he laughed and said he'd always carried it that way, ever since he was a kid. Then he patted me on the ass and said, "Okay, let's us go find ourselves a drink and have some talk. I think we need it."

We sat at a table in a bar he knew, just up the hill. George tried to make small talk while we waited for our drinks but I'm afraid I wasn't paying much attention. I couldn't get the image of his dick out of my head and the thought of what I'd just done with it was keeping me about half hard. What I really wanted was to get my hands on him again and make that thing of his buck around and shoot another load for me.

When the drinks were served he lifted his and toasted me. "I sure did like that," he said, "what you just did to me. I guess you kind of liked it too, huh?"

It was a statement really, not a question. "Yeah," I said, still thinking about his dick. "I liked it a lot."

"You didn't mind that, uh, well that I didn't, you know, help you?"

"You didn't need to. I came anyway."

"You did?" He looked at me with questioning eyes.

"Yea. It happens once in a great while – when I'm really turned on. But I think I know what you're getting at. Some guys just like to get their rocks off and let it go at that." I shrugged. "If they find someone who likes helping them get their rocks off what's the big deal? It seems to me everybody wins." I took the bull by the horns: "You want to do it again?"

He sipped at his drink and signaled the waitress for another. "Well, that's what I wanted to talk about," he said. "Besides with me, would you maybe like to do it with some other guys? I mean a couple of my buddies? Sort of like help us get our rocks off without, uh, you know, without us having to..."

My heart began to pound. "You mean would I like to jack you and your buddies off together?"

"Well, sort of but – I mean, maybe not together exactly and maybe a little more than just hand jobs. Maybe doing some other stuff too, you know." He hurried on, "But only if you like it. I mean we wouldn't do anything you didn't want to do, just stuff that felt good. I mean to you, too." He finished his drink in a single gulp, obviously very uncomfortable.

Something that had been growing in the back of my mind suddenly bloomed. He was talking about guys who considered themselves to be straight. "You know my reaction to that?" I waited until the waitress had finished serving the new drinks. "I've got the biggest hard-on of my life." George squirmed around in his seat and it suddenly occurred to me that he had one too. "You know, you really shouldn't carry that big dick of yours between your legs if it's going get hard. Must be kind of painful."

He laughed, recovering his stride. "Yea, it is a little. So would you want to do it?"

"Maybe. But where? I mean, we can't just take over the locker room at the union hall for an orgy. Someone's bound to notice."

He laughed again. "You bet your sweet ass they would." He stopped for a second, wondering if maybe he shouldn't have mentioned my ass. "Anyway, one of the guys has this cabin up in the country. It isn't much really, just a converted bunkhouse but it does have a pool and it's very private. We could go up there for a weekend and just relax, lie in the sun, have a few beers and, you know, sort of play around."

Would I do this? "What about the other guys? Do they know you're arranging this little party to help them get their rocks off? Some guys get a little funny about that, you know, doing it with a guy, even if they aren't expected to reciprocate."

He grinned at me, back on familiar territory. "Oh, well, we've sort of talked about that. I mean we sometimes go up there and get to watching videos and stuff and we end up horny as hell. We talked about bringing some women up with us but a couple of the guys are married and they wouldn't feel right about doing that. So Ken, he's one of the guys, Ken said maybe we should just get a guy to take care of us. We talked about that some and I know all the guys really want to do it, it's just that none of us knew how to, you know, find the right guy. Then when you started smiling at me – watching me work the dozer and all – I thought maybe this was our chance. Then today you seemed to, you know, to like doing it so much and everything, I thought I'd just ask if you'd want to come up to the place with us and kind of..." His words were beginning to tumble over each other.

"I tell you what," I said. "You go into the men's room there and rearrange your dick so you don't rip your shorts and let me think about this for a minute." He nodded and got up. By the way he walked I figured his dick was probably pretty near hard and probably cramped up like hell in those tight jockeys.

I didn't need to think about it much; hell, I would have jacked off a whole platoon of guys if it meant I'd get my hands back on George's giant dick again. It also occurred to me that the guy George sometimes had coffee with was probably one of the guys involved and I thought it would be nice to get my hands on him, too.

I looked up and caught George walking back to the table. He probably wasn't more than half hard but with a cock as big as his there is no way to hide even that, no matter how loose your jeans are. A couple of people turned to look and I thought to myself that he'd probably cause a riot in a gay bar.

"You must be the envy of all your buddies," I said, looking directly at his crotch.

"Yea, well that's the thing," he said sitting down, "we don't just sit around in a circle jerk up there. I mean, sure, I guess we've all seen each other jacking off one time or another, some of those videos really make you horny, and a couple of the guys like to run around naked most of the time but we really don't, uh, you know, we don't fool around together. You know what I mean?"

I had the picture. Just a bunch of regular guys who like to get it off and have figured out that it would feel a lot better if somebody else got it off for them. "By the way," I asked, "just who are these guys, anyway? What do they look like?"

He smiled, knowing I was going to do it. "You've seen one of them. You know, the guy I have coffee with? That's Ken." He paused and thought for a second. "I tell you what. I'll get them all together the day after tomorrow, you know? In the coffee shop. That way we can all see each other, make sure it's okay with everybody. That okay?"

I agreed. I wasn't truly sure what I was getting into but I agreed.

The next day in the coffee shop he nodded to me just like he always did, just like nothing had ever happened between us. I wondered if his dick was still tucked up between his legs and decided if I ever had the chance I'd try and get him to let it ride off to the side and maybe show a little. I thought it was something he ought to be proud of.

On the following day I approached the coffee shop with great anticipation. I had tried not to fantasize too much about the others but I hadn't been very successful. As soon as I walked in I spotted them: five guys, all looking the part of construction workers. Just guys, joking among themselves over coffee before they go to work. I caught George's eye and nodded; he smiled back.

I looked them over as I waited to pay for my coffee. The one I had seen before smiled at me, showing a set of beautiful, even, white teeth under a heavy dark mustache. The one with his back to me turned around and raised one eyebrow. He was a bit shorter than the others and had a big tuft of dark hair sticking out over his tee shirt. I smiled at him and he grinned back. All in all I thought they were a friendly – and good- looking – group of guys.

I wondered what the drill was but George took care of that by beckoning me over to the table. "Mark," he said a little formally, "I want you to meet my friends. This is Ken, you've seen him before, and this is Miles and Billy and Doug." We shook hands all around. Doug, who was sitting on the far side of the table, stood up when he shook my hand and I could see that he, at least, was proud of being a man and let his pride show in his jeans. Billy, who also stood up, was the shorter one who had grinned at me. He had a very sweet face but didn't show much of anything at the crotch. Miles, a blond with close- cropped hair and beard, stayed in his seat and threw me a mock salute. Ken smiled again, showing me his incredible white teeth. His eyes were dark, almost black, and they seemed to have a brooding look about them.

I threw the salute back to Miles and smiled at the rest of them. "Glad to meet you guys." I glanced at my watch. "I sure would like to spend some time with you now but duty calls. I gotta get to work."

George nodded. "Yeah, we do too. Starting a new job this morning. Tell you what, though, can we meet for a quick lunch? Say 11:30, here?"

I agreed, hoping we were going to carry this thing off.

I walked into the coffee shop just a little late and found George alone at a table in the back. "Hi, Mark," he said when I pulled out a chair. "I got here a little early so I got you a burger and a Coke. Hope that's okay."

I sat down, uninterested in food. "Well?" I said.

"Hey, all the guys thought you were neat. What'd you think of them?"

"Nice. Seemed like a great bunch of guys. I think it'd be fun to spend a weekend with them – as long as you're there too."

He smiled. "Oh, I'll be there, don't worry about that. Hell, I'm still thinking about the other day." One of the counter people brought our food and we waited until he was gone. "Okay, we all talked about it and everyone wants to do it. In fact, we'd like to do it this weekend if you can make it. Miles has a van so we can all go up together. We get off at three but we could go any time. What do you say?"

I hesitated a little. "Well, I won't be able to get off at three, that's for sure. And then I have to get home and change..."

"Hell, just bring your jeans and stuff with you to work and you can change in the van or when we get there, whatever you want. Okay? What time?"

I thought for a second. "I can probably swing four or a little after. What do I bring?"

"Nothing, just you. Maybe a pair of shorts and a tee shirt or two. We're pretty informal up there so you don't need much else. Ken said he'd get us some videos, maybe even one or two that you'll really like." He lowered his voice. "You know, just guys and stuff. Okay? Friday at four o'clock?"

And so it was decided. We would have a weekend in the country I was pretty sure I would never forget.

# # # # #

It was a little after six when we arrived at the cabin. After some initial tenseness the ride up had turned out to be fun. I didn't change my clothes, it being a little crowded in the van, but I did take off my vest, roll up my sleeves and drink beer with the guys sitting around the table in the back. It wasn't long before I proved that I could talk sports and cars with the best of them and I became just one of the guys. Even so there was a sexual tension hanging in the air, thick enough to smell.

The cabin was small but very well done and it had a real pool, not the "ole swimmin' hole" I had expected. Billy, who owned the place, showed me around with a lot of pride. The building had originally been the bunkhouse for a good-sized ranch, which had been broken up and sold off in 25-acre parcels. On the first floor the sleeping quarters had been turned into a living room which Billy had fitted out with some comfortable old furniture and some very good video and sound equipment. The bathroom had been left pretty much alone, including its original trough urinal which looked like it would accommodate two – or three if everyone was desperate. The bathroom was small because part of its space had been taken to enlarge an old storage room, which had then been turned into a very usable kitchen.

Upstairs the layout was exactly the same except, of course, there was no kitchen and the bathroom was bigger; along with the urinal it had a gang shower with three heads in it. What was the living room downstairs was the bedroom upstairs. The bunks had been replaced with double beds but that was about the extent of the changes. "We all sleep here," Billy said, gesturing at the four beds. "Just help yourself, we aren't real formal about it. Or the bathroom either. If the door's open, go on in. And leave it open unless you really need privacy." It was my kind of place.

I watched Billy as we changed clothes. When he pulled off his shirt I saw that the tuft of hair that frothed out over his tee shirt was only the beginning. His chest was covered with a wiry fur, like a little bear, and it continued, unbroken and untamed, all the way down his belly and into his pants. I could hardly wait until he got out of his jeans so I could see if that fur thinned out any before it got down to his cock. I didn't find out though, because he was wearing what looked like silk boxer shorts under his jeans and he didn't take them off. He just stretched himself and said, "That's better. I'm going downstairs and see what's going on. Hurry up and get into some shorts or something and come on down." Off he went to join the party wearing nothing but electric blue silk boxer shorts. I decided right then that I was going to like him.

When I got downstairs George handed me a beer and asked if everything was okay. I told him it was and asked if I could do anything to help out in the kitchen. "Not a thing," he said. "Your job is to go out to the pool, relax, and get to know the guys. Ken's going to toss a salad and I'm going to throw some steaks on the grill and that's about it. Very basic."

Outside Doug was standing by a little bar, opening a beer. He had exchanged his jeans and shirt for a pair of gray gym shorts which showed a very promising bulge. I was looking forward to, as George put it so delicately, helping him out; he was a very good-looking man.

Miles was in the pool and called out, "Hey, Mark, come on in and get wet!" I guess I hesitated because Doug added, "You don't need a suit. Not up here. Come on."

With that Doug pulled off his shorts and jumped in the pool. Miles pushed off the edge and I could see that he didn't have anything covering his ass either so I unbuttoned my shorts, slipped them off and splashed in.

The water was fairly warm and it felt good after the long drive. I heard another splash and pretty soon Billy bobbed to the surface, shaking water out of his ears. I'd missed seeing him get out of his shorts but from what I could make out in the water that heavy pelt of his covered him all the way to the crotch.

Miles wanted to play war. "I'll get on Mark's shoulders, and Billy, you get on Doug's. We'll see who can stay on the longest." Miles moved in behind me and put his hands on my shoulders; I ducked down in the water and he climbed on. I grabbed onto his legs to steady him as he wriggled into position and was surprised at how firm his muscles were, especially since he'd said on the way up that he never went to a gym. "Hang on a sec," he said when I started to move towards Billy and Doug, "I have to arrange things up here." I felt his hands at the back of my neck and then something that could only be his dick flopped down beside my ear. I wanted to turn my head and see if I could kiss it but I decided it was a little too early for that. I still wasn't sure I knew the whole drill and I didn't want to do anything to upset what was surely to come.

Billy had gotten himself up on Doug's shoulders and they were coming squarely at us. I couldn't see Billy's cock of course but the beautiful brown fur that disappeared behind Doug's head really caught my attention. It was covered with tiny water droplets that sparkled like little diamonds caught in the hair.

While Miles and Billy were attempting to knock each other down Doug and I jockeyed for position, trying to give them some leverage. Miles crossed his legs on my chest for stability so I moved my hands higher on his legs, catching him on the thighs. In the excitement I managed to get my fingers around his cock for a minute; it was firm – I don't mean hard, just firm, like the muscles in his legs – and cool to the touch.

Getting my hand on Miles' cock made me lose focus on the game and Doug took advantage of that to move Billy in for the kill. Miles had been paying attention though, and grabbed Billy around the chest, trying to push him off sideways. I lost focus again because Miles' strategy forced me up flat against Doug and all I could concentrate on was the feel of Doug's cock brushing around my crotch. I began to get hard and maybe that's what broke Doug's concentration, I don't know, but suddenly both Billy and Miles tumbled into the water, pulling Doug and me with them.

We splashed around in the pool for a little longer before George came out brandishing a Bar-B-Que fork and saying that dinner would be ready in ten minutes or so. When we climbed out I watched Doug drying himself and thought what a really handsome man he was. His body was nearly hairless except for a sparse, silky looking growth at his crotch. His cock was as handsome as the rest of him, bigger than most guys and uncut, with a short, neat foreskin that barely covered the head. He had big balls too, pulled up against his crotch in a smooth, tight sack. When he walked over to get his shorts his dick swayed like it was heavy, maybe not completely at rest. The thing I liked best about him, though, was that when he pulled his shorts on he still looked very much a man, his dick evident as a thick bulge centered at his crotch. He was obviously very proud of what he carried.

Dinner was good: salad, steaks and potatoes from the grill and icy cold beer to wash it all down. When we finished I volunteered to help George with the clean up. He was wearing a pair of loose khaki shorts and I could tell he still had his dick tucked in between his legs. While we did the dishes I told him I didn't think it was a very good idea for him to wear it that way. For one thing, I said, it seemed to me that keeping it bent back like that was probably depriving it of some of its blood flow. For another, it was just too handsome to hide.

"Well, there are two factors here, Mark," he said wiping down the counter. "First, if I wear boxers or loose jockeys I get embarrassed because it shows so much and in the boxers it sometimes even hangs out. Second, I know how big it is and I know a lot of times that really puts people off. Guys get jealous and women are afraid of it." He sighed. "The other thing, if you must know, is that I like the feel of it between my legs, especially when I'm sitting on my dozer."

I had to admit that I couldn't argue with anything he'd said. Nevertheless I still thought he should let it hang free some of the time and to hell with fear and jealousy.

"Well, maybe one day you'll convince me. We'll see," he laughed. "But for now let's just go watch some movies."

Everyone else was in the living room and Ken was just putting on the first video. "You guys'll really like this one," he said. "It's three men and one terrific lady. Man, she really knows how to take care of these guys. She even takes it up the ass a couple of times with..."

Billy snorted. "They always have to take it up the ass, don't they? You really must love that, Ken."

"Oh, come on, Billy, they don't always. And anyway, I think it's sexy seeing some guy's big cock going up there and how good it must feel and... You know..." He threw up his hands. "Oh, hell, just watch the damn movie." He jabbed the play button and went out to the kitchen for another drink. It struck me that he was somehow a little embarrassed.

The movie started out okay with two pretty good-looking studs and another one who wasn't much except that he had a fairly big cock that seemed like it never got soft. She was actually nice-looking too, but I didn't pay much attention, especially since the other two guys couldn't seem to keep it up very long and didn't look like they had very much interest in what they were doing anyway. Nobody else in the room looked very turned on by the movie either and after a few minutes Billy got up and said he was going for a swim. I decided to join him.

We splashed around in the pool for a while and then Billy pulled himself up on the deck and sat with his legs dangling in the water. I swam over and hung onto the edge next to him, waiting to see what would develop.

"That movie bore you too, Mark?" he asked and then laughed. "Actually I guess you don't really need a movie what with all these naked guys running around..."

"Well, yea, it is kind of nice for a guy like me."

Billy put his hand on my shoulder and squeezed. "I didn't mean it like that, I just meant..."

I laughed. "Hey, I am a guy like me and I mean it, it is nice looking at all these naked men running around. 'Course, I haven't seen everyone yet. You for instance."

He looked over at me and smiled. "Well, you might be a little disappointed with me. I'm nowhere near as big and showy as they are. Of course no one's as big and showy as George, even if he does hide it, but... You know, Doug and Miles..." His voice trailed off for a moment, then picked up again. "And I'm circumcised too... I sort of wish they hadn't done that." He sounded kind of wistful.

"Aw, come on Billy, circumcised isn't the worst thing in the world. Besides, some of the other guys are clipped too, aren't they?"

"I suppose. Miles and Ken are circumcised but it's different for them because they've both got more actual dick than I do. A little skin hanging down might..." I wanted to ask might what? but he went right on. "Besides, those guys look so neat and mine's kind of ugly where they did it."

I laughed and put my hand on his thigh. "Billy, trust me on this. There are no ugly dicks. Some of them are big and some are small and some got clipped but not one of them is ugly. Now since I'm the expert on these things let me see just what kind of job they really did." I moved over until I was between his legs and looked closely at his cock. "That's actually a pretty nice job there," I said, taking his cock in my hands. It wasn't terribly big but it was no smaller than some guys I know. I thought maybe it looked smaller than it actually was because it was buried in the longest, thickest tangle of pubic hair I had ever seen. I ran my fingers around the head, feeling the skin on the underside. "That isn't very much of a scar and the skin is wonderfully smooth Billy, just like sheared velvet. All in all I'd have to pronounce it a nice, clean job. And don't forget, I'm the expert here." He began to harden in my hand.

"Whatever. Anyway, I can do something I don't think any of them can do," he said, feeling the stiffness coming into his cock.

"What do you mean?" He was completely hard now, and bigger than he thought.

"Well, like a lot of guys I guess, I never learned how to hold it back so I come pretty fast but what I don't have in staying power I make up for with repeat power. What I mean is, I can do it probably twenty-five times a day."

"You're kidding me. No one can do that."

"I can. If I jerked myself off right now I'd probably come in about two minutes. But then I could do it again in twenty minutes. Of course, I'd still shoot off in a couple of minutes but then I could do it again and again. And every time feels just as good as the first time."

I kissed the head of his dick and then looked up at him. "You gotta be putting me on, Billy. No one can do that."

"Want to bet?"

Of course I wanted to bet. "What are the stakes?"

"I don't know. Whatever you want."

I thought for a moment. "Okay, I tell you what. If you can do that, if you can get off twice in, say, thirty minutes and not take more than three minutes to do it each time, I'll give you a Roman bath."

"What's that, a Roman bath?"

I laughed. "You know, like Tony Curtis did to Larry Olivier in 'Spartacus?' You get a trim, wash, dry and massage. Okay?"

"The bet is on," he said and took his cock out of my hand. "Here comes the first time."

I stopped him and took back his cock saying, "I think, just to be sure there's no question about your getting off, you'd better let me take care of that." He sucked in his breath as I leaned down and took his cock into my mouth. It really was a nice cock, big enough that it was very satisfying to suck on but not so big as to threaten lock jaw. I could take the whole length of it into my mouth and bury my nose in his hair and not have to work at it at all. I could even tongue his ball sack without letting go of his cock. He began to shiver as I held his cock in my mouth and ran my tongue over the shaft. I slid up on it and then back, down to his balls, my lips tight along the shaft.

"My God," he whispered, "oh, my God." I stopped moving on it, holding it still in my mouth and rubbing that wad of skin just under the head with my tongue until he sucked in his breath again and let go. He sat very still while he came, the only movement his cock squirting out its load of cum and the only sound a low moan from the back of his throat.

When he was finished and I slid off of him I realized that the whole thing had taken less than two or maybe three minutes. He was right about that part: he was fast. But after the intensity of that orgasm could he do it again in half an hour? I doubted it.

He laid back on the deck, breathing hard. "My lord Mark, that was wonderful. Lots better than I can do with my hand, that's for sure." He sighed deeply and sat up. "Meet me back here in thirty minutes and let's do it again."

I pulled myself up on the side of the pool. "Sure... We'll meet in a half hour but I'll bet you can't do it again," I said. "At least, nowhere near that fast."

He laughed. "You'll see, you'll see. Now come on, let's go find ourselves a drink or something."

We dried off, put on our shorts and went back inside. Ken was in the kitchen making himself another drink and raised an eyebrow at Billy as we came in. "Was it fun?"

Billy didn't miss a beat. "It sure was. You ought to try it. The water's great."

Ken took a long pull on his drink and looked at me. "Yeah, maybe I will. Later." He poured more scotch in his glass and went out to the living room. Billy got down a couple of clean glasses and smiled at me. "Funny guy, that Ken. Drinks too much, but I guess that's his business. Come on, let's go see what's on at the movies."

What was on at the movies was a couple of guys lustily giving it to a couple of women. I watched for a minute and chuckled to myself. It was a typical straight porno flick, the guys completely naked while the women were wearing spike heeled shoes, net stockings and earrings. I hoped they were being careful with those heels!

The audience was fairly intent on the movie. Doug was sitting in one of the easy chairs, slowly rubbing a much bigger bulge in his shorts than I had seen before. George was sprawled on the couch and I noted with some satisfaction that he had a pretty good bulge in his shorts too. At least that huge dick of his wasn't still clamped in between his legs.

Ken was in the other easy chair with his legs spread wide apart. I could see his cock hanging down the right leg of his jeans but it obviously wasn't anywhere near hard yet. He was pretending to watch the movie but actually he was keeping an eye on George, his gaze almost fixed on George's crotch.

Miles was lying on the floor, on his belly, and I thought I detected just a little hip movement. I sat next to him and let my hand just touch his jeans, to see if he really was fucking the floor. He was.

The guys in the movie changed women and went at it some more. "Man, those guys are real fucking machines," Doug said. One of the guys pulled out, stroked his cock a couple of times and sprayed cum all over the woman. "Geez, look at that guy come!" I wondered if Doug was coming along with him but evidently he wasn't; at least I didn't see any wet spot develop at his crotch.

Miles rolled onto his side and gently pushed himself against the back of my hand. "When's that other guy going to come? He's been fucking non-stop for about an hour." I turned my hand and quietly brushed along the length of Miles' hard cock which had been pulled up so it rode just behind his fly. I tucked my little finger under the waistband of his jeans and let it play over the head.

When the movie ended – the other guy finally did come – Miles rolled back onto his belly, pretending nothing was going on. Billy stood up with an obvious hard-on poking a tent in his silk shorts and went to the door, giving me a significant look as he went out to the pool. I didn't think we had been watching that movie for a full half hour but what the hell, if he wanted to try it again now I was willing. I followed him out.

I found Billy stretched out on an air mattress by the pool. He'd taken his silk shorts off and his neat little cock was sticking straight up in the air. I sat down between his legs and gently took his balls in my hands. "You haven't been working that thing up now, have you? That wouldn't be fair, you know."

"I don't have to work it up, not with you around," he said. "Come on, I'm looking forward to that Roman bath – not to mention getting my rocks off again." He thrust his hips out, wanting his cock sucked.

"Three minutes, right?" I closed my fist around his cock.

"Probably less, horny as I am." He flexed, making his cock swell in my hand.

I stretched out on my belly, between his legs, and slowly took his cock into my mouth, clear down to the base. I really liked sucking that cock and I found I could do things to it that I can't do with a bigger one. And he loved all the things I could do, especially when I buried my nose in his pubic hair and licked at his balls with his cock still in my mouth. That sent shivers through him and caused him to rear up, trying to get those balls into my mouth along with his cock. I ran my tongue around the shaft and across the head, prising at the slit, trying to get my tongue in it. His moans were getting louder and I knew he was about to win the bet. His cock suddenly jerked and he came with a rush, giving me my second taste of him. It was salty and there was a lot of it; his balls must have been working overtime. When he was finished I let his cock slip out of my mouth and sat up. "I didn't think you could do it, Billy, I really didn't but I guess you did."

"I told you I could." He sat up and straddled the air mattress. "Now about that Roman bath. How about tomorrow morning when we're both fresh?"

"That's okay with me. Whatever you want." I was glad we were going to wait because I had some ideas forming in the back of my mind and I wanted to work them out.

Billy got up and pulled on his shorts. "I can do that again by the way, if you're in the mood later."

I nodded and got into my shorts. "I think that can be arranged. In the meantime, I'm going to go in and finish my drink. I want to see how scotch tastes in a salty mouth."

He was still laughing when we went in the house.

Inside everyone was pretty much as they were, watching another movie. This one featured a fairly plain looking woman jerking some poor guy off with her huge boobs. Someone, Ken I imagine, had finished my drink. As I picked up my glass to take it out to the kitchen Ken opened his eyes and slurred out something about going to bed. He tried to get out of the chair and nearly fell flat on his face. I put my glass down and grabbed hold of his arm to steady him. "Here," I said, "let me give you a hand."

George started to get up. "Want some help, Mark?"

"No, that's okay. I can manage him. Which bed is his?" It occurred to me that this was probably normal behavior for Ken since none of the others seemed to be very concerned about it.

"Any one. No one has his own special bed up here." I thought Billy's eyes twinkled as he spoke but I was too busy holding Ken up to be sure.

Ken protested that he could get upstairs by himself but it was pretty obvious that he couldn't. I got his arm around my shoulder, grabbed his waist and we stumbled our way upstairs.

It was fairly dark in the bedroom but I managed to find one of the beds and sat Ken down on it. He slumped over and fumbled at his shoes so I squatted down and got them untied for him. He lost interest so I pulled them off, along with his socks. He somehow managed to struggle out of his tee shirt and tossed it away, hitting me in the face with it. "Gonna pee," he mumbled.

I unbuttoned his jeans and told him he'd have to get out of them first. I wasn't going to let him pee in his pants.

He kept mumbling "I Gotta pee," but he let me tug his jeans off. At least he wasn't wearing shorts under them.

I hoisted him up and somehow got him into the bathroom, standing him up in front of the urinal. He fumbled around, looking for his dick but gave it up and laid his head back on my shoulder instead. I was afraid he'd piss all over the floor so I steadied him with an arm around his waist and grabbed his cock with my other hand, aiming for him. He slurred something about doing it himself but he didn't try to push my hand away and finally let go with a veritable waterfall. His bladder must have really been hurting.

For fear of shutting him off I held my hand still while he peed but what I really wanted to do was wave his cock around and see how far he could throw that stream. I also wanted to check his cock out a little more thoroughly. It was kind of exciting, holding his cock and feeling the water rushing through that thick tube on the underside and I began to get hard.

The force of his stream finally diminished and he said he was through. I told him to push and get it all out. He grunted a little and then pushed his ass back into my crotch so I guessed he really was finished. I milked it down a few times and was surprised when it began to firm up.

I figured I couldn't stand there all night, holding him up and playing with his cock so I steered him back to the bedroom and got him on the bed. He flopped down like a sack of meal, his breath already coming in a light snore.

Now in normal circumstances I would avoid fooling around with a drunk because it generally turns out to be dull and very unrewarding.

But these were anything but normal circumstances and I really did want to get the feel of that nice cock so I took it in my hands and began to play around with it. It was very nicely shaped, silky along the shaft and velvety across the head. I hefted it and it felt heavy, like it had been – or was going to be – hard. I fondled his balls and found them as silky smooth as his cock which was actually beginning to rise.

Since I had never come across anyone so horny that they could get a hard-on while dead-drunk-asleep I decided to see just how far he could go. I nestled down between his legs and took his balls in my mouth which even in his drunken sleep he must have liked. I was amazed when it brought his cock up fully hard.

I shifted my attention and licked along the shaft of his cock, up to the little slit and then drew the head into my mouth, tasting that wonderful muskiness that always seems to come out on a horny man. Ken grunted and spread his legs wider but his breathing remained deep and regular so I went on, sliding my mouth slowly up and down on his cock.

I heard someone come into the room and then a warm hand touched my back, sliding down my spine until it came to rest on my buttocks. I pulled up, letting Ken's cock slip out of my mouth but then sucked it in again as another hand pushed my head back down. Very quietly he said, "No, go ahead with that. We'll just slip these off."

Two hands went under my belly and unfastened my shorts, then began to ease them off. I helped by lifting up a little and he slid them off, dropping them on the floor. The warm hands came back to my ass, massaging my buns and then gently spreading them to find what they protected. Something was pressed into me and my ass was suddenly flooded with a cool slickness. I knew what was about to happen and I shivered with anticipation.

He pushed my legs apart and I felt the bed sag as he climbed in between them. I wondered who it was and hoped it wasn't George. I didn't think I was ready for him yet. When the man pressed his cockhead against me I knew immediately that it wasn't George and I relaxed to enjoy the sensations of a cock being gently but firmly pressed into me. Once the head had slipped inside he paused for a moment, letting me get used to him but I was anxious and pushed back on him, starting his long drive home. The more cock he fed into me the more I thought it must be Miles because none of the other guys in the group had a cock anywhere near as long as the one going into me. By the time his balls were brushing up against mine I felt the head of his cock pushing against another door, deep inside me. No one had ever been in me that far and the sensations were indescribable.

He rested a moment before pulling back a little and then pushing the last of his cock into me. I felt him opening that second door, pausing and then pushing again, through the door. The sensations in my ass were so incredible that I almost forgot the cock in my mouth and it began to go soft. I swallowed down on it, wondering if the two cocks were going to meet somewhere in my middle.

The man with his cock in my ass – I was certain now that it was Miles – lay against me, pressing me into the mattress with his weight and resting for what was to come. My own dick was pulled up against my belly and I could feel the precum oozing out of it. He tried his first stroke, pulling back a few inches and then pushing in, all the way. He found that door again and shot bolts of icy electricity through me. He was liking it too. He pulled himself up on his elbows and began a series of very long, slow strokes, almost pulling out of me and then making a smooth push all the way back in. Ken's all but forgotten cock slipped out of my mouth and I buried my face in his balls, reveling in the sensations flowing through my ass.

Miles stroked in me for a long time and then slowed, then stopped. He was breathing hard but he hadn't come. He pushed his cock all the way in to me again, prodding through that inner door and then lay on my back, resting his cheek against my ear. I felt his jaw muscles work and thought he was going to say something but he didn't. I felt Ken's cock brush against my cheek but I let it be, enjoying the feel of Miles resting in me.

Ken's cock fell against my cheek again and Miles whispered, "That was very nice. We'll do it some more, a little later. Right now I think I'll go and have a shower." He moved against my back and began to pull out of me. When the last of his cock slipped out, he got off the bed and I heard him padding off to the bathroom. I went back to Ken's cock which was lying against my cheek and still very slick with saliva.

Ken must really be drunk to sleep through that, I thought as I went back down on him. Drunk and asleep or not, he still had a nice hard-on and I still wanted to see if I could make him come.

I didn't hear anything else, probably because of the noise of the shower, so I was startled when I felt another hand probing my ass. When he found that I was already slick and well lubricated any idea of preliminaries went out of his mind. He simply climbed in between my legs and shoved his very thick, very hard dick into me. It surprised me and I let out a little gasp as he went in.

He bent over my ear and whispered, "Oh, God, I'm sorry. I don't want to hurt you but I'm so horny. I'll do it better tomorrow but right now I just gotta fuck some of this cum out of me." And that's just what he did. He fucked me with long, fast strokes, slapping his balls up against mine as he shoved his dick into me and then yanked it out so he could drive it in again. Once I caught his rhythm I went right along with him, pushing back to meet his thrusts and then pulling away as he yanked his hard dick out of me. My mouth slid up and down on Ken's cock in same rhythm as the dick ramming into my ass and my own dick was being ground into the bed with every stroke. Ken began writhing around too, moaning deep in his throat like some sort of animal. Or was that the man driving his dick into me? Or me? I couldn't tell and I didn't care, all I cared about were three hard, throbbing cocks, all getting ready to explode.

My mouth was suddenly flooded with hot, bitter cum and that set my own dick to firing off under me. At the same time the man in my ass made one final slam home and it was over for him, too. Cum seemed to be spurting everywhere and all of us were gasping for breath.

When the body above me collapsed on my back I let Ken's cock slide out of my mouth and I laid my head in his soft pubic hair. We all three lay still for a moment, savoring the release and then the man on my back gently pulled out of me. "I guess the shower's free now," he said and climbed off the bed. I lay between Ken's legs for a moment or two more, then got up myself. The sheets were slick where I had come but it would dry and I figured Ken wouldn't notice anyway. I wiped myself off, pulled my shorts back on and went looking for a drink.

I found George and Billy downstairs in the living room, cleaning up. "Anybody want a fresh drink?"

"Oh, no, not me" George said, waiving the idea away. "I'm going to get some sleep, assuming it's quieted down up there. And I assume it has since you're down here." He grinned and winked at me. "You guys can stay down here and drink all night if you want but I'm going to bed."

I assured him he would find it quiet upstairs except, possibly, for Doug in the shower. "And I'm pretty sure he'll go directly to sleep when he's finished," I added, winking back at him.

George went upstairs and I helped Billy finish straightening up the living room. When we were through, he fixed us a couple of drinks and we took them out to the pool where we sat, naked, dangling our legs in the water

"You okay? Guys being good to you?"

"Yea, I'm having a good time. Why..."

"Sounded like it might be kind of rough up there for a while..."

"What? Oh, that." I laughed. "That was Doug. He was pretty strung out. So horny he didn't have time for finesse, you know?"

Billy nodded. "Well, I'm not surprised. He'd been playing with that thing of his through his pants most of the night. I'm only surprised that he hadn't come all over himself before he... Well, before he went upstairs."

"Miles was up there first. What's with him, anyway?"

Billy looked at me sharply. "Why? What'd he do?"

"Well, it's more what he didn't do... I mean, he was very enthusiastic about it and everything, but he didn't..."

"Didn't come?" Billy smiled. "Don't let that worry you. I don't think Miles ever comes when he's up here."

"Never?"

"I don't think so. I think maybe he saves it, you know, to carry home." He grinned at me. "Not that he doesn't love that cock of his. I've seen him work quietly on it for hours while we're watching movies but there's never any sign that he's come." He shrugged. "But he seems to enjoy playing with it so what the hell?"

"Yeah, he does that," I said, rattling the ice in my drink. "You want another?"

Billy smiled again. "You want something to drink? Just bend over here."

"You're kidding, Billy!"

"No I'm not. See?"

Billy leaned back on his arms and sure enough, his cock was sticking straight out into the air, hard as I'd ever seen it. I hopped into the water, pulled myself up between his legs and slipped my mouth over it. He gave a sigh and hunched his hips forward, pushing his hairy balls up against my chin. I ran my tongue around his cock a few times and then pushed down hard so I could lick his balls at the same time. He let out another sigh and my mouth was flooded with his salt again. If anything, I thought, the man is getting faster!

I climbed out of the pool with a slowly shrinking hard-on sticking out of my groin. Quick as he was – and as often as I seemed to be doing it – I found sucking Billy's cock to be more and more exciting.

We decided that another drink was probably unnecessary and went up to bed.

"Who are you going to sleep with?" I asked him. "I don't advise Ken – the bed's probably still a little damp."

"No, I never sleep with Ken. He thrashes about too much, grabs onto you in the night and you never get any sleep. No, I think I'll go with Doug. He sleeps like a baby. Unless you want him?"

"Me? No, I think I'll sack out with George tonight."

Billy chuckled and clapped me on the shoulder. "Be careful of the monster."

We went into the bathroom and I watched Billy pee as I brushed my teeth. When we were through we traded places. Billy eyed me as I was waving my dick around, washing down the urinal. "That feels good too, huh?"

"Billy, just about anything to do with a cock feels good, mine included." I pointed at the shower. "Is this the site for tomorrow's bath?"

Billy looked thoughtful for a moment. "No. I think I'll run everyone out of the pool and we'll use the shower out there. It'll be much nicer out in the sun." He gave me a little waive and went in to bed.

George was sound asleep when I got into the bed with him. Sensing that someone was there he moved over, rolling onto his side, facing me. When I'd settled in I carefully reached out, searching for his dick. It was soft when I found it and took it into my hand. I still found it hard to believe how big it was and that it grew even bigger when it got hard. I drifted off to sleep holding on to it.

Sometime later I woke, not quite sure where I was or what had awakened me. Once I remembered where I was it didn't take long to figure out what woke me. George had his hand on my ass and was petting it very gently. After a while he fumbled around and I felt a coolness entering my ass. I tensed up, knowing what was about to happen.

"Easy," he whispered, his lips so close to my ear that I could feel his breath against it. " Just trust me and it'll be okay. Now relax and let yourself go slack. There's no hurry about it and I won't hurt you, I promise." He rubbed my back for a long time, relaxing me, and then he slipped an arm around me and fondled my nipples. And all the time he was whispering in my ear: "That's it. Don't push, just let it be there. Gently now. Easy. Let me do it, you just let it happen."

George's huge dick pressed for entrance and the pressure against my ass was intense, almost demanding, but it was gentle too. He kept touching my nipples and kissing the back of my neck and whispering in my ear as he kept up the pressure, telling me how much he wanted to be inside me. I felt my whole body relax, as if it was turning to jelly and as my body relaxed my dark flower bloomed, slowly opening itself to him. I lost all track of time and place, everything but George's touch, his quiet, soothing voice and the feel of his dick slowly finding its way inside me.

I don't know how long this went on. It seemed like minutes and it seemed like hours, all at the same time and all that time George's huge dick was slowly inching its way into me. At one point I found myself pushing back on it, trying to hurry it but George stopped me, making me let him do it, let him decide how fast I could take it.

When he finally settled in against my ass the realization that I had all of him inside me almost made me come. And the fullness! The pleasure of being so completely filled with him was almost more than I could bear and I was amazed that my ass could accommodate him. I took a deep breath and let myself fall apart, completely in his power.

We lay still for a long time, our bodies pressed together, joined by the solid bridge of George's dick. When he did begin to move it was slowly, pulling back just a fraction and then waiting a moment before gently pressing himself back in. Another movement, a little more this time and less of a wait until he gave it back, pressing himself tight against me again. I responded by squeezing down on his dick and he moved again, this time faster and with more of him. I ached to grab on to my cock but I knew I couldn't. Any touch would push me over the edge, releasing the orgasm I wanted to save.

George's movements got longer and longer but never very fast. He seemed to be savoring what he was doing, making it last, but in the end he had to give into it. He pushed his dick into me as far as he could make it go and I felt its spasms as he let his cum flow into me. I gave in too and emptied my balls onto the bed, waves of pleasure washing over me until it seemed they might never end.

When George began to withdraw I wouldn't let him. I kept pushing back against him until his back was against the wall and he had to give in. He pulled me up against him and we drifted off to sleep with him still inside me.

We woke with the morning light in our eyes, the smell of coffee in our noses and George's dick still inside me. We had slept the night without disconnecting and there it was, still filling me. George stirred when I squeezed down on him and he began to harden, filling me even more. I tested myself and found I was already there, as hard as I had been the night before.

"I gotta pee," George mumbled sleepily.

"Let's do this first." I squeezed down on him again and he tried a couple of experimental short strokes.

"You sure?" he asked, more awake.

I pushed back against him and squeezed again. "What do you think?"

He ran his hand down my flank and took hold of my hip, pulling me in tighter against him. "Where is everybody?"

I looked at the beds around us. "Downstairs, I guess. We must be the last ones."

He moved his dick in me again. "After last night we deserve to be." Another couple of strokes, then: "Roll over."

I pulled my cock up against my belly and did as he wanted. He pulled himself onto my back and straddled my buttocks with his thighs, reaching under me and finding my nipples with his fingers. "You like that, don't you?" He chuckled. "I guess I'm helping after all." His strokes got longer and a little faster, faster than the night before but they were still very gentle. The more he squeezed my tits and thrust his dick in and out of my ass the deeper I fell into a new wash of pleasure.

He pulled his knees forward and straightened up, grabbing my ass cheeks with both hands and driving his dick into me at a new angle. I bucked back on him, meeting his strokes, trying to get him in deeper. "Like riding a bronco," he said, almost to himself, and began slapping my ass, urging me on and making me buck harder against him.

When I heard him suck in his breath and moan "Oh Geez-us!" I knew he'd fallen over the edge. I savored his orgasm, loving the feel of his big dick thrashing around in my ass, spewing out its load of cum and filling me with it. I felt it so strongly it seemed like it was my very own orgasm and then I realized it was. My own cum was shooting out under me and sending waves of pleasure through me, making me clamp down on his dick which only made him come all the more.

When it was over he fell back on me, pressing me down with his body. We lay like that, filled with our collective pleasure, until our breathing came back to normal.

"Now can I go pee?"

"Sure," I laughed, "as long as you don't take that thing with you. We worked so hard getting it in there that I think I'm going to keep it in there all day."

He lay quietly for a moment, still covering my body with his, and then I felt an odd, warm sensation in my ass. "Well I'll be damned," I whispered and squeezed down again so nothing would leak out.

He sighed. "You're going to make me hard doing that. Besides, I don't think there's room in there for both my dick and all that beer I drank last night." He raised up and I let him slip out of me. I sighed too, my ass feeling very empty.

Downstairs I found Billy in the kitchen. "I have new respect for you," he said with a smile, handing me a cup of coffee. "You certainly jump right in, advice or no advice."

"What advice is that?"

"I told you to beware of the monster but you hopped right on, went where no man has ever gone before. Something like that."

"Uh-oh. We keep you awake?"

"No, but two guys don't sleep together the way you were this morning unless there's something... ah, something between them as it were. I'm surprised you can walk."

"Actually, so am I. And I think we need to change the sheets."

"Several sheets need to be changed. Don't worry about it. Ken likes to take care of that sort of thing. It's his domestic side. All the beds will have pristine sheets again tonight." He laughed again, "At least until you get into them."

"Billy!"

"Hey, Mark. Relax. You're the best thing that ever happened to this group. We owe George a big vote of thanks for finding you. Now come on, go outside with the guys. And tell Ken to get his ass in here for kitchen duty – after last night we need fuel!"

I took my coffee out to the pool and found Ken lying naked in the sun. He smiled up at me, showing those beautiful white teeth. I gave him Billy's message and wondered what, if anything, he remembered from the night before. Was he aware that he'd gotten blown by a guy who was getting fucked?

"I guess there's no rest for the house help," he said, flashing that smile again as he got up and headed for the kitchen. From his manner it looked like he didn't remember anything.

Miles was naked too and was cleaning the pool. He looked up and saluted. I hadn't realized quite how good looking he was. With that close-cropped beard – little more than stubble, really – and his sun-bleached hair he looked pleasantly rugged. He had a light sprinkling of dark blond fuzz across his chest too, which ran down his belly in a broad band and then spread out into a patch of thick, almost white pubic hair. Usually a guy's pubic hair is darker than the rest but Miles' was about five shades lighter. His cock swung freely as he pushed the vacuum across the pool floor and I studied it for a moment. It sure didn't look as long as it had felt the night before when it was working its way into my ass. Of course it had been hard then but even so... Then I saw that it was like an optical illusion: his balls were so big and hung so low that they made his cock look shorter than it really was. And I had been so intent on the feel of his cock pushing so far up inside me that I hadn't even been aware of his balls against mine. Next time would be different – and I was pretty sure there would be a next time.

I turned away from Miles and watched Doug setting the table wearing nothing but a pale blue jockstrap. The pouch was obviously well filled and I wished he'd take it off. There was a dick in there which I had yet to get my hands on, even though it had been up my ass. He smiled at me, "Hungry? Breakfast will be out shortly."

George came out of the house, carrying a coffee cup. He grinned at me, ran his hand over his crotch and winked. I hoped there'd be more of that, too.

Breakfast was wonderful: scrambled eggs, sausage, fried potatoes and rolls. We laughed and joked around the table, just like any bunch of guys off for a weekend by themselves. When the meal was over and the dishes had been cleared up, Miles announced that he was going up to the meadow to cut some fire wood and George said he was going out on the back deck to read, out of the sun. Doug decided the van needed washing and Ken just disappeared, presumably to change the sheets.

"Bath time," Billy said to me. "You didn't forget about it in all the passions of last night, did you?"

I laughed. "No, I didn't forget. Just let me run in and get what I need while you get dressed for the part of Spartacus." He gave me a puzzled look. "You know, get naked."

I went into the kitchen and found a clean plastic scrubber then went upstairs to get my toiletry kit. As I had suspected, Ken was pulling the sheets off the beds and he directed me to the clean towels. "All set, Billy," I said, back outside. "Now help me move this table over there by the shower." Once the table was in place I put one of the air mattresses on it and covered that with one of the towels.

Billy was already hard, his cock jutting rigidly out of its thick bush of dark hair. I turned on the hot water and soaked one of the towels until it was hot enough that I could barely wring it out. "Okay, up here." I indicated the mattress on the picnic table.

"What for? What're you going to do up there?"

"Just keep quiet and do it," I said. "I lost the bet so this is my party."

He dubiously climbed onto the table and I laid him out on his back, tucking the hot towel around his cock and balls. He gasped with the heat when I first put it on him but then he lay still, enjoying the sensation. I took the comb and scissors from my kit and began combing the thick hair on his chest and belly with one hand while I played with his nipples with the other. I was startled when he let out that sigh I had come to recognize and his body jerked under my hands. I had intended for him to come, but not quite this soon. "Don't worry," he said with a mischievous smile. "That was only the first time."

Good lord!

I took the hot towel from his crotch, wanting to see his cock soft but it was still sticking straight up into the air. I wondered if it ever did get soft.

I combed the long, thick hair away from the base of his cock and trimmed it short. Then I carefully trimmed the hair on his balls. I found the tube of hair removing cream that had come, free, with my toiletry kit. Billy looked up. "What's that?"

"You keep quiet," I said. "I told you, this is my party. Now lift your legs up." He bent his knees and I spread the cream thickly over his ball sac and up around the base of his cock. A little more went behind his balls, down just short of the little pucker of his ass. A final dab went in the center of the pubic hair I had trimmed.

After washing my hands I worked on the hair covering his abdomen, shortening it a little and using my razor to give it cleaner definition. I trimmed around his nipples, too, exposing the dark little circles. About then he began to squirm and said, "My balls are burning up," so I guessed the hair remover had done its job. I got him off the table, took my own shorts off and put him under the shower, positioning him so that the spray hit him squarely in the crotch.

I knelt down beside him and lightly rubbed his balls with the plastic scrubber. The hair sloughed off, exposing baby pink skin, probably the first time since puberty that it had seen the light of day. Then I scrubbed around the base of his cock, taking away the hair nearest to it. When I finished his cock looked bigger somehow and I realized that the base part of it had always been hidden in the thick hair, making it look stubby. It still wasn't huge but it didn't look tiny anymore. It also still wasn't soft.

I shampooed him all over, rubbing the rich lather into the hair that still covered his body. Turning him around I was surprised to note how sparse the hair was on his back but I took the razor and cleaned it off anyway. I lathered the cheeks of his ass and washed down into the crack, lightly massaging the little pucker hidden there. He squirmed a little but I could tell he liked it. He liked it when I kissed him there, too.

A very brisk overall rub with a wash cloth finished the shower. I turned off the water and took him into the sun to towel him down. When he was dry I took some baby oil and gently worked it into the newly pink skin of his ball sack and around the base of his cock. I wrung a towel out in very hot water again and put him back on the table, wrapping his still hard cock and balls in it. Then I had him roll over and I massaged him, starting with his shoulders and working my way down, over his buttocks, to his feet. By the time I finished he was nearly asleep.

"My God that was nice," he said when I patted him on the ass and said it was all over. "Now can I see what you've done to me?"

He stood up, dropped the towel on the ground and ran his hands slowly down his body to his crotch. He fingered his balls and looked down in surprise. "They're so soft. And my cock looks bigger! Wow, that is really... What's this? Some sort of trademark?" He was pointing at the little spot, just above his cock, where I had cleaned the hair away.

"No, silly," I chuckled. "That's for my nose. It seems to be buried down there all the time and I'm getting tired of suffocating. Speaking of which..." I dropped down on my knees. "Let's see if I got it in the right place." I sucked in his cock and found that my nose fit perfectly into the little clearing in the hair. He gently pulled me off and said, "Let's lie down."

We went over to one of the air mattresses and he stretched out. I dropped down between his legs and took his balls into my mouth. I couldn't believe how soft the skin had become without all that hair on it. The taste of baby oil was pleasant in my mouth and I began to roll the balls around inside the sack. I reached up, stroking the fur along his belly and chest and when I caught on to his nipples he jerked and shot cum all over my hair. I hadn't even been down on him.

"Sorry," he laughed. "I guess you need another shower. Help yourself to the shampoo." He stood up and looked at me. "Thank you. That was the nicest Roman bath I've ever had." Then he did something that really touched me. He reached down and squeezed my hard dick. "And that's the nicest complement I ever had, too." He turned, hiding, I think, a little embarrassment. He recovered quickly though and laughed, "The guys are gonna love this. How am I ever going to explain the little bald spot?"

"That's your problem," I said, getting under the shower. "But whatever you say, they'll probably figure it out. After all, it's not like they don't know where your dick has been spending its time the last 24 hours."

Since I was wet from the shower anyway, a swim seemed in order. I jumped into the pool and swam thirty fast laps, enjoying a somewhat different sort of exercise than I'd been getting since I'd arrived. After a while Ken came out to hang the sheets up to dry and he joined me in the pool when he finished. We horsed around for a while, me trying to get my hands on his dick and him trying to decide if he wanted me to or not. He never did make up his mind and seemed relieved when Doug came up and announced that the van was once again clean. He jumped in with us, still wearing his pretty light blue jockstrap.

Shortly after Doug, Billy came to join us. He walked out of the house naked and Ken saw it right away. "That must have been some bath, Billy," he called out. "Looks like you lost half your hair."

Doug tossed his two cents in too, "And you got a bigger cock. How'd you do that?" Billy just laughed and dived into the pool.

Someone found a volleyball and we threw it around for a while, mainly trying to splash each other, laughing and having a fine time. Pretty soon George wandered out to see what was going on and he pulled off his shorts and jumped in with us. I swam over to him and looked down at his dick floating out in the water. He held me at bay with his hand flat against my chest and chuckled, "Oh, no, you stay away from me. I can't swim with a hard-on." The other guys got a very big kick out of that.

"What's so funny?" Miles asked, appearing out of the trees and heading for the shower, sweaty after his wood-cutting chores.

"George just announced that he can't swim with a hard-on," Billy answered. "Hell, I'm surprised he can swim at all with that thing hanging down between his legs!"

"Hey, Billy, show Miles your hair cut and your new cock." Doug grabbed Billy and attempted to lift him out of the water but he only succeeded in ducking them both.

George turned to me, neatly avoiding my hand which was sneaking out towards his dick. "Billy got a new cock?" he asked.

"Well, let's see it," Miles said, walking over to the pool. "Come on, Billy. Show us your dick."

Billy's face was red but he pulled himself out of the pool with great dignity and turned for all to see. "It's the same old cock, guys, only now you can see it." He put his hand behind his balls and pushed then out. "These are the same ones too but they have new life in them now that they're naked." He realized that his cock was beginning to rise up so he jumped back in the water, his face turning red again.

He wasn't quick enough for Ken, though. "Yep, that's sure the same old cock you've always had, Billy. Can't keep the damn thing down with a brick."

"Probably the same old balls, too, always working overtime," Doug added. "But tell us, what's the little bald spot in the middle for?"

"I know," said Miles. "Something fits in there, doesn't it, Billy?" He looked over at me. "And I guess we all know what it might be, don't we?" He jumped in the pool, joining the rest of us.

A minute or two later Miles swam over to me and gave me a quick, affectionate hug. "You done good, kid," he whispered. "We've never seen Billy as happy as he is right now. Thanks." He patted my cheek and swam away.

We played and swam for a while and then, gradually, one by one, we got out of the pool and stretched out in the sun. A little after noon Billy decided it was time for lunch and he and Ken brought out platters of cold cuts and salad and some good, cold beer.

After lunch we were all in a very lazy mood. George had fallen asleep on the deck and we let him be since he wasn't in the sun. Doug decided to take a walk and I went upstairs to find the book I had brought with me. Everyone else decided to have a nap.

I took my book out to the pool and sat on one of the lounges where I could admire the sleeping bodies. George was stretched out flat on his belly and looking very content. I wondered how, lying as he was on that huge cock of his, he could be comfortable. I decided that unlike the princess and her tiny pea, he must be used to sleeping with a thick lump under him.

I looked over at Billy and had to chuckle. He was lying on an air mattress, on his back, and he was hard again, his cock tenting his silk shorts.

Ken was also lying on his back, snoring softly, his hand lying protectively over his crotch, the head of his dick just peeking out through his fingers. He was a very handsome man I thought, almost pretty in the face but with a definite aura of maleness about him too. Like Miles, he had a well-defined, natural body, the sort that never went near a gym and didn't need to. I thought it was a shame that something was gnawing away at him, making him drink too much and robbing him of his confidence.

I looked around for Miles but didn't see him. I didn't think he had gone for a walk with Doug – who had made a great point of changing before he went and then appeared wearing only sandals and a new jock strap. This time it was a neon yellow one and had his name embroidered in blue across the waist band.

I tried to read for a while but the book was not very good and I figured out who did it before the deed was even done. I chucked it and went in search of a beer.

On my way to the refrigerator I looked out on the back deck and found Miles. He was napping in the hammock, one of those rope things that always leave funny marks on your body and he was lying on his stomach, his dick and balls hanging down through the mesh. His slow, regular breathing caused his dick to sway back and forth like a slow pendulum. When I noticed the air mattress stashed under the hammock my cock began to stiffen, knowing even before I did what I was going to do.

Quietly I went over to the hammock, adjusted the position of the air mattress slightly and then lay down on my back. I had only to turn my head a little for that long, low hanging cock to drop right into my mouth. Miles made no sign that he was even aware of what was happening but his cock knew. It began to grow hard, lengthening on my tongue like it was seeking the back of my throat. I reached up and fondled his balls and that made his cock grow faster and push deeper into my mouth. I laid there for a long time, licking and sucking on that long cock that hung weightlessly above me. I guess I even dozed for a bit, sucking on Miles' cock like it was a baby pacifier and I was the most pacified baby in the world.

I slowly became aware of someone else, someone kneeling over me. Strong hands undid my shorts and slid them off, gently taking hold of my half hard cock so it wouldn't tangle in them. I saw the neon yellow jock strap out of the corner of a sleepy eye and knew it was Doug lifting my legs and gently working his way in between them, seeking my ass with his dick. He must have lubed himself with something because his cock was slick when it pressed against me and gently opened me to its entrance. For a moment I hung there, like the cock in my mouth, suspended in pleasure.

Doug continued to move slowly and steadily, pressing his dick further and further into my ass until his hips were pressed up against me and my legs were held tight against his chest. When he began to move in me Miles matched him, slow stroke for slow stroke, sliding his cock in my mouth exactly as Doug was sliding his in my ass.

Doug's angle was perfect for his cockhead to press against my prostate with each inward stroke, massaging it and making my dick dribble like a slow faucet. Every time he pushed into me he pressed a little harder there until I was breathing heavily, sucking in air around the cock that filled my mouth. With every stroke Doug whispered to himself like he was chanting, "Easy now, easy now." And his strokes were easy, and very gentle.

I could hear Miles' breathing too. He was still moving his cock up and down in my mouth but the strokes were short now and he paused between them, losing Doug's rhythm. I was right on the edge and I knew I wasn't going to be able to control myself much longer. Doug's chanting got louder, "Easy now, easy now."

When I felt his hand on my balls I went over the edge and started firing cum all over my chest. That did it for Doug and he stopped, holding his breath, waiting. Then he let go with a long sigh, and his dick started spasming inside me, shooting its load of hot cum into my guts.

When he was through he stayed inside me for a long minute, my balls still in his hand. Then he pulled out, picked up his yellow jock and went into the kitchen. Miles quietly said, "Let's do some more of that later," pulled his dick back through the mesh of the hammock and turned over. By the time I was up and looking for my shorts he was dozing again, holding on to his cock. I retrieved my shorts and followed Doug into the kitchen where I could hear the shower running in the bathroom.

# # # # #

I showered upstairs, wishing that Doug were there with me instead of downstairs by himself. Regardless of the fact that he'd fucked me twice now, I still hadn't gotten my hands on his dick.

Billy came into the bathroom while I was drying off. He stood at the urinal with his back to me, talking over his shoulder. "Where've you been?"

"Out on the back deck."

"Oh, with Miles." He grinned at me and I could hear him peeing, hitting the back of the trough.

"Yeah, Doug too."

"With Miles? My, my. Doug has certainly taken a shine to you."

"What d'you mean, Billy?"

"Well, you must have noticed how shy Doug is about... well, about that sort of thing. He's not one to show off the way the rest of us like to. Not that way. I mean, I don't think any of us have actually seen him do anything except rub himself through his pants. The rest of us sometimes get so horny we just pull it out and jerk it off in the open, you know, like when we're watching one of those movies, but not Doug. So if he, uh... if he actually let you do him with Miles around, well, he's obviously very taken with you."

"I didn't exactly blow him, Billy. I was busy doing that to Miles so he... well, he fucked me."

Billy was silent for a moment and then let out a long laugh. "We've obviously underestimated you, young man. That or we've been way off base with our man Doug. In either case, I suggest you begin shopping for your trousseau. And girding your loins in case the divorce is messy." He was silent for a moment and then said, mostly to himself, "That must have been something to see, you with Miles and Doug at the same time. I wish I'd been there."

I leaned in and looked at him. He'd stopped peeing, I guess because you can't pee through a hard cock. The sight of him like that made my own dick begin to rise. "I can't help it," Billy said, looking down at himself. "It just happens."

"It also happens that help is here," I said, turning him around. I went down to my knees, grabbed him by the ass and pulled him against me, slipping his cock into my mouth until my nose was buried in the little bare spot I had made for it in his hair. I took his balls in my hand, still amazed at how smooth they were without all that hair, and I managed to get one of them in my mouth along with his cock. My tongue had a field day, running along the shaft of his cock and then sliding back to the silkiness of his ball sack. It wasn't long before he let out that long sigh I had come to recognize as the beginning of the end. His body shook and he filled my mouth with his salty cum. We stayed that way for just a moment, me on my knees with Billy's cock in my mouth, Billy with his back arched, holding rigidly still, both of us enjoying the aftermath.

I relaxed my grip on his ass and let him slip out. "Now take your shower, Billy," I said as I stood. "I'm going down and have a drink." I smacked my lips and grinned at him. "Scotch – with salt."

He laughed. "Fix me one too, will you? I'll be down in a minute."

Doug was standing at the kitchen sink, dropping ice in glasses. He'd exchanged the neon yellow jock for an emerald green one although I guess it wasn't technically a jockstrap. It didn't have any straps and the pouch was more like a sack, held around his equipment with elastic. When he moved the whole thing swayed, just like his dick would if it had been free. "Hey, Mark, you want a drink?" he asked without the least recognition of what we'd done together less than a half hour before.

"Yes, please, but you better make two. Billy will be down shortly. Where is everyone?"

"Out at the pool." He poured and handed me one of the drinks. "Come on."

We sat in the late afternoon sun, joking and talking, five everyday guys enjoying a stag weekend out in the country. If you were a stranger coming into the group, if you didn't know, it would never occur to you that every one of them was having sex with the same man. It was weird too, the way all of them – except maybe Billy – pretended not to notice that I was doing it with the others. They obviously knew, even Ken who was kind of out of it all the time, and Miles and Doug had actually done it with me together, but nobody recognized it. I decided that there was so much sexual tension in the air all the time that anything was okay just as long as they each got their rocks off. My dick began to firm up, anticipating the night to come and I pulled myself out of my reverie. "Got any good movies for us tonight, Ken?" I asked.

He was enthusiastic. "Oh yeah, a couple of really good ones. And I brought one you'll really like too, I think. We'll see."

Billy came out to tell us dinner would be ready soon and ask if anyone wanted another drink.

"Yea, Billy," I said. "I'll have another Scotch – with salt."

His cheeks turned pink but he held his ground. "You have to do that one yourself," he said.

"What's a scotch with salt?" someone asked. "Sounds terrible."

"Not at all," I said, "if you get your salt from the right source." I turned and followed Billy back inside.

He was standing in the kitchen. I didn't say a word, I just dropped to my knees in front of him and yanked his shorts down. His cock was already hard in anticipation, thrusting out of his newly trimmed brush. "My god, Billy, don't you..." He cut me off by grabbing the back of my head and shoving his cock into my mouth. I think he tried to hold off but it still didn't take more than three or four minutes before I tasted his salty cum again. Where the hell did he get it all? I stood up and stuck my hand into my shorts to arrange my hard-on to a less cramped position. Billy reached down and gingerly felt me. "After all these times," he murmured, mostly to himself, "and it still makes you hard..."

"Well," he said aloud, "another drink?" He pulled up his shorts and began adding ice to my glass. "You really shouldn't have said that, you know. About the scotch and salt. Now it's going to be a joke around here forever." He handed me my drink and slapped me on the butt, pushing me towards the door. "Now get out of here. You go face the guys this time."

Out at the pool George said, "I hope dinner isn't burned." Miles threw me one of his mock salutes and added, "I hope nothing's burned." Ken looked up and said, "Wait, wait. I want to hear about this salt and scotch thing." Jokes were still going around the table when Billy announced dinner.

After the dishes had been cleared away and taken care of we sat in the warm twilight, shooting the breeze and enjoying each other's company. Finally Ken stood up and asked if any of us were ready for a movie.

Doug said he was going for a swim but the rest of us went into the living room and arranged ourselves in front of the T.V. While Ken readied the movie I positioned myself on the floor where I could look up the leg of George's shorts. He had evidently taken my advice because he wasn't wearing anything under them now and I could just make out the foreskin that covered the head of his dick. He grinned at me, knowing where I was looking, and pretended to scratch, pulling his foreskin back a little so his cockhead could look back at me.

"... is a really great one," Ken was saying. "I know you guys are going to love it. It's got an orgy with about fifteen people, all goin' at it at once. Really hot!"

"What'd you do, watch them all first?" Miles asked.

"No, I didn't watch them all first. But where I rent them, there's these little booths and you can preview any movie for a quarter. So I just look at a little bit to be sure I'm getting good ones."

"Sure," George chimed in. "I bet you spend twenty dollars in that little booth, previewing."

"Not to mention what else gets spent," quipped Billy. "Come on, Ken, on with the show."

"Where's Doug?" Ken asked. "He'll especially like this one." He went to the door and hollered at Doug. "Here he comes. Now we can start."

Doug wandered in, a towel wrapped around his waist. "What happened to your pretty green posing strap?" Billy asked him.

"It isn't a posing strap, it's a cache sex, and it got all wet," Doug answered, stretching out on the floor next to me. "What's the movie?"

"Swinger's Orgy Club," Ken said, switching it on. "You're going to love it."

I watched the screen for a little while. It actually was a pretty good movie – lots of nice-looking studs waving quite nice cocks around. As they turned to serious fucking on the screen I turned to watch George's big dick start to get bigger. Doug rolled onto his side and propped his head on his hand. As he did so his towel fell open and I finally got a good look at his cock. It was just beginning to harden and the head was still partially covered by his foreskin.

Doug made no move to retie the towel and as the movie progressed his cock began to lift, the head slowly emerging from its nest of skin to glisten darkly in the dim light. I glanced up at George. He winked at me and flexed his dick, which was almost fully hard.

Looking back I caught Doug watching me with hooded eyes. When I moved closer he gave me an almost imperceptible nod and then let his eyes drift back to the movie.

Doug made no sign when I took the head of his cock in my mouth. He laid quietly on his side, seemingly totally absorbed in the movie. The only sounds in the room came from the screen and our collective breathing. I slid further onto his cock, until it was comfortably in my mouth with just enough room to maneuver my tongue around it. I suppressed a sigh and laid there, silently massaging his cock with my tongue. It was a cock made for long, slow sucking and I intended to give it what it was made for.

I found that Doug's cock had a distinct, pleasant taste and I let it lie still in my mouth for a long time, savoring it. I brought my hand up and held the velvet of his ball sack, feeling the heavy globes inside roll smoothly under my touch.

We lay that way for quite a long time, my mouth quiet on his dick, my tongue moving lazily over the underside of the head and my fingers lightly stroking his balls. He had his head down now, cradled on his arm, lost in what I was doing to him. He might almost have been dozing

When I felt him begin to tremble I stopped, laying my tongue along the length of his cock and holding his balls still in my hand. As his trembling subsided I moved my tongue again, slowly, taking him back to the edge and then letting him back off from it. I forgot the movie, the guys sitting around us, everything but Doug's cock and bringing pleasure to it, keeping it just on the edge of release

Doug began trembling again, this time insistently. I held my breath, not moving a muscle. He gave out a low growl and I felt his cock swell in my mouth but I didn't move until he thrust forward, telling me it was time. When he came it was like an explosion in a silent movie, all fury and no sound. His dick jerked and throbbed and shot its heavy load in complete silence; I didn't even hear a change in his breathing. I guessed maybe he was so quiet because there were four of his buddies sitting around the room pretending they weren't watching him get blown.

Silent or not, he took a long time with it, finally giving in and stroking his dick between my lips, making it last all the longer. When it was finally over for him he lay still for a long time, letting himself go soft in my mouth.

When he finally did slip out of my mouth he rolled over onto his stomach and sighed as though he might be drifting off to sleep. I looked up at George and saw him slowly run his hand along the length of his dick which was pressing up against his shorts. He caught my eye and smiled, then he glanced at the door, telling me something. I nodded and went to the bathroom.

Billy was standing at the urinal. I dug out my half-hard dick and stood next to him. "I told you Doug has taken a shine to you," he said, looking at me. "He's never, ever, done anything like that before. I mean, with all of us watching and everything. You should have seen Miles, whacking away at his dick and even George had his out in his hand for a while." I stopped waving my stream around and aimed it squarely across his making them splash together.

"Oh, no you don't," he said, "and if you look at my shorts you'll see why." He turned a little, showing me the large wet spot on the front. "I'm fast to recover but not that fast." He patted my ass, "Give it a while."

Miles and Ken were watching another movie and Doug was asleep on the floor when I passed through the living room. I went outside to find George.

He was lying on one of the lounges, slowly stroking his dick. He had taken his shorts off and his dick was pointing straight up into the air. I reached down and took his balls in my hand, pinching on the sack the way I knew he liked. He sighed, continuing to stroke his dick. I found a nipple with my other hand and squeezed it; George pushed his chest out, liking it, so I knelt down and began to suck on one nipple while I pinched the other and tugged on his balls. His breathing became ragged when my mouth left his nipple and found his balls. I sucked one of them in and rolled it around with my tongue, then lightly nipped at the sack. I pinched his nipple harder when he began to groan and he let himself go, his cum shooting into the air and falling back on his belly like warm rain. He sighed contentedly.

"And now to bed. Alone. To sleep." He stood up. "You?"

"No, I think I'll just sit here for a minute."

He went inside and I stretched out on the lounge, looking at the stars and enjoying the quiet.

When I went in everyone else seemed to have gone to bed except for Ken. He was in the living room watching a movie. He had taken his clothes off and was lying on the floor, playing with his cock.

"What're you watching, Ken?"

He looked up. "Just a movie. Actually, it's the one I got for you."

"Me?"

"Yeah, I thought you might like one with just... Well, you know, with just guys in it. You want to watch? I'll back it up if you want."

"Sure. Can I get you a drink while you do that? I'm going to have one."

"Yea, sure."

When I came back and handed him his drink he punched the button to start the movie. I unfastened my shorts. "You mind?" I asked as they dropped to the floor.

"No. Go ahead. Make yourself comfortable."

I sat down beside him and watched the movie. There wasn't any story, just a crew of big-dicked studs romping around on wall to wall mattresses wrestling around with each other, touching and sucking whatever cock happened to be within reach. I looked over at Ken. His dick was hard and he was stroking it, obviously enjoying the on-screen action. When one of the studs got down to some seriously fucking, though, he stopped, holding his cock in a tight fist, eyes riveted to the screen.

"My god," he whispered as one of the guys pushed his ass out to take another guy's dick, "how can he do that? How can he take that cock up his ass? God, that must hurt. Mark," he turned to me, his eyes bright, "how... Why does a guy do that? I mean, it must feel good to the guy who's doing the fucking but what does the other guy get out of it?"

The other guy suddenly came, shooting cum all over his belly.

"Oh, Jesus, he came! He came with that big dick up his ass. How... I mean, why..."

"Oh come on, Ken. He came because it felt good. You have nerves in your ass, you know, just like you do in your cock. Or in your tits, for that matter. It feels good having a dick up your ass, sometimes so good it makes you come without even touching yourself."

He looked at me like I'd lost my mind. "No. Guys don't have, well, feelings there. Not like women. A guy's ass or his tits? No way, man." He gave his cock a couple of strokes as though proving that it's the only place a man gets his pleasure.

"You want to bet? Didn't anyone ever suck on your tits or lick your ass?"

"No." He looked puzzled. "Why would they?"

"Because it feels good, dummy."

"No." He looked at me like a starving man at a delicatessen but he couldn't bring himself to ask. I saved him the trouble.

"Yes. Turn over."

"What? Oh, no. No. I couldn't take..."

"Don't worry. You're not going to take anything you don't want to. Just turn over and relax." I rolled him onto his belly and pulled his cock down, between his legs. He resisted a little but finally gave in with a little puppy whimper.

I started with his cockhead and then licked my way up the shaft. I spent some time with his balls, sucking on them and quickly flicking my tongue up towards his crack, teaching him a little anticipation. When he started to moan softly I moved further up, spreading his cheeks with my hands and running my tongue in close to his little flower. The more I did that the more he tried to push his hips back on me, urging me on. The first time I grazed my tongue over his little pink hole he bucked back like a pony but I held him down and pulled his cheeks wider apart, burying my face between them. I teased him a lot with the tip of my tongue and then pushed it in a little, forcing saliva ahead of it to ease the way. While I was busy with his ass I groped my way up to his chest and found one of his nipples. When I rolled it around in my fingers it got hard and he began to shiver.

After awhile I realized that he was mumbling something, talking to himself and I listened, trying to make out what he was saying. Finally I caught it. Over and over he was whispering, "Put it in me. Please. Put it in me."

I fumbled around to find my shorts and dug out the small packet of lubricant I always carry in my pocket. I applied the stuff liberally to his ass and my dick and then lay over him, supporting myself on my hands and knees. "Are you sure, Ken?"

He didn't answer, just kept whispering over and over: " Put it in me. Please. Put it in me." There were streaks on his face where tears had run.

I laid the head of my cock against his ass and held it there, not pushing, just letting him know it was there if he wanted it. It took only a moment before he pushed back on it. All my preparation paid off; he was wide open and my dick slipped easily into him. Even so, I still wouldn't push; I made him do it, pulling his ass up on my dick until he was on his knees with my balls swinging up behind his. I let him pull me back down with him until I was resting on him, my weight on his back and my cock up to the hilt in his ass.

We rested that way for a while, letting him get used to the sensation of having a man inside him. When he squeezed down on me a couple of times I knew he was ready and I began, very gently, to fuck him.

I rolled him onto his side so I could get at his cock. From the first touch I knew he wasn't going to last long so I lengthened my strokes, trying to catch up to him. I didn't quite make it but when he clamped down on my dick, squirting his cum out on the floor, I went off right after him and bathed his ass with my own hot juices.

Afterward, we lay together, my arm around his waist holding him tight against me and my dick still inside him. When I finally did pull out he turned over, grabbed my head and kissed me.

"Whoa, boy. Not so fast there."

He kissed me again and then pulled back so he could look at me. "No. I gotta face it now. I've wanted that for a long time. A very long time. And it felt so good. Not just your dick inside me but all of it, the way you held me, the way you took charge of me. I guess I've always wanted a man to do that but I was always afraid... You know?"

I knew. We lay on the floor together and had a long talk. He told me that he was always a little afraid around the guys, afraid he might do something that would turn them against him and he thought that might kill him – literally. These guys were his male world and he was happiest in a male world. He also told me he was in love with George and had been for years only he was more afraid of him than anyone. He also feared George's dick which both fascinated and frightened him. There were other things too, and we talked well into the morning.

When, finally, sleep became overwhelmingly important we took a shower together. While we were drying off he dropped down on his knees and slowly took my cock in his mouth and held it, playing his tongue over it until it grew hard. I smiled down at him and he released it, standing up.

"I know. We need sleep. But I just had to do that, had to finally feel what it's like having a cock in my mouth." He smiled sheepishly, "I liked it."

On our way upstairs I turned to him and said, "Here's my one and only piece of advice, Ken. Be true to yourself first and you have nothing to fear. Self-honesty makes you free and lets you do anything you set yourself to. Anything." I had a pretty good idea what he was about to set himself to do.

"What..."

I just smiled and pushed him towards the bed I knew he wanted to sleep in. Then I crawled in with Miles, hoping he wouldn't wake up. For a while.

I woke from a confused dream – something about being an acrobat and learning to fly. What woke me was Miles, who had laid his cock up against my ass and was gently pressing it into me. I moved back a little and pushed against him, wanting to take him inside. He put a hand on my hip and slowly came into me until he was up against me and his cockhead found that inner door again and pushed against it, slowly opening it. Then he stopped, letting me savor the feel of him so far inside me.

When he began to move in me I lay still and let him do it. His strokes were easy and slow, without any urgency but filled with great pleasure for both of us. I drifted in and out of sleep, waking to feel my orgasm rising within me, dozing to let it subside.

After a long while he took hold of my dick and stroked it in time with his strokes in my ass. He pulled me closer to get a better grip and then moved his hand a little faster. I gave myself up to him and then, finally, to a long, slow orgasm which seemed to flow through my cock forever.

I woke again, finding myself turned over to face him. He was asleep but he still had his hand on my dick. I kissed him and went back to sleep; when I woke again it was morning and he was gone.

When I went to the bathroom I saw that everyone else was up too, except for Ken and George. They'd thrown the sheet back and I could see that they were lying spoon fashion with George's arms around Ken, holding him tightly against his chest. Further down I could just make out the base of George's dick, the rest of it still inside Ken. I smiled to myself, wishing them well, and went to pee.

Downstairs Billy, Doug and Miles were out by the pool. "Well," Billy called, "we thought you were going to sleep all day."

I wasn't sure what he was talking about. "Is it late?"

"Only if you call lunchtime late. You sleep well?"

"Yes, very well." Miles looked up and threw me one of his salutes. I sent a smile back to him. "Very well indeed." I sat down next to Billy and he passed me his coffee cup. It was nearly cold but it was something.

"What'd you do to Ken last night?"

"Nothing. Well, nothing he didn't want done to him."

Doug laughed. "Well, it's about time someone did something to him. God knows he's wanted it for a long time. Maybe now he'll calm down a little."

"Yes," Billy added, "and maybe now the liquor bill will go down a little, too." He patted me on the arm. "Seriously, Mark, you think he's okay?"

I thought about it for a while. Doing what he'd done last night, admitting what he was and what he wanted, is a very hard thing to do. "I think he will be, as long as he has you guys as friends. He's taken a big step and it might take him a little time but, yes, I think he'll be okay. He took a big risk you know, tossing that sheet back so you all could see... the way he was. If you guys can deal with that he'll be fine. Just as long as he has friends."

"Oh, he has friends all right," Billy said. "What he's not gonna have is lunch if he and George don't get out of that bed pretty soon. Come on, guys, I'm hungry. Who's going to grill the burgers?"

Doug volunteered for grill duty while Miles and I set the table and Billy put the rest of the stuff together in the kitchen. When the table was ready Miles brought out a couple of beers and we sat down. He turned to me and said, "I told you before, Mark, you're the best thing that ever happened to this group and I want you to know we all appreciate it." He raised his beer bottle and touched it to mine. "Thanks. From all of us." He grinned. "Especially from me!"

George wandered out just as we started to eat. "Burgers and beer for breakfast?" he asked, "how can you?"

"If you hadn't been doing whatever you've been doing up there all morning you'd know it is well past lunchtime," Billy said. "Where's Ken?"

I thought George blushed a little. "He'll be down. He's just... well, he's feeling a little shy right now."

"That's dumb," Doug said. "I mean it's not like he's any different this morning than he was yesterday at lunch." He went into the cabin and we heard him yelling: "Ken! Get your ass down here. Lunch is on."

Ken finally did come out, looking a little sheepish. He sat next to George and we were all quiet for a moment. I saw George put his hand protectively on Ken's thigh and then Ken looked around the table, looking each one of us in the eye. After a moment he grinned and said, "Okay, okay. So I... Look, guys. No jokes, okay? At least for a while?"

Doug reached across the table and chucked him under the chin. "No jokes, Ken. At least until after lunch."

So that's the story of my weekend in the country. Well, not quite. Billy caught me once more before we went back to the city – and damned if I didn't get a hard-on when I went down on him.

I've become a permanent fixture in the group now and I manage to go up to the cabin with them once or twice a month. I can't say things have changed much though. Miles still doesn't come, no matter how much he plays and Doug still wears his bright little jockstraps – he must have a hundred of them. Billy still comes five or six times a day and I'll be damned if he still doesn't give me a hard-on every time I go down on him.

What has changed, of course, is Ken. Every time we're all up there he makes it a point to have sex with someone, generally George or me, where everyone else can watch, usually on the living room floor while the movies are on. We all know he's proving something but none of us are quite sure what. Doesn't matter. If he needs to do it who are any of us to not watch. He also doesn't drink very much anymore.

George has changed too. He's become very protective of Ken, always looking out for him and sleeping with his arms around him. I think they're finally talking about getting a place together.

BOYS ON SPRING BREAK
Thomas C. Humphrey

"Uncle Mark? This is Kevin." The unfamiliar voice gradually displaced the remaining fragments of the deliciously erotic dream which had been shattered by the jangling phone. As I struggled to shake the cobwebs out of my head, my erect cock throbbed in protest against awkward confinement beneath the covers and required immediate adjustment.

Before long I was awake enough to realize that the voice on the other end of the line belonged to the son of my very best high school buddy years ago. Roger and I had played basketball together and had been inseparable, even after he got his girlfriend pregnant during our senior year and married her the weekend after we graduated. I had secretly wanted Roger for years, but I swallowed my jealousy and served as his best man at the wedding. When Kevin was born not long afterward, I was his godfather, and he grew up calling me "Uncle Mark."

Then several years ago I had been transferred to Florida and kept contact with Roger only through occasional phone calls. I had not seen Kevin since he was thirteen or fourteen, when his family made the obligatory trip to Disney World and spent a weekend with me before heading back north. As I listened to his explanation for the middle-of-the night call, I hurriedly calculated and was shocked to realize that Kevin had to be going on nineteen, though his dad and I were only in our late thirties.

In very hesitant, apologetic tones, Kevin explained that he and a couple of friends were on their way to Lauderdale for spring break when their car slung a rod and stranded them on the outskirts of a tiny town about fifteen miles north of me. Nothing was open in the town, and he wondered if I could come to get them and put them up until they could figure out their next move.

I hurriedly dressed and made a quick sweep of the house, popping a Jeff Stryker tape out of the VCR and secreting a couple of skin magazines I had left on the coffee table. I am completely open in

Florida, but nobody in my hometown knows I'm gay. I wasn't sure whether I was more concerned over shocking Kevin or having word get back to his dad, whom I guess I'm still half in love with, after all these years. As I drove to pick up Kevin and his friends, I agonized over having three straight college kids in my house for god knows how long without being able to do more than look and lust.

As I pulled up in front of their disabled car and my headlights illuminated them forlornly slouched against its hood, I immediately knew I had cause for concern. In the reflected glare, I confronted the ghost of Roger at eighteen. Kevin was the spitting image of his father, with the same raven-black hair falling in tight curls over his forehead, the same tall, lithe build, and the same leonine grace in repose that had made his father an ideal point guard and had fed my near-maniacal lust for him throughout high school.

The three of them sauntered over to my car, and as Kevin introduced his friends, the growing pressure in my crotch told me I was in deep trouble. Joe and Jesse were identical twins, taller and huskier than Kevin, of Nordic stock, with deep blue piercing eyes and hair the color of wet corn silk. All three were dressed in the mod style which I have come to hate: baggy shorts that fell to nearly mid-calf and too-large sweatshirts that hung well below their buttocks, completely disguising all the best parts of their youthful physiques. Still, they exuded enough raw sensuality that I knew I would have a struggle to keep from doing anything foolish.

Next morning after a leisurely breakfast, I arranged to have their car towed to my mechanic, who would not be able to repair it over the weekend. I let Kevin use my car to go to meet the tow truck and talk with the mechanic. Jesse went with him, but Joe elected to lie out by the pool and work on his tan before hitting the Lauderdale beaches. I sat in a lounge chair planning to review a report that was due the following week.

Immediately, it became apparent that I would get no work done. First, Joe asked if I would rub sunscreen on his back, an offer I couldn't refuse. I had a hard-on by the time I finished. Then he placed his towel directly in front of me and lay on his stomach with the orbs of his beautiful ass just inviting a caress through his tight swimsuit. Before long he sat up to oil his chest and gave me a shot of a crotch so full I wondered why the fabric of his swimsuit didn't rip. By the time he got around to coating his inner thighs, I had an overriding urge to rip it myself. "He's straight; hands off," I had to keep admonishing myself.

Suddenly, he got up and made a running dive into the pool and so captivated me with his gamboling and cavorting that I laid the report aside and feasted my eyes; maybe I couldn't touch, but I could store some magnificent visual images!

"Why don't you join me?" he asked teasingly on one of his trips to the side.

When I declined, he swam the length of the pool and then was back. "I love this secluded yard," he said. "You could swim nude and not have to worry about neighbors."

"Yeah, we're totally alone," I agreed.

He remained propped on his forearms a minute and then disappeared into the water. Before I knew what was happening, his wet trunks plopped at my feet and he stood grinning like a Cheshire cat. For the next ten minutes, he practiced his diving skills, spending more time preening and posing and showing off his magnificent equipment than he did diving. I was totally transfixed, and my eyes followed his every movement. His behavior showed that he knew I was captivated, but I no longer cared.

Finally, he sauntered around the pool toward me, his thick cock swinging several inches beyond low-hanging balls. As he approached, I kept thinking that water was supposed to make it shrink! He grabbed my forearm with both hands and tugged me to my feet. "You gonna swim with me, or do I have to throw you in?" he challenged good naturedly.

I shrugged my shoulders in mock resignation, kicked off my sandals, and slipped off my shorts. We had barely hit the water before we were grappling and splashing playfully. As we laughed and frolicked, I was afraid my imagination was running away with me. Joe's thigh just happened to wind up pressed tightly into my crotch too often, his hands just happened to stray down to my ass and linger too long. Then he made his intentions quite obvious. His hand roamed down my abdomen and his fingers encircled my semi-erect cock.

"Let's go inside," he said hoarsely.

We had hardly hit my king-size bed, wet hair and all, before he was all over me, kissing my eyelids, my cheeks, my mouth, all the while fisting my cock. My own mouth and hands were just as busy. I've always been considered exceptionally well hung, but this kid easily matched me – in fact, exceeded me in thickness. His shaft was almost as big around as my wrist, with a noticeable curve to the left. When I went down on him, I was afraid my jaws wouldn't open wide enough to accommodate him.

"That's it, man, suck it," he moaned, running his fingers through my hair and raising his hips slightly off the bed. "I was holding off for Lauderdale, but this feels so good!" he whispered. His obvious pleasure made me try even harder. I licked all around his enormous cockhead and down the thick shaft until I reached his balls, which had tightened against his body. When I took one of them in my mouth and swirled it around with my tongue, he clutched desperately at my back and lifted his trembling thighs completely off the bed. "Oh, god, stop, or I'm gonna shoot," he protested.

He pulled my head from between his legs and toppled me onto my back. He grasped my cock tightly in his fist, licked around the glans, then abruptly plunged down my shaft, and swallowed me to the roots. As he kept rising and falling on my cock, taking it all each time, it was my turn to moan and gasp in ecstasy.

Barely breaking his rhythm, he shifted around on the bed and thrust his rigid pole in my face. Once again, I mastered its girth, and we settled into a long mutual suck session. I got one and then two fingers up his ass and contemplated trying to fuck him, but what he was doing with his mouth was too beautiful to interrupt. Just as I felt an explosion building, Joe began bucking and hunching and grunting while trying to cram all of that massive meat down my throat. I felt it swell even larger and twitch against my cheeks as he unloaded a stream of jism that I couldn't possibly handle completely, especially with my mouth already overfilled by his huge dick. Just when I thought I couldn't handle any more without gagging, my own cock exploded in his mouth, and I forgot all about his come dribbling down my chin.

When the paroxysms of orgasm finally subsided, Joe sat up straddle-legged beside me. "Thanks, I needed that," he laughed.

"My pleasure," I said, reaching to stroke his hairless chest. "But how did you...why did you – ?"

"Make a move on you? You're a good-lookin' dude, with a terrific body for your age," he said. "Besides, I just like to live dangerously. And count on it, I'm not through with you yet."

"But what about Kevin and Jesse? Won't they – ?"

"You let me take care of that. I'll figure out a way to bed you again before we leave," he promised. When Kevin and Jesse returned, the three kids spent all afternoon in and out of the pool as I lounged nearby watching. Around the other guys, Joe acted as if nothing had happened between us that morning, and in both talk and behavior all three of them were just typical all-American boys. Nobody could possibly have guessed that one of them was a master cocksucker.

As much as I was reminded of our morning tryst every time Joe emerged from the pool, his huge cock bulging his skimpy red trunks, I had to admit that it was Kevin who demanded most of my attention. All afternoon I was carried back to my own teen years with Kevin's dad, and, although I felt a powerful sexual attraction toward Kevin, I wondered if it was only some form of transference, some attempt to relive my frustrated youthful infatuation for his father.

The kids declined my offer to take them to dinner, opting to call out for two large pizzas, which they quickly devoured along with a gallon of soda. Then we settled in to watch TV and engage in typical kid-adult conversation about college and career plans. The boys also groused about the expense of repairing the car and the prospect of severely curtailed fun in Lauderdale. All evening I noticed that their talk was almost entirely devoid of girls. Well before midnight, they all were stretching and yawning, and we decided to go to bed.

I lay restless and horny for a time, thinking about my morning session with Joe and lazily fingering my hard-on. I had about reached the point of jacking off so I could get some sleep when the bedroom door eased open and closed behind a silhouetted figure who moved silently to the bed. I threw back the sheet invitingly, only a little anxious that Joe had made his move too soon, before the other kids were guaranteed to be asleep. The anxiety faded quickly as he embraced me and deep-kissed me passionately, his hand groping for my erect cock.

I reached between his legs, and my whole body tensed as my hand encircled his cock. He must have felt the change, for he sat up and asked, "What's the matter? Not what you expected?"

I explored his cock again to be sure before I spoke. "No, it curves in the wrong direction, Jesse."

He chuckled with obvious amusement. "We wondered how long it would take for you to catch on. Joe and I are not identical in everything; he curves left and I curve up. Are you disappointed it's me instead of him?"

"How could anybody be disappointed with this?" I asked, again squeezing his cock, which was every bit as thick and long as his brother's. "But you mean you guys talked about what we did this morning?"

"We share everything," he said, "especially sexy guys. So, you want to talk or fuck?"

We went at it hot and heavy, and as I lay on my back with him curled on his side, head on my abdomen, most of my cock in his mouth, the door again opened and closed. His twin silently crawled onto the foot of the bed, lifted my hips, and began tonguing my ass, spreading my cheeks and probing deeply. When he had me thoroughly laved with saliva, he raised my legs to his shoulders and pressed his huge cockhead against my opening insistently.

I tensed up and shrank away. "I can't handle that big monster."

"Well, you're gonna get fucked by both of us, so take it like a man," he said. He pushed against me again, and as the head made its initial intrusion, it felt like he was shoving a baseball up my ass. As he patiently worked more and more of himself into me, it was like he followed the baseball with the blunt end of a Louisville Slugger. Once inside, he started thrusting deeply, and I feared I would split open, but Jesse went back to work on my cock and got me so excited that soon I was reaching for Joe's ass cheeks to pull him even deeper into me.

The bedroom door opened a third time, and Kevin moved to the head of the bed.

"You guys got him good and warmed up yet?" he asked.

I almost panicked. Much as I had been aroused by Kevin since I first glimpsed him on the highway, actually doing anything with him seemed somehow almost incestuous; he was my best friend's son, my godchild; I was his "Uncle Mark." "Hey, I...I don't know about this ..." I stammered.

Kevin knelt by my head and shoved his cock into my face. "Shut up and suck my dick, Uncle Mark," he said gruffly.

I opened my mouth to take him, and as I ran my tongue around the extra folds of skin below the glans, I recalled Roger's telling me after Kevin was born how he wanted him to grow up natural. I silently thanked my old buddy for that decision; uncut meat has become an especially intense turn-on for me in the past few years.

Though not as long or as thick as the twins', his dick was perfectly formed and enough to grace the centerfold of any skin magazine without apology. I attacked it ferociously while Jesse worked mine over and Joe pounded his huge rod into my ass. Without withdrawing, Kevin straddled me, most of his weight on his legs, sat back on my chest, and began gently face-fucking me. "God, I've wanted this a long time," he whispered.

"He's got something else you're gonna want, too," Jesse said, removing his mouth from my cock.

Kevin reached back and grasped my dick. "Yeah, man, I want it," he said. He craned his head around and Jesse rose up to kiss him, while I reached to tweak his nipples and Joe continued to pile-drive my ass.

As if by some silent means of communication, Kevin and Jesse exchanged positions and Kevin started deep-throating my cock while Jesse forced his thick meat into my mouth. I lay impaled front and rear, top and bottom, by the twins as Kevin expertly led me toward imminent explosion. Just as I felt the first spasms of orgasm, Joe started humping my ass at a murderous pace, grunting and moaning, and I felt his hot come scald my insides just as I shot my load into Kevin's throat. Unbelievably, almost at the same time, Jesse began creaming in my mouth, as copiously as his brother had that morning, until it dribbled down my chin.

When they were completely drained, Jesse and Joe left the room, but I wasn't allowed any rest. Still unsatisfied and hot as a poker, Kevin got between my legs and replaced Joe up my ass. I wrapped my legs around his waist and pulled him down on top of me, arms tightly encircling his back, and began gyrating my hips to match his rhythm. In no time, he was whimpering and moaning and frantically trying to get deeper inside me. His cockhead excruciatingly massaged my prostate, and my spent cock came back alive. I began contracting my ass, milking Kevin's dick until he made a couple of sharp, deep lunges and collapsed on me as he spewed out his load.

Just as he extricated himself from my clutches and rolled off, the twins came back in. "Damn, the old man's up and ready again," Jesse said. He slobbered on my dick awhile and then straddled me and eased down, sinking my entire shaft in his ass. As he rocked back and forth on it, Joe stood on the bed and fed his cock to his brother, and Kevin pushed between them to take Jesse in his mouth.

I decided to show a little initiative. I maneuvered Jesse onto his hands and knees and knelt to fuck him while he continued to suck his brother and Kevin crawled up under him, fondled my balls, and worked on Jesse like a calf at teat. After awhile, I withdrew from him, shoved Joe down, and plunged into his ass.

While I fucked him, Kevin moved to suck his cock, and Jesse knelt behind Kevin to ream his ass. When I thought Jesse had Kevin ready for me, I moved behind him and grasped his hips.

"Uh-uh, I can't do that," he protested, twisting away from my probing cock.

"Won't is what he means," Jesse scoffed.

"Yeah, he's a pussy virgin who won't give up his cherry," Joe added.

"Not to you guys," Kevin admitted. "Those monsters between your legs scare me to death. And you're not much more comforting, Uncle Mark."

"Okay, everybody to his own thing," I said. "But come here, Jesse; you love it."

We kept switching around and changing partners until everybody except Kevin had done just about everything possible. Kevin and I had gotten off twice more, and I think Joe and Jesse had come four times; I finally lost count. When everybody finally was exhausted, it was after three o'clock and we had been at it nearly four hours practically non-stop.

Completely drained, we took Sunday as a day of rest, but we did a lot of talking about a lot of things, with no inhibitions. I discovered that everything, from Joe's remaining behind that first morning to test me out to the four-way the night before, was part of a plan concocted by Kevin while they waited for me after his phone call and elaborated upon as things unfolded.

"But why did you think I'd be interested?" I asked.

"I had your number that time we came to visit, from the way you couldn't keep your eyes off Dad. That and what I already knew about you and Dad being best buddies in high school, and you living alone and not having a woman in your life. It all just added up," Kevin said.

"But you were only thirteen then."

"Fourteen. And this is the nineties, man. I already knew I was gay, and you turned me on something fierce. I kept a cock stand around you all that weekend, even if you did treat me like a snot-nose kid."

"I was that obvious, huh?" I fretted. "Did your dad pick up on it?"

"Are you kidding? He and Mom are so straight they think Divine's a real woman. He's always talking about how he wishes you'd settle down and start a family. I don't even want to think about how I'm going to handle being gay around him."

Before we went to bed, I had extracted a solemn promise from the three of them to stop back by on their trip home for at least one more session.

The next morning, over their protests, I wrote out a check to cover their car repair.

Kevin drove me to the office so they could use my car to retrieve theirs. He picked me up early to go home. The twins already had their car packed and were eager to head for Lauderdale, but Kevin grabbed my hand and led me out of the room.

"Come on, Uncle Mark, we need to talk in private," he said.

"Yeah, I'll bet you're gonna talk," Joe or Jesse leered. I couldn't tell them apart with their clothes on.

Kevin closed the bedroom door behind us and immediately was in my arms. He seemed completely different this time. The night of the foursome, he had been just a horny kid eager for hot sex which he approached with crass impersonality. This time, he made love to me, and it was gentle, tender, and intensely intimate and personal.

"Fuck me, Uncle Mark," he whispered as he broke our embrace after some elaborate foreplay.

"Are you sure?" I asked hesitantly.

"Yeah, I'm ready for it, and I want it to be with you." He laughed as if at a private joke. "You know, after we visited you that summer, I bet I whacked off five times a day thinking about having sex with you, and most of the time I imagined you being inside me."

After much patient effort, with a lot of grimacing and groaning and shrinking away on his part, I managed to penetrate him completely. He wrapped himself around me tightly, and we established a slow, easy rhythm which we sustained until the very end, when I was thrusting frantically toward the most intense orgasm I have ever experienced.

Later, as we lay exhausted and content, Kevin propped up on one elbow. "Can I ask you something?" he asked tentatively.

"After this, you should be able to ask me anything," I said.

"I don't have anything lined up for the summer, and I don't want to spend it at home. If I got a job and paid rent, could I come and stay with you?"

I wanted to tell him I'd pay him for the pleasure, but I restrained myself. "Sure, but I won't charge you rent; you can bank whatever you manage to make," I said.

As the three boys backed out of my driveway, a wave of sadness swept over me but quickly was replaced by calm anticipation. After all, they would be back in a few days, and, better yet, Kevin would be mine for an entire summer – and maybe for many summers to come.

ISLANDS
John Patrick

*I've always been fascinated by islands. There's nothing more
seductive than a scratch of earth surrounded by sea, cut off from the
mainstream, with its own distinctive personality. I love the intimacy
and smallness of an island, how it can give perspective to the larger
things of life.*

I drank my coffee and had a muffin, with my back to the bed
looking out onto the balcony, the doors flung open to the pond behind
the Parliament House, a place I had begun to think of as an island in
Orlando. It was a desultory day and the afternoon stretched invitingly
ahead.

I went to the bed, propped the pillows against the headboard,
and lay back on them. I unzipped my jeans and reached inside. They
were much too tight and I wriggled my hips out, aching for my own
touch. It was lovely, this gentle probing with my fingers on my
erection. I took my hand away. It was too good not to prolong. I pulled
my shirt off, then wet my fingers with my own saliva and circled my
nipples, first one and then the other, while the ache grew. I rolled onto
my stomach, up on my knees, pulling the pillow down, brushing just
the tips of my nipples on the cool cotton, and with my fingers once
again, needing no saliva now, stroking my erection, gently at first, then
harder and harder, and my hips moving, as they were inclined to move
with Barry, slowly, with my ass high in the air, my chest against the
pillow, until with each twitch of pleasure, each rocking motion, my legs
widened and spread, and I came, moaning, sinking, spreading myself
wide onto the bed. I was ready to start the day.

Barry arrived just when he said he would. He finished a trick at
four, went home, showered, changed, and showed up looking fresh and
relaxed.

"Hard day?" I asked.

"No, hard all day," he laughed, groping himself.

My hand instinctively went to his groin. His cock grew hard as
I stroked it. Ah, youth! It was our third afternoon of sex. I intended to

keep working him until I lost interest or left Orlando, whichever came first.

I tossed off my robe and lay on the bed on my back, fidgeting for no good reason while Barry took off his clothes. He was well-built, with a lightly furred chest that I loved to run my hands through. When he got into bed, he spread my legs and he entered me. His huge uncut cock slid in, each magnificent inch slowly impaling me. But he was going too slowly, I wanted more. I held his ass, pulling him into me, pleading with him to fuck me harder. Instead, he slowly eased his cock out of me. I can't stand that; the sudden void drives me wild. He rolled me over. I looked in the mirror across the room and saw him shoving his cock into me. He was a beautiful sight, hovering over me, plunging it in. I tightened my muscles around the cock and thrust upward, thousands of tiny fingers gripping the cock. I exploded but he kept right on fucking. I knew he probably had another date that night, shouldn't really come now, but he did anyway, leaving me full, warm, satiated.

He pulled out of me, quickly showered, dressed. I handed him two fifties and we kissed goodbye, perfunctorily, and he left.

I had left the curtains open and we had gathered a small crowd on the balcony during the fuck. Barry did not look at the men as he left but I did. If they had any sense they would have been applauding but they just stood there, unsmiling. They dispersed quickly – all but one, a tall, bearded man in his late thirties dressed only in a black leather jockstrap. He bunched his balls and I gave him a half smile.

After he entered the room and closed the door, he drew the heavy curtains, plunging the room into almost total darkness. I got on the bed on my stomach, raised my ass to him. He climbed over me and rubbed the leather across my buttocks, then roughly probed my asshole with one finger, then two, Barry's load easing the entry. The finger-fuck lasted several minutes before I turned to see him lower the jock and release his erection. It was much smaller than Barry's, perhaps only six inches, but felt wonderful just the same as he drove it into me and, within moments, came. It was a perfunctory fuck; he barely touched me and when he was done, lifted himself off the bed and quietly left the room without uttering a word.

I was exhausted and dozed for an hour, then went out to dinner. When I returned the cruisers on the balconies were out in full force. I walked those long balconies for what seemed like hours, watching through the windows, wondering how men could give themselves up to such decadence. I paid for sex earlier so that I wouldn't be tempted, yet the group scenes held a fascination for me I couldn't explain.

\# \# \# \# \#

The following June I returned to Orlando with Paul, a wealthy man much older than myself. The first night we sat at a table by the pool and Paul talked on and on about "the good old days," the '60s and '70s, when he visited the Parliament House often, but I was often distracted by the music in the disco. It reached us faintly on the breeze and made me anxious.

In my youth, I felt I had to work as hard as possible to make up for my lack of beauty and charm. But my parents had left me well-fixed; I could afford to be choosy. I didn't have to put up with Paul, but I did. He made life comfortable for me.

Eventually, though, I was sick of dreaming. I decided to find Barry, or someone like him, no matter what, no matter where. After Paul went to sleep, I went into the bar where a thin, dark-haired man in his early thirties asked me if I wanted to go to a party. He reminded me of the leather man from the year before: someone you wouldn't marry but for a night of lust, he was perfect.

The party was in his room at the complex. He left the door open and soon we were surrounded by men in various stages of undress. We said nothing to each other as we sat together on one of the two double beds in the room. I reached out and touched the bulge in the stranger's jeans. He arched his graceful back and met my mouth. He was rather beautiful in the dim light, and I was aroused beyond belief, the public nature of our caresses making me all the more excited. So turned-on was I that I fell off the bed.

When I lifted myself from the floor and looked up to his face, his perfect white teeth glowed in the light coming from the fixture over the sink at the far end of the room. At first I thought his smile was mocking. I kept thinking of Paul, asleep in our room. Why had I agreed to come with this stranger? What would Paul think of me now? The stranger began to kiss me passionately with his full lips. I slowly began to open his pants. His puzzling, maddening smile never left his face, as though he were challenging me to go down on him. He wrapped his arms around me and, as he did, I could feel his cock harden against my leg. He began kissing my chest and unbuttoning my shorts, his hands taking hold of my cock and, before I could protest, he fell gracefully to his knees, his mouth over my cock. His tongue flicked over the head

147

and then he took the whole length into his mouth. I could feel his hair brushing my bare chest as his head fell lightly against my stomach, his cheek moving up and down against my lower abdomen. I lifted my hips to thrust my erection into him. He took it eagerly and I started to press his head hard over my throbbing penis as I felt an orgasm filling every nerve of my body. He was touching his own cock and turned his body so that I might see it at full mast. Incredible desire blazed inside me.

In the midst of my orgasm, I looked up to see Paul, the corners of his mouth turned up in a wicked smile as he saw the man from behind, his dark-haired head moving languorously up and down against my belly. I opened my mouth to explain, then thought better of it. Paul moved toward me, but there were four hands on him, holding him, caressing him. A man dropped to his knees before him and yanked his shorts down.

The man grabbed Paul's cock and slowly pumped his shaft. A drop of pre-cum blossomed at the tip. The man licked it off his cockhead and I was pleased to hear Paul groan at the man's touch. The man started sucking and licking him until he pulled away saying that the man was going to make him come too fast.

The party giver had moved on to another man and Paul came over to me. Paul's cock felt like a lead pipe in my hands and, as I squeezed him, he groaned, "Suck it, darling." I took him into my throat and another man, a dirty blond, reached down and started squeezing my cock. His big cock dangled before me, begging to be sucked. The shaft was thick and heavily veined, and his balls were big, round and firm. I left Paul's cock and went to the blond's. I opened my mouth, took his soft cock inside and licked him until he began to grow. It grew to such mammoth proportions there was no way I could hold it all. Soon only the head was in my mouth. I massaged his meat with both hands and Paul got down on the bed beside me and I let him take the huge penis in his mouth. I lay back on the bed and the blond spread my legs. Paul let go of the cock and the blond slowly pushed it into my ass. I felt every heavenly inch as he stretched me wide open. My ass had never felt so full. Eyes misty and half-blind with passion, I turned my face to see another couple had gotten on the other bed and had begun to fuck. I wrapped my legs around the blond when he finally hit bottom. My cock tingled as he pulled out, then plunged back in and pumped harder and harder until I thought I would come again. Suddenly I felt him stiffen. His cock throbbed as he pulled out and I felt juice ooze down my leg.

He stepped aside and another man, muscular, with golden-brown hair, older than the rest, but not as old as Paul, was standing before me, his long cock swinging between his legs. I smiled as Paul stroked it, getting it ready to enter me. With each of the muscleman's thrusts my body tensed with ecstasy. He obliged by fucking me harder and harder. I was starting to come again when he pulled out. Another man, even bulkier, with massive shoulders, took his place. His cock was thicker than all of the others and hurt at first. As I cried out, Paul knelt behind my head so that he could watch. He stuffed his cock back in my mouth, silencing me. The two men began to move in a steady rhythm. Other men surrounded us, jacking off, depositing their loads on my body and then backing away to let others in.

After penetrating me again and again, the bulky man finally came inside me and, overcome now with desire, Paul came, his load joining the others on my belly. I was left vacant and filthy, sweaty and spent. Paul went to the sink and came back with a towel and helped me clean up. After he tenderly wiped me off, he leaned over and gave me a long, slow kiss. He moved my matted hair away from my face and helped me up. I couldn't believe how easy it had been for me to abandon myself to this crowd. I turned to see the couple on the other bed were still fucking. I realized the man on the bottom was the party giver. We stood there, Paul's arm wrapped around my waist, for a few moments, before Paul took me back to our room.

The next day, the smell of sex still clinging to us, we talked at length about the orgy. Far from being angry with me, Paul was delighted to discover I was as great an exhibitionist as he was a voyeur. As we talked my body pounded with desire, making me feel a little dizzy, drunk on the possibilities that lay before us. During that glorious but far too brief summer with Paul, we visited many islands, real islands, Key West and Manhattan in particular, but I will always revere the wicked, wonderful environment of the Parliament House, the island that isn't really an island, where something deep inside me had broken wide open.

LUSH LIFE
John Patrick

I was tired after a long day at the beach, but before going home I wanted to stop across the boulevard at the Backroom for a drink. I hadn't been there in months, but after seeing a picture in the local fag rag of a sexy new bartender, I thought it might be worth a return visit.

It turned out the bartender's name was Ken and he didn't start work until six. Waiting for Ken, I drank. I was proud of the fact that I was drinking slow and steady, like a submarine sneaking up on its target, and still had most of my money in my pocket. When I was younger, one of my favorite ways of communing with nature was to drink as much as I possibly could as fast as I could. I'm much more mature about it now.

At about five o'clock, a young man in a tank top and running shorts entered the bar and asked me if I could give him change for a dollar. He said he needed to use the phone. I handed him some change, watched his hand tug a dollar out of his sock and slide it onto the bar, and ogled his ass as he walked off to use the phone. At that point in the day, I thought he had the most splendid ass I had ever seen.

A few minutes later, the young man came back to where the dollar still lay on the bar and sat down. He ordered a beer. His long lashes fluttering, he acknowledged with a smile and a nod the man across the bar who quickly paid for his drink.

His drink had been bought and paid for, but he was not drinking it. He leaned back and I could feel him staring at me. Finally he said, "You don't like it here, do you?"

I smiled. "No, that's quite true. I came here looking for somebody but he isn't here yet. So I wasn't too happy until about five minutes ago."

His brown eyes brightened. "Oh?"

"Yes, when you walked in ..."

He grinned. His face was deeply tanned and he had small, perfect teeth. I introduced myself as Toby: "in real estate in Tampa." He said he was Jimmy: "student." Student of what, he didn't say.

"I'm here to see Ken," he said.

"That's funny, so am I."

Ken was worth the wait – good-looking and muscular, with blue eyes and wavy brown hair, a collegiate-type like Jimmy. He kept glancing over at me and giving me "that special look" that made my cock twitch. He had something on his mind, and it wasn't just tending bar. Mostly, though, when he wasn't pouring drinks, he was smiling at Jimmy. They were old friends, probably lovers. I didn't really want to know.

I didn't notice the sun go down. There was no window and you don't think about those kinds of things when you're sitting in a gay bar swilling down beer or bourbon or both and talking with a boy as pretty as Jimmy.

Suddenly Jimmy said he was hungry. I hadn't had anything to eat since my cereal that morning so I told him I'd take him to dinner. We went to Max's Diner down the street. I ordered coffee, eggs over easy, hash browns, and whole wheat toast.

"Breakfast?" Jimmy said, raising an eyebrow.

"I like breakfast when I can order it out," I said.

Jimmy ordered a steak and French fries. I tried to ignore the waitress as we ate, but it wasn't easy: Bunny was bustling around pretending to be busy, leaning forward to show me her cleavage and bending over to show me her legs and ass. I had the impression she was trying to get me to order something that wasn't on the menu. My attentions to Jimmy finally left her miffed and disappointed, and she went into the kitchen to pout.

"Bunny seems to think all she has to do is jiggle her tits and wiggle her ass, and a guy will get a hard-on for her."

I said, "She's an attractive girl."

"But you don't like girls – as sex partners, I mean." It was a statement, not a question.

"I can take 'em or leave 'em. How about you?"

"Mostly I leave 'em."

Impulsively, I gulped down the rest of my breakfast, napkinned my lips, rose and said, "Your place or mine?"

Jimmy's grin got wider. "I'm staying just down the street."

It was a cozy enough place with the bathroom and the kitchen in the rear, a sparsely-furnished living room overlooking the gulf, and one bedroom in the back. Jimmy fixed each of us a brandy and I drank it standing in the doorway looking at his bed and wondering how many thrashing bodies it had known. The faded white sheets were discolored, a crusty landscape of cum spots. Jimmy finished his drink in the living room, put on some soft music and stepped up to me. I gulped what remained of my brandy. Jimmy took me in his arms, held me close, and our lips met and pressed tightly. Before long, our tongues were working back and forth in each other's mouths, our crotches rubbing together in a sensuous dance that had my cock rising quickly.

It had been almost a week since I had come and my balls rumbled with pleasant anticipation. Releasing him, I stepped back and went into the bedroom, setting my empty glass down on the bureau. I started unbuckling my trousers. Taking the hint, Jimmy followed me into the bedroom, then rapidly removed his shorts and tank top. He wasn't a big guy; he had a runner's build – flat, lean, tight. What most interested me was the bulge in his jockstrap.

My own seven-incher was hard and jiggling in front of me as I went to him. Dropping to my knees in front of him, I stared at his smooth, tanned legs leading up to that magnificent crotch. I ran my fingers along his sweaty inner thighs. I fondled and squeezed his balls gently, began gnawing on the thick cock that hid behind his grimy jock. As I pulled the strap down, his meat lunged at me. I tongued his shaft, shaking my head as if to loosen the iron-grip hold he now had on my hair, knowing he wouldn't let go, not when I start sucking his love muscle. He bucked his hips, fucking my mouth and aiming for the bottom of my throat.

"Come on, slut, come on, open wide. That's it. Wider, wider, aaaaahh."

He stuffed his dick so far down my throat my eyes began tearing up.

"Oh, yeah, choke on that big dick! Choke on it, choke on it! Come on, harder, harder!"

He wanted to prolong it so he pulled out of my mouth and I stroked his cock with slow determination. I took the cock in my hand and a drop of precum formed in his slit; my tongue instinctively lapped it up. It was delicious – and Jimmy responded by shuddering. More precum formed. Once more, I dipped my tongue into the tiny puddle, lifted it, then swirled the sticky fluid around the knob of his cock in slow, sensuous circles.

"Oh, shit, that feels good."

I ran the flat of my tongue up and down the front of his hard, throbbing shaft and then dragged it tantalizingly down to the ball sac, which I kissed and then sucked between my lips.

As I glanced up at Jimmy's pretty face, contorted now in passion, I reached down between my legs and stroked myself with one hand while using two fingers of the other to encircle the root of Jimmy's cock. I held it steady while I reluctantly let his balls slide from my warm mouth in order to put my lips over his knob. I swirled my tongue all over the head, then I opened my mouth wider and pushed my face down into his crotch so his cock could slide along the roof of my mouth and down my throat.

I decided it was at least eight inches long and so fat it completely filled my mouth. Keeping my lips tight around the head, I moved up and down, enjoying the suck as much as he was.

Seconds later he was twisting and gasping, sighing and pumping. He was close to coming, and I didn't want to delay it. I sucked even more furiously; my tongue went into action over his cock and soon he was coming, slamming his cock against the roof of my mouth and squishing down my gulping throat.

The extraordinary force of his orgasm pushed his cock back and almost out of my mouth, but I managed to keep his cockhead between my lips so the final dribbles would be on my tongue. I kissed his belly, coating it with his spunk.

Spent, he fell back on the bed and promptly dozed off.

I wandered around the apartment, got another brandy, then went to the bathroom. In a heap in the corner were T-shirts, sweat pants, and socks – and a few jockstraps. I grabbed them like a prospector finding gold, bringing the dankest one to my face. A stray pubic hair clung to the pouch. I inhaled, then licked the strap and stuffed it in my mouth, jacking my cock furiously. I came in moments, my cum landing on the pile of clothes.

I returned to the bedroom and lay beside him. The bed reeked of the dried funk of his many jolts of nightly spew. I humped the sheets and clutched the pillows that nightly supported his head, then brought to my face the jockstrap he'd been wearing that day. I dozed off. When I awoke, the clock on the nightstand said it was nearly one. Jimmy was still asleep. Carefully, I rolled from the bed and began to search for my clothes.

"You leaving so soon?" Jimmy said suddenly, rubbing his eyes.

"Yeah, I think I'll go back to the Backroom, have a nightcap."

"You needn't bother. The only nightcap you'll ever need from the Backroom will be here at two."

I crawled back into bed next to Jimmy. We talked about Ken. Jimmy was obviously crazy about him. Ken already had a lover but often stopped by Jimmy's on his way home. "He likes three-ways. He said he liked your looks. I told him to join us. I hope you don't mind my using you like that."

"No, not at all. You can use me any way you like," I said, stroking his cock.

He pushed my hand away and said, "You'd better rest. You're gonna need all your strength when Ken gets here."

And how right he was. I fell asleep again and when I awoke with a start I was confronted by the sight of the largest cock I had seen in years. It had to be at least three inches longer than mine and two inches longer than Jimmy's. The head resembled a dark purple plum. Jimmy was rubbing his hands over it, working up and down the scandalous length of the shaft and then cupping the low-hanging balls. When it was finally erect, he gave the cockhead a big kiss. That kiss said a lot more than welcome to my apartment.

Ken got on the bed and took Jimmy in his arms. I couldn't help but stare at them. I wanted to touch them both so badly. They made a beautiful couple.

Jimmy brought his lips to Ken's and kissed, a long soulful one that I thought might never end. Ken was soon reaching over to caress his body. Imagining the touch of his warm hands on his young friend's arms, shoulders, and nipples, sent shudders through me.

"I can hardly wait for Toby to taste you," Jimmy said when Ken finally leaned back.

"There's time enough for everything," the bartender said. "I don't know about him, but we have all night."

"We do?" Jimmy said, as if he was surprised.

"Yeah, my lover's out of town. I'm spending the night."

"All night's just fine with me," I said, submitting to the pressure of Jimmy's hands inviting me to lie back on the bed.

I was still a bit nervous being in the company of these two strapping studs, but they spent a long time helping me to relax. Ken, still playing bartender, brought out a bottle of Jack Daniels which we passed between us. Jimmy began spilling it on Ken and licking it up.

This led to me getting bathed in it and then they began to run their hands all over me, spending as much time on my arms and legs as they did to my chest and my cock and balls. I lay back, soaking it all up, moaning softly at the touch of their fingers and tongues. Finally Jimmy leaned down and parted my legs gently, then flicked his tongue over my hard, aching cock.

My whole body trembled at the touch and I moaned. A delightful rush came over me when I looked down and saw Ken had replaced Jimmy between my legs, licking me, while Jimmy's practiced hands went to my pecs, twisting my nipples. Never had foreplay felt so good.

Ken moved very slowly over my crotch, licking everything he possibly could. He ran his tongue along the top and bottom of the shaft, then up my thighs. He moved down to lick at my ass, pulling my cheeks gently apart with his hands and kneading them with his fingers. He made long laps on my balls, then made a point of his tongue so that he could slip the tip of it into the entrance to my anus. Everything he did seemed to feel better than the last, and I moaned loudly.

Ken told Jimmy he had prepared me and ordered him to get into position. Jimmy took Ken's place between my legs and Ken knelt over my face. At first, I could only stare – and breathe deeply. I couldn't get over how beautiful Ken's cock was and how good it smelled, his pubic hair laced with Jack Daniels, suspended so close over my face. Before I even touched the cock, I knew that this was going to be a rare experience, one that lived up to the expectations of my fantasies ever since I saw his photo in the fag rag.

I reached up and held Ken's strong thighs with my hands and pulled that hard cock down so that I could reach it with my mouth. I touched it with my tongue. The taste was delicious and I savored it. Ken didn't rush me, content to hold himself there, enjoying what I had to offer. Slowly, sensuously, I reached down with my hands to hold Ken's balls while I took the head of his cock in my mouth.

So absorbed with Ken was I that I had nearly forgotten Jimmy was at my ass. The jolt of his entry momentarily took my breath away and I gagged on the head of Ken's prick. As Jimmy ground his cock into me, I went almost crazy with desire for Ken's cock to be in as far as it would go. I would be impaled on both ends – as if this was the place I was meant to be!

"Take it easy," Ken said, "we have all night."

But I couldn't help it – I was so desirous and so close to coming that I felt weak.

When Jimmy was all the way in, he took Ken in his arms and began bathing him with his tongue, exploring every inch of his shoulders and back.

I was finally filled completely: Jimmy in my ass, Ken in my mouth. I thought I would come, but Ken prolonged the ecstasy by moving around on the bed to face his substitute lover. I eagerly resumed sucking his cock. As they kissed, my inhibitions left me completely and I reached over and touched Ken's sweet ass with my fingers. Unable to stop myself, spurred on by Ken's moans, my mouth left his cock and I slipped a finger inside his ass, amazed at the heat I found there.

Just then, Jimmy began his orgasm. The lovers kissed all through it and then Jimmy pulled out of me.

With his cock gleaming with my saliva, Ken crawled to the foot of the bed and took Jimmy's place. I spread my legs wide apart, waiting for him. As he crouched down over me, I could feel the head of his cock at my anal passage, and when he pressed it into me firmly, he soon filled me until his hard belly was right on mine. "Fuck me," I begged, and he did, vigorously, until my need was so great that I pushed my hips up to meet his thrusting.

"Harder!" I urged, and he ground into me, slamming that cock deep into my ass. I clenched his ass cheeks and pulled him into me, then pushed him away, rammed him back into me. Our chests were mashed together, our breath coming hard, our bodies gleaming with sweat. Jimmy returned to the room and brought his fingers to Ken's ass. Soon he was jamming his fingers in and his hand against it so that all three of us were in ecstasy.

Ken came before I did, and as he trembled and cried out, he continued to ram the mighty cock into me. I exploded myself, holding him tightly and moving my hips to get every last thrust of his body. Then we lay together, his weight warm and comforting on top of me, and Jimmy lay next to us, playing with his renewed erection. My eyes bulging, I reached out for it. I told them I wanted to give them both head at the same time. That was fine with them.

I had them kneel alongside each other while I sat in front of them. I pulled their pricks together until they were touching. I rubbed them gently against each other for awhile, then began to lick them both at the same time. Ken began to stiffen. I hadn't thought it possible, but I managed to stuff both of their cockheads into my mouth at once. It wasn't easy, but I did suck on a few inches of both simultaneously, then lick the heads with my tongue.

As I sucked them both at the same time, I reached around and cradled their buns. Jimmy was kissing Ken hard on the lips. His tongue found Ken's tongue and his chest rose and fell against Ken's as his breathing quickened. I teased their cockheads for a long while, licking, kissing and nibbling. Then I ran my tongue along their shafts, pausing now and then to suck their balls. They laughed and told me to suck harder. I was really getting into it, with my nose buried in Jimmy's pubic hair and his cock halfway down my throat, when he came again. I did not swallow all of Jimmy's cum.

I rose up and gave Ken a kiss and pushed some of Jimmy's load into his mouth so we could share it. It was the perfect nightcap.

Ken collapsed on the bed and Jimmy saw me to the door. Jimmy invited me back the next evening: "It'll just be the three of us."

I told him I wouldn't consider anything less.

THE TRESPASSERS
Edward Bangor

Warren looks good today. He's wearing his black laced shoes; grey ankle socks; over-tight black trousers which cling to him front and back in the correct places; crisp white shirt; red and white diagonally-striped tie; and oversized black blazer with a badge over the left breast matching the tie. He is the picture of the perfect senior schoolboy.

A flicking motion of his crystal-blue eyes shows he's aware of the two boys following him. Both are the same age, but several sizes larger, say, rugby prop-forwards to his hooker positioning in the front row of the second team scrum.

Making sure to keep a decent distance from his followers, Warren continues down the narrow school corridor for several yards before turning sharply into a door marked "Changing Room."

On the other side of the door, three boys stand together in front of a broad wooden desk, behind which their teacher, Mr. Mallory, sits in his blue track-suit, complete with whistle around the neck.

"What are we doing today, sir?" Gareth, the more articulate of the two larger boys, asks.

"Cross country," Mr. Mallory snaps, not looking up from his tabloid newspaper. "Get changed."

Warren chooses a spot down the far end of the L-shaped room. Sitting on the wooden bench running around the walls he unlaces his shoes, only looking up as a couple of shadows fall across him. "What do you want?" he asks the bullies.

"You to be silent," Gareth barks, reaching down and pulling Warren to his feet with his tie, choking the boy.

"S-sss-sss-orry!"

Gareth wraps the lose end of the tie around a low peg, forcing Warren to stay on tip-toe. That complete, his accomplice speaks for the first time. "So you should be, but we do want something." The bullies exchange glances. Nervously Warren's eyes jump from one hard face to the other. Then he heard the words he had long been dreading: "We want your bum."

He'd spent many a lonely night in his own bed thinking about such a moment as this. What would he say? What would he do? How would he react? How should he react? Should he shout for the teacher? Just say "No?" But if he did that, would he be denied what he really wanted? Yet, if he didn't he'd be known as a "tart" and that wouldn't do, either. It really was a paradox.

But Warren has matters taken right out of his hands. No sooner has Kelvin delivered his threat than two hands are assaulting the smaller boy's crotch. "You're going to get a good hard fucking, right up your little arse-hole, and these ..."

Suddenly Mr. Mallory appears behind the threesome. "That's enough of that. Leave it for the girls."

"Yes, sir," the teacher's two golden boys chorus, and slip away to take up their own changing position on either side of their freed victim.

The three boys began to disrobe. Ties, jackets and shirts are quickly discarded, but the rest takes a lot longer. For a succession of minutes the two better-endowed boys pull a series of muscleman poses as the smaller-framed Warren watches, wide-eyed.

Then they turn to him. "Your turn."

Reluctantly Warren does his best but can barely raise more than a slim pebble on top of his right upper arm. The rest of his body remains as flat and hard as a sea-washed stone.

Laughing, Gareth and Kelvin chorus: "Wimp!"

"A girl could do better."

"Maybe he is a girl!" adds Gareth, completing Warren's humiliation with a highly successful grab at the boy's groin.

"I'm not."

Gareth tugs down on the recaptured crotch: "Prove it."

"You've got to change anyway," Kelvin reminds him.

Warren's eyes begin to tear but he naps open his beit, runs his zip and opens the two flaps of cloth giving a tantalizing glimpse of the white underpants beneath before he literally peels the tight black cloth down his legs and steps out of them. Turning his back on his tormentors, he reaches up to hang the garment up on a peg by a belt-loop.

A hand flicks into the sweaty crack in the tight white briefs and Warren springs back around. "Show us your muscles then. Let's see what you've got!" Kelvin demands.

Warren tries in vain to get the muscles on his slim legs to toughen up.

"Wimp!" from Kelvin and, from Gareth, "Show us your love muscle."

"My what?"

The two bigger boys exchange a look of horror, then Kelvin grabs one of Warren's wrists in one hand and tugs down the lad's underpants with the other.

"Make that go stiff," hollers Gareth, "and we'll let you go. I'm sure you know how: just think about us in the shower yesterday."

Standing naked between his tormentors Warren blushes as he remembers the larking about in the showers, but Warren wasn't the one trying to balance the soap on the top of his oversized erection; he'd just been trying to avoid having it pushed up his bottom. Still, nothing was fair about the way Gareth and Kelvin picked on him, especially the way he was beginning to derive pleasure from it. He was close to admitting to himself that he always looked forward to his times with Gareth and Kelvin. That's why his hand was slipping across his thigh even before the order had been given.

He pinches his penis, just back from the head, peeling the skin back like an over-ripe banana until the quickly swollen purple knob stands out proudly from the creamy white of the shaft. The rest of the length quickly fills with pulsating blood as he works over it, his testicles jiggling in their sac beneath the gently flogging wrist.

"What's going on here?" Mr. Mallory asks, suddenly appearing behind the wanker, who he seizes violently by the ear before turning his attention to the audience. "You two get changed."

Gareth and Kelvin hurry to obey. Warren also moves quickly, his hands rising up to relieve the pressure being asserted on his ear lobe, leaving his penis to twitch nervously, gaining him a tutorial reprimand. "Oh, no. Don't stop. You enjoy yourself."

Thus Warren, while still hanging from his own ear, is forced to continue to masturbate as, before him, the two more mature teenagers undress down to their swollen, damp underwear.

"Off ..." Mr. Mallory barks at Gareth as gym shorts are snatched from a bag. "You know the rules. No underpants." Never once does he take his eyes from the shiny head of Warren's penis as it appears and disappears inside its protective sheath.

Once more the friends look at each other and smile. They have a very good reason for wanting to keep their modesty covered but they know Mr. Mallory would be bound to check even if he wasn't standing right in front of them now. At the start of every lesson the first thing the muscular teacher does is get the boys into a line and pull out the front of their shorts so he can peek down and search for contraband. Making sure their coach and classmate are watching, Gareth and Kelvin strip, and their healthy erections bounce into view.

"Look!" Mr. Mallory shouts. "Look what you've done, you dirty little pervert." As each word is spoken Warren is shaken violently from one side to the other. "You've corrupted my finest athletes!"

Gareth and Kelvin turn sideways so the full extent of their erections can be seen, long and straight, the ends glistening in the dull light as the precum drips down to the cold changing-room floor. Mr. Mallory's eyes glare, his chin drops open and he speaks the most dreaded word in his limited vocabulary: "Punishment!"

Warren stands facing the teacher's desk which has been cleared. Gareth and Kelvin stand at either end. None of the three is attempting to hide what the situation has done to their bodies: Their erections make a highly lubed triangle across the surface of the desk where their pre-cum endlessly drips.

Slowly Warren bends forward, lowering his chest onto the desk. His legs part to drop his hips down to the table-top. His arms stretch out on either side where the wrists are eagerly grasped by the nearest teenager and pulled to the breaking point.

The boys cheer as the coach swings the paddle onto the boy's unprotected bum. A second one lands even before Warren's flashed brain can register the pain from the first. Soon the eight inch diameter ping-pong bat is flying back and forth as the tally mounts up. Four. Five. Six. Seven. Eight. Nine. Ten times Warren is struck until his bum is covered in a waffled red pattern that starts at the small of his back and goes all the way down to the upper part of his thighs. His small body racks with the sobs he holds back. A cry escapes his lips only as the coach pulls him from the desk and sends him back down to the changing room with an eleventh blow to his unprepared rear. "Get dressed."

Gareth and Kelvin whisper urgently as they pull crisp white shorts from their kit bags and step, bare-arsed, into them, pulling them up snugly against their groins, erections pressing tightly into their hips.

The lower hems of their white T-shirts barely hide the soggy patch at the end of each boy's length.

Warren, meanwhile, roots around in his bag, as if looking for treasure.

"Hurry up," Mr. Mallory demands of the nude boy. "What's wrong?"

"I can't find my kilt, sir."

Mr. Mallory slaps Warren again with the paddle.

Gareth and Kelvin are forced to hide their giggles behind their hands as Mr. Mallory goes to his desk and tosses something at Warren. "Put this on."

Warren holds it up, his faces twisting in disgust as he recognizes the garment. "But it's a skirt," he complains, quickly following that up with an "Ouch!" as the paddle hits his rear for an unlucky thirteenth time.

"Just put it on, wimp."

The older boys laugh more openly at the familiar insult. Warren does as he is ordered, wrapping the short black cloth tightly around his loins, where it covers only to the tops of his battered thighs.

"Get going," the coach says to all of them, "and don't come back here until you're all hot and exhausted."

"Oh we won't. I can promise that," Gareth says standing next to the skirted boy.

"But, sir..." Warren's protests are cut off as he is dragged out into the autumnal air by his teammates.

The three boys run down a quiet, overgrown country lane. Warren leads the way, his skirt flying up to expose a rapidly maturing groin at each step.

They turn a corner alongside a chain-link fence beyond which an old house is protected by warning signs, threatening trespassers Will Be Prosecuted, OR WORSE. Gareth and Kelvin increase their pace until they are alongside Warren. They hold themselves level as they goad Warren into making a reaction against their attempts to flick the hem of the skirt up. But just as Warren tries to fight back Gareth grabs his arm, twisting it high up his naked back and slams the boy face-first into the chain-links, the metal rattling against its worn fixings with the force of the impact.

Kelvin takes a handkerchief out of the rear pocket of his shorts, spins it into a rope and stuffs Warren's mouth full of the foul-smelling cloth. His hand remains on the back of the gagged head as Gareth pulls out a short length of cord which, once untangled from prominent parts of Gareth's anatomy, is quickly wrapped around Warren's wrists before being looped, for good measure, around his waist, holding his hands tight to the small of his back.

With their captive safely trussed, the boys have a quick look around to see if they've been spotted, then lead the prisoner through a peeled back section of chain-link and up towards the empty house.

In an obviously disused lounge, Warren stands facing his seated kidnappers. "Dance," they order.

Warren begins a half-hearted jig. The two boys spread their legs, reclining in the over-stuffed arm chairs covered with tarps, secure in the knowledge Mr. Mallory won't blame them if they are late getting back, or even if they didn't return at all. In no time at all, hands are caressing swelling shorts until it looks as if the thin white cloth is about to be split in two by the sizable objects pushing up from below. These squeezes and strokes becoming more urgent on the occasions Warren's skirt flies up.

Eventually Gareth can take it no longer. "Come here, boy," he orders, mimicking Mr. Mallory. Warren executes an elaborate turn that almost takes his balance from him. "Come closer. Come and see a real love muscle."

Warren mumbles something through his gag that is taken as his agreement. Grinning like a maniac, Gareth pulls down the front of his shorts, letting his erection roar up in all its splendor. Warren's eyes gape: it seems even bigger than it looked yesterday in the showers.

"You like it, don't you?"

He nods, unable to help himself.

"Want to pay homage to it?"

Warren's head bounces, just as his penis does.

"Want to kiss it?"

He nods.

"Bend over then, and have a real good look."

Intrigued by the size of the thing, Warren does as he is told. Gareth holds himself steady with one hand, while his other comes to rest on the back of the Warren's head, pressing the smaller boy's face ever closer until the damp tip of the penis is brushed over his face, soaking the gag.

"Want to suck it?"

Warren nods, getting an erection pushed in his eye. He just has time to blink the precum out when he realizes the gag has fallen to the floor between Gareth's hairy legs.

But before Warren can collect his thoughts enough to speak, Gareth has his erection rubbing across the soft boy's lips. "Kiss it," he instructs.

Warren does.

"Lick it."

Warren does this as well.

"Open up and let it in." Gareth comes close to begging as he pokes the boy's face. "Let me in."

It takes Warren slightly longer to comply this time. Nervously Gareth's hand tightens in the blond locks but soon releases again as Warren's jaw starts to part. The lips separate, letting the swollen end of Gareth's sex sink against the teeth. Warren opens his jaw slightly. Judging correctly that the moment is right, Gareth jams the whole upper section of his penis into Warren's mouth.

"Ohhhhh, yes," he groans, his eyes looking up for the first time from the tight red lips locked around the middle of his penis. "Someone should punish you for doing this to us."

"Someone will," Kelvin laughs hoisting himself from the chair.

Warren's body jerks as his skirt is lifted up over his bound hands but Gareth isn't going to let him raise his head from where it is impaled on the swelling erection; if anything, he wants it to go farther down, not up.

Almost gently Kelvin begins to stroke the recently paddled boy's bottom. His fingers tenderly trace those marks left by Mr. Mallory's ping-pong bat. Warren shivers in anticipation at the unexpected feel of the goosing fingers. He hasn't felt anything like this since the last time he'd been debagged in the middle of a rugby scrum a week before. At that time someone had poked a finger up his bottom while his arms were trapped around his teammates' shoulders. Could that have been Kelvin?

Warren's body shoots forward, then jumps back and forth as the teenager spanks his up-turned bottom. Eventually Kelvin is forced to hold him by the bond wrists, but by then, Warren already has his face pressed as tightly into Gareth's belly as it will go, the swollen head of the seated boy's erection pressing into the entrance to Warren's windpipe. Inch by throat expanding inch, Warren is forced to accommodate Gareth's prick until soft but wiry pubic hair is pressed into his nostrils and his chin rests on sperm-loaded testicles.

"Enough!" Gareth suddenly gasps more out of breath than either of the others.

The spanking ceases but the hand remains on Warren's bum, and reverts to stroking again. Kelvin spits on his fingertips and slides them into the gap between the reddened cheeks, fanning his fingers out to spread the flesh inside.

"Go on, do it," Gareth yells over Warren's bent body. "You've got to lose your cherry sometime. You and him both."

With a snort of annoyance Kelvin crouches down, releasing Warren's hands so he can better part the young boy's bum. For a second it seems as if the tight circle of Warren's sphincter opens, winks, and closes again. Kelvin smiles to himself; it is the sort of invitation he can't refuse. He plunges his face in, his long slender tongue teasing the tight opening, and then easing its way inside the boy.

"Get it up him, before it's too late," Gareth says harshly.

Quickly Kelvin stands and tugs down his shorts, the end of his shaft glistening almost as much as Warren's hole. Carefully he lines one with the other. Then, with the knob resting nicely in the correct slot, he takes hold of Warren by the hips, and speaks to his peer. "Here it comes."

Both Gareth and Warren's bodies tense up as Kelvin takes a deep breath and shoves forward. Warren yelps with the sudden forced entry, but Gareth pushes the soft-haired head back down into his lap welcoming the uncontrollable shakes that have overtaken the smaller boy's body. Kelvin starts a grinding motion with his hips, forcing Warren's virgin anus to accept his erection. Meanwhile, Gareth is pounding Warren's hollowing cheeks up and down on his shaft. Juices begin to flow copiously from Warren's two over-stuffed holes. His whole body tenses with the battering the athletes are giving it.

Suddenly Kelvin draws back and his erection plops out of Warren's red-lipped rear, pumping his semen all over the abused buttocks. At the same time Gareth finally allows Warren's head to rise out of his groin only to shower the pretty boy's face with his load.

"That'll teach you," Gareth says. "Time for a wash."

They kick Warren over onto his back and then flush him from head to two in two highly powered jets of steaming piss. Warren squirms from side to side, trying in vain, to avoid the heated liquid. The burning pile-drive effect soon reduces itself to a mild tickling as the liquid drains along the natural creases of the boy's body. When the last drops have been shaken off the two boys tuck themselves into their sports kits and leave.

Warren finds the bathroom and steps under the shower. He begins to wash his abused body, ignoring his head – which isn't getting wet anyway – soaping his gradually slopping shoulders and working down from there. Over his nipples he travels, pausing to tweak the upstanding buttons of tense flesh, then on down to rinse out his belly button. Suddenly he jumps on down to his ankles and works upwards, coating his slender, dancer's legs in the gleaming mixture of soap suds and water until they shine. Then, and only then, do his hands begin to rub and roll over his penis and testicles this way and that. Idly Warren begins to masturbate his rapidly stiffening shaft. He turns sideway, his left hand running back and forth over his blushed buttocks in time to the right-handed manipulations. A finger slips up between the most curved potion of his body.

Warren rests his forehead against the shower-room tiles. His legs open. His finger pushes up into the hole. The first knuckle rapidly disappears, then the second, until a third rests against the hot flesh. He pulls it out and rams it back in again, imagining it to be Gareth's shaft roughly taking him from behind. Warren's moans and groans of self-satisfied sexual pleasure are lost in the hissing of the cool water. His right hand moves in time with the fingers.

"Yes, yes, yes!" he cries as he comes.

Moments later Warren is drying himself using the only towel he could find. Finished, he wraps the soiled, skimpy towel around his waist, knotting it where it only just manages to meet over his right hip, in an unintentional imitation of the skirt Mr. Mallory had given him. The boy steps in front of the toilet. Raising the hem of the towel, he removes the partly erect penis from beneath it and, with the foreskin neatly retracted and held as lightly as possible between thumb and forefinger, he pees.

In the background, beyond the boy's line of vision, a shadow moves into the doorway. Gradually getting closer to the unsuspecting boy, the brass buttons on the private security guard's uniform glint. An old-fashioned straight baton-like truncheon swings widely across the urinating boy's bottom, pushing him up against the wall.

"Spread 'em, thief," the guard demands, holding his weapon firmly in place on the toweled buttocks.

Warren raises his arms high above his head, palms flat to the wall, his legs already spread either side of the toilet bowl. Carefully, though needlessly, the guard's free hand frisks the virtually nude boy, ending up probing the bum and then down over the front of the towel to grab the boy's groin, the blunt end of the truncheon jamming itself into the tight crack of the boy's buttocks, as hard as the towel would allow.

"You're nicked, big boy."

A pair of handcuffs are produced, Warren's wrists soon encased in steel behind his back.

"I hope you're not hiding anything," the guard laughs, repeating his search by feeling up Warren's bare legs, and under the towel to grasp the boy's privates, rubbing the penis just twice before pulling away.

Warren looks up at the handsome face leaning over him. He tries to kiss the lips but the guard was having none of it. "Move!" he cries, giving the lad a shove that loosens the toweling knot, followed by a single spank with the truncheon to make the towel slip further, the soggy covering only just staying on Warren's hips as he is lead away to his fate.

In a third room of the deserted house the guard positions the nearly naked, handcuffed boy in front of an old leather-topped desk while he picks up a telephone to call his boss. "This is Morgan, sir. I've caught another trespasser," he says. "No, it's only a kid... No, no police... Okay then... I'll sort it. 'Bye."

Morgan returns the hand-set to its base, sits on the desk and looks at his captive. "You heard that, I take it?"

"Yes, sir."

"I'm going to have to punish you myself. Understand?"

"Yes, sir."

"I don't normally do this, but boys like you have to be taught a lesson, don't they?"

"Yes, sir."

A large hand goes out and tickles the soft fuzz on top of Warren's upper lip. The boy makes no attempt to move away. "You're a pretty young thing, aren't you?"

"I guess so, sir." He'd been told so, many times, and knows just what is meant.

Morgan's hand moves to close around the back of Warren's neck and pull him forward, slightly bending him over. Morgan's other hand clasps the cuffed hands, lifting Warren up and depositing him onto his lap as if the boy weighed next to nothing. Two spanks land on the towel. The hand remains after the second blow, just resting there, waiting for a reaction that doesn't come. A finger slips up inside the waist and then down the crack of the arse, taking the towel with it, until the latter drops, finally, to the floor.

Warren's pale, youthful erection is caught between his pubis and the blue-trousered leg.

Morgan begins spanking the boy, giving it his all. Warren's cries of pain become real after just a few of the heavy-handed blows. Warren wriggles and drops his leg from Morgan's knee, parting his buttocks so the tight ring of his sphincter opens up.

The spanking stops. Morgan releases his hold on the chained arms and uses both hands to further spread the bright pink, almost purple, bum cheeks. With his fingertips alone, he opens up the boy. Morgan reaches back and takes a small biro pen from a pot on the nearly bare desk. He spits on the pointed end before pressing it into Warren's hole. Easily it slips inside, as far as it can go while the man still has hold of it.

Morgan removes it, spits on his forefinger, and pushes the fat digit into the anus. He withdraws, pauses for a moment or two, then pushes for a second time. Warren's blond head snaps back as the second over-sized knuckle enters. His neck continues to crane and his mouth goes slack and eyes begin to tear as the rest of the long, thick finger disappears up his ass. A second finger joins the first, the pair of them pushing up inside Warren as the boy pants and moans.

Pleased with the result of his test, but far from finished, Morgan pulls his fingers from the clinging muscle. The boy relaxes as the remainder of his upper body is twisted around in the man's lap. Morgan produces some hair oil and coats the anus. Picking up his truncheon from where it had been resting on the desk, he rests it provocatively between Warren's legs. His knuckles whiten as they tighten around it. He puts his considerable force behind that shaft, both pushing down and twisting the truncheon in order to literally screw it into the boy. Warren's rectum opens up like an electronic sliding door, complete with the appropriate hissing sounds coming out of the lad's mouth. The arse hole stretches, gaping wide as the anal lips engulf the rod.

Suddenly the boy is shoved from the man's lap. Warren somersaults over his head, banging it on the floor, rotating until he lands on the handle of the truncheon. Two more inches go into him with a jolt until his cuffed hands take his weight from his internal organs. Warren rolls onto his side and then up onto his knees before the man. With one hand rubbing the front of his tented blue canvas trousers, Morgan takes the boy by the hair, twisting a clump of it into his fist. Smiling, he presses Warren's face into his crotch, his legs twisting about the thin shoulders to hold him there as the lips were drawn up and down the swollen mass of his out-sized penis. Morgan opens his trousers. Warren's eyes bulge. The cock is nearly eleven inches long, dwarfing anything he's seen previously.

"You know what to do, pretty boy."

Warren smiles. He certainly does. Pleased to be back on familiar ground once more, he tenderly licks the pulsating crown, running his tongue down the side, trailing over the purple membrane. Then his teeth move in, nibbling as if this were the sweetest damn corn-on-the-cob in the world. One of Morgan's hands cup the back of the boy's head, drawing it forward, needlessly forcing the youth's mouth to stretch wider and wider. As the man feeds his vein-popping shaft into the boy, the lad sprouts a raw erection, standing up in salute from the soft round marble-like testicles to point at the much larger organ resting firmly below the pleadingly wide eyes and the bulging lips and cheeks.

At first Warren swallows the best he can but soon it becomes clear he is having some difficulty with this penis. Morgan, however, doesn't seem to notice, or care, just keeps on pulling the lad's head down onto it, forcing him towards his testicles, jabbing with his hips whenever he encounters an obstruction. With less than an inch still remaining Warren starts to cough and splutter. Progress is halted. The boy's mouth is full.

Morgan tries in vain to find the correct angle to complete what he has started. The final breakthrough comes when, as a desperate measure, he pushes Warren down on his hunches. The truncheon handle bangs onto the floorboards, ramming itself up the boy's bum. Warren feels a spasm of pain mixed with pleasure rush up his spine. He opens his mouth to ask for help but all he receives is a large throbbing erection pushed mercilessly down his throat. Pubic hair presses into his nose, threatening to choke off his limited air supply, while heavily slung testicles swing at his chin. The lad coughs and sputters as he tries to remove the blockage from his throat.

A split second later Warren finds his mouth free once more. His eyes focus on the erection now waving in front of his face, glistening with his saliva. Raised up by the hand in his hair, Warren stands on his shaky feet. Another hand clutches his testicles but leaves the smaller erection to flop and flick like a fish out of water. They swap places, Morgan standing while Warren lands on the desk, face down, with a thump, knocking what little breath he had left out of his lungs. The hand that had once been giving pleasure to his testicles gives pain with the sudden, unexpected withdrawal of the truncheon from his anus. A bunch of keys is produced from Morgan's fallen pockets and the handcuffs are unfastened from one wrist before Warren is rolled over onto his back and fingers dig into the soft flesh of his thighs and hips.

With his legs now dangling over the edge of the desk, Warren's arms are pulled back behind his head and the cuffs re-applied, threaded through a drawer handle. Two more sets of cuffs and chains come from a second drawer. One snaps onto Warren's right ankle, allowing the limb to be pulled sideways, painfully parting the lad's legs while the other sticks up vertically from his loins in a magnification of his erection.

Taking the hand towel from the floor Morgan drags the once white square up and down his hairy crack. He then repeats his actions to the drying sweat around the boy's groin and anus, before wrapping it in a tourniquet around his erection and proceeding to flood its fibers with urine.

Once the towel is so wet it drips, Morgan goes to the head of the table. "Open wide!" he sneers, trickling the sodden material up the boy's body. Warren's hair is grasped as he tries to turn his head away. The towel is laid out flat across his face. Fingers part his jaw to force-feed him the towel, piece by piece into the crater of his mouth until once more Warren's jaw can take no more.

Now the boy is successfully gagged and Morgan completes chaining up his body. Snapping the sole remaining cuff into place, he yanks on Warren's leg, pulling it away from its twin to be tied of to the opposing corner, stretching the boy out horizontally along the desk edge. Morgan again spreads the lad's anal lips and brings his erection to them. The muscles of his back tense and his hips give an experimental jerk forwards, making Warren leap up from the desk despite the bonds which hold him. Morgan's fingers dig into the young boy's thighs as Warren is stretched open by the cock being thrust into him.

Warren cries out, bellowing through the gag but he isn't heard. The man goes right on in regardless, pushing in, back and forth, forcing himself as deep inside as he can each time. His erection swells as he bends over the captured boy, his hips pistoning back and forth as he gives Warren's prostate the fiercest work out it has ever received.

Suddenly the man's body stiffens. His back arches until it looks as if his spine will snap. Slowly he pulls himself all the way back until the roughed-up sphincter is about to force the intruder out. Then he rams himself all the way back in with enough force to heave the table a full foot across the floorboards.

Wave after wave of semen flood into the lad, burning a path right up inside his bowels until he's convinced it would come out of his foul-smelling gag. His own penis becomes so hard it hurts as he tries to force out sperm that no longer remains. His testicles ache with the weight of the man's heaving body lying between his legs. His wrists and ankles are chapped from the chains securing him but Warren has never felt so good. So fulfilled. So relieved. So happy. And so keen on returning to school to see what Gareth, Kelvin and Mr. Mallory will cook up for his next adventure.

TEAM EFFORT
Greg Bowden

"God damn it, Ferguson, just what does it take to get your attention out there anyway?"

Coach Bowers was pissed and I guess he had every right to be. We had just lost a game we should have won and we lost it through a series of really stupid mistakes and, as he said, not paying attention. It was a lousy end to a lousy season and now we had just one game left – the biggest game of all: the Alumni Homecoming game against Crocket.

"Don't yell at me, Coach. I tried. All of us did, but it just..."

"Ferguson," he said, spinning around and glaring at each of us. "All of you. Let's get a few things straight around here. First of all, as a ball team you stink! Ferguson here couldn't hit the God damned ball if his mother threw it to him..."

We all laughed at that, which was the wrong thing to do. Coach Bowers went ballistic.

"And the rest of you dickheads couldn't catch it if it fell into your glove! Baker," he snapped at me, "what the hell was the point of that little juggling demonstration out there? Is it really too much to ask you to just hold on to the ball?"

I guess I blushed. I'd had a perfect set up – the ball practically homed in on my glove but I'd been thinking about something else and when I caught it I just couldn't seem to hang on to it. They scored twice before I managed to get the ball to Adam at third base.

Coach's voice suddenly got low and ugly, almost a growl. "And am I to understand, Mr. Garcia, that what you were doing out there is called pitching?" Billy Garcia hung his head and mumbled something but the coach had moved on to Garret Hammond, the second baseman.

I felt kind of sorry for Coach Bowers. I mean, here he was just out of college, not much older than we were, and he's trying to make us into a baseball team. Not that it couldn't be done, I guess. We all played some in high school but somehow now that we were in college lots of other things seemed more important than playing ball. But the poor coach was trying to prove himself to the administration and I guess we weren't helping him much.

"Guys, look." The coach's voice lost its sarcastic edge and became almost pleading. "In just eight days – a week and one day from this moment – we play Crocket College. We have not won a game with Crocket in over ten years and I really wanted this to be the year we did it." He balled up his fist and smacked it into the palm of his other hand. "If I could only think of some incentive to get you to pull together as a team, I know we could do it. I just know it." He looked around at us. "What would it take, men? What do you want?"

We stood in silence for a moment, hanging our heads and wishing this was over. Then, very quietly someone said, "Me, I want your ass."

"What? Who... My ass?"

"Yea, your ass." It was Randy Sloan, the catcher. "Gettin' my dick up your ass would be a real incentive to play good ball. Right, guys?"

Most of the guys laughed nervously, but quite a few of them nodded, too. Including me. I mean, Coach Bowers is one hell of a good-looking man and he has a grin that always reminds me of my dad. I guess I'll work that out in Psych III when I'm a junior but in the meantime, the idea of sliding my cock in between Coach Bowers buns put me well on the way to a hard-on.

The coach stood there for a long time, staring at us. Finally he let out a long sigh and nodded. "Shit. Okay. If that's what it takes, that's what it takes."

Randy took a step towards him. "You mean it?" He had an odd look in his eyes; I guess maybe it was lust.

"Yea, I mean it." He held up his hand and waited for us to quiet down. "But only on my terms." He looked around as he spoke, locking eyes with each of us, one by one. "First, my part. If you guys can pull this team together and win that game with Crocket then whoever wants it can have my ass. In here, after the game." He paused for a moment, thinking. "Now, your part. You're gonna work. You're gonna practice. If necessary you're gonna bust your asses but you're going to become a team." He waited a second, his mouth slowly breaking into a smile. "Oh, and one other little thing gentlemen. Between now and the end of that game – for the next eight days – you don't so much as touch your dicks. You also don't let anyone else touch them. You got that? I mean no jacking off, no rub jobs, no milking it down, no girlfriends or boyfriends getting it off for you. I mean no sex of any kind! None. You got that?"

Now it was our turn to stand and stare but then, slowly, the guys nodded, one by one. Adam, the third baseman, poked the man next to him with his elbow and said, "Geez, Randy, I don't know if I can go eight days without, you know, without relievin' myself a time or two."

Several guys laughed and someone said, "Probably more like twenty times," but Randy just fixed him with a hard stare. "You mess up this deal, Adam, and it's your ass I'll be getting after that game. You got that?" Adam just shut up and nodded.

"Okay, then, I guess we have a deal?" The coach looked around the group again and everyone nodded. Then he sighed and shook his head. "God, I hope this works," he said under his breath and then, to us, "All right, that's enough standing around. Hit the showers and then get out of here. Go study or something. Just be ready to work your butts off as a team at practice tomorrow."

Practice for the next five days was sheer hell. Coach Bowers cursed and swore and screamed at us like a madman. Drop the ball and you were a shit-faced stupid prick and you had to do twenty-five pushups right then and there and God help you if another ball came your way while you were doing them. Miss that one and it was fifty or sixty pushups. A couple of times he made me so mad it was all I could do not to slug him one – or cry. Poor Kirt Daly actually did cry a couple of times, once not even trying to hide it, just standing there at first base banging his fist into his glove, tears running down his face.

Then the coach kind of backed off, suddenly hollering "Good catch, Baker," or "Great hit, Ferguson, good work." A couple of days before the game he brought a cooler full of Cokes and stuff for after practice and made sure everyone got all they wanted.

He dressed differently, too. At first he'd wear these baggy sweats but then, about the time he brought the cokes, he showed up in some sort of knit gym shorts and a tank top that really showed off his physique. The shorts were cut extra snug across the butt too, as if he was showing us what we were working for.

We changed, too. At first all we did was bitch about what a lousy deal this was and how horny we were and how that made us walk around with half a hard-on all the time. Then we began to see that somehow this was paying off; we were actually beginning to operate as a real team out there on the field. Finally, when the coach began being a human being again, I think a lot of us began to seriously anticipate the pay off. We all dealt with it differently (I decided it was just a phase I was going through) but most of us were developing a serious case of the hornies – for Coach Bowers.

The day of the game finally arrived; a warm, windless, perfect day for baseball. We all showed up for the morning rally, cheered a hokey speech by the college president and generally strutted our stuff for the other kids and the alumni. Later, in the locker room getting into our uniforms, the coach gave us a short inspirational talk wearing nothing but white socks and a jockstrap. When he turned around and walked down the hallway to his office Randy Sloan quietly said, "Oh, don't you worry Coach. We'll win this game if we have to kill Crocket to do it." The bulge at his crotch was obvious.

The guys on the Crocket team were a pretty cocky bunch when the game started and I suppose they had good reason to be. After all, they hadn't lost a game to us in years and we had a reputation for being the absolute worst team on the circuit. I guess they thought the only way they could lose was by not showing up. Anyway, they spent the first couple of innings fooling around, acting like a team of dads playing with their twelve-year-old boys, always shouting advice and instructions to us. Then, around the fourth inning, it began to get serious.

About that time too, Coach Bowers began to pace up and down in the dugout, flexing his buns and telling us we were doing okay. And we were; no game with Crocket had ever gotten to the fifth inning nothing to nothing.

In the top of the sixth we thought we might have it when Cliff Ferguson connected with the ball and sent it way out in center field but their guy managed to catch it and then shot it to third where Kirt Daly got caught and was called out. Jerry Evans jumped up and screamed "Shit!" I could see that he had the pretty good beginnings of a hard-on.

At the middle of the eighth, when we were coming in from the field with the score still zip, I heard Peter Warner say, "I don't care. I just want it to end. I've got to get my rocks off, I don't care how." Someone answered, I think Billy Garcia, "I know. I got the worst case of blue balls ever and damn it, they hurt."

We went into extra innings. At the top if the tenth it was still zero to zero and I think we were getting a little desperate. I know the Crocket guys were. They were beginning to pick at each other and the field chatter had turned a little ugly.

And then we did it.

Randy, on the first pitch, connected with the ball so hard that he cracked the bat; he also sent that ball across the field, over the fence and across the road. For a moment he just stood there, watching the ball sail through the air. Then he turned around and grinned at the coach before trotting slowly around the bases.

Adam, sitting on the bench next to me sighed, "Oh, Jesus, we did it. We did it." Then he suddenly doubled over, groaning and I thought he was having an attack of some sort until I got a whiff of him. He was coming in his pants.

We dispatched the rest of the game with three quick strikeouts. 1 – 0 was good enough.

Back in the locker room one of the guys handled the folks who came to congratulate us by telling them we had to have a private debriefing session and we would see them at the dinner planned for that evening. Once the door was closed – and locked – the coach began a speech of thanks but Randy cut him off.

"The reward, Coach. Remember the reward? I think we're ready." He proved it by pushing down his pants and letting his dick slip out of his jock. It was hard and leaking some clear fluid which Randy smeared all over the head.

The coach looked a little shaken but nodded his head. "Yeah, I know. Okay." He stripped down to nothing but his white socks and then looked around at us. "Where?"

"Right here," Randy said, indicating a pile of towels laid out on the bench between the lockers. "Prepared 'specially for you. I also brought this," he held up a large tube of lubricant, "which I think you're going to need."

Coach Bowers straddled the bench and then laid himself over the pile of towels. His buns opened up giving us a good view of the little brown pucker between them. I looked over at Randy and then back to the coach's ass; it didn't seem possible he was going to take anything the size of Randy's hard dick up there.

Someone called out, "Come on, Randy, get on with it before I come in my pants like Adam did."

"That doesn't count, does it? I still get my turn don't I?"

"Sure you do, Adam. Sure you do." Randy coated his cock with the lube and then kneeled between the coach's legs. "So I'm a slimy shit-eating prick face, am I?" he said in a low, dark voice. "Well, my man, I'm also a big-dicked ass-fucking stud, and yours," he rubbed the head of his dick against the coach's ass pucker, "is the ass I'm going to fuck!" Then he shoved his dick into the coach, all the way to the hilt.

The coach yelled. "Easy, Randy! Go easy!"

"Easy your ass!" Randy pulled himself back and then shoved in again, connecting with a loud smack. The coach sucked in his breath but didn't say anything more. It didn't take long before Randy went all rigid and then let out a groan and you could tell he was coming. It seemed to take a long time before he caught his breath and then slowly pulled his dick out of the coach.

I went around to the other end of the bench and straddled it by the coach's head, to see how he was doing. "You all right?" He had a grim look on his face but I swear there was a twinkle in his eyes too. "Yeah, Baker, I'm okay. Who's next?"

Garret was slicking some of the lube on his dick but I guess he was too close because he suddenly arched his back and shot his wad all over the coach's back. There was a lot of it, more than I ever knew a man had in him. He got up with a sheepish look and Cliff took his place.

I guess I'd seen Cliff a hundred times in the shower and I never thought he had anything special as far as his dick goes; I mean it was just an average dick, like we all got. But I'd never seen it ready for action. Up and hard it looked to be the biggest, fattest dick any man ever had on him. I kind of worried for the coach but he took it like – well, like a man. Cliff pushed it in real slow, giving Coach Bowers time to get used to it as it worked its way up his ass. Then when it was all the way in Cliff just braced himself and didn't move for the longest time.

The coach was sweating like crazy so I picked up my tee shirt and wiped his face. For a man just lying there he sure looked like he was working hard. Cliff leaned down and whispered in the coach's ear. Sitting where I was at the coach's head I heard what he said: "I don't know what muscles you have up there or what you're doing with them but it's going to bring me off. Yes sir..."

The coach looked up and gave me that grin that turns me on so. Then Cliff let out a low growl and began to shiver all over. He pulled his dick a little way out and I could see it throb as he shot his juice up the coach's ass. When he was finished he patted the coach on the buns and looked around at the other guys. "Best fuck I ever had, bar none." He reached out and grabbed on to Jerry Evans' hard cock. "Go on, man. Get in there."

Jerry didn't even bother with the lube but just began feeding his dick up the coach's ass. As soon as he was all the way in he slid it back out and then pushed in again. He went on like that, fucking in long strokes without a pause until he called out, "Gonna come, gonna come now," and switched to short, jerky strokes. A moment later he pulled out, his cock still dribbling out cum.

The rest of the guys took their turns, including Adam, who went off before he'd even gotten it all the way in. At one point the coach reached up and took hold of my balls. "When's it your turn, Baker?"

"Pretty soon now." I brushed his hair out off his eyes.

He grinned at me and then laid his head back down on the bench but he didn't let go of my balls. Randy came back, fresh from the showers and smelling of cologne. As Billy Garcia pulled his cock out of the coach, Randy took his place, gently patting the coach's ass. "I did it in anger before," he said. "Now the other way." Very gently he pushed his dick into the coach and, when it was all the way in, he began to massage the coach's back, working his hands along the muscles to ease the tension in them. He leaned forward and kissed the coach's neck while he established a slow, easy rhythm with his dick, pulling out until just the head was inside and then slowly pushing back in until his bush rubbed against the coach's ass.

All the while Randy was fucking the coach that second time the coach held on to my balls, gently kneading them and rolling them around in their sac. Randy caught my eye and smiled at me, then leaned down and kissed the coach's neck again before putting his lips close to the coach's ear. "Go on, coach. It's okay. You know you want it."

The coach raised his head up and nodded. "Yeah, I do." He let go of my balls and put his arm around my butt, making me scoot forward. The next thing I knew he had the head of my cock in his mouth and was slowly sucking in the length of my shaft until his nose was buried in my pubic hair and the head of my cock was partway into his throat.

Randy began to fuck faster and the coach began to moan and squirm around on the bench. He pulled up on my dick and worked his tongue along the shaft until he found that really sensitive place just under the head. He played there for a bit and then took my dick back into his throat. Then he began to swallow. After that I don't know who did what because I was in another world, a world where the only thing there was my dick and Coach's mouth and the biggest, longest orgasm of my life. Soon Randy started groaning and shooting his second load into the coach and the coach began making a lot of noise of his own. Randy finally quieted down and then he pulled himself out of the coach. "I think we all need a shower, don't you?" he said, helping the coach up off the bench. I don't know why but it surprised me to see that the coach's dick was slowly coming down from being hard and that it was dripping cum. Coach Bowers put his arm around my shoulders and gave me a little hug as we followed Randy down the hall to the showers. I surprised myself by speaking out. "I didn't get your ass, you know. Like you promised."

He laughed. "I know. You'll get it, though. Tonight. After the dinner and all the celebrating." He hugged me again. "Now we both have something to look forward to."

AT THE WHITE HOTEL
James Medley

Karim calls his cock the black dragon. He is luscious and warm. On a steamy day, I meet him in a bathroom. The toilets are stained and the place reeks of urine and filth, and I feel so delectably decadent, kneeling in the stench and worshiping the black dragon.

I notice we are being watched by another, whose eyes are like fervid agate marbles. He has his hands in his baggy pantaloons, stroking his hardness.

Karim, breathing deeply with a beautiful mouth, his pantaloons sagging to his ankles, hips thrust out, looks down at me as I gaze upward as he ejaculates.

I come in my pants.

I ask Karim to return with me to the white hotel. He nods toward the other youth. I nod.

The white hotel blinds us, blazing up from the dust, its stucco surface glaring in the sun. The boys are barefoot and their feet are whitened by the dirt. I want to lick them clean before we pass through the open arches of the lobby.

The fan in my room hums and listlessly dusts the soft air over their brown bodies as they undress. The other boy's name is Kebir and Karim knows him.

They lie down together. Kebir is still hard, Karim quickly so. I strip to my white underwear and see the spreading patch of moisture from my ejaculation. I kneel at the foot of the bed. Their cocks are not huge, but beautifully proportioned, glistening in the amber of late afternoon.

Karim cradles Kebir to his smooth sculpted chest. Kebir licks, not tentatively but with an experienced tongue. He goes to the hardened nipples, sucking, teasing, tasting, savoring. Then to the sun-washed belly. He makes a saliva trail as he kneels.

Karim bends and strokes Kebir's cock, a sense of wonderment on his dark young features. Naked innocence comes to mind – as innocent as the helmet of flesh which sheaths their maleness in fleshy folds. Innocent of the knife. Kebir goes for the sucking kiss upon Karim's plum-like knob. Karim allows but three engulfing swallows before he drags Kebir's dark face to his. I feel an intruder. Karim senses this. He reaches behind Kebir and pulls me to him. Their lips are soft and yielding, moist and warm, wet. We kiss. Tongues distended and dueling, exploring nether reaches, alternately.

My cock is hard. Their flesh is like satin, velvet, silk all at once. A softness so fast upon the hardness of their maleness. A distilled essence of BOY.

I eat them.

Now on Karim. I suckle and feed at his cock. Kebir masturbates above me. Karim kisses him. I pull his globes to my face and revel in the feel of him, the smooth black dragon pulsing in my mouth is bone hard and throbbing with need. The skinned-back head a part of my throat, my tongue loving the downside tube. His muscles jerk and quiver. He shudders.

I drink his sweet milk as he comes.

Kebir comes all over Karim's face and I think there is nothing so perfect and pure as the white cream as it splatters onto Karim's dusky skin.

Kebir leaves and Karim falls asleep in my arms. I cradle his warm and damp skull to my shoulder and smoke a cigarette.

I see my white uniform draped over a chair. My cap lying across the thirteen buttons of my fly. Bell-bottomed legs draped to the floor. One week of shore leave. Not enough.

I wriggle from under Karim's draped arm and slip into my underwear. Two doors open to my balcony and I go onto the bare unpainted boards and stand there, looking and smelling the fat city. The wrought iron railing is rusted under my palm.

In a bazaar across the way: Darting youths, piled clothes, canvas tents and lean-tos. Men in robes and burnoose. Women masked. The sun is low, cooling for the night.

A man across the street spies my semi-nudity and, leering, smacks his lips. Has he tasted the treasure just behind me, on my bed? I turn to reassure myself. The sprawled dark mass of Karim's limbs, are a shadow on the whiteness. I am nothing compared to him.

I dismiss the man with the harsh, learned glance of my comrades, feeling traitorous. He sullenly leaves. My eyes drift back to the bazaar. If only there were a boy stall. A thousand Moroccan dirhams, I want this boy. I will take him home, keep him, protect him from others like myself. I would buy him everything his bright brown eyes can see, send him to college, dress him in the finest latest fashion. Love him. Or would I just corrupt his innocence?

And to my shipmates, I would say, He's a servant.

They would laugh and know but it's all right.

I become aware of the towering mosque when the nearest minaret wails the mueddin for the evening call to prayer. I shake myself and gaze at Karim. He sleeps. The fan turns. As I approach him, Karim shifts slightly, draws one leg further to his chest. A bit of spittle seeps from his fleshy lips. I kneel beside the bed, sip it. He stirs, wipes his lips with his tongue, touches mine. His eyes open, confused.

He relaxes as I kiss him, nuzzles into my enfolding arms. My cock is hard. Karim languorously strokes it and I roll him to his belly, strip, climb onto him. As I push in, he moans and I moan. I come in him. He comes in my hand. I lick his seed from my fingers and kiss it into his sweet mouth. He takes it as communion. I suck his tongue and lie with him.

Night. He does not ask but I pay him. We find a restaurant on the crowded avenue. We order lamb and vegetables and grease drips from Karim's lips as he eats. I want to kiss him right there. Resentment wells up, but I stifle it.

- Can you spend the night with me?

- No.

- Tomorrow?

- Yes.

I give him the key to my room.

I sleep until the sunshine is bright. I breakfast in the white hotel. The eggs are a miracle. Karim appears at ten. What did he do last night? Where did he lie unconscious? With whom? I don't ask. He is beautiful in the morning light, his hair back lighted against the sun, gleaming black as the cooing pigeons in the square.

We explore the city. Karim leads. Cul-de-sacs and chattering babble, brick streets and stucco walls, shadowed arches, mysterious byways, hidden gardens and darkened entranceways. We move far away from the intensity.

In a secluded niche, against a rough stone wall, hidden by a giant eucalyptus tree, Karim fumbles with my pants, pushes me down, turns me to face the wall. He grapples his cock from the baggy pantaloons, opens his voluminous white shirt. He holds his cock, rigid and stiff and pushes against me. Soon he is fucking me, my hands raking the crumbling mortar. His shirt conceals the pumping of his ass. His cock fills me and he comes.

But we are caught. There are loud whistles, scurrying officials. My uniform is searched. I am thrown against the same wall but not to fuck.

We are separated and I do not know where they have taken Karim. In a crowded cell I am terrified of the alien speech, surly stares. I refuse to eat or drink the water.

We stand before a magistrate. Karim is next to me.

- Sodomy. Prostitution.
- No.
- Six months.

The embassy and military staff wash their hands of me. Time passes slowly in the moldering city prison. I violate and am violated. I see Karim at meals. He is kept in a different sector.

From the tattered robes we wear, Karim shows me a knife.

- Kebir.

My eyes are wide.

- How?
- Tonight. You come with me?
- Yes.

After dark, Karim opens my cell. We slip into the passageway. There are no guards. We make it to the wall. As we climb, Karim is behind me. I hear the shot. The boy falls. I drop back on my side. I cradle him to me. I hold him tightly and he is still.

- Karim!
- What?

It is night outside the white hotel. Karim has slipped back into my bed. My clock shows three in the morning. I have only one more day of leave.

- Oh, Karim, it was an awful dream.

He sucks me. I suck him.

I have breakfast with Karim and we explore the city. Back at the white hotel in the afternoon, we remain dressed, lie with one another, my hand inside his baggy pants, feeling him and moving his cock head against the rough fabric. His cock is a secret treasure. All mine, from the dewy ridge of skin which runs from the firmness of his shaft to his sweet, tiny hole.

His hand explores inside my fly. Buttons open and he wondrously palms over the flaring head, greasing.

Soon we are naked on the bed. Every tactile inch of my flesh is exploding with raw, red nerves of passion for Karim. His erection is hard and tight in its sheath of skin, running with lubricating juice as I stroke and love.

Karim rolls over and propels me to my back. We embrace tightly, kiss. He lifts my legs, gets his cock in me. He ruts. He fucks me violently, ravenously. His cock is all I want in the world, his cock in me, filling me. Karim bites his lips, clenches his teeth. He jackknifes his spine, grunts and wheezes, pants.

I shoot. Slathering ropes of cum arc out over my body and onto my face and hair. Love cream. Love Karim. My son.

I buy Karim a motorcycle. His face glows. The last I see of Karim, he is standing astride the black machine, legs spread. In the Levis I also buy.

The touch of flesh is cheap. The love of a boy cannot be bought. My plane takes off and I can hardly breathe.

TAKING VOWS
Trebor

I. Layover in Tokyo

I was just stopping in Tokyo briefly on my way to Bangkok and, from there, a monastery in the north to study the dharma and hopefully learn how to meditate. I had grown tired of the scene in San Francisco, bored with everything American, was ready for something completely new – and hopefully meaningful. While I was looking forward to the monastery and taking the vows, the commitment to celibacy still bothered me. I'd never tried it and actually had little confidence I could follow through. I was already fantasizing about lifting those ochre robes on young monks and thrusting my stiff prick deep up their little brown asses. I felt a bit guilty for these thoughts, but they were just thoughts, and, as a good vipassanna student, I was supposed to watch them – but not get caught up in them of course! That was the hard part.

My dreams were wild on the flight over. I had entered a large temple in one of these dreams and had gone to the Buddha statue and lit a stick of incense. Out of the shadows came a thin young man in orange robes, smiling. He dropped his robes, revealing a nice, straight, slender cock that smoked like an incense stick before it began gushing cum endlessly, then I awoke to soiled shorts.

In Tokyo I was impatient, wanting to get to Bangkok, stop in at a brothel and get sex out of my system, then move on to the monastery, when I saw the Japanese boy standing over at the newsstand. "Damn!" I thought. He was young, dressed in those silly American Gap clothes, baggy on his little Japanese body, with that pale skin running from his close-cropped hairline down his neck, under his shirt and to who knows what blissful places of beauty.

He was looking at a magazine and I was looking at him. He must have felt I was staring dumbstruck at his round little ass, because suddenly I looked up and saw he was smiling at me. I smiled back. He put away the magazine and began walking down the wide aisle of the airline terminal. I followed, my crotch tight with a rising half-boner.

Every once in awhile, he'd look back and sort of smile and went where I thought he would, into the bathroom. I followed him into the stall. He grabbed me and began kissing me deeply, wantonly. "Gaijan, gaijan," he whispered as he licked my neck. I grabbed his belt and began pulling him back and forth toward my crotch. He pulled away, smiled, and put his hand out as if to say, "Wait."

"I can't wait," I murmured back, reaching for his crotch. He grabbed my wrist, smiled again. He flung open the stall door and led me down a passageway to a room that housed what looked like a bunch of sideways plastic gym lockers. It turned out that they were intended for drunken businessman who couldn't get home but didn't want to pass out on the street. The boy was putting his coins in to rent one! We both climbed in. It was cozy, and so, I imagined, was his sweet round ass. We began mauling each other's mouths again and tearing off each other's clothes. It was awkward getting things off and at one point I simply tore his white cotton shirt right down the back and snapped all the buttons off with a couple good tugs. He was laughing. Now his pretty pale chest was revealed with a few little hairs around the dark nipples and a nice dark line of hair running from the navel toward the beltline. He had broad shoulders and deep, dark hairy armpits. His biceps were well-shaped and his forearms had sexy veins close to the surface. His stomach was flat and lined with the muscles below. He was cock bliss heaven! He lay back panting and smiled as he pulled me toward him. He grabbed my still Levi-clad ass and pulled my crotch into his. I went for that chest, sucking his tits, then I licked him right down the middle and into that line of hair at the belly. I stuck my tongue deep into his bellybutton thinking about how deep my cock ached to go into this boy. I grabbed his belt hard and undid it in a few motions. I yanked his pants down and he lifted his butt up to help me. A sweet, slender boner popped out, bobbing in front of a fine mass of black hair. I immediately went down on him, chewing the musty cock and sucking his balls. Damn, I felt like coming a gallon, filling that little cubicle with my jism. I wanted to just hose this boy down like a driveway, drench him, drench the unutterable and almost too-much-to-stand beauty of his pale body. I lifted his fine legs, very hairy on the calves but smooth on the inner thighs, and just sparsely hairy on the outside. He had fine dents for flanks, and when I got my hands around to his butt to lift him for my cock's entry, I felt a perfect hairless white-yellow roundness. I grunted as I forced my 8-incher into his puckered hole. I almost started crying as I pumped like a maniac. I felt the tightness of his sphincter rhythmically grabbing and releasing as my thick, veiny cock pushed in and pulled out. I could feel the pre-cum oozing out of my cock, sliming the inside of his rectum. I kept pushing deeper and he kept pulling me in. I grabbed his butt on each cheek tightly with my hands and lifted him higher as my fucking got more and more violent. His feet were pushing into the ceiling to increase the power and resistance of my fucking. My big round balls were slapping loudly, against his butt cheeks. He started murmuring something, loud, deep and guttural, as I thrust at him. He was holding his cock when it just went off, globs of cum hitting my chest and belly and I leaned down and caught one in my mouth. It dripped over my lip. "Damn," I cried, "I'm gonna cum! I'm gonna fill your sweet boy ass till you swell with my cum." I pulled my cock out on a sudden impulse and shot cum right onto the puckered part of his expanded hole. Watching it drip off, I was coming and coming like the monk in the dream. Now I thrust it toward his face and came on his nose, his brow; it ran down his cheeks. "Damn," I kept saying, "damn, damn!"

He had his tongue out, getting all he could.

Then I grabbed his legs again, put them up onto my shoulders and drove into him again, pumping and panting till I came again, this time my cock so far up his ass my balls actually hurt, pressed so tight against his firm buttocks. I let out a gasp as he began shooting again, almost clear cum now, arcing up onto his neck and chin. He was breathing hard. We smiled as I pulled my big cock out of his ass.

A buzzer went off; our time was up in the booth. I looked at his balls rolling into post-fuck relaxation among those black hairs, the cock now half-hard, bending and falling across the lightly-haired thigh. I kissed him with his cum still on my lips, my cum all over his mouth. We kissed in our cum and slobbered it around. We wiped each other up with the torn shirt and laughed as we shredded it some more to share it. I kissed his sweet ass before he pulled on his pants, even licked the hole, tasting my own cum. I gave him my undershirt to wear and we climbed out, but not before I nabbed a gob of his cum off the wall and slapped it over the Japanese stamp in my passport.

"So this is Japan," I thought, "a nice memory."

Back in the terminal, we went our separate ways. He didn't look back for awhile, then came a smile as he rounded a corner. I smiled to myself.

Later, on the plane, I jacked off thinking about that fine round pale need-so-bad-to-be-fucked ass, spurted on the mirror in the jet's bathroom and went back to my seat. I had said goodbye to civilization and civilized fucking. But I was going to the jungle and I was going to fill that damn passport with Thai sperm. That was my final vow.

II. Thai Driver-boy

Arriving at the airport in Bangkok, I was overwhelmed by an onslaught of cute youngsters offering me rickshaw rides. I stood there assessing them all, and picked the cutest. He never said anything, just grinned. It was the biggest smile I'd ever seen. He was maybe five feet five, thin and brown, with a mop of shiny black wavy hair he combed out of his eyes periodically. His skin was smooth and his eyebrows dark and large. But the smile, with all those teeth, really got to me. I kept fantasizing about putting my cock in that mouth, pulling out, and as he flashed his big smile, jetting cum onto those white teeth and watching it drip off. Meanwhile the scenery was amazing. Temples and tropical trees. And cute boys everywhere. All smiling!

I never asked my driver-boy to stop the rickshaw so I guess he figured he'd just keep going. He would turn around and smile every once in awhile, and I'd just smile back. Pretty soon we were getting to the outskirts of town, the streets were looking muddier and the houses more dilapidated. Suddenly, he slowed down and pulled over. "You stay my hass," he laughed. "Fie dullah!"

I nodded yes. Why not, I thought, but I reminded myself I was due at the monastery next day. I figured he'd probably know where it was and could take me there in the morning. I went inside with him and saw that it was his family's house, with all sorts of folks of various ages. I never did figure out all the relationships between them, though at dinner I tried to piece it together. There were about five little kids, four elderly folks, a middle-aged man, three middle-aged women, a couple of other young men around my driver-boy's age and a pretty girl who must have been tricking the way she kept distance from everyone and loaded on the makeup. I started worrying that my driver-boy might be pimping for her and felt that urgent need to stand up and scream "But I'm a fag!" But I was in Thailand; I thought I better sit tight and just keep my head.

As we ate, they all talked among one another and smiled at me. I think the driver-boy was the only one who knew any English and that was very little. I figured I should bring up the monastery now that we were finishing up and they were offering tea. I pointed to myself, held my hands in prayer at my heart and bowed, hoping to communicate I was a Buddhist. I think they thought I was thanking them, which was fine, but logistically I'd failed to make my point. So I pulled out the piece of paper I had with the monastery's address on it and gave it to the driver-boy.

He laughed and nodded his head furiously, almost shouting: "I know place! I know!" He kept laughing as he communicated something to the rest of them about my note and then they all started laughing.

Suddenly the girl prostitute got up and stormed out.

"Come me," my driver-boy said and he led me out the door and along the street. We entered a bar, walked through it and out the back into a patio. A group of young monks were sitting around joking with one another. He said something to them and they all looked at me. I figured maybe they belonged to the monastery I was looking for. They all got up and motioned me forward. We went through a gate in the back fence and came into a beautiful grove of banyan trees. It was dark but there was a moon and the light of it played in the wide-fanning branches of the trees. The monk's bright orange robes shone almost like flitting flames as they walked ahead of me. They all stopped under a particularly large tree and they all quickly took off their robes, revealing a group of precious brown skins, skinny arms and tiny little butts. All were turned with their back toward me and driver-boy.

Suddenly the kid started coming on to me, standing close, smiling and looking down. He pushed his pelvis into my crotch. I was getting very hard, what with him there and a dozen naked monks beyond doing I didn't know what. Driver-boy and I were kissing, every once in a while those teeth flashed in the moon's light. We started tearing each other's clothes off. He was as beautiful as I had imagined. His slender cock shot up out of a little patch of black, shiny hair I'd only seen the likes of once before with a Sioux boy I'd dated. I pulled our cocks together as I fondled his sweet brown-skinned balls. I'd almost forgotten about the monks when I noticed them moving toward us. All of them were erect and I stopped kissing the driver-boy momentarily to watch their beauty approach us. He turned too, holding my hand in his, our cocks bobbing in the night breeze.

A dozen boys walking toward us, all brown-skinned, hairless and smooth, with varying cocks. Oh, how could I choose which to worship! The rakish bent ones, the stiff, straight ones, the thick ones, the big-headed ones. They all mobbed us and I felt all those different cocks pushing against my legs and buttocks. That meeting when cock skin, with its hair frame and wrinkled rough scrotal touch, presses against me is the sexiest moment of all.

The one with the big-headed cock pushed it up my ass and I groaned with pleasure as he began pumping in the grip of my expanding sphincter and sucking hard the back of my neck. Meanwhile the driver kissed me deeply, matching the cock's deep thrusts with his tongue. Other Thai cocks were pushing into my flanks. One boy was on his knees, licking my thighs while he jerked off. I wanted my fantasy and forced the driver-boy to his knees. Smiling, he gobbled my cock up.

In front of us two of the monks had mounted. One fucked the other furiously from behind, his tortured blissful face looking at me as he drove his cock into the boy beneath him, who pulled furiously on his long cock till it shot and splattered cum on my feet. I jiggled my toes in it as I felt the big-headed Thai cock explode in my ass. I grabbed the driver's beautiful, shining locks and pulled him off my cock and watched his smile and found my fantasy as I shot cum onto his teeth. He smiled and started to laugh as he lapped it up and pulled me to the ground.

"I fuck you," he said as he put me on my back. I could feel the rough leaves grinding into my skin as he lifted my legs and pushed that wild root into me, all the time smiling. We kissed and he whispered many things, I don't know what, as he pumped into me. I felt his arms and skin and played with his tits. All of him was so incredibly soft.

Another boy began fucking him from behind and two more got onto their knees on either side of us, jerking their cocks. Before long I felt the splash of their cum on my belly and looked at their faces radiant with joy as they squeezed out what was left. I grabbed both their asses, searching to shove my fingers up their little holes. They pushed their butts into me and started getting hard again.

Driver-boy was getting close and my ass must have been a foot off the ground as he scrunched me forward and came with a loud grunt. I shot onto his chest a moment after, white cum on brown boy, dripping from his tits.

The boys with the hungry asses came next, onto my belly again, and I rubbed it all over me. I wanted to kiss all of them and thank them for being so beautiful and giving. Suddenly they all came to me at once, then started licking the cum off of me and kissing me all over and combing my hair back and massaging me and making me feel so loved and like a king. It was like some crazy, fucking colonial dream; I was full of imperialist guilt that only a white boy could know.

Then they were up and ran away with their robes in tow. Like a dream, it came and went. Even driver-boy was gone. I went to put on my clothes and found my wallet was gone, but I didn't feel robbed. They were fun and good to be with. They were poor, I only lost a hundred dollars or so; they more than earned it.

As I got settled in at the monastery, I discovered the boys at the bar were ex-monks. They'd been asked to leave the monastery as they couldn't keep the vows. I could understand this. Unlike Christians, the Buddhist monks just ask you to go if you don't like the program; they don't excommunicate you. And you're always welcomed back. In the next few weeks, I saw some of them return. I was surprised they recognized me. They soon got caught fucking again. I was torn between joining them. Not only in fucking but the romantic life of monks on the lam.

The second time they came back, I fucked with one of them. The one with the big cockhead who'd fucked me hard from behind and made my sphincter grab tight. God, it was good after six months of no sex. I spread my legs for him and begged him. My asshole felt like a giant flower the size of a satellite dish, I was so hungry for it. I just clung to him as he drove his cock in again and again. I marveled at the veins in this cock, the casualness of his loose foreskin, the innocence of those tits and the determination of his brow and his big cockhead. Why had I given this up? I wanted to go with him, I wanted him to stay. But I'd made a commitment; it had cost me a lot of money to escape America. And somehow I knew he'd be back.

"But one thing before you go, please?" I asked him. "Fuck me from behind, and before you cum, pull out and put it on my passport." He didn't understand anything I said so I got on my knees and fingered my hole, then I picked up the passport and held it at his cock and stroked his cock a few times and pointed to the page where the Thai authorities had made their stamp. He laughed heartily, then grabbed my ass by the flanks and shoved that big cockhead in slowly. Soon it was home free and deep for the rest of that well-marbled cock. The friction of it in my tight ass, the veins straining, the rubberiness of his cock bending, the lust in his eyes, the little shock of black shiny hair, his strong little hands holding my butt cheeks, his sucking on my neck, pulling out, so swollen, drove me wild.

I kissed the cock lightly before he put it in my passport, bending the poor little booklet around his cock and soaking it like a sponge.

Later, at the border, they gave me some trouble about the messiness of it, but I'd kept my vows.

BAJA BOYS
Jose Roberts

Paco and Ruben, friends since birth, lived in Linda Vista, one of Tijuana's many poverty-ridden barrios.

Paco, tall for his age, was considered muy guapo (very handsome). His face was beautiful: lips full, sensual, almost feminine. His soft curly hair was black as were his eyes, with a slight oriental tilt, their blackness emphasizing the whiteness of his teeth. He had an athlete's body: wide chest, slim hips, his legs muscularly lean. He was embarrassed that his smooth, coffee-colored skin was hairless except for a small pubic fluff at the base of his penis. It embarrassed him to not have even the hint of a mustache above his upper lip. Basically shy, he remained a virgin, even though nearly every girl in his barrio of Linda Vista letched after his body.

By contrast, Ruben, a few months older, had been sexually active since early puberty. He too was handsome, an inch shorter than Paco but more muscular. His skin was a slightly darker shade, and he proudly sported a fuzzy but noticeable bigote, considered macho among young Mexican males. In order to make it thicker, he had shaved it since he was 13.

While Paco was quiet, unassuming, Ruben was gregarious, easy to meet, with a smile for almost everyone. Paco was slow to anger, but once angered, he was a ferocious fighter, fearing no one, regardless of size or age. Ruben respected the speed and deadly accuracy of Paco's fists.

The two had been looking for jobs in Tijuana, but the continuing recession in California had decimated the economy of the town, which depended upon tourists who came south to bargain for trinkets or get drunk and chase whores along the streets within the Coahuila, the city's red light district. Neither boy was old enough to work in the only places paying a decent wage, the cantinas or restaurants which sold liquor. However, as with most laws in Mexico, many owners ignore them. When things are tight they choose to risk paying fines or mordida (bribes) when caught hiring underage employees.

When they got to the wide highway which paralleled the fence between Mexico and the United States, the boys raised thumbs, hoping to hitch a ride back to their barrio. Not many hitchhiked in Mexico, public transportation being cheap and frequent, but they were broke, so it was hitch or walk.

Several cars passed before a yellow Cadillac sedan stopped and the driver, an American, motioned for them to get into the front seat next to him. Ruben slid in first. Paco sat next to the window, relieved they did not have to walk the entire way home. The man at the wheel was in his early forties, well-dressed, smoking a big cigar.

"Where you headin', muchachos?" he asked in heavily accented Spanish.

"Our barrio," Ruben answered.

"Let me know when you want to get off." Chuckling, he patted Ruben's thigh.

"It's about ten kilometers from here," Paco said.

The boys watched the Americano toss the butt of his cigar out the window, then raise a pint of Jose Cuervo to his mouth and suck down tequila. "Want some?" he offered, holding the bottle out to Ruben.

"Sure." Ruben tilted the bottle for a shot, coughing when it caught in his throat. He liked to have others feel he could hold his booze. Paco refused his offer of the bottle.

"Come on, Paco. Don't be a panocha."

Paco hated to be called a pussy, even in jest by his best friend.

"Go ahead, muchacho. It's damn good stuff, the best."

Paco would like to have skipped it but took a small swallow, careful not to cough as Ruben had.

"Take another snort, then pass it back," the Americano pressed.

Paco took a second, bigger than he intended, then passed the bottle to Ruben who grabbed a quick swallow before handing it to the gringo.

"Our barrio's just over the next hill," Ruben said, pointing ahead.

"What time you boys have to be home?" asked the Americano.

"No special time," Ruben answered. "We're just cruisin'."

"Great. Why don't you come on down to Ensenada with me and have dinner? Maybe we can chase a few whores." As he ended the sentence, he ran his hand up Ruben's thigh, giving it a long squeeze.

"Fine with me," Ruben said. "How about you, Paco? You got nothing to do tonight."

Paco had expected to be home before dark, but with the gringo paying, why not?

"Bueno," the man said. "Have another shot of the Cuervo. We gotta finish it before we hit Ensenada."

Ruben took another swallow then passed it to Paco, who followed his example. Paco, not used to drinking, felt the effects of the first two swallows. Relaxed, he looked forward to the drive down the Baja coast.

"Hey, my name's Pete." He reached across Ruben to hand Paco the bottle. "What are yours?"

The boys gave their names. When Paco handed the bottle back, he noticed the gringo's hand on Ruben's upper thigh. That was Ruben's business, so he ignored it.

By the time they passed Rosarito, the bottle was empty. Pete pulled into a liquor store and bought a full liter of Jose Cuervo and a bag of potato chips. He thumbed off the top of the bottle and took a long swallow before pulling back onto the highway. Ruben was slurring his words and giggling at everything Pete said, be it in bad Spanish or English. He appeared to pay no attention to the man's hand which was now groping his crotch. Paco, feeling the booze more than his friend, was amused that Ruben enjoyed having his balls fondled so much, even leaning back and spreading his legs to make his bulging cock available.

"God, you're big," the gringo mumbled, zipping open Ruben's pants and pulling out his fully erect cock. "Jesus, you gotta have more'n eight inches."

"Mi amigo's is mucho mas grande," said Ruben, kneading the bulge in Paco's jeans.

Paco pushed his hand away. He had heard his pal brag of the money he had made letting guys blow him, and although he did not hold it against Ruben for making a quick buck, he was not into having anyone touch his cock. Nevertheless, he could not take his eyes off the gringo's finger as it spread Ruben's oozing precum over the surface of the mushroom-shaped glans. Actually it turned Paco on to see his friend lean back and moan, and his own cock started to thicken. He also knew he was getting drunk.

"Oh, boy, I gotta get that big pole of yours in my mouth." Pete swung the car onto a dirt road, bumping through dry brush until he found a secluded spot. Flicking off the ignition, he bent to lick Ruben's glistening glans clean, then slid his mouth down the thick shaft until his lips pressed into the hair at its root. A couple of minutes later, Ruben was crying, "Mecos!" (cum) over and over and shot his load into Pete's mouth. Some of the cum oozed out through Pete's lips and ran down the long prick and over his hand.

Pete, having taken his own cock out, jacked violently as he licked Ruben's cum off his hand, then sent a long stream of cum across both boy's thighs.

"Don't stop," Ruben gasped, "I'm ready to mecos again." He grabbed his cock and began to jack it, but Pete pushed his hand away and went down on him again. Less than a minute later, Ruben came a second time, then leaned against Paco, his energy drained. He did not even react to Pete's running his tongue up and down the wet shaft to retrieve every bit of cum clinging to it.

Paco, grossed out by Pete's cum streak across his pants, tried to wipe it away, but merely smudged it into the fabric.

Pete got out of the car to take a piss and Ruben stuffed his cock back into his pants. Paco, silent, gazed out the window.

Back in the car, Pete drove to a roadside restaurant specializing in locally-caught lobster. After eating, Pete took the boys to a cantina near the waterfront and ordered a big pitcher of Margaritas. The sign behind the bar stating Mexico's law against serving minors liquor was ignored as the waiter placed salt-rimmed glasses in front of the three. While the boys were obviously underage, they were with a gringo.

Pete was feeling his liquor a bit by the time they got back into the car, spewing gravel as he raced onto the road ahead of an approaching truck. Two miles down the road, a siren and flashing lights shook him back to sobriety. When he pulled over and stopped, a swaggering transito (Federal highway patrol), moved to his window and in Spanish demanded his driver's license and registration papers for the car. When the officer leaned to take the papers, he noticed the two boys sharing the front seat and asked their names. Both answered in Spanish, so the transito turned his attention back to Pete.

"You were speeding, senor," the transito said in halting English. "I clock you at more zan one hundred kilmetros por hora." When he noticed the lack of comprehension on Pete's face, he continued, "That ees more zan seexty milas por hora. Zee limeet esta seexty kilomteros por hora aqui...here, not seexty milas por hora."

"I couldn't have been going that fast," Pete said.

"Do not argue weeth me. I clock you," he lied. "I weel have to take you to the comendancia, unless you would prefer to pay zee multa (fine) to me."

"How much is the fine?"

The transito stepped back to look the expensive car over, then said, "Cuatro cientos pesos."

"How much is that in dollars?"

"A hundred dolares."

"I don't have that much cash."

"Then I must take you to the commendancia."

"Okay," said Pete, disgusted with the turn of events.

"How much you got, senor?" the transito asked.

"About fifty bucks, I guess."

"Then I will take that, so you do not have to go to zee commendancia."

Pete shrugged and handed the man two twenties and a ten. The officer stuffed the money into his shirt pocket, turned on his heels and got back into his car.

Pete waited until he had driven off before pulling back onto the highway, pissed at being taken for fifty bucks. Even though he might have been going a few miles over the forty miles per hour limit, other cars were passing him.

"Stinkin' puto, el transito," blurted Ruben. "You should not have paid him."

"Yeah, and spend the rest of the night in some shitty jail."

"He would not have taken you to the commendancia. Paco and I witnessed him ask you for money. If you told his commandante what he had done, he would be arrested and lose his job."

"Look, it was worth fifty to get rid of him. It's lucky he didn't bust me for driving drunk."

"If he had seen you had been drinking," Ruben said, "he would have taken the car and made us walk back to Tijuana."

In Ensenada, Pete took the two boys to a bar where he ordered another pitcher of Margaritas. The three were feeling good by the time they had finished their third pitcher.

As they walked back to the car, Pete grumbled, "Christ, I don't want to drive back to Tijuana tonight. How about us gettin' a room at the hotel across the street and headin' back in the morning?"

Feeling the full effects of the liquor now, neither boy objected.

In the room, Pete started to undress. "Let's all take a hot shower, then get some sleep. We'll have an early breakfast then head back for Tijuana."

Ruben followed his lead, dropping his pants, kicking off his shoes and tugging at his shirt. He was naked before Pete could get his shoes untied and pants off. Paco took his time, annoyed at the stickiness left on his leg from Pete's cum. It had seeped through the fabric and dried. He decided he too needed a shower.

Ruben was in the big shower, adjusting the hot water, by the time Pete joined him. Ruben loved any chance to take a hot shower. There was no hot water in his home; he had to dip cold water from a topless barrel to bathe. The shower was like most in Mexico, spacious, but with no curtain to divide it from the toilet and sink. Ruben moved over so Pete could join him under the steaming spray.

When Ruben saw Pete take water into his mouth, he warned, "Don't swallow it or you'll get the shits."

Paco entered the bathroom and Pete's eyes fell to his long, flaccid cock, its head halfway down to his knees. "God, you weren't kiddin' Ruben! Paco's got the biggest cock I've ever seen, and he isn't even hard."

Paco looked up to see Pete's good-sized cock rising from his body, surprised that the man had such a good build.

Pete stepped aside and motioned for Paco to step into the shower with them. "I'll wash your back," offered Pete as he ran a bar of soap up Paco's spine.

It felt good, so Paco relaxed and let the man soap his entire back, spending more time than necessary on his firm, round buns. He was too drunk to mind the man's hands lingering on his ass, but he began to object when Pete's hand slipped around his body and fondled his cock. When he looked down and noticed he was fully erect, he relaxed and let the man soap its length then wash his balls and run the bar of soap up the crack of his ass.

"Hey, how about washing me, too?" asked Ruben.

"Okay," Pete said.

Ruben became hard the moment the man's hands slid over his round ass and up his back, and his thick cock was curving upward by the time Pete began washing it. Ruben groaned with pleasure as the man ran a soapy finger up into his asshole, and played with his balls.

"Lemme wash your back," Ruben said, turning off the water. Moments later, Pete's body was soap-covered, his cock hard. He reached back to guide Ruben's rigid cock up into the crack of his ass, bending to make the entry easier. He grunted once, grimacing in pain as the boy moved his pelvis forward jamming the full length of his impressive cock deep into his ass.

Paco's own cock became painfully hard as he watched his buddy bend his legs to squat low, the muscles of his thighs tightening as he rammed himself up into Pete. His muscles relaxed as he slid the glistening shaft back out, his cockhead coming into view before he rammed it back in. Ruben had taken only six or seven plunges when the muscles in his legs again bunched as he shot load after load of cum deep into Pete. His movements became jerky before he quit and backed off, his cock flopping free, cum still flowing from the massive head.

"Now you fuck me, Paco," begged Pete, backing his white ass onto Paco's pulsating cock.

Paco had never butt-fucked anyone before, but the steamy warmth of the shower rising up into his crotch and the feel of Pete's soap-slippery ass rubbing on his cockhead was more than he could resist. Besides, his balls ached. Grabbing his throbbing cock with one hand and spreading Pete's ass cheeks with the other, he moved the head up and down the cum-slick crack until he found the opening. Taking hold of Pete's hips, he pressed the cock head against the sphincter until it opened enough for him to enter the man's already sperm-filled asshole.

"Slow, muchacho," Pete begged. "You're bigger than any cock I've ever taken."

Paco backed off, letting Pete back into him slowly, soon taking all of the toadstool-shaped glans. As the thick shaft slid a couple of inches into Pete's body, Paco was surprised how warm the man's insides were. It felt even better when it slid in to more than half its length.

"Shove all of it in, Paco," Pete begged.

Paco rammed his cock all the way, and gripping the man's hips with both hands, he began sliding the shaft back and forth, the head almost coming free before he jammed it back in. Pete began to jack-off as Paco speeded his thrusts. Finally Paco slammed his pelvis forward, crushing his pubic hair against the cheeks of Pete's ass. Pete groaned.

The power of the approaching orgasm took over Paco's mind and body, his movements becoming automatic, beyond his control. His slim body jerked sporadically as he capitulated to the sensual power of his first butt-fuck. Just before he shot his load, he felt the man's sphincter flutter then tighten around his cock stem. Pete was well into his own orgasm, ejaculating a stream of cum onto Ruben's stomach and chest, the boy too amazed to jump out of way.

Paco squirted at least six times before pulling out of Pete and turning on the hot water. The three stood rinsing the mixture of suds and cum off their bodies and cocks before drying.

Ruben was already in one of the double beds when Pete followed a naked Paco into the room.

"Sleep with me, Paco," Pete said, taking the boy by the shoulders and directing him to the empty bed.

Paco was too tired to resist and fell naked into bed and let Pete crawl in beside him. He was almost asleep when the Pete took him into his arms, kissing him on the lips. He could feel his cock harden against the man's stomach before he drifted off to sleep.

When Paco awoke in the morning, he was surprised to find Pete had moved into Ruben's bed, and was sucking his friend's cock. Paco slid out of bed and walked naked to the bathroom, his piss-hard cock waving back and forth in front of him. Turning on the shower, he stepped in, letting a stream of yellow piss mix with the hot water as it pounded into his copper- colored skin.

Paco was just finishing as Ruben and Pete entered the bathroom, both hard, Ruben's cock glistening with Pete's saliva. Over the next few minutes, they repeated the scene from the night before, except this time Paco went first into Pete's ass, followed by Ruben, and Pete sucked Paco's semi-flaccid cock while Ruben was fucking him.

Exhausted, Pete crawled back into bed, but the boys insisted on eating breakfast. Pete covered his head with the sheet, but the boys playfully dragged him out of bed and dressed him.

After breakfast, Pete cashed some traveler's checks at the front desk and led the boys back to the room. Pete handed each boy a fifty-dollar bill. Before they left the room, the boys let Pete suck them one last time.

Shortly after noon, Pete dropped the boys off at the road into their barrio. Before they got out of the car, Pete handed them each another fifty-dollar bill.

"You boys were the greatest I ever had," he said, his green eyes flashing. "I'll never forget this trip." It was true. On his twice-yearly vacations from his commodities business in Los Angeles, he had picked up many boys for sex in Mexico. The sex had always been pretty good and only once had he been robbed. But these boys were special, utterly guileless and into sex as much as he was. He smacked his lips and, as the boys slammed the door of the Cadillac, Pete took two more fifties from his wallet and pushed them out the window. "Just the greatest," Pete said, nodding his nearly bald head.

Beaming, the boys grabbed the bills and waved as Pete pulled away, both pleased to be so rich from only a few hours of "work."

PETER FROM PITTSBURGH: ANDY WARHOL'S BEST BOY
Thom Nickels

Sad to say, my lover had grown chubby even though he was still in his twenties. Most people considered him attractive, but I hated having sex with him because his belly was getting bigger and he didn't care. "Take me as I am!" he'd say. "Don't I love you for you?"

"Which is?" I asked.

"Over the hill. Bald," he said defensively.

Which wasn't the case exactly. I was only partially bald. In chronological years I may have been over the hill, but people rarely took me for a forty-something man. My lover, on the other hand, was doing everything to make himself undesirable. Like drinking beer three times a week, sometimes getting so drunk he'd throw major temper tantrums. This was when he'd start to throw things. Like ashtrays or expensive knickknacks. In the meantime, his belly kept growing and lying on top of him was like laying on rumpled sheets or two huge pillows.

"Take a long look at yourself!" I'd say, "if you'd only do sit-ups every other night you'd lose that thing. But you're lazy. All you want to do is party. No wonder you say our threesomes don't work. How do you expect guys to be attracted to a belly like yours? They pull away because nobody wants to lie on top of the Matterhorn."

Which was the truth. Guys we picked up during our walks around town usually snuggled up to me. I don't say this because I have a big head. I say it because I work to stay slim. Sure, these guys may have liked my lover's twenty something face and his full head of hair, but once his clothes were off – wham!, they came to me. This infuriated him. Especially when he saw that I was enjoying a particular guy while he sulked near the edge of the bed.

"What do you expect me to do? Stop sucking a guy because he's more attracted to me? That's not fair to the guy," I said.

"Whose more important, me or him? Who is the person you say you want to spend the rest of your life with – isn't that supposed to be me?" he'd say.

I'd answer in the affirmative. If I didn't, there was always the chance he'd belt me. I never knew when a shoe, an ashtray, a vase, or even his fist would come flying into my face. That's the way he was. To stay safe, to remain unhurt, you had to appease him. You had to make an extra effort.

"So what was to prevent you from massaging his ass? You just lay there and did nothing. You sulked. You withdrew. I can't feel sorry for you," I'd say. "As I said, maybe he didn't like your beer belly. Did you ever think of that?"

"Oh, so you think I'm fat. You think I'm an ugly pig!"

"I never said an ugly pig."

Sometimes he didn't throw anything but just sat on the living room floor, rocking back and forth to music such as Abba or Elton John. He rocked like a person on a rocking chair, moving his upper body fast or slow depending on the music or how angry he was. At times he rocked so fast I could barely count the sways. Other times he looked as if he was lulling himself to sleep. His swaying always looked odd. Sometimes when he rocked he'd take a break and go out to buy himself a six-pack. That's when I'd make preparations to leave the apartment. This meant packing a small overnight bag and hiding it in case I had to make a quick exit. Once I grabbed the bag, I had to make a quick bolt to the door because he'd always try and stop me.

Whenever I saw him rocking I knew he was mulling things over. Would the rocking lead to more sulking, screaming or violence? I never knew, though I'd wait in another room, unable to relax and preparing for the worst. It was a sick relationship for sure.

It wasn't always a sick relationship. There were good times when he cooked dinner, when I took out the trash with a smile, when we'd go food shopping like ordinary couples. We even had many moments when we laughed together, went on picnics, took walks down by the river. The outdoors appealed to him and he was often his best when there were a hundred chores to do. He did the chores fast – shopping, laundry, cleaning the house, walking the cat, making lunch. It was as if he'd taken a pill that turned him into a speed demon. His habit was to do the chores before I could get to them so he could say later that I was shirking my duty because he had to do all the work.

Experts call this manipulation. He'd talk about all the work he rushed to do during regular arguments or after some guy we picked up showed me too much attention. Usually I followed him around when he did the chores and tried to pick up the slack. That's because I didn't want him to have ammunition for future fights.

Our hunt for the perfect threesome had us shivering in below-freezing temperatures in every part of the city. We'd walk down by the river, wind reddening our noses. Or we'd circle the same city blocks, then head back to the river again. This back and forth motion sometimes lasted several hours. "What about him?" he'd say, pointing to a guy sexy from the neck up but with a beer belly and love handles like his own.

"I don't know. Child-bearing hips, don't you think?" I'd venture.

"You mean fat. Fat like me, right? I know, you want these skinny-winnie Auschwitz victims. Okay! Let's go!"

This was a mark against me, a mark I knew he was filing away for a future fight. "You never like people I'm attracted to. I'm always the one who compromises. I like somebody with meat on their bones," he'd scream under a streetlamp.

"Look, I don't want a fight. Let's go back and talk to him. I can find something about him to be attracted to. Maybe he has nice legs. Or nice feet. He did have a nice face," I'd say. Which was true in most cases provided the guy was not too fat. Most fat guys have handsome faces.

"No, I'll let you pick the person like you always do. But of course they'll have to have a big dick – bigger than mine anyway!"

One night we went into a straight peep show not far from our little apartment. It was our last stop on the way home on this particular night. We just did a cursory check – peeking into booths, checking the corridors, that sort of thing. We were on our way out when we ran into a man who later identified himself as Peter Mara from the Andy Warhol museum in Pittsburgh. He was a handsome Hercules-type, about 28, blond, bearded, masculine. The three of us connected right away. We started to talk and before I knew it we were headed back to our little apartment.

That's when he said he was in Philadelphia to find extra stuff for the museum. We didn't ask him too many questions at first. That would come later. Though Peter was handsome, my big concern was whether or not he was fat. He wasn't as skinny as I like my men, and his clothes were baggy so I couldn't be sure what he looked like nude. But my lover seemed confident that we were in for a treat. I was somewhat disappointed that Peter wasn't more boyish looking.

I knew we had a unique package, however, when he told us he was straight and that he was dating a black female police officer in Pittsburgh. This made him very sexy to me.

In our apartment, we lit a candle and sat on the living room furniture I paid $999 for when my lover and I first got together. The furniture still had a new cedar smell, though both the sofa and the love seat had been soiled dozens of times with spilled Pepsi (my lover), beer (my lover), and semen (sloppy threesomes). Two or three times I knocked a cup of coffee into the cushions, so depending on which way the wind was blowing (or where you were sitting), the sofa reeked of coffee beans.

"Maybe I should take off my shirt to get things started," my lover said after a short silence.

My lover was never embarrassed about taking off his shirt. I thought it odd how it never once occurred to him that a guy might be turned off by what he saw. My approach would have been to start feeling the guy up, but never take off a piece of clothing and just sit there. There were times when I'd make the first move, though it was more along the lines of "Let's go into the bedroom and relax!" Once or twice I suggested that we all remove our shoes, but that was only when the atmosphere was uptight.

Peter didn't seem to mind my lover's beer belly. This is often the way it is with straight guys. They're not as fussy or as picky as gay bar clones. A bar clone will say: "Get away from me, you're not pretty enough!" while a straight guy, even the handsomest of them, wouldn't think of saying that.

By now I was sitting on the floor near Peter's shoes and moving my right hand towards his feet. Caressing a guy's foot, even with shoes on, was one way of turning up the heat. Guys usually started playing with themselves when I did this and the next thing I knew they had their clothes off.

"What kind of museum artifacts are you looking for?" I asked Peter, whose huge hard-on formed a lump under his cotton trousers.

"Old and new. Unusual. Things the artist may have touched. Things the artist might have touched if they hadn't killed him at St.

Vincent's hospital. Some lithographs, serigraphs, that's all," he said, touching the head of his cock.

We moved into the bedroom, passing the kitchen on the way. My lover stopped to introduce Peter to the cat. Ajax was on a countertop and my lover was talking baby talk to her. He pointed to Peter and said, "Yes, this is Peter. Say hi to Peter. Shake hands." He grabbed Ajax's paw and made little handshaking motions. Then he started in on his 101 cat stories. For a while the three of us stood around petting Ajax. Peter accepted this in good humor, though I could see his mind was on what would occur in the bedroom.

Forty-eight hours before we met Peter, my lover blunted the tip of a butcher knife when he brought it down hard on the kitchen countertop. I was glad when he didn't come after me with it. When Ajax saw the knife she hid under the big sofa. The memory of the knife, mixed in with the sound of baby talk, made me think of clowns and John Wayne Gacey.

When Peter had his clothes off, I couldn't believe what I saw. He was body beautiful: small-waisted, big chest, pointy nipples, perfect ass, dick the size of a small fire hose. I was beside myself.

I crawled into bed, leaving room for Peter in the middle. My lover crawled in next to me. I panicked, thinking he would stay, but he quickly repositioned himself so Peter had enough room between us. When Peter moved towards us he lunged forward like a gladiator on all fours. His mammoth cock was three or four times the size of mine (and I was big), nine or ten times the size of my lover's (who was small). Far thicker than a silver dollar, it made me think of the quip, "It was quite a stretch" as originating from this man. Peter was so horny he dripped long spidery lines of cream onto the bed sheets.

"I've never seen anything like this," I said. Even my lover was transfixed, touching and pulling the gigantic organ. I held back but let him get in the first lick. Part of the psychology of avoiding arguments was to act casual, to not get too excited about a sexy catch. My lover would note my every reaction, every groan and gulp. I watched him go hog wild on Peter's organ, then decided it was time to make my move. When I slid my body down underneath Peter's balls I could feel my lover stiffen up. I knew he was getting out his mental checklist. I put Peter's cock in my mouth anyway, no easy task; I had to open my mouth so wide I felt as if two people had their fingers inside my cheeks and were stretching it sideways. For some reason I then started to wonder if Peter had ever appeared as an extra in a Warhol film.

Peter did not touch or suck us but was content to be worshiped. I jerked him off onto our chests (we were both nestled underneath his legs). He came in a huge arch. The arch collapsed and sputtered sideways before finally dissolving into a trickle.

Afterwards, he said he had to get back to the Holiday Inn on 18th Street. He gave us his business card: Peter Mara, Assistant to the Curator, Andy Warhol Museum, Pittsburgh, Pa. He said we could call him at work anytime and leave a message. He also promised to call us whenever he returned to Philadelphia, which would be fairly frequent, he said, because there was a special serigraph in a Villanova estate he wanted to get his hands on.

As he dressed, Peter told us that Warhol had appeared at a Philadelphia bookstore in the seventies for a book signing and had left some signed napkins lying around. The bookstore's owner was now willing to part with the napkins, as well as the chair Warhol sat in. There was also a section of the bookstore's bathroom wall on which Andy had scribbled erotic graffiti – a line drawing of a glory hole with flames around it so that it looked like the sun. Peter said he wanted to cut that out and move it to Pittsburgh where it would be remounted in a mock john.

"What did you think of him, honestly?" my lover asked me two days later.

"Big cock, the biggest I've ever seen. Incredible. Plus, he's handsome and has a great body. A real nice supermodel type. If he were gay he'd be insufferable," I said. "He's a nice guy."

"I know," my lover said. "If he were a bar clone he'd walk around like his shit didn't stink. Do you think he'll call?"

"Yes. He seems like the kind of guy who wants a regular connection rather than fishing for new contacts every time he comes to Philadelphia," I said.

"For once we met someone who's much bigger than you. He made you look small ..." He didn't finish his sentence because he probably realized that if Peter made me look small, what did that make him – hopelessly microscopic, pathetic?

"Cock size is an accident of birth. He didn't do anything to earn it. It's not like he should be congratulated or anything," I said.

"You loved it. I saw the way you were sucking on it. You were in heaven. You don't suck on me like that," he said, taking out his mental checklist.

"But nobody comes like you. You can loop across a room, go up a wall, hit the ceiling, zoom around in all kinds of circles. You're incredible. Big cocks may be big but they generally don't spray far. I don't know why that's true, but it is," I said, hoping he'd drop the subject.

"But you don't suck on me. I want to know why you don't suck on me. You take licks but you never go over the head and suck – suck up and down like you did to him. Do you think I'm diseased? I'm the person you say you want to spend the rest of your life with, but you won't suck my cock all the way down. You must be saying you think I have AIDS," he said, raising his voice.

"You don't have to get excited," I said. "He was only a passing ship in the night. I've never seen a cock like that. I was mesmerized. I broke one of my rules. I'm human. Look, I give you lots of licking, especially around the balls."

"I don't like my balls licked. It tickles. I want you to go over my head and suck up and down like I do to you. What makes you think you're not diseased? I take chances on you. Besides, oral sex is safe. You can't get AIDS from sucking cock. I don't know what you're afraid of. I'm just your sexual plaything, something you take off the shelf when you want to have sex with. You're using me," he screamed.

Ajax disappeared into the other room. I tried to look and sound relaxed, hoping it would tranquilize him. "You're putting too much energy into this," I said. "It's not worth it. Look, we had a nice two days with no arguing. We agreed we had a nice time with Peter. So why the change?"

"It's my stomach, isn't it? You liked him because he didn't have a stomach? You won't suck my cock over the head because I have a fat stomach?"

"No, no," I lied. "I'm just very safe. I admit I made a mistake with Peter. I'll never do it again. I don't usually suck any cock over the head – for too long a time anyway. This AIDS business has me scared to death. I'm sorry if you think it's because of your stomach. You're very attractive. Handsome, even. People are always commenting on your face. You have a full head of hair and that should count for something!"

"You're a damn liar," he said, standing up. "You think I'm a fat ugly slob. All you care about are big cocks. I'm too small. I'll always be too small. I can't change that." Before I knew what was happening he grabbed a small statue of the Buddha I'd inherited from my grandmother's estate. He threw it against the wall where it broke into a hundred pieces. "I am your lover," he screamed. "I am supposed to be the most important person in your life!"

I saw Ajax cower under the big sofa. My lover's face was red and he was getting that cross-eyed look again. I was glad he hadn't been drinking. Because he was sober, his tantrum would probably fizzle. Still, my Buddha was broken. I liked Buddhas. He broke my grandmother's Buddha. I wanted to tell him, "I'll never go near your cockhead now, never, not in a million years. And yes, your stomach disgusts me. You're fat. You let yourself go to pot," but I didn't. I only said I hoped he realized what he'd just done. "Breaking a Buddha is bad luck. There may be a curse attached to it. I could never break a Buddha. My grandmother had that Buddha since 1928."

For several days I lamented the broken Buddha. He tried to make it up to me by cooking me dinner four nights in a row. Meat loaf, mashed potatoes, green beans, applesauce, coffee, apple pie. That didn't bring back the Buddha. Nothing could do that. I was glad that at least he wasn't harping on my adoration of Peter's cock. I was glad about this, even though he wanted me to suck his cock with the same gusto. At night he would climb over my face and pretend he was Peter. I wanted to scream.

"Suck it!" he said, his belly hanging over me like a pillow. I'd make a feeble attempt, just to keep the peace, then start licking his balls because I didn't like the taste of his organ. It was sour, like his stale beer and mood swings.

Three weeks later, I was on the telephone talking to Peter. When I put the phone down, my lover asked me, "Is he at the Holiday Inn?"

"Yes, at 18th and Market. Room 208. I told him we'd be over in an hour. Is that okay?"

I could see that it was okay because he seemed excited.

"I don't want you measuring everything I do," I said. "Just let me have fun. Leave your mental checklist at home. Please, just be a free spirit this time."

He seemed to be in a good mood. Two hours earlier his identical twin was over and the two of them were on the floor rocking to Abba. Sometimes one rocked one way and the other one rocked in the opposite direction. His brother was having problems with his Korean wife. She kicked him out for beating her up and he came over to our place to tell us the latest. He wanted our sympathy and understanding – and beer. He also had a worse temper than my lover, though he never got mad at me. Since they usually had a fight whenever there was beer around, the idea was to never let them get drunk at once. Once they almost killed each other at a party that was supposed to be in my honor. The guests could not restrain them as everybody ran screaming into the street.

Peter was in his bathrobe when he opened his hotel room door. The lights were dim in the room. My lover started chattering right away; I could tell by Peter's facial expression that my lover was talking about all the wrong things. That's the kind of person my lover was. He never stopped to study a person's facial expression in order to gauge the flow of a conversation. He just kept talking. He had no perception of what a person wanted to listen to but he'd force-feed lots of chatter on them.

"How's the Warhol business?' I asked Peter, eyeing a package of small paintings in the corner of the room, as well as the crotch lump in his bathrobe.

"Good. We found three in an old mansion off Rittenhouse Square. The bookstore gave us the signed napkins," he said. "Two of the serigraphs have never been documented. There's one more I'm trying to get. I'd show you the ones I have now only they're all wrapped up and taped in brown paper."

"I'm not crazy about Andy Warhol," my lover said.

Peter's erection was poking through the folds of his bathrobe. He didn't do anything to cover it but let it air itself. "Okay," he said, meaning it was okay to not like Andy Warhol.

"You guys are more than welcome to come to Pittsburgh when the museum opens," he added. "I'll let you know."

"That's a Golden Triangle," I joked.

"Well, I don't know about you guys, but I have to work tomorrow. I think we should get started," my lover said. "I'm going to take off my shirt."

Peter's cock seemed to shoot upwards. My lover saw me staring at it and frowned. Peter took off his bathrobe as I unlaced my shoes and stripped. My lover was the first one on the bed. He occupied the center, legs spread out, belly protruding like the bulbous Buddha he smashed against the wall three weeks ago. "He has some nerve, stretching out in the middle of the bed like some supermodel," I thought. "Probably wants to prevent me from enjoying Peter."

I was worried that he wouldn't change positions, that he'd occupy the center of the bed during the entire session. He was always testing me. I hoped Peter would ask him to budge, but when he didn't, when nothing happened, I reluctantly took my place on one side as Peter took the other. That's when I felt my lover studying my face for signs of disappointment. I tried to mask things as best I could; I even ran my hand over his hairy chest and big belly and moaned a soft "Ahhhh." That's how afraid I was of him losing his temper and of having something else I owned smashed to smithereens once we got home. But I was dying inside.

He kept me there for ten minutes as he stroked Peter's arms and pecs. Peter looked at me as my lover squeezed him into his belly. The look in Peter's eyes told me he wanted to be in the middle. When I had had enough I stretched my right arm over my lover so that it touched Peter's butt. Then I stroked and patted it. As I did this I noticed my lover stopped sucking Peter's cock. He turned around in a quick about-face and started to suck me. The maneuver was a ploy. Now I was obligated to suck him before sucking Peter. To ignore him now would surely lay the groundwork for a big fight.

I held my breath and went down on his four inches. I groaned and snorted, keeping one eye on Peter, who was feeding his delicious member to my lover. "Ten more strokes and I'm switching to Peter," I told myself, as my lover's belly hit my forehead the more he tried to thrust like a stud.

As if by telepathy, Peter suddenly straddled both my lover and me. We grouped ourselves together under his legs, with Peter turned in my direction. This was a cue for me to take his cock. My lover watched as I took my turn and tried not to act too excited. I reached for my lover's organ (an act of charity) while manipulating the Warhol man to orgasm.

On the way home, my lover said he hadn't been satisfied and wanted to look for another threesome. "Peter likes you," he said, "he doesn't like me. Now I'm going to find somebody who likes me. You had your fun."

"I don't know what you're talking about," I answered, "that was 50-50. I can't help it that he came when I was touching him. Take that up with him. Cocks don't have a conscience. They come when they want to."

"It's obvious he's more attracted to you. It's because I'm fat," he said.

"If you think you're fat, lose weight. Do sit-ups. It's not like you can't change it," I suggested.

"So you do think I'm fat!' he said.

"Isn't that how you see yourself? Don't you keep talking about being fat? I almost never tell you you're fat!" I said.

"That's because you're afraid I'll throw a temper tantrum. You're afraid of violence," he said.

He started to walk up our street but instead of walking past the apartment, he headed inside. "I thought you were going cruising?" I said.

"I'm going to bed! Nobody wants me. I'm fat," he said, going in before me and slamming the door.

A week later I was home by myself when I got a phone call from Peter. He said he'd just come from a Main Line estate where he was able to get the last known Warhol lithograph in Philadelphia. He wanted to know if he could stop over on his way to the train station. I had Ajax on my lap when I told him yes. I knew my lover wouldn't be home for another three hours, so we had plenty of time to play. It was not my intention to cheat, since our agreement was to meet people together, but the temptation proved too much. Besides, I was still thinking of the smashed Buddha. Why honor a commitment to a person who beats you up and who has no respect for your property?

No sooner was Peter in the apartment than his insatiable boner showed through his cotton trousers. He had the lithograph in a paper bag on the kitchen counter. It was wrapped in white tissue paper. Ajax sniffed it, then retreated to the sofa. Peter kept groping himself through his business suit. He wanted it bad.

I asked him what he wanted me to do and he suggested I get on my knees and do him right there. "I wouldn't even have to take my clothes off," he said with a wink. I didn't think I'd have trouble doing this, but then something hit me. Earlier I'd been thinking that if I worked a little harder remaining faithful to my lover (I hadn't always been in the past), maybe, just maybe, he'd stop having temper tantrums and we'd get along. In those days, I believed that monogamy, gay or straight, was the will of God. That's why it was so easy for me to tap into the superstition that the reason we were fighting was because we weren't "listening" to the Word.

It was hard not to go down on my museum friend. He hung around for a while, trying to cajole me. There was no way he could know that I was having mental battles with my soul. He wanted it bad, yes, but I never gave in. Eventually, he gave up, picked up his package and headed back to Pittsburgh. I never told my lover what happened.

That night my lover broke three brass ducks off a knickknack shelf that had been in my family since 1941. This time the argument was not about sex but about money. We were having a calm discussion about the telephone bill when he suddenly went off. He reached for the ducks and threw them across the room before I knew what was happening. One of the ducks hit the coffee table, two ricocheted behind the sofa and the third struck Ajax. I didn't wait around for a follow-up attack, but bolted and ran out the front door before he had a chance to block my exit. He managed to catch hold of my shirt when I was in the hallway, but I swung around so fast he was forced to let go.

On the street, I headed for the porno cinema around the corner, my usual place of refuge after a fight. It was a sleazy, smelly place filled with homeless men, criminals and assorted bums, but occasionally one could find a sailor or a clean cut youth who wandered in by accident. I'd sit there and ponder my sick relationship, though more often than not I found no one to cruise. My frayed nerves often had me buying lots of chocolate bars from the theater candy machine. My lover never chased after me, though I'm sure he knew where I was. Even in the relative safety of the theater, I was still cautious whenever anybody entered. (I certainly didn't want my lover sneaking up behind me.) Boredom sometimes had me propositioning men I'd never approach otherwise. These were shady characters in knit hats or white men from South Philadelphia, old-style queers with a penchant for white Levis and cheap cologne.

Many times I'd ponder the women in these films, who to the men were nothing more than human sperm receptacles. Their heaving breasts and moans reminded me of the sounds of patients in hospital intensive care units. The women made me think of Peter and the fact that my lover and I were his sperm receptacles. I was the biggest potential receptacle because Peter often telephoned me during the day from the same Holiday Inn and asked if I could come to his room.

Peter sensed I was having trouble with my lover and it was my feeling that he wanted to catch me on a down day – a day when I was feeling weak and would say yes. I said yes only once.

When I went to his room that one time he was sitting on a chair in his bikini briefs. He barely said three words to me as he slouched down to make himself look sexy. He looked so delicious, I gave myself the green light. When it was over, he pulled up his bikini underwear and thanked me in his usual polite way. I felt terrible because there was a part of me that still believed in my sick relationship.

When he called again and said he had a Warhol serigraph of his cock, I was suspicious. He knew I'd do almost anything for art.

"What do you mean a serigraph of your cock? I've seen most of Warhol's work. He doesn't have any cocks. You must be thinking of Mapplethorpe," I said.

"I'm thinking of Warhol," he answered, "I told you, there's a wealth of stuff not yet seen by the public. Warhol did it first. Mapplethorpe copied. My cock is in black, white and blue – American colors."

"And you have it now," I said, "right there in your hotel room?"

"Right here. It was hanging in the Villanova estate. The matriarch of the house relegated it to the billiard room, but her son, who's a real queen, insisted on framing it like a Russian icon."

I was not going to fall into the trap and tell him his cock was like a Russian icon. "Well, that's nice," I said.

"Would you like it?" he said.

"Would I like it? Aren't Warhol rare-finds worth a fortune?," I asked.

"Depends," he said. 'This one, not especially. It was done quickly on bad paper. Andy crumbled it up and was going to throw it away but I rescued it from the trash can. I had to sneak it out. He always used to guard his trash."

"Did you have sex with Andy?", I asked.

"Once," he said. "He knelt down in front of me and played with it. He wanted to see it shoot. The stains on the serigraph are from that session. That's me in there. The Villanova guy knew this but his mother, the matriarch, had no idea the picture was built on a bed of semen."

"You want me to come over and get it?" I asked.

"If you'd like. Of course, I really can't give you this particular work, but I can give you something by Andy if you're willing to wait a while," he said.

"Talk about a quick-change artist," I said. "Did Andy teach you to be such a tease?"

I never saw the serigraph because at the exact moment I said "tease," my lover walked in the door. He seemed to have a chip on his shoulder and I sensed trouble. I quickly hung up the phone after saying, "Thanks for calling." The first thing out of his mouth was, "Oh, so who was that, one of your daytime boyfriends?" Right away I imagined myself running to the porno theater. I wasted no time moving knickknacks and putting away the new book I'd been reading.

"Don't worry," he shouted, "I'm not going to throw things. I'm not going to hurt your precious book!"

He began to pet Ajax. "You're the only one who loves me for who I am. You're always there for me," he said to her. Ajax meowed, then ran to me and began rubbing up against my leg. This was her vote for peace and harmony. I ran my finger over her cold nose, tapping it twice.

My lover put Abba on the phonograph, sat down on the floor and started to rock. I waited for his litany of lists: had I sucked his balls and not his cock when we last made love? Had I kissed him properly? Did I mention Peter's name in my sleep? As things turned out, he was just worried about something at work. There was no fight.

Two weeks later, a package arrived in the mail. It was addressed to me and had a Pittsburgh postmark. I opened it in a hurry, knowing it was from Peter. Taped to an inside package was a note which read: "AIDS has scared everybody, me included. I'm sticking to my policewoman for a while. Thought you'd like this. It might help to spur you on – if you know what I mean."

I opened the package and saw a copy of a red, white and blue serigraph of a hairy man's stomach. The stomach protruded outward like a bloated rendition of the Matterhorn. There was no face or arms, just the bulbous stomach and close-ups of dark hair follicles. There were also views of the circular bands inside the belly button, and a penis, which looked very small.

Off to the side was the famous "AW" (for Andy Warhol) scrawl.

SHARING
Matthew Rettenmund

It's a selfish world out there, but me and my buddies share everything.

When Andy gets paid (he strips at Rosebudz), he splits his tips with us by keeping us in the liquor all Saturday night; when Dave's prude roommate takes off for the weekend, the pad's ours to use like our own.

Even I have something to contribute to the kitty, something I enjoy sharing. It's my ass, because I'm the only bottom of the trio. So, I swap a little hot and tight for some of the big and hard. People could do worse, and have.

Recently, we three found something new to trade to each other. I'm pretty bad – some "thing." Someone; this guy Rich, a new addition to our clique.

We all met Rich at the exact same moment, the only reason our trading deal ever came to pass. I mean, if any one of us had even met Rich alone, he would've kept Rich all to himself.

Instead, we all met Rich at Rosebudz, me and Dave sitting a few chairs apart at the bar, Andy dancing on top of the bar, naked except for a wringing wet Holiday Inn towel he clutched with no particular modesty to his hairy crotch.

Andy's an exception to the hairless rule with strippers, a big, bulky man who insists on keeping his expansive chest and heavy groin (and even the small of his back) as hairy as Mother Nature designed them. Whenever he danced and I was at the bar, we had this routine where I'd make a to-do about slipping him a fiver as a tip, then he'd squat a little and let me reach up under his towel (or into his jockstrap, depending on what look he'd gone with that evening) to play with his fat, hairy balls. Nearby customers would trip over their pencils to give Andy a five- or ten- or twenty-spot for the shot at groping nuts or prick or shoving five rude fingers into the crack of his ass.

I got to feel Andy completely up – the others lucked out to make full contact before he swiveled coyly, expensively away. Highly unethical to rope 'em in like that, but then what sort of ethics do you expect from a damned stripper and one of his fuck buddies?

Furthermore, I don't even look like I should be trusted. I'm a little dark-haired guy with a good haircut and a lean body that doesn't betray much indulgence, just a lot of conditioning. I must be good-looking, not because so many guys tell me so right before they fuck me, but because so many pretend not to look at me on the street.

I'm pretty self-aware and I think I look dangerous – well-kempt, attractive, even sexy – but untrustworthy, like I'm so fed up I just might bulldoze your feelings without realizing it. It's in my eyes, in the way they squint at you, cutting through the bullshit. I have an old man's eyes, and some would say a cantankerous old man's cynicism. I feel old at thirty. There's definitely something wrong with that.

The night we met Rich, I was buzzed on good booze and a day-long marathon of getting mercilessly reamed out by Andy. He'd been unusually aggressive and horny after an ill-fated, celibate, quasi-relationship with a pious college-bound Mexican boy who'd thrown him over for a fucking priest. Hail Mary.

Tipsy with alcohol and afterglow, I was antsy to do the old five-buck scam with Andy as an excuse to fondle the fuzzy nuts I'd recently drained. Andy was scanning the bar for potential tippers. Dave? Oh, him – the quiet one. I almost forget to include him in any stories I tell about us, even in sex stories where he's my partner. Mousy, bespectacled Dave, who, at six -two, with transparent blue eyes, boyish bangs, and the longest non-female eyelashes in circulation, is by far the "cutest" one of us, and the most generous in bed. Dave was there, too, just giving up on trying to engage a Franco phonic towhead sitting on the other side of him.

As if on cue, we all three laid eyes on Rich for the very first time.

Rich is not Hercules. He isn't even Steve Reeves. He's just a real good-looking sandy-haired guy with a little more chest than belly, and a little more shoulder than chest, and a sweet, straight-looking face that belongs in a college track team group photo. In that homespun, wholesome way, Rich is very average to the eye, but there is also an extra something, a warmth and a pleasing enigma. It's the simultaneous familiarity and mystery you see in posed faces from vintage family photos sold unceremoniously in stacks at flea markets.

Knowing that since all three of us saw Rich plop down between Dave and me at once, I realized he was about to be assaulted from every direction. Regardless, I also knew that I felt the intense need to share myself with this guy. The feeling shocked me, scared me.

Rich saw me before he noticed Andy or Dave, and smiled at me nervously. I could picture myself on my knees, his knees at my ears while my tongue licked his swollen prick, sucking salt from skin, coaxing semen. He would smile in gratitude–not smugness – as I sucked him off, this I could tell from the unpretentious pull of his lips at his teeth when our eyes met.

Then Dave extended his hand to Rich and received a similar grin. Then Rich...

"Nice to meet you guys – I'm Rich,"

...spotted the white of Andy's towel and gawked at Andy's beautiful body. When Andy danced, it was like watching The Thinker standing and straightening to stretch and gyrate and flex and arouse.

Within the hour, Andy was done with his performances and his pockets were fatter than even Rich's promising, black jean-ed basket. The four of us were doing the egg thing at our favorite dive, 24, an all-night diner.

Rich charmed us with his Midwest disposition and funny stories of being a closeted frat boy in Michigan. When he compared the state of Michigan to the shape of his hand, pointing to his thumb and saying, "I'm from here," I felt my heart doing flip-flops. It'd been so long since I'd had a crush, a bona fide crush, that I'd almost forgotten how much more exciting crushes are than plain old lust.

That Rich had only been "out" for a short time and confessed to minimal sexual experience endeared him to me all the more; not like chicken appeals to a chicken-hawk, not in a sleazy, cherry-mongering way. I found myself coveting Rich's inexperience, planning how to start over with him, innocent again myself just by association.

Crazy.

Around 3 a.m., Rich bravely gave all three of us pecks on the cheek (though Andy managed to slip him a hunk of lip, I noticed) before leaving us at 24 with his phone number and mutual promises to "stay in touch." Andy and Dave were just as smitten as I was, though if either had the alien romantic notions I was having, they were well concealed under macho talk of virgin assholes and bronco-busting.

We came to a group decision I'll always regret. But I was always a joiner (God, it sucks to say so). We had always shared, and Rich would be no exception. Each one of us would seduce him singly, then we'd persuade Rich to join us in our usual old-fashioned gangbang with Rich doing double time as a top and a bottom.

"Can your little ass handle three dicks going at it?" Andy asked me lewdly, playfully pounding my arm. Dave's foot had been brushing my inner calf all evening.

After meeting Rich, these guys were climbing the walls for more action. I knew we'd be in our monthly three-way soon.

"I'm always up for anything."

Forty-five minutes later, I was sandwiched between two beautiful men. I was lying with my upper body across Andy's lower body, his erection gleaming, freshly slipped out of my mouth. Dave hovered above and behind me, his strong arms ramrod straight at either side of me, his lower body flush with mine. He was screwing me, literally; Dave only thrust occasionally, mostly just swiveling his hips and swirling his buried dick around inside me.

Nobody fucks like Dave – it just feels so good-natured, like he's doing it for you and not to you. Of course, he was really doing it just the way he liked it best. If he'd liked to fuck me rough (like Andy did), he would've.

"Mmmmmm – you're tight," Dave moaned wetly in my ear, "Squeeze my dick – yeah, that's right, that's it, there it is..."

I could feel my butt burning like I was going to come soon so I went back to working Andy's prong furiously, mouthing the head and then sucking it like I knew made him hot to come.

"Suck me, suck me, suck me," he chanted, legs as far apart as nature allows, his forearm draped over his eyes, head thrown back limply on a pillow. "He likes taking big dicks on both ends, loves that big dick..."

"...lovin' it," Dave joined in, "He's lovin' it all the way up his ass...Shit, he's shooting it! I can feel his asshole twitch..."

- SKINHAIRSWEATPAINPAINPAINRELEASE –

"Yes, fuck, fuck, fuck–yeah, yeah, yeah!" I howled.

God, it's incredible to come with a fat prick in your ass, especially when you're fantasizing that the dick is attached to a guy you're crazy in love with.

I worked Andy's meat until he shot all over my cheek, my lips. I was a wreck, just barely conscious of licking come from the corner of my mouth when Dave tugged out of me and sprayed my sweat-soaked back.

No, we never use condoms. We were best friends, and had all tested negative more than once. We trusted each other to play safe outside the circle so we could play unsafe within. It's stupidity all dressed up to sound smart, and it's the kind of craziness millions of guys fuck around with every day. Welcome to gay sex in the '90s.

We lay entwined, Dave sliding in his own semen on top of me, my face buried warmly in Andy's musky balls. Andy's palms were protectively over my ears.

In a lot of ways, I love my buddies. But already I was setting up Rich in my mind's eye as an alternative. Why jeopardize such hot sex? Well...

"So, who screws Rich first?" Dave asked from on top of me (and he's the shy one).

"Me," Andy said with swagger.

"Why you?" Dave asked.

"I have the biggest dick," he laughed, nudging me with it and cuffing my ears.

Rich.

I decided to break the agreement and beat Dave and Andy to the punch.

Three days after our breakfast at 24, I had Rich alone in my apartment. I'd asked him over to help me pack since I was moving the following weekend and needed a hand. But it was obvious when I called him that I was interested in him. That he came over made it obvious he was interested right back.

"You have tons," he observed of my scattered possessions. Rich showed up in a red sweatshirt, a matching (but just barely) cap, and faded jeans so worn the back pockets sagged outward loosely, making his sprawling ass seem a perfect bubble. He lifted his cap and scratched the side of his head through just-woke-up-and-pulled-on-this-cap hair.

"Yeah," I agreed. I'm a pack-rat, more out of boredom than sentimentality. "Let's fill boxes."

We worked for four solid hours stuffing boxes full of stuff to move, stuff to throw out, and stuff to donate, the latter of which I'd secretly throw out as soon as Rich left. I kept an '80s classics station on the whole time so our work was continually interrupted by mutual exclamations of recognition, frenzied dancing, and Boy George impersonations. It's scary how quickly the present becomes nostalgia.

Rich was so much fun that day, so "on" and infectiously cheerful. I couldn't take my eyes off him – the always smile, the forever arms, the never-going-to-let-you-down. I wanted this spark plug, this little firefly in a man's big body. I could smell his sleep-sweat seeping from the neck of his sweatshirt, and kept fantasizing that my fingers were in his hair.

As we wound down our work, the tension in the room was palpable, our mutual glances meeting every couple of minutes. My time with Dave and Andy and a lot of other buddies like them over the years has conditioned me to be aggressive.

"It's getting hot, Rich," I said, plainly manufacturing a situation. He looked up at me from where he squatted, taping up a box. "Why don't you go ahead and lose the sweatshirt?"

He stared at me silently, his eyes so round and warm and ready. He knew what I needed. He knew. Slowly, he stood up. I could hear his back crack and I was counting the seconds.

"Okay," he said hoarsely. "That'd be great." He pulled his sweatshirt up and over and off with a graceless but brief struggle. His chest was broad, his torso so thick and firm, but with a welcome layer of softness that betrayed irregular visits to the gym. He had dark chest hair between dark nipples, which were erect and probably tingling.

Tentatively, he asked, "How's this?"

I knew I looked aroused. I couldn't help it! I was so horny and liked him so much that I just knew, knew, that fucking with feeling was going to be incredible. My cock throbbed in my jeans, my asshole twitched in anticipation.

Have to have it.

"It's great," I said, coming up to him, "You look fucking great." I reached up with both hands and squeezed his pecs, rolling the rock-hard nipples between my thumbs and forefingers. Rich groaned softly, leaned back a little with his hands in his back pockets.

"Oh, that's good," he said shakily. "Do more...I like it..."

I felt up his entire upper body, my fingertips rubbing over skin slick with perspiration. I felt him deliberately, screwing a finger in his navel, pressing my palms into the curves of his furry underarms, gripping his powerful biceps with both hands, telling him what a hot man I thought he was. Rich loved it, let me explore him at length, then took my head in his hands and brought our lips together for the most leisurely kiss. He pulled me against him and we gently chewed each other's lips, sucked tongues up and down like sucking a cock. Our own cocks were grinding together, our bodies locked.

"Suck me," he whispered, "Love my dick with your mouth." I sank to my knees and he undid his belt, unzipped, pulled my face into his crotch. "Suck me...I need it so bad right now..."

I pulled out his big, uncut cock, its musk stinging my nostrils – unwashed but salty-clean. I was blind with hunger for it. Immediately I took it all, couldn't wait, no time to spend on heading now, only time for fucking face. He held my head still and thrust his long prick in and out of my loving mouth, forcing it over my rough tongue.

"Oh, I could come," he moaned. "I'd love to just lose it in your mouth."

I took him out of me and kissed his belly. "No," I gasped, "Save it up for my ass. I want you in my ass."

"Yeah." He lifted me up and turned me around, holding me against his body, rubbing his cock against my butt. I tilted my head back and slipped my tongue into his mouth, more turned on than ever. I was going to have the fuck of my life. I lost it...

"I want you up me now," I begged, tugging my jeans down to mid-thigh and bracing my hands on my knees. I thrust my hairy ass back against his hot prick, feeling it throb against my crack.

"God, you're hot," he grunted. I could hear him spit to moisten his dick, the slick sound of his fist working the spit over his tool. "I wanna slip it right in..."

"Yes! Do it all the way in..."

His cock pierced me of a sudden, just sluiced into me with no resistance, my sphincter trained so well to take that big dick.

At once, "Yes..."

I almost fell forward from his eager thrusts, full-body slam-slam-slams as he sent himself all the way up me again and again. I couldn't talk, my teeth gritted, my eyes squeezed shut in ecstasy.

"I'm going to ..." He slowed and gasped and I felt that fullness, that incredible burn as he shot his nut in my butthole. It was so hot, the hottest fuck, and his kisses caressed the back of my neck as he slumped forward, exhausted and panting.

"That was incredible," he said through a satisfied grin. "I want you to come for me now."

"Finger fuck," I said, and he replaced his slowly shrinking penis with a pair of stiff fingers. He fucked me to the knuckles while I beat my meat with abandon, wriggled my ass on his fingers. When he started doing big circles and I heard the wet smacking of his fingers in my asshole and the...

- HOTCOMESWEAT –

"I'm coming, oh, yeah!" I shouted, tears in my eyes it felt so good, so, "Goddamned good!"

"Yeah, shoot it... Come!" Fingers unrelenting as my asshole gripped them for dear life.

It was more than fucking; it was redemption.

We cleaned up, kissed, slept.

I woke up madly in love! Kissing and stroking Rich's furry chest, I knew I could never share him with Andy and Dave – no way. I needed Rich all for myself. Things could only get better.

"Andy was so right," Rich said dreamily.

I froze, the sound of hope drowning. And then Rich crushed me, oblivious. "You do have the best ass." He hugged me close, but my face was flushed. Andy had said no such thing.

I was suddenly over-hot and tried to move away, but Rich thought I was playing, so he held me all the tighter.

"When did he say that?" I asked, my ears ringing.

"Two days ago at his, you know, at that crash-pad of his."

"Where he fucked me," the unspoken.

Seems I'm not the only untrustworthy one in this neck of the woods. But I may be the only dreamer.

Since then, Dave's had his crack at Rich, too, and we have regular three- and four-ways, just buddies trading a little meat for some of the best sex anyone out there's ever had. I like it a lot, it feels great, it's incredible to crawl into a bed full of gorgeous men and suck any available cock, feel them sliding inside you, rubbing over you.

How can I complain?

Still, more often than not, I find myself seeking Rich's parts in the tangle, extra-thrilled when it's him I'm sucking or taking in the ass. But even when I find him and he takes me or lets me take him all the way to blinding, raging orgasm, I'm still not satisfied, you know? Every time we fuck I just feel another year older.

FUN & GAMES
Jarred Goodall

I'd just been minding my own business, at least that's the way it had started out.

There was no law against going over to the other dorm. And nobody said you had to make a lot of noise walking in. I wasn't the only kid going around the campus in gym-shoes.

So when I got close to the rec room door I didn't stomp my feet and whistle or anything. Nobody did that. I just slipped in. And stood there with my mouth hanging open. I didn't know whether to laugh or puke or start kicking asses – bare asses!

Six guys were lying on the floor, semi-naked – totally naked in their middles where it counted! They were jacking each other off! And what they were doing it in you didn't want to even think about.

When I got over my amazement I started calling them sodomites and queers, and I don't know what else that came into my head.

But, I should have known. They were hopeless. They were perverts. They acted like I was the guy who ought to be forcibly taken to the local shrink. "You don't do that yourself?" one of them asked, calm as a Sunday school preacher talking about Godly love.

"None of your fuckin' business!" I shot back. "If I did, I sure as shit wouldn't be doin' it in public."

"Oh, is that right?"

"Any other guy touch it, or flob on it and it'd shrivel right up!"

And then Cameron said, "Oh, yeah?" in a way that suggested maybe my boast had been a mistake. "How'd you like to prove that?"

"Jesus, I don't have to," I said.

"Oh, yes you do!" And, perverts, super perverts, they grabbed me and hauled me over to this bed they had there to sleep their guests on, perverts attaching themselves to my wrists and elbows and ankles and neck, after which I couldn't fucking move.

Of course they had to drag my pants and skivvies down and pull my T-shit up over my face. Now, is there anything more humiliating than getting de-bagged? You're used to going around with something covering you, so you don't have to have a bunch of perverts staring at your cock, comparing and watching for when it goes stiff, as sometimes you can't help it doing.

But that was just the beginning. "We'll see about what you told us," one of them said.

"We figure you're being just an eentsy bit hypocritical," said another.

I tried to fight them off. I thrashed my head back and forth and shouted and spat at them but they just laughed and wiped the spit off their faces, not mad at all – and then Cameron picked up my thing and started handling it!

It was awful – and the worst was that it was exciting, in a definitely queer sort of way.

Queer was the right word. That's all they were, a bunch of queers, six queers, Cameron the worst of the lot – and he'd been voted the handsomest boy in the sophomore class. Not far behind him in looks was his little brother Donny, with his turned-up freshman nose like it was left over from kidhood, and that oh-so-cute, oh-so-innocent, oh-so-pretty face, a regular landing field for a spray of oh-so-cute little freckles. Donny had no business being in the sophomore dorm. He'd obviously just come over there to perv with his big brother and friends.

"Looks like you've volunteered," Cameron said to Donny.

"You mean it? Can I?"

"Can you? – you got to!"

"Terrific!"

"So take hold of this thing... and make it sit up and do tricks."

"We'll all provide the lube," said one of the other boys, "the kind His Holiness here says he hates."

So it was Donny – Donny's hand, not Donny's face – I had to deal with, because Donny's hand took over from Cameron's. I wasn't hard, nowhere near, but that damned freckle-face Donny started squeezing it and rumpling it. I allowed myself a grin – this wasn't doing anything for me. What Donny worked on wasn't much stiffer than cooked spaghetti.

"Told ya," I said.

"Gimme time," Donny answered. "I'm saving."

"What, Kroger stamps?"

Donny grinned. "No, spit."

Well, if they tried that I'd stay limp forever, that was for sure. Just let them try!

A half a minute later I felt Donny let go of me and lean forward and – Jesus, I couldn't look! – but when that hand came back and started doing what it had just left off doing, the difference was unbelievable!

I felt myself getting stiff, then stiffer, then, very quickly, rock hard. I didn't want to think about what was giving all that fantastic lubrication down there, but the feel was perfect – and shitty and humiliating, and I hated every minute of it!

Something cold hit my chest and I jumped. Ray was listening to my heartbeat with, would you believe, a doctor's stethoscope! "What the fuck you doing?" I demanded.

"When a guy gets close to cummin', his heart speeds up," Ray explained. "We want to know. Donny's got to know, that's all." So young freckle-nose could stop stroking on me, they thought!

Well, they could think again. No way was this going to turn me on that much. Ray was supposed to be the great all-time woman-slayer, with his long face and blue eyes and mop of fine blond hair and thin eyebrows and perfect teeth. For a woman-slayer he sure showed a lot of interest in a guy's thing and how it went off!

Shit, I had to stop looking at Ray! Every time I really saw Ray I'd get a jolt through my groin, which was the last thing I wanted, so I shifted my gaze from Ray to Donny, but now Donny flashed me a grin and half-whispered, half-mouthed, "Nice? Does this feel good?"

Goddamnit all to hell and back through purgatory, I found myself floor-boarding, roller-coastering, jetting off toward that final rise. I tried to think of all the disgusting things they were doing to me, but it didn't help. Another couple of strokes of Donny's hand and...

"Quit!" Ray said. Donny let go. I shuddered and bit my lip, and when I'd got my feelings back under control I gave them a big splattery raspberry and said, "You really think you guys can blow my nut? Come on!"

"Right!" Ray said. "We'll let you calm down for a minute or two." Now the sons of bitches brought out two pairs of handcuffs – Big Gene was a cop freak – and locked my ankles to the foot of the bed and my arms above me to the bedstead.

Then they walked away and went to the other end of the room where I couldn't see them. Someone changed stations on the radio.

Maybe, I thought, they'd got tired of their perverty game and were going to let me go. I couldn't hear what they were talking about.

But pretty soon Donny came back, all by himself. By then my thing was all dry. I could tell because its skin was no longer cool from evaporation. Donny patted it and said, "Well, you haven't gone sloppy, anyhow."

Now Ray and Gene came over. "You ready to do what we told you?" Gene asked Donny.

"What d'ya think?" Donny pointed to my cock. "It's all yours."

I felt Gene's fingers wrap themselves around it. The contact was dry and sticky and not very sensual. Gene's hand pulled the loose skin up until the tip it enclosed disappeared from sight. "There," he said, grinning up at Ray, "I made a nice little cup for you."

With hard-beating heart, I watched Ray lean over and... again I couldn't look – but, shit, that's just what I should have done, look and look hard so I wouldn't be so hard down there! 'Cause now there was nothing I could use to block out of my mind the feel, first the warmth on the cool skin of my cock, and then, as Gene's hand started to move, that fantastic, mind-destroying slipperiness.

"Oh, Jesus, here we go again!" I moaned.

Ray plugged the stethoscope into his ears and resumed listening to my heartbeat.

Up and down Gene worked his hand, slow, steady, warm, tight and cozy. And now Donny dropped to his knees beside me and grinned at me with his kid-like smile that crinkled all those freckles on his nose and cheeks.

After about twenty slow strokes, Gene looked up and said to the others, "Lube's starting to wear out."

Tom came over and put a hand on Gene's shoulder and asked me, "Is it?"

No way was I going to tell him.

"He's not sayin'," Gene replied.

"How does it feel to you?"

"I'd say go for it."

Tom nodded, bent down over where Gene was working, and – yuk! – the feeling immediately got a hundred percent better again!

This time I looked, really looked. "Chris sake, quit goobering me!" I shouted.

All they did was giggle. And now Donny was on his feet beside me and I could see – from close up, real close up – his fingers fiddling with his belt-buckle, then the buttons on his fly, and the light blue denim springing open to a V, and in there, behind a couple of layers of white Jockey-short cotton, was his cock, sort of folded up against itself, making a bump big as a cheerleader's tit. Donny's face might look like it belonged on the little kid next door with baseball glove and skateboard, but he sure had a man's crotch, with a man's strong smell, and a real man's thing.

Which now came uncoiling itself damply out of his skivvies as they were shoved down by a pair of thumbs. He took hold of it, pointed the blunt, circumcised head down at me. "Chris sake, no!" I shouted. "Not piss!"

But Donny just laughed. "Hadn't thought of that. Maybe I ought to."

"No way," yelped Gene. "My friend's gotta sleep in this bed tonight."

Donny grinned. "Didn't really mean it." He sank slightly to his knees, and as he did I watched his cock's tip lowering, coming closer and closer to my face, targeting my nose and lips. The crazy thing was I couldn't look away; I couldn't turn away. His cock-sweat was rapidly drying off, shedding its strong boy-man scent of everything that was masculine: all the smells you get on your hands when you jerk off, pube and ball-sack odors and – oh, Jesus, this was tearing me up! – the darker, stronger, filthier smells of further back.

The tip of this thing touched down on my upper lip. I'd never thought about what a guy's... penis... would feel like on my face, never wanted to think about it, but I was about to learn. The purple tip was soft to a depth of at least it's first quarter-inch. It's skin was smooth and very smelly. "Dig it?" Donny asked.

"No!" I cried. "It's horrible!"

"I don't think so," said Ray. "He's getting close again."

Gene's fingers came off my cock and I was left gasping on the wrong side of an orgasm I hadn't even realized I was about to have.

It just seemed to go on and on, at first with Donny rubbing his cock over my face, trying it put it between my lips as it firmed from a rubbery hose-like thing to a formidable hammer handle, then with more boys doing the same. Down below, Gene or one of the other boys kept working on my thing, calling for fresh mouth-lube when he decided the old was "wearing out". Every time I thought I could sneak off a cum, Ray would call a halt and they'd leave my cock in limbo, go off and talk about football or something at the other end of the rec room. After a few minutes, they'd come drifting back to the bed where I was spread out helpless and frustrated. A couple of them would bring out their smelly things and start giving my face a multiple penis massage again, and someone would get hold of me down below and re-lube it up and go to work. I'm telling you, the feeling those hands gave as they slid around on the most private part of me, making all those disgusting squidgy noises, was awful, mind-blowing, pure torture.

Tom claimed Donny had the smoothest hands for jerking off – Tom ought to know; he'd probably been onanized by every pervert in the sophomore dorm. Anyhow, Donny was the youngest – and the youngest boy in any crowd has to do what the older guys tell him to do, otherwise he can look for his company somewhere else. So Donny was put back on masturbation duty. Donny may have been the low man on their totem pole, but when his hand started to torture me once again, he was pretty high on mine!

Now Cameron kicked off his cut-offs – that's all he was wearing – and squatted over my face, forcing my nose into his ass-crack, moving his butt back and forth. I couldn't help breathe in the rich, masculine smell of him. It was awful, degrading and the shittiest thing yet they'd done to me, but my thing seemed to have a different opinion of the feel of Cameron's ass cheeks closing in on both of my face cheeks, and the strong, male stink of him went right up my nose and into my brain, and that signal, too, went zig-zagging down to my crotch. Meanwhile, up and down, up and down went Donny's hand, squeaking a little, moving not too fast, just slow and easy, like the two of us had all the time in the world, like we were riding together in perfect harmony – which we sure as hell weren't! – an easy stroke, warm and gentle and teasing.

But time, for me, like my feelings, was actually on end, as Donny and all the rest of them must have known. Inside of me all had gone haywire – grandfather clocks striking crazily off tune, church bells ringing out in the middle of the night, alarm clocks crying their hearts out and bouncing off the bedside table! Time had entered another dimension: it was beat out by my heart in response to that warm, steady stroke on the root of my feelings; it was measured in squirts of testosterone into my veins, great build-ups to cataclysmic comes and sudden stoppages short of fulfillment, Donny saying, "Nice? Do I got the stroke you like the best?"

When Donny was at it, when my face was being smothered in Cameron's ass or his classmates' penises, I could hardly breathe. Against the quiet, distant conversation of the other boys – they were still going on about football, as best I could make out! – I could hear the slippery sounds of Donny's hand sliding on my thing. It was awful. I'd never been so degraded. I never knew such perverts existed – or that I ever would fall into their hands if they did, and that Donny's fingers could do to me what they were doing now. The feelings that breeze brained freshman were giving me were stronger than anything I'd ever got just by doing myself. And each time when Ray cried "Stop" and Donny quit, it was worse than the time before.

"Man, I hardly have to touch it now," Donny said.

"Yup, here he goes again!" said Ray.

Did I ever need my cum! This had been going on much too long. I'd risen at least ten times to an almost-there, but always Ray had spotted it and Donny's hand had let go just at the worst moment.

I decided to try one last time to fool them. Maybe I could sneak a come after all. If I pretended calm and tried to control my heart. If I told all my muscles not to knot up and jerk the way they usually did as the moment of relief approached. If I told my breath to stay even. If my sweat glands behaved themselves. If...

Man, I would give it my best.

Cameron was squatting once again over my face. To my amazement, I found my tongue was sneaking out and roaming around the rim of his asshole. Jesus, I thought, was queering off catching?

"Hey, hey, hey!" said Cameron. "Prude-face here is starting to get with it!"

Well, if licking out that smelly pucker got me up and racing quick enough, who cared? It wouldn't matter if Donny stopped. The momentum would carry me over the top.

"Hold it, kiddo," Ray said. "I think he's on the rise again."

Donny's hand froze. "Are you sure?"

"Not absolutely, but you better let go of that thing to be safe."

Donny let go. I gasped – and raised my head under Cameron's ass just enough to look down. Streamers of the fluids of my agony – theirs and mine – still connected my cock to Donny's fingers like miniature high-tension lines after an ice storm. "Shit!" I shouted. "Fuckin' queer bastards!"

"I guess you were right," Donny said, grinning.

Gene wandered over. "You give him another near miss?" he asked.

"I guess so! And he was trying to trick us."

"Nothing wrong with this guy's equipment," Ray said.

"Or my little brother's technique."

"You better believe it!" Donny told them.

"How'd you get so good?" Cameron teased. "I didn't realize froshers had lived long enough to have gotten in all that much practice."

Donny jabbed his brother with an elbow. "You showed me, remember? Way back when I didn't know nothing from nothing."

Now, if that wasn't the pits! "Typical!" I told them. By now my feelings were back under control. "Teaching a little kid how to pollute himself. And then the two of you bragging about it."

But nobody paid attention to me. "That makes a dozen," Ray said. "Maybe it's time to stop, before we kill the guy."

"It was time to stop before you fuckin' started!" I shouted.

"All we really want is an apology," Cameron told me. "And you admit you like our cocks and asses... and getting masturbated... and you agree you're not going to bother us any more with your big mouth."

"No way!" I shouted. "I hate this. You're degenerates. I'll..."

Cameron sat back down on my face to shut me up – I'd have bit him if there'd been anything there protruding to bite – and said, "He's really asking for it, isn't he? Let's pull out the stops."

And then they were all over me, and I mean all over me. They were licking, wet-lipping, chewing on whatever part of me was handy – my toes, my wrists, my upper arms, the outside and the inside of my thighs, my nipples (and that sent a whole new set of nerves in me jangling and short-circuiting). One kid was actually sucking on one of my armpits. I looked up and saw two hands jerking off two things right above my nose. "God!" I cried, "let me up!"

"So you can get off?" Cameron smirked.

"What I do after I'm free is my own business," I growled. "Or maybe you can tell your little brother to get busy with his hand again."

Cameron chewed his lip for a moment, thinking, then said, "Good idea. That's exactly what we will do."

Donny reached for my dripping thing he'd been handling and slathering for the last hour, but Cameron grabbed his wrists and said, "No. Rub his face off."

"What?" Donny said in surprise.

Amazement, shock, disgust and arousal shot through my body, mingling and fighting with each other. "Oh, no!" I shouted. Because then, just then, the two objects being rumpled on above me let go, sprinkling my face with gobs and globs and drips of white sticky stuff, and Donny's hands folded themselves across my face. Immediately he started rubbing everything in, the spit and pre-cum on his hands, the sperm already there. I thrashed my face from side to side, but Donny's hands went with it. There was no escaping Donny's hands.

It was just the worst thing I'd ever been through – horrible, humiliating, degrading and – God, I had to admit it – unbelievably arousing.

I broke. I started to sob. "Do it! Oh, Jesus, Jesus, Jesus!" I was mumbling and weeping through Donny's fingers. "You gotta do it! Please!"

The hands came off of my face and I found myself staring through sperm gobs hanging in my eyebrows up at Donny and his older brother.

"I'll never ever do that again," I sobbed. "I'll never bad-mouth you guys, not about jerking off, not about nothing else, either. Just get me off, for mercy's sake!"

Smug smiles of satisfaction broke out on all their faces, but I couldn't have cared less right then. All that mattered was that Donny, or any one of the boys, get a hand back on my cock.

"I think he's learned his lesson." Cameron said. "You guys think we can trust that?"

The others just shrugged and looked back at Cameron.

"Anyhow," Ray said, "we gotta quit some time. We can't just leave him hand-cuffed here to the bed with a hard-on, can we?"

Cameron turned to his younger brother and put his hand on the boy's shoulder.

"I get to do it?" Donny said. "I get to make it spurt?"

Cameron smiled. "If you think you're good enough."

"All right!" Donny elbowed a couple of the older boys out of the way and took up his old position. "You ready?" Donny said. Then, without waiting for my reply, he said to his older brother, "Look at that old thing stream! Don't need any of you guys to lube it up this time!" He looked back down at me again and said, "You ready for my magic fingers? You ready to let me let you shoot?"

"Cock-sucker!" I shouted. "Do it! Oh, Jesus, do it!"

Donny brought his hand to my cock. His fingers tightened around it. As before, he started moving it up and down, slowly at first, gliding in the excess pre-cum providing the most wonderful smoothness. Again in me the shudders started, the galvanic spasms which seized all my muscles, from my neck to my stomach to the thighs and calves of my legs. My toes knotted and unknotted. Were they really going to do it? Were they really going to allow me to go over the top? Ray had put his stethoscope away – that was a good sign.

Donny's hand sped up, the grip got tighter. Donny's head was jerking in rhythm with his hand. I could see the tendons in his neck pulsate as it did.

And then – no time to think, now – I was rising, boomeranging out into space – Jesus, they better not stop or I'd tear up the bed and my wrists and ankles as well! – rising, rising – too late, now to stop – if they did I'd just go over the top without them – but Donny had no intention of stopping this time – if anything the grip tightened, the stroke got faster and faster.

And then I shot, the first squirt tangling in my hair, the second decorating my left cheek, the others puddling on my chest.

"Man!" Donny said, full of admiration for the trajectory of my shot, "that was something!"

"Yeah," I said, panting, "it was awful... and revolting... and the last time ever!"

But Cameron wasn't buying. As Gene unlocked the hand-cuffs, Cameron said, "Well, Donny likes you anyhow. You know where we are. Come back after you've thought everything over. Maybe we can dream up some new fun and games."

Like I said, these guys are beyond hope!

TYING KNOTS
Jarred Goodall

"I got a suggestion," Tom said.

"What's that?" I immediately had the feeling that something was up, no pun intended.

"Knot practice." He looked at me shrewdly out of hazel eyes shaded by a tousled shock of brown hair. "Um, actually a kind of exam for us."

"We don't do exams," I said.

"Oh, this'll be different. We'll tie you up. Then you try and see if you can get out of our knots, and if you can't we'll all know you've taught us perfect."

He smiled, the north woods sun sparkling on his teeth and lips. How many times, especially during the past week of our canoeing and camping trip, had I made love to my hand imagining my tough, slender leader-boy wrapped around my body, those brilliant white teeth nibbling on my neck, ears...and down below!

"Taught us well," I couldn't help correcting him.

"Whatever," he shrugged.

I thought about his proposal for a minute. I'd always tried to make woodcraft fun, but to most youngsters, tying knots can get pretty boring, no matter how badly they want to become competent woodsmen. Maybe if they had a hot body to work on they would go at it with more enthusiasm. It would also pass the time until supper: it would be an hour before someone was going to have to start the cooking.

So I agreed. "All right. Good idea, Tom. We'll do it right here...." – meaning the canvas cot I was sitting on.

Tom called the other boys over. "He's agreed," Tom told them. "Stormy, go get the ropes."

Stormy was a happy-go-lucky blue-eyed, wide-faced blond farm boy – not tall but growing beautiful shoulder muscles and a well set-up chest.

I lay back and stared at the tops of the pine trees and the August blue sky. My young companions crowded around me, pushing each other with their elbows. There's nothing like being in the great out-of-doors, away from town or city life, to break down the inhibitions young men normally have against touching each other. When my crew wasn't play-wrestling they were poking, shoving each other, draping arms around one another's shoulders.

All eight of the boys on our little canoeing expedition, without being glamorous or anything, turned me sexually on. I couldn't, I reasoned, do anything outright, but there was no harm in looking. And listening. And smelling!

Day by day, as they left behind their city ways, grew absorbed in activities which required all their young energies, they had become more physically appealing. Their skin had darkened, their faces dirtied, their hair tousled. All of us wore less and less clothing. The boys went around just in their swim trunks or old pants cut off well above the knees, until the coolness of evening chased them into their jackets.

At the moment, I, like the boys, was barefoot, and the only clothing I had on was a pair of corduroy cutoffs.

Tom thoughtfully put a pillow under my head. Stormy came back with the ropes, and they started tying me down: first my ankles, then my wrists, then ropes about my chest and across my lower legs – sailors' knots, woodsmen's knots: running bowlines, bowlines with a bright, cat's paws, clinches, sheepshanks, slip knots, square knots, in a few places a couple of carelessly thrown half-hitches. How wonderful it was to feel their hands working, even if somewhat brutally, over my body; how delightfully my nostrils twitched to the pleasant aroma of eight proximate, sweaty youths!

"Does anything hurt?" Tom asked.

"No," I admitted.

"Now, see if you can get loose."

I tried – first my wrists, then my legs. "No," I said, "you got me."

"Come on, you can do better than that!"

I gave it another try and was satisfied that all but a few of the knots were going to hold.

"I'm afraid I'm helpless," I said.

"Good!" Was that a mischievous glint in Tom's eye?

"Maybe my right ankle... I might be able to work it loose in time."

"Yeah, okay." One of the boys loosened and then re-knotted the rope more carefully. "Now, how's it feel?"

"Like I'd never get away till the snow flies."

Tom smiled. "That's the way it ought to be."

The afternoon was warm, insects absent, I was the center of the boys' attention. I couldn't say I was uncomfortable, but I became more and more sure that the boys had been plotting. When you are a youth leader you develop a sixth sense about such things.

After what I thought was a decent interval for them to admire their handiwork, I said, "Okay, if this had been a test, you'd all have passed. I'm helpless."

"Um, this is sort of a test," Tom said.

"Good. Have it your own way. Now let me up."

"You know, sir," Tom said, "we were talking about staying up here a few days longer?"

"You were talking about staying up here longer, not me."

"Will you lose your job if you're a week late?" Tom asked.

"Maybe."

"Come on. Your boss needs you more than you need him."

A nice compliment, and perhaps true. But, "I wouldn't want to test that proposition."

"Mr. Carter," said Bob, Tom's tent mate and closest friend, "you're a man of your word, aren't you?"

"Of course I am..."

"So if you say we can stay you won't go back on it?"

"Naturally not, but..."

"So... can we?"

"No."

"And that's final?" Tom asked.

"Yup. I think you better untie me, before this gets un-nice."

"Uh, we will... eventually."

The boys went into a huddle and whispered for a half minute or so. When they came back they all had suspicious grins on their faces. "Mr. Carter," Tom started, "you know you were worried about things getting un-nice? Well, they won't. In fact, pretty soon they're not going to be un-nice at all."

What, I wondered, was going on in his head?

Bobby hung a chin over Tom's shoulder and agreed, "Not for you, anyhow."

"So, let me up."

Tom ignored me. "Stormy, come here."

Stormy moved over and stood in front of Tom. "Breath check."

"What's Stormy's breath got to do with untying these ropes?" I asked.

They still ignored me. Stormy raised his chin and, opening his mouth, exhaled upwards into Tom's face.

"Now Bob."

Stormy repeated the operation, breathing into Bob's face. Tom and Bob exchanged a look, and Tom told Stormy, "Okay, fine, you do it first."

Stormy turned around and squatted beside my shoulder, his face looming large above me. I could see drops of sweat on his forehead. Velutinous down swirled softly over his cheeks – some young men don't have to shave until well after they've fathered their first child. Stormy's body and his breath gave off a lovely sweet-sweaty scent.

"Stormy, what do you want?" I asked him.

"Huh?" Stormy turned around and looked questioningly up at Tom rather than me.

"Go ahead," said Tom.

"Yeah, get started," said Bobby.

Stormy looked back at me and shrugged, almost apologetically, I thought. Then he bent down and started running his lips over my face.

"What the hell!" I shouted. I was so surprised I wasn't even aware for a moment or two of the sudden charge of sex that surged through my stomach and took root immediately under my cut-offs.

Stormy's lips were very wet, and they spread his scented wetness all over my cheeks and nose and lips, his tongue even pushing a bit of bubbly/crinkly spittle up each of my nostrils. Like a cat, he was putting his scent on my face, making it his territory. And all I could do was lie there and shudder and gasp.

"See what I mean?" Tom said. "That wasn't un-nice at all, was it?"

"Get him off of me!" I pleaded.

"Not a chance. Go ahead, Stormy, work your way down a bit."

Stormy's hands came to my face and began caressing it, sliding in that remnant wetness.

Now, the sweaty palms of a guy's hand can take on a lovely sweet scent redolent of honey, clover blossoms, lips, teeth and penis skin. One time, as a teenager, I'd had to ride squatting on the floor of a station wagon, backing up into the crotch of an attractive older boy who, for some reason I've long forgotten, clamped his hands over my face, and it seemed that in the scent I inhaled was all the essence, aura, physicality of the older boy. I'd sprung an immediate hard-on and for weeks masturbated to the memory of that casual caress which, on the part of the other, was probably not erotically intended in the least.

Not so with what Stormy was doing to me now. Forced to breathe through my nose, I got the full impact of the odor of the boy's not very clean but very busy hands.

Meanwhile, his lips were working their way down my neck, across my clavicle, to one nipple, on to the other. And then, to my horror, I felt someone fiddling at my crotch. My zipper tab was being lowered, my shorts slid down. And – my God! – my penis was bared; I knew, I just knew, it was quickly firming to rigid attention in the full sight of my troop.

These kids were definitely on to me. But how? What had I done?

Stormy's hands, still clamped over the lower part of my face, moved an inch or two down, uncovering my eyes. His cute farmer-boy's grin swam into my vision.

"That feel nice?" he asked ingeniously.

I couldn't have answered, even if my mouth hadn't been covered, but I saw, couldn't help seeing, that there was no anger or contempt in his blue eyes. He was watching me closely, gauging my reactions, as were Tom and the other boys crowding around me.

Now Tom pulled Stormy away from me and pushed Mike down in his place. Mike was a fairly average-sized youngster, with rather thick medium-brown hair and intelligent grey eyes. There was always a kind of sweet odor about him, no matter how sweaty and grubby he got portaging or paddling his canoe against a hard wind. He was wearing nothing but a pair of undershorts, standard attire for him since he'd split out of his trunks a couple of days ago.

"Do I gotta do the same thing?" Mike asked Tom.

"Sure. What's the big deal?"

"Well... maybe you'd better explain everything to Mr. Carter."

"And it'd better be a good explanation!" I just managed to croak out.

As Mike began to mouth my face as Stormy had done, Tom said, "Remember, Mr. Carter, when I came to your house to talk about arrangements for our trip, oh, maybe a month ago?"

"Yes."

"Well, you'd been working at your computer and when you went out to the garage to pack up the cots I started going through your directory and found a file called `Camping'. I figured it had something to do with this trip so I brought it up on the screen...."

"Oh, my God!" I moaned.

"...and it was, like, a jerk-off story you'd made up..."

"Jesus fucking Christ!"

"...starring us."

What he said was all too true. I'd had a big fantasy-writing and masturbatory fling – the most recent of many. I should have archived all those files onto well-hidden diskettes and deleted them from the hard disk, but of course I hadn't, forgetting that young Tom was a computer fanatic. There were more erotic files there, and, unlike `Camping', most of them played heavily upon something I thanked my lucky stars Tom hadn't learned about – my Special Thing.

"Oh, man, this is the pits!" I whispered.

"Aw, don't sweat it, Mr. Carter," Tom said kindly. "Now, are we going to stay up here next week?"

"No. I told you no."

"Okay." Tom shrugged. "Billy, you're next."

Billy was a dark-haired, narrow-faced boy whom I'd only in the last month or so begun to dream about erotically. He positioned his mouth above mine, lowered his lips and began to kiss me in the most knowing way.

This was incredible. Boys just didn't kiss men, or other youths, I'd always believed. Maybe a few would allow themselves to be impersonally jerked off by a buddy, or even sucked off by a prosperous man in exchange for favors or money, but Billy was actually giving me a wet-lipped, erotic kiss, sucking on my upper lip, nibbling on it with those incredibly even, white teeth I'd recently come to admire so much. He could only have learned that from personal experience!

"You'll get a chance, Mr. Carter," Tom was saying, "to test all of us – like, am I better or is Stormy or Billy better?"

"Let me up and I might tell you," I mumbled through Billy's slippery lips.

Now big, dark Andy elbowed Billy out of the way. Once again I was staring upwards at a familiar boy, feeling his soft, moist lips melt themselves into mine.

This was all turning out so differently than I had expected! Of course, you can dream of getting it on with the objects of your lust, but you're always absolutely certain that at best they would cut you short if they discovered how attractive you found them. But here were eight boys I'd been dreaming about for months kissing my lips, breathing their sweet breath into my face, caressing me with their young, wilderness-horny hands, and it was all almost routine; it was, to them, completely okay! My horror at being found out began to fade – and made room for an even stronger arousal.

When Andy was finally through, Tom hunkered down beside my right shoulder. "How about our proposition now, Mr. Carter?"

I shook my head. "I don't accept that there was a proposition. All I heard was a demand."

"Oh, we'll give a little."

"Like?"

"We'll let you up."

"You've got to do that anyhow."

"Eventually, sure, when we've got what we want."

"No."

"This is just the beginning, Mr. Carter. There's more we can do."

I knew there was, if he had read enough of that 'Camping' file. But... if you're going to be raped, best lie back and enjoy it. That was what I intended to do.

"Stormy, come here again."

When the blond boy presented himself, Tom, without asking permission, started unbuttoning the boy's fly, shoving down the cut-offs and revealing his pendulous masculinity which hung from a luxuriant bush of curly blond hair. With a hand on his bare ass, Tom urged him over to my cot, until he was standing over my face, looking down, and I was staring at the lavender tip of his cock – and smelling it, too, for it was only inches above my nose.

Stormy handed it and, bending his knees slightly, brought it down until the whole rubbery shaft was lying horizontally across my lips.

Now I could really smell it. Stormy hadn't swam in the lake that day, but had made a strenuous hike to the top of Mt. MacIver with two of the other boys and recently returned, sweaty and pungent. His cock smelled of that sweat, the musky, nearly cheesy stink of young penis skin, of ball-sweat, the scent of ass-crack.

And then, to my surprise, and strangely accelerating my lust, he dropped a long string of spittle onto it (some of the spit plopping down onto my nose), and began to slide his cock back and forth over my lips. I could feel the gristle of that cock rapidly hardening up.

This was glorious, this was frustrating, this was torture! All the boys now took turns rubbing their penises over my face, sometimes two or three at a time. My vision was completely restricted to their rubbery and sometimes fully erect cocks moving like snakes above me, to ripe ball-sacs, and, way above, the faces of boys I'd thought I knew, every so often dropping strings of youth's masturbatory lubricant of necessity.

And so it went for the next half hour, while my straining cock reached for the sky and dripped and dripped and dripped, with no one deigning to touch it. But that was just the point, wasn't it? It was getting harder and harder to keep on the anticipatory side of orgasm and my sanity at the same time.

In the erotic contest we were engaged in, all that the boys had on their side was their attractiveness and youth. They had evidently never heard of psychic orgasms. They'd obviously always got sperm by playing with themselves. Their repertory of sex was perhaps rather limited.

Two cocks were sliding over my lips. I let one in, sucked on the warm, loose skin, and then, without even having to work for its relief I found myself smoothly, magically rising toward orgasm, in ecstasy and agony. With a hoarse moan I shot what they later told me was one solid arc of sperm over my head and jetted out five or six others that spilled onto my chest, decorating even the trunks of one of the boys who was standing too close.

I came back down to earth. The boys were looking at me with new respect, and I began to laugh. There was nothing, it seemed, like an ejaculation with real trajectory to impress young males!

"I win, you lose," I said. "No extra week. And, by the way, you kids gave me a great time."

"Aw shit!" Tom said.

"You going to let me up?"

"Yeah, sure."

A dozen hands loosened the knots. When they'd finished I sat up, kicked off my cut-offs and skivs and said, "I don't know about you guys, but I'm going to take a swim."

I ran off and dived into the lake, followed by a somewhat subdued bunch of trainee canoers.

After supper, Tom took me aside and said, "Uh, Mr. Carter, can we negotiate?"

"What about – now?"

"If we stayed on up here, we could give you the sexiest week you've ever had in your whole life. Any one or all of us any time you wanted."

"Come on, Tom," I said, "making out is a two-way street." "How do you mean?"

"Well, once in a while getting a going-over like you kids gave me this afternoon is exciting, but sex really has to be enjoyed by both parties."

"So?" Tom was staring boldly and seriously into my eyes.

"You guys like girls. I know you like girls. I've heard you talking about them."

"Doesn't mean we don't fool around, or want to fool around."

"With each other, I can understand that. But with an old man like me...?"

Tom smiled. "You're in pretty good shape for an old man. Not many of us can shoot a jiz-stringer like you did."

"That's because you don't leave your things alone."

"No point in holding out when you don't have to. Anyhow, how about it?"

"No."

"Come on, Mr. Carter, that just doesn't make sense. In those stories you were doing everything with us – me, Stormy, Billy, Bob, Andy. And then, there's your – what'd you call it? – your Special Thing."

"What!!!"

"In the other story."

247

My knees started to feel weak. "What other story?"

"The one called something like 'By the Waters of Babylon'. After I read the 'Camping' file I started looking around for more like it, and that Babylon thing was a bit more explicit, wasn't it?"

"Jesus, you sure don't respect a man's privacy."

A confident grin. "I thought maybe you'd like to have all of us know..."

"Well, you were wrong, and I don't."

"...seeing as how we were all going to be up here in the woods together and letting everything hang out – except you made no move and we had to bring things to a head, didn't we? And, on your Special Thing, all us guys talked it over, and, well, we're willing."

"You are?"

"Okay, okay, it'd be nothing in itself for us, but it's your thing, no problem. Here's our deal. We stay up an extra week. Each night you take one of us to sleep with and zip together the sleeping bags into a double, like us guys do half the time. And sometimes, when you're in the mood, we'll do the... you know."

"You're talking for all the seven other boys?"

Tom nodded.

"You can't possibly know how they feel."

"Do we have to tie you up again to convince you?"

"No, I..."

"Guys, come here," Tom shouted to the others. "I think Mr. Carter is weakening. It's Special Thing time!"

The boys closed around me. Hands reached for my T-shirt and pulled it up over my head; others slid down the zipper of my fly. I found myself being lowered to the cot, gently, politely, now looking up at their shadowed, fire-flickered faces silhouetted against the deep blue evening sky just beginning to be pricked with stars.

I felt my resolve weakening. Eight days and eight nights, each with a different boy, and, every so often...

"Guys, let's get started," Tom said. The boys gathered around me in a tight circle. Now in the flickering firelight I was looking at eight cocks pointing at me like the guns of a firing squad.

They all seemed to let go at once – hard streams of yellow piss, some arching a little, all splattering down on my chest, my neck and – oh my God, my face! – with a wet, warm, noisy clatter. I closed my eyes, had to close them because one of the boys was playing his stream on my nose. I groaned and bubbled with my breathing, felt foam at my lips as warm boy-pee trickled into my mouth, salty and bitter and stinking.

I'd never felt anything like this in my whole life. It was harsher, more thrilling than I'd ever dared dream.

"Okay!" I yelled, spluttering from my lips a shower of urine drops which, flying away from my face, sparkled bright orange in the firelight.

"Hurray!" the boys cheered.

With one mind, they all turned their streams upon my cock. It was as if a fire-hose was played upon it, a sweet-but-harsh vibration which I prayed wouldn't cease, wouldn't ever cease (but knew it would have to). Yet I was faster than their endurance, for in seconds I was reaching for the sky, the stars, dripping, spluttering, exploding my sperm far beyond the little island where we were camped, far into the Milky Way and, who knows, maybe beyond.

SWIMMERS' MEAT
Sean Michael O'Day

Mr. Bradshaw, our swimming coach, who looked like pictures I'd seen in my history books of Attila the Hun, called us into his office a couple of days before a big meet with our arch rival, Northeast High, and gave us a good dressing-down. We weren't performing and we knew it. My buddy Kyle looked like a lazy tortoise sliding into the pool rather than a high diver, and both Brad and I looked like sluggish snails rather than competitive swimmers. Our excuse was that final exams and graduation were looming, and our minds were on millions of things besides swimming.

"Is that right?" the coach barked, before going into a long tirade.

The three of us stood in front of his desk with our hands behind our backs, looking down sheepishly at the floor.

Finally Mr. Bradshaw said: "Oh, and one more thing. Since you wimps can't improve through practice, why don't you try shaving. It might psych you up. And if it doesn't, you'll at least look like the babies you are."

Wimps? Babies? Well, Brad certainly wasn't a wimp; he was one of the toughest guys I'd ever met. And I sure didn't consider myself a wimp. Kyle . . . well, maybe he was a little wimpy, but he was still a good buddy, and on his better days, Kyle could dive like a porpoise.

Sulking, we stamped out of the office and down the corridor, not saying anything to one another until the front doors flung open, and I yelled: "Shaving! Hell, I shave almost every morning!"

"No, no, no, dummy," Brad said, shaking his head. "He didn't mean shaving your face; he meant your legs. I once heard that shaving makes your body glide faster, and propels it more smoothly through the water."

"Bull!" I said. "Besides, that's the sickest goddamned idea I've ever heard. I'd look like a plucked chicken."

"Naw, you wouldn't," piped up Kyle. "I heard that once, too. Shaving's supposed to get a person psyched up."

Kyle, Brad and I had been buddies since grade school, but I sure as hell knew that they didn't shave their bodies. We never even talked about it before, and now, it sounded like a downright goofy idea to me. I did know for a fact that Kyle, a redhead, was covered with soft, fine, downy hair, which thickens on his legs. And Brad was the most hirsute guy I've ever seen: hairy chest, hairy belly, hairy legs, hairy balls. He's even got hair growing out of his bellybutton and all over his buns.

I knew this because I had taken some real good looks at Kyle and Brad in the school showers (and I noticed them eyeballing me a couple of times, too), but apart from the usual pranks – hiding their soap or towels, or playing touch-tag in jockstraps, comparing sizes and talking dirty, we never seriously messed around with one another.

That's why the more I thought about body shaving, the more I liked the idea. Maybe, I decided, it would lead to other things.

"How would I do it?" I asked. "I can't shave my neck without nicking myself, yet the coach expects me to shave my entire body without slashing myself to ribbons? Hell, I couldn't do it!" I tried acting coy as the devil, but my dick was already thumping around in my jockstrap, leaking precum.

"For chris sakes," Brad said, "you wouldn't shave yourself. You'd get somebody to do it for you."

"Oh, I get it!" I said, feigning both repulsion and total stupidity. "If you think I'm gonna ask my mom or dad to shave my whole body, you're fuckin' nuts!" I glanced at Brad and Kyle to see if they were crawling into my web.

"Well," Kyle said very softly, "we could shave one another."

"The hell we could!" I said, pleased with the success of my plan. "I'd feel like a goddamned Munich!"

"Not Munich," Kyle corrected. "It's eunuch. But I don't think you would; I think you'd enjoy it."

"Within a day or two, our hair would start growing back," Brad said, coaxing me. "C'mon, let's try it."

"I'm not sure . . ." I said, noticing that the bulge in Brad's crotch was straining the fabric of his tight Levis. "I guess I'm willin' to do it, if it would help us win the big meet."

Kyle smiled primly and said: "Since Friday's a free day, and both my parents will be at work, want to come over to my house about noon?"

"Just two conditions," Brad demanded. "If anybody asks some dumb-ass questions, we gotta swear to each other that we'll blame the coach. We'll say he told us to do it. And second, we gotta swear that each of us shaved in the total and absolute privacy of our own individual bathrooms."

Our handshakes sealed the plan.

I arrived a bit early, around 11:45 a.m., and Kyle and I were lounging in his parents' living room, watching MTV, when the front door swung open and Brad walked in carrying a gym bag.

The three of us went trooping down the hallway beside the kitchen to Kyle's bedroom and bath, located at the far end of the house from his parents' bedroom. Tossing his gym bag on Kyle's bed, Brad said, "I stopped at Mr. Top Dollar." Without naming his purchases, he pulled out three cans of shaving cream, brand new safety-razors, his own electric razor, and an attachment for shaving our heads.

I can't even remember all the times we stood together nude under the water jets in the school shower, but there were always dozens of other guys running around nude, and we generally had to rush back to home room before the bell rang. But today was different. Our sole purpose was to psych each other up, to see one another naked, to touch our bodies, shave our hair, experience our nudity. Hell, it was almost like a ritual. And I loved it!

Suddenly my heart was pounding, my brain pulsing with excitement.

"Should we take our shirts off?" Kyle asked in some half-assed geeky voice, shy and shaky, "and shave the pectoralis major first?"

"Aw, hell," Brad said, "strip completely so that we can enjoy ourselves. Don't you ever sit around nude, watching porno videos and jacking off?"

"Here!" Kyle said, dumbfounded, glancing toward his wide-screen TV.

Tired of words, I pulled off my muscle shirt and unbuttoned my 501s. Looking at Kyle and Brad, I laughed, for I really wanted to turn them on, make them hot. I stretched my shoulders and swiveled my hips, pretending to be a bodybuilder in competition, and then I shoved my jeans down over my hairy hips till my cock and balls plopped out of my pants. After kicking my Reebok Runners into a corner, I did a little dance, still laughing, trying to arouse them. Apparently, it was working.

Brad and Kyle slowly began shucking their clothes, theatrically and enticingly, imitating what I had done, till they stood nude, staring at me.

I found myself looking at Brad and Kyle in a new way, and they responded by giving my cock and balls a long, hungry look. I felt my dick growing, snaking out long and fat. When I slid my hand under my balls to massage them, Brad said, "For chris sake, Butch, I get horny just watching you." I got excited, because he had never said anything like that before.

Brad straddled his legs wide, brash and rugged, with his hands on his hips. Of the three of us, he had the most hair, raven-black that glistened midnight-blue in sunlight. His face always carried a five o'clock shadow, his beard grew so fast, and the thick mat of hair covering his chest and stomach reminded you of a tough, brawny construction worker.

I always enjoyed sitting in class beside Brad, because his pants legs would creep up and his swarthy, hairy legs would show above his socks. Often during class, when I'd glance over at him, his hand would be moving back and forth like the slow, steady pendulum of a grandfather clock, his palm stroking his crotch.

Once in biology class during a movie about cells and chromosomes, I looked over and he had his fly open, tugging gently on the end of his dick. I got so turned on watching him that I shot a load in my Levis without even touching my prong.

Kyle had a sparse patch of downy fur in the middle of his chest, but much more on his legs. His hands and fingers are something else! Once during an assembly in the auditorium, Kyle sat beside me and I began to dream that he had let his hand slip over into my lap, rubbing his long, slender fingers along my dong, feeling its outline, helping it grow. By the time the assembly was over, I leaked out a load right inside my pants. Kyle just laughed.

Today, for several moments we stood looking at one another in Kyle's bedroom, hands planted on our hips, watching as our cocks squirmed, bobbed, wiggled and grew, without our touching them. Brad's stocky balls dangled in his humpy sac like two giant goose eggs hanging between his swarthy legs. His basket was always so big in his Speedos I never got tired of watching him during practice.

"Somebody has to go first," I said, interrupting our lusty gaping at each other. "Might as well be me."

I extended my bare arms, urging Kyle and Brad to start shaving me.

"How about armpits?" Brad asked, shoving his face into the sweaty hair under my arms, licking the tiny beads of fresh musk. "Jeez," he said, "this smells good!"

"Let me do that," Kyle said.

While Brad slid his electric razor up and down my arms, its motor buzzing faintly throughout the room, Kyle snipped away under my armpits with scissors, not removing all the hair, but trimming it severely. Having four hands fondle my arms sent me spinning into a whirlwind of pleasure.

I glanced at the rain of hair drifting to the bathroom floor, and then rubbed my fingers over my shaved arms. My forearms had never felt so smooth, nor my armpits so sexy.

Within minutes, Kyle was extending his arms, and then Brad. Shaving the downy, reddish-blond hair from Kyle's arms, and the thick, jet-black hair from Brad's was causing my cock to twitch uncontrollably. Just thinking of how Kyle and Brad's hands had felt running over my body sent my dick jerking upward.

I checked out my pecker. Although it wasn't yet rock hard, it would have been a chore to try and shove it into a swimmer's jock. It stuck out seven inches from my pubic hair, curving upwards like a saber, arching to get nudged into a wet mouth or a warm asshole. But I reminded myself that wasn't what we were here for. At least, not yet!

"Butch is hairy," Kyle said, examining my nude body from stem to stern. "Almost as hairy as you, Brad."

Kyle had this butthole-knack of making every one of his goddamned statements sound like a judge's decree.

Answering Kyle, while glancing sideways with admiration at Brad, I said: "Brad's ass is hairier than mine. Besides, my butt is as smooth as two ripe melons; his are like furry coconuts."

Brad laughed. Kyle winced and pursed his lips like an offended spinster. They studied me, slowly circling my body, rubbing their sweaty palms over my hairy chest, then sliding their warm fingers to my furry legs. Brad dropped to his knees to examine the jungle bush that grew at the base of my banana.

Feeling Brad's hot breath hovering around my balls vaulted my dong out another inch or two, so that now it was arching upward about nine inches. Kyle, too, had dropped to his knees and was fingering my pubic hair, plucking the strands like violin strings, saying: "Should we use a straight razor here, or an electric?"

Sliding his fingers back and forth through my dense jungle thatch, Brad said: "Use your scissors to cut off the bush, then I'll use the safety razor to trim away the stubble."

"Now that you've planned your work, when will you start?" I asked, getting hornier by the minute. I wanted to feel their hands on my chest, shaving me, working their way down to my balls. Their talking, their fingers slithering around my cock, their playing with my balls brought my dong to a full raging hard-on. I had never seen my all-day sucker thump so big, straining at ten inches, thick as Kyle's smooth wrist, brawny as Brad's biceps, purple veins throbbing.

"Let's go," Brad ordered, briskly shaking his can of shaving cream, its contents billowing out into his hands like thick, frothy clouds. While Brad's palms filled with white lather, Kyle's fingers washed my chest. He seemed to relish the task. Feeling his slender fingers slide a hot, wet cloth across my pecs, my belly, my groin brought a surge of passion to my balls that tingled my entire spine.

Because I use an electric razor on my face, I was unprepared for the exotic sensation of Brad smearing soapy lather all over my chest and belly, clear down to my balls. He rubbed it in deep, causing my stomach muscles to ripple, while he pinched my tits, then reached for the razor to shave me clean.

With the care of nurses, the precision of surgeons, they set about their task. My body suddenly felt light, weightless, cool, as the metal razor slid across my chest. I had difficulty keeping my balance, so great was my pleasure. Finally, to prevent myself from falling, I leaned beside the sink, against the dressing table.

I glanced down at my cock, where a long thread of pre-cum was swinging lazily between my legs. Brad's cock, too, was leaking oily strands of gooey drops; our lube juice swung slowly, idly attaching to each other's hairy legs.

While Brad continued shaving my chest, I closed my eyes and moaned. Suddenly I felt Kyle's slender fingers gently probing my buns apart, and then I felt his wet, warm tongue exploring my raspberry. My body tensed, my cock twitched, my butt pushed backward, coaxing more of his tongue up my ass, and my chest arched outward as Brad spanked my dong against his hairy leg.

Brad was about to rinse the razor, heavy with clusters of thick hair, under the faucet in the sink, but Kyle called out: "That'll clog the drain! Wipe it on paper towels."

When Kyle leaned over to begin rubbing the wet washcloth over my chest, the icy-warmth of my shaved chest sent shivers from the base to the tip of my dong. I reached down and swapped my fist around Kyle's slender, long dick. Rubbing my palm against his oozing precum, I leaned forward to tongue my way between his moist lips. Much to my surprise, Kyle started French-kissing me with fiery passion. The judge was mellowing!

I arched my chest forward till my tits jutted into his pecs, and I slid my palms over his shoulders, his back, his buns. He released his grasp, stepping away.

Smooth as satin, pink as sunrise, my pecs were warm from the shaving; but below my pecs, a dark mat of hair remained. The contrast psyched me up; rising low through my balls, surging through my cock like an electric current were orders to proceed, full-speed ahead. My dong looped up, bobbing and twitching, like a foot-long sausage, thick as a beef log, ready to get chomped on, primed to plug any hole that Kyle or Brad wanted to shove at me.

"Hey, guys," I said, "go easy! I can't take any more of your shaving without coming. What say we stop for a jerk-off break! How about a suck or a fuck! Please, Kyle! Brad, give me some head, huh? I need it before my whacker clogs up and splits apart!"

Brad laughed hoarsely, saying: "Man, you're just getting psyched-up, that's all. And that's why we're here. You wanna win that swim meet, don't ya?"

"Win it?" Kyle purred. "After this, who gives a shit?"

And that from the mouth of our mild-mannered Kyle!

"If you're psyched-up now," said Brad, "wait till you take a razor to me and Kyle."

Kyle was already wetting Brad's chest with a sopping-wet cloth, and so I shook a can of lather and dispensed it directly onto Brad's hairy chest, my hands smearing the foamy cream over his muscular pecs, my fingers feeling his nipples sticking out, begging to be bitten. Soaring high as an eagle in ecstatic pleasure, I continued spreading the soapy lather over his belly, his balls, his cock, and between his legs up under his asshole.

"The idea," said Kyle, "is to shave him, not drown him."

My chest heaving, I grabbed for the razor. Carefully, nervously, I touched the blade to Brad's skin, sliding it over his upper chest, down, past his nipple, watching a clear path of smooth skin appear. I worked the razor like a doctor, holding his swarthy belly with one hand, shaving around his tits with the other, until his rounded pecs glistened with the flushed smoothness of a baby's skin.

Brad began moaning, grunting with husky roars, writhing his brawny shoulders, flexing his thick biceps. "Suck my cock, Butch," he whispered. Then more loudly, "Forget the shaving and whack my cock in your mouth. Go on," he demanded. "I want my piss pole shoved down your horny cock suckin' throat!" He grabbed me by the waist, I pushed him away. "I'm gonna cum!" he hollered.

"You shit!" I barked back. "You made me wait when I was hot; now you can wait. Shaving's just getting you psyched-up."

Brad's body shook with convulsions of pleasure; his eyes closed and he threw his head back, trying to suppress his climax. But he couldn't do it. A torrent of cum splashed out of his cock – even though he wasn't touching it. The thick load of hot cream sprayed all over my chest.

"I told you I couldn't hold it back any longer!" Another load of spunk hit Kyle's belly.

"Okay! Okay!" I demanded. "That's enough. We've got work to do. Let's finish our shaving before we start playing."

After a brief pause, Kyle and Brad settled down. I couldn't wait to get my razor back on Brad's hairy body.

When Kyle and I slid our razors over Brad's hairy belly, shaving him clean, watching his body squirm and his cock pound, I realized that shaving hair off my buddies was creating a bond that we had ever before experienced. Maybe that half-assed coach was on the right track after all.

While shearing Brad's belly-thatch, I noticed Kyle drop to his knees to slurp Brad's piston between his lips. Too delectable for Kyle to resist, Brad's fat mushroom disappeared into Kyle's mouth.

"Take it out, you horny cocksucker," I ordered Kyle. "When we're finished shaving, we'll mess around. Not before!" I jerked Kyle away from Brad, brought him to his feet and slapped his ass.

For the next fifteen minutes we worked in silence, but once the three of us were smooth from the waist up, we took a shave-break, staring at one another lewdly, admiring ourselves. Our bodies, from the waist up, glistened with sweat. As we looked each other over, our chests heaved with excitement. The lusty energy that passed between us had made our dongs fill out fire hose-thick. I had already dropped a load of cum on the floor while I was shaving Kyle's stomach. And as I watched, Brad arched his back, his hands on his hips, his pelvis thrust out, his monster cock spurting a shower of cream on the floor.

"For Chris sakes," I said, "don't waste it; we can milk each other after we've shaved."

Brad groaned then said, "The way I feel now, I could shoot my wad the rest of the day." His throbbing cock hadn't shriveled an inch.

"I decided that I don't want all my cock hair shaved," said Kyle, unexpectedly, almost apologetically. "I'd be embarrassed to be seen in the showers at school."

"But we agreed!" yelled Brad.

When Kyle turned to me for support, I shrugged and said, "Brad's right. We agreed to shave one another."

"And that includes cock hair," Brad said. "All of it."

"No, please," Kyle whimpered. "Not today. Some other time, maybe. Guys at school would know . . . they'd know that we were messing around with each other."

"Messing around," Brad murmured, "you should've thought of that yesterday, you little coward!" He reached for a wet washcloth and suddenly lunged behind Kyle, grabbing his arms from the rear and locking him into an iron grip. Kyle couldn't escape, Brad's strength overpowered him. After sloshing water on Kyle's crotch, Brad squirted mounds of shaving lather over Kyle's thatch, spreading it roughly, massaging it into his groin.

"Go on, dammit," Brad ordered me. "Shave it off! All of it!"

Kyle's cock hair was dripping with water and lather when I touched the razor to his groin. His whimpering turned to tears. Brad struggled to restrain Kyle's thrashing, but Kyle flailed his legs so savagely that I was afraid of getting kicked, and even of accidentally cutting him, so I stood back and let Brad handle it.

Brad swung one arm around Kyle's chest, clamping them together, restraining him so forcefully that only Kyle's legs were jiggling; with his free arm, Brad began whipping Kyle's butt with his bare palm.

Each thwack resounded in the bathroom; I winced each time Brad walloped Kyle's ass, for Kyle let out a shrill howl. By the time Brad had smacked Kyle's buns seven times, Kyle had been subdued. His thrashing had stopped, his flailing arms had quieted, his butt had turned apple-red, and he was reduced to immobility, sobbing.

Hearing his cry only intensified my desire to shave him; it also produced a thrill of pleasure along the length of my pulsing cock, causing a load of cum to well up and splatter onto. Kyle's belly. Trying to soothe Kyle, I rubbed my rock-hard dick against his belly, sliding my dong back and forth in my hot jism.

"Let's get back to work," Brad murmured, nodding for me to shave Kyle's cock hair.

Slowly, gently, I began shaving the reddish-blond hair from around Kyle's piston. Although he still whimpered softly, his throbbing cock continued growing; it was coiling out longer and harder, thicker and heavier; its silky smooth skin sliding out into a raging hard-on like I had never seen on Kyle. Coaxing him, reassuring him, I dropped my hand holding the razor, and let my lips circle the end of his arrowhead wang. Brad was now petting Kyle's shoulders, kissing his ears, licking his neck, rubbing his cheeks against Kyle's head.

Kyle's whimpering had turned to groans of pleasure and he was thrusting his hips forward so that his beef log was worming deep down my throat, nearly gagging me as it slid down the narrow tunnel. Kyle's moans were deep, sexual, mature; his fingers were gratefully stroking me and Brad. With my free hand, I reached between Brad and Kyle's legs and found Brad's piss pole, grabbed hold of it and dusted Kyle's virgin shit chute with Brad's fat, sweating mushroom head. Kyle let out a yelp of pleasure the moment Brad's pole touched his crack, begging, "Don't stop! Shove your shaft clear up my ass, Brad!"

Brad had his cannon in position, aimed to shoot a monster load up Kyle's virgin tube. Now, I thought, was the time.

"Knock it off," I ordered. "Let's get back to work, shaving our bodies. That's what we're here for, right? Playtime can wait." I figured I'd pull the same trick they had played on me back when my balls had been about to explode.

"Give us a break!" yelled Kyle.

"Yeah, what the fuck! Just when I was about to get my first piece of real ass!" Brad hollered.

But then we all broke out laughing, turned-on and psyched-up at our powerhouse bodies primed for action! Kyle and Brad grabbed razors and came toward me with a determined gleam in their eyes. But with me, they weren't going to get a fight. I stood motionless as a statue as they scissored off my pubic hair, shaved my groin, then started on my legs.

Having their fingers paw at my crotch, my cock, my balls, my legs – all sent spasms of pleasure through my body. Feeling them smear lather over my hairy legs nearly sent me through the ceiling! As they shaved and scissored, stroked and fondled my lower body, I let my fingers slide to my crotch, sliding my palms over my shaved skin. My meat basket was sizzling hot, as though charged with high voltage electricity. My super-long dong stuck out suggestively, and my heart beat faster, as I looked down at my smooth legs, pink belly, rounded pecs, not seeing a hair in sight.

"On your hands and knees like a dog," ordered Brad, as he roughly shoved a sopping washcloth along the length of my crack. Kneeling, crouching between my widespread legs, he soaped my ass crack, then took a razor to it. Carefully, he removed the last traces of hair from my ass and beneath my balls. I remained motionless as I felt his nose sniffing around my clean hole.

Kyle and Brad used hot washcloths to wipe away the last traces of soapy lather from my body. I had begun moaning, then begging, pleading for one of them to chomp down on my sizzling sausage and give me head.

"You guys are cruel," I yelled, but they only laughed.

Brad ran to his gym bag, pulled out an attachment which he stuck on the electric razor, and motioned toward his head. Within five minutes we had given each other crew cuts so short that our heads looked like billiard balls.

For a long, silent moment we stood staring at each other's shaved bodies. Secretly, I had feared that the shaving would cause me to feel weak, helpless, unmanly; but, in reality, I felt just the opposite. I felt strong, independent, yet bonded, to Kyle and Brad as never before. We had done something unique to one another that joined us together closer than brothers.

Standing with our legs spread wide, our balls dangling loosely, we were so full of hot spunk that we forgot the mounds of lathered hair smothered on paper towels in the bathroom; we made a mad dash for Kyle's bed, jumped on it, and began our meet right there, except it wasn't a swimming meet. It was, we agreed, a fuck-meet.

Having our body hair shaved off, even our buns and cracks, made our bodies stick together for the first several moments, but our sweaty skin provided the grease we needed for slipping onto one another, sliding, rubbing, and gliding across each other's bodies.

Although I lost track of the loads we shot, I do know that every couple of minutes groans would turn to heavy gasps, and I'd feel a torrent of hot cream shooting from me, under me, over me, on me, or in me.

When we finished playing, we lay there, completely relaxed, totally spent, yet ready to conquer the world. Maybe that's what the coach had in mind.

At the swim meet, we assured Mr. Bradshaw that we had "come out... to win!" And we did.

CAGED
John Patrick

It was one of those weekends when I had no parties to go to, no house guests, no deadlines, and, frankly, I was depressed about it. I decided to spend Saturday morning with the animals – they always seemed to cheer me up. So there I was at the zoo, standing in front of the gorge separating the humans from the lions. The lions weren't caged, exactly; they just weren't free to go. One male and one female were slumbering on fake rock ledges. Raw meat was nearby.

The sky was overcast and a light breeze carried the smell of peanuts and animal dung up my nostrils. I coughed and turned to see the peacocks making their stilted progress across the sidewalks. Just then a youth walked up and stopped a few feet away on my right. I had cruised the zoo on weekends many times but had never encountered a boy quite so enticing, in a sloppy, raw way. We immediately made eye contact and he stepped up next to me. In an up-all-night voice, he said, "What would you do if I shot that lion?" He nodded his head: he meant the male, the closer one.

"Shot it?"

"That's right."

"Gee, I don't know." Sometimes you have to humor people, pretend as if they're talking about something real. "Do you have a gun?"

"Of course I have a gun." His green eyes were fixed on the lion. "I have it in my pocket."

"I'd report you," I said. "I'd try to stop you. There are guards here. People don't shoot caged animals. You shouldn't even carry a concealed weapon, a boy your age."

"This is Cleveland," he explained.

"I know it is," I said. "But people don't shoot caged lions even in Cleveland."

"It wouldn't be that bad," he said, nodding at the lions again. "You can tell from their faces how much they want to check out."

I said I didn't think so.

He turned to look at me. His hair was brown and shaggy and his skin was so pale it seemed bleached. He was wearing an over-sized trench coat and a pair of high top sneakers and jeans with slits at the knees. He looked like a fifteen-year-old homeless person. "I don't know why you can't see it," he said. He shivered and reached into his pocket and pulled out a crumpled pack of cigarettes. "Lions are so human. Things get to 'em. They experience everything more than we do. They're so romantic." He glanced at his crushed pack of cigarettes, and in a shivering motion tossed it into the gorge. He swayed back and forth. "They just want to be loved," he said.

"Are you all right?"

"I guess. I slept here last night," he said, pointing vaguely behind him. "I was sleeping over there. Under those trees. Near the polar bears."

"Why'd you do that?"

"I wasn't alone all night." He was answering a question I hadn't even asked. "This guy, he was with me for a while ..."

"Oh." I didn't want to hear the details, yet I did.

He was really shivering now, huddling inside that long overcoat.

"Are you hungry?" I asked. "You want a hamburger?"

"I'll eat it," he said, "but only if you're buying."

We went to the snack shop and took a booth by the window. I brought him one of their giant cheeseburgers. He held it in his hands familiarly as he watched the cars passing on the street. The grease dripped out of the bun onto the plastic plate and I turned to let my gaze follow his. When I looked back, half the cheeseburger was gone. He wasn't even chewing. He even didn't look at his food. What was left of his burger he gripped in his skinny fingers.

"You're looking at me."

"Yes, I am."

"How come?"

"A person can look," I said.

"Maybe." Now he looked back. "Are you one of those creeps?"

"Which kind?"

"The kind of troll who picks up kids and drives 'em places, and, like, terrorizes 'em for days and then dumps 'em into cornfields."

"No," I said. "I'm not like that. And I'm not that old."

"That's too bad," he said with a shrug, as if he was disappointed I didn't have an adventure planned for us. "Maybe it's the accent," he said. "You don't sound American."

"I was born in England," I told him, "but I've been in this country for thirty years. I'm an American citizen."

"You've got to be born in this country to sound American," he said, sucking at his chocolate shake through a straw. He had returned to gawking at the traffic. Then he looked at me and smiled. "I guess you're okay. But, anyhow, I'm not worried because, like I told you, I've got a gun."

"Oh yeah," I said. "I'd almost forgotten about that gun in your pocket." I thought of what Mae West used to say -

"You're not a real American because you don't believe!" Then this man-child fumbled in his coat pocket and clunked down a small shiny handgun on the table, next to the plastic containers and the French fries. "So there," he said.

"Put it back," I told him. "Jesus, I hope the safety's on."

"I think so." He wiped his hand on a napkin and dropped the thing back into his pocket. "So tell me your name, Mr. Good Samaritan."

"John," I said. "What's yours?"

"I'm Jason. What do you do, English John? You must do something. You look like someone who does something."

I told him I was in advertising and began to describe my work but his eyes glazed and he cut me off.

"Oh yeah," he said, chewing his French fries with his mouth open so that I could see inside. "You try to get people to buy things they don't really need."

"Well, I think you're trying to get me to buy something I do need."

"Oh? Like what?" he asked playfully.

"A good time."

He chuckled. "Maybe."

I drove him home. He admired my dark green Jaguar XJS, the car phone, the six-speaker stereo. He gave me directions on how to get to where he was staying with a "friend." He took me down fast-food alley and then through a series of right and left ninety-degree turns on streets with bungalows covered by aluminum siding. Here, a few minutes from the airport, there were few trees, not much green at all except the lawns. "We're close," he said, nodding, as if any one of the houses would do. "You can come in."

I was going to drop him off at what he said was his driveway, but there was an old chrome-loaded Pontiac in the way, one of those vintage '50s monstrosities, its front end up on a hoist and a man working on his back on a rolling dolly underneath it. "That's my friend," Jason said. "You want to meet him?"

I parked the car and got out. The man pulled himself away from underneath the car and looked over at us. He was in his mid-thirties and was attractive in a grease-monkey sort of way. He stood up, began wiping his hands on a rag, and scowled at Jason. He wasn't going to look at me right away.

"What's this?" he asked. "What's this about, Jason?"

"This is about nothing," Jason said. "I spent the night in the zoo and this dude found me and brought me home."

"At the zoo. Jesus Christ. At the zoo again!" He turned to me at last. "Is that what happened?"

"That's where I saw him," I told him. "He looked pretty cold. I bought him something to eat."

He dropped a screwdriver I hadn't noticed he was holding. He was standing there in his driveway in a white T-shirt and grubby blue jeans next to the Pontiac, looking at Jason and me and then up at the sky. I'd had those moments too, when nothing made any sense and I didn't know what to say next. Finally he said to Jason, "Go inside and take a shower. I'm not talking to you here on the driveway."

We both watched him go into the house. He looked like an overcoat with legs.

"He thinks he's so damn smart." He said something else, but an airplane passed so low above us that I couldn't hear him.

He ended his speech by saying, "I don't know who you are but ..." and extended his hand.

"John," I said, "and I don't know who you are either."

"Earl."

When I shook his hand, I could see a fading tattoo on his forearm of a broken heart. "Well, I guess I better be going."

"No, wait. Let me thank you for bringing Jason home. Unhurt."

I nodded to show I understood.

"You know, I was awake most of the night. I didn't know what had happened to him. He does such crazy shit. Jesus Christ. The zoo. He loves the lions, you know?"

I nodded. "Yes, he certainly loves the lions."

"He'll do anything. And it isn't an act with him." He looked up and down the street, then up at a second floor window. Jason was standing there watching us. He was bare-chested and smiling.

"Jason wants you to stay," Earl said.

"Okay," I said.

On the way up to the house, Earl said, "I don't know what I'm gonna do. Here I have this cute young lover who goes off to the zoo and spends the night and that's his idea of a good time." A light rain had started to fall. He glanced up at the sky. "You want a beer?"

It was eleven o'clock in the morning. "Sure," I said.

We sat in silence on Earl's cluttered back porch. We sipped our beers and watched the rain fall on the crabgrass. My morning gloom was on its way out. It wasn't lifting so much as converting into something else, as it does when you're in someone else's house, going with the flow. I didn't want to leave as long as I felt that way.

His quick shower had perked Jason up. He was getting more and more playful. His robe would fall carelessly so I could get a glimpse of thigh, then cock and balls, resting. He was a little temptress. Earl was oblivious to the show; he sat next to Jason on the aluminum-framed settee talking about all the work he had to do on his car that day and now it was raining. I smiled at Jason and he smiled back, swinging the robe back up, covering himself again. Earl asked me if I ever had much to do with "bad kids" – that was his phrase – and I said that sometimes I did. He put his arm around Jason, the first sign of affection I'd seen. I decided Earl was rather handsome in the details, and when he looked at Jason his eyes sparkled, his love large and naked and obvious.

"Well, then you know how hard it is to keep 'em occupied," Earl went on. "You gotta keep 'em occupied or they run off to the zoo and spend the night."

"I only spent the night in the zoo once," Jason spat. "And besides, I was protected."

"Protected?"

"You know, protected." Jason pointed his index finger at his lover with his thumb in the air and the other fingers pulled back, and he made an explosive sound in his mouth.

"You took that?" Earl said. "You took that to the zoo?"

Jason shrugged. At this particular moment, Earl turned to me. "John, did you see it?"

I assumed he meant the gun. I nodded. I was so involved watching Jason I didn't want my fantasies disturbed.

"He always said I should watch out for myself," Jason said to me, bringing the beer can to his lips, "now listen to him."

"Not with a gun," Earl said.

"You showed me how to use it," Jason said loudly. "You didn't want me to be ignorant about firearms."

"That was just information," Earl said. "It wasn't for you to use." His face was tightening up, his flesh stiff, but he didn't know how to go on, the right choice for the next word.

Jason finished his beer, belched, and then ran into the house. Seeing him in flight did something to me, and I knew I had to either follow him or get the hell out of there.

I glanced at Earl. He was shaking his head, gazing out into the backyard. The rain was coming down hard now.

"Have to go, Earl," I said. Everything about me was getting just a little bit out of control, and I thought I had better get home.

"You're going?" Earl said, trying to concentrate on me for a moment. "You're going now? You're sure you don't want another beer?"

"I'm sure."

"But, John," he said, looking at me, his right eyebrow going up, "you know where Jason is right now?"

I glanced into the house. "No."

"He's in bed, waiting for you."

"No, I couldn't."

"You've come this far, you might as well give him what he wants."

"But ..."

He had a wearisome look in his big brown eyes. He'd been at this point many times I imagined. "It's the only way I can keep him," he said.

I turned and again looked into the dark cavern of the house.

"It's the first bedroom at the top of the stairs. Don't mind the mess. You know how teenage boys are. Messy and everything."

"Yes, I know."

It was as if I had been placed under some strange spell. I wanted to go, at least to see what was waiting for me in the upstairs bedroom. As I started to move towards the door, Earl's hand touched my thigh. "Do you mind if I join you in a few minutes?"

I looked down into his face, smudged with grease. He was a pleasant man, in his way. I wouldn't have picked him as a sex partner but, no, I wouldn't mind if he came in. "No," I said without hesitation.

The bedroom door was partially open. Jason was laying on his stomach in the middle of the bed. He had pulled the shades but even in the dim light I could tell he was naked. He began to undulate his hips when he heard me push the door completely open. I stepped over the bathrobe he had carelessly dropped on the floor and went to the rumpled, filthy bed. I caressed the hairless, plump ass cheeks. It was a sublime ass.

"It'll be okay," Jason murmured. "Earl just likes to watch."

I quickly undressed and Jason made room for me on the bed. We began slowly, stroking each other's erections. He had a nice, cut cock about six inches long.

"Oh, yeah," he said, holding up my cock. "This must be eight inches at least."

"I guess."

"Does that feel good?" he asked after a few moments of feverishly jerking me.

"Oh, yes. Yes," I said as desire for him washed over me.

"Then fuck me."

"First get it ready ..." At first he refused to put the slippery head of my cock into his mouth, content to lick up and down its length, so I grabbed him under the chin and rubbed my wet cock all over his smooth cheeks. He gagged when I pried open his jaw and pushed my cock in, but he drew his lips tight around it, applying a suction that was painful in its intensity.

He sucked my cock contentedly for awhile, then withdrew it, spreading the glossy pre-cum up and down the shaft, before kissing the tender pink head.

Finally he rolled over on his stomach and, kneeling in front of his ass cheeks, I ran my fingers along his sweaty ass crack and felt his pink pucker twitching. He handed me a tube of K-Y. I applied some lube to my cock as I leaned down and kissed his ass. He bent forward slightly and I pressed my cockhead against his hole. He bucked back onto me, and with a little gentle prodding, my cockhead slipped inside him. He clamped down on my erection while I reached under him and squeezed his tits. Soon he began whimpering, his asshole spasming around my cock. I bit into his shoulder, holding his hips and grinding his ass down on my pubic bone.

I heard the door close. Earl stood leaning against a KISS poster thumb-tacked on the wall. He had removed his T-shirt, revealing a sculpted chest with a veil of black hair. His jeans were open and he pulled out his erection. It was about the same length as mine, but thicker. Wet with a dab of pre-cum, it was so hard it must have hurt.

I pulled out of Jason until just the head was caught by that quivering anus, letting Earl see, and then sent it in again. Jason was so tight it was like a fist around it, only better.

Jason turned and looked at his lover. Earl stepped over to the bed and soon Jason was slurping the oozing precum off his cock, giving it a good tonguing, then sliding his mouth down the shaft. Earl's eyes alternated between watching my cock fucking Jason's ass and his cock fucking Jason's mouth.

After awhile, Earl's hands came to Jason's head and stopped him. He got the K-Y and lubed up his cock, then crawled over me. He didn't waste any time, didn't use any foreplay, just positioned himself over me and drove his cock into me. I cried out with the jolt but I continued fucking Jason. Earl's thrusting was expert; he gave me the full length, pulled it out, gave it to me again and again. I captured his hard-driving rhythm as I fucked his lover. Earl's balls banged against mine each time he was in me fully, and soon Jason was getting off on it, moaning and jerking his cock. Jason tightened his muscles around my cock as he exploded and, hearing him, Earl grabbed my shoulders and came in my ass. Between them, I felt like I was caught in a vise.

Panting, Earl pulled out and padded out of the room, slamming the door behind him. I remained in Jason's ass while the boy maneuvered himself onto his back. I lifted his legs over my shoulders and shoved my cock in to the hilt.

He kissed my cheek, then brought his lips to mine. We kissed deeply as I felt the tension build inside me, then burst with tingling waves that seemed to electrify even my fingertips. It was a memorable orgasm. We lay naked, pressed together, my cock softening inside him.

At last he smiled, "This is better than getting drunk."

"It'll feel better in the morning too."

He sighed. "Will it?"

# # # # #

I didn't think I'd hear from Earl or Jason again, but about a week later when I returned from a business trip there was a message on my machine. I called Earl right away.

"I found his diary," Earl said. "How was I to know he had a diary? He never told me."

"They often don't, Earl. Was it locked?"

"What?"

"Locked. Sometimes diaries have locks."

"Well, this one didn't."

"Sounds as though you read it."

Earl was silent. I decided not to get ahead of him again. Finally he said, "I thought that maybe I shouldn't read it, but then I did."

"How much? How much of it did you read, Earl?"

"All of it," he said.

"It must be hard, reading your lover's diary," I said. "And not right, if you know what I mean."

"It's hard, but not the way you think." He took a deep breath. "I don't mind the talk about fucking other guys. You can wish it won't happen, but it does. You know what I'm saying?"

"Yes, I do, Earl."

"He's very aggressive. Very aggressive. The things he does. You sort of wonder if you should believe it."

"Diaries are often fantasies. You really shouldn't be reading your lover's diary at all. It's his, Earl. He's writing for himself, not for you."

"He writes about me, sometimes."

"You shouldn't read it, Earl." I felt my anger rising, as usual. I was like my father in that respect. My mother, who was from Brighton, used to say to me, "Watch your tongue in front of these people." "These people" always meant "these Americans." Among them was my father, who had been born in Cleveland and who had married Mother after the war. "Your father," my mother said, "has the temper of a savage." Mother always thought that anger was peculiar to Americans.

"I can't help reading it," Earl went on. "A person starts prying, he can't stop."

"You shouldn't be reading it."

"You haven't heard what I'm about to say," Earl told me. "It's why I'm calling you. It's what he says."

"What's that?" I asked him.

"Not what I expected," he said. "He pities me."

"Well," I said.

"Well is right." He took another breath. "First he says he loves me. That was shock number one. Then he says he feels sorry for me. That was shock number two. He feels sorry for me because I work on the line at the engine plant and I drink a six-pack a day and I live in this dump. Where does he get off? That's what I'd like to know. He feels sorry for me! My God, I always hated people feeling sorry for me. I don't drive a Jaguar with a phone in it but I do all right."

"Sure you do, Earl."

"I could never stand it. I never wanted anybody on earth pitying me, and now here's this punk doing it."

"Earl, put that diary away."

"I hear you," he said.

"By the way, what did you do with his gun?"

"I threw it in Lake Erie."

"Sure you did," I said.

"Well, anyway, thanks for listening, John." Then he hung up.

Earl called me a few more times after that, in irate puzzlement over Jason. Each time I thought he was going to tell me something new about the boy, or invite me back for a re-run, but he didn't.

When Earl called for the last time, he apologized for bringing me to the phone on Memorial Day. I said it was okay, that I didn't mind, although I did mind, in fact. "He's gone. Been gone for a week now," Earl said.

"I'm sorry to hear that."

Earl raged on and on. Finally he begged, "If you see him, John, please call me."

"I haven't been to the zoo lately, Earl. Why don't you try there?"

"Maybe I will."

"You never know, Earl."

After I dropped the phone back in its cradle, I turned to the naked boy reclining next to me on the bed and said, "You can put that silly gun away now, Jason. I said exactly what you wanted me to say."

About the Editor

JOHN PATRICK was a prolific, prize-winning author of fiction and non-fiction. One of his short stories, "The Well," was honored by PEN American Center as one of the best of 1987. His novels and anthologies, as well as his non-fiction works, including Legends and The Best of the Superstars series, continue to gain him new fans every day. One of his most famous short stories appears in the Badboy collection Southern Comfort and another appears in the collection The Mammoth Book of Gay Short Stories.

A divorced father of two, the author was a longtime member of the American Booksellers Association, the Publishing Triangle, the Florida Publishers' Association, American Civil Liberties Union, and the Adult Video Association. He lived in Florida, where he passed away on October 31, 2001.

HOTHOUSE
BACKROOM
.COM

Join today and get instant access to:

- 1st Run Hot House Movies
- Backroom Exclusive Videos
- 100s of Hot House Scenes
- Free BelAmi Bonus Content
- Thousands of XXX Hardcore Pictures
- Premium Member Discounts on DVDs

Hot House Exclusive
TONY MECELLI

g any underwear. "Excuse me," I said, having a hard time looking

ed by that bulge in his crotch, "but don't I know you?" "Maybe,"

of t   bout a m

Ray   God, you

er?   in?" he a

'Lik   s stronges

ody   e on Gree

he l   I ever sa

to t   any ideas

king   he same

coul   ery long

rac   me swell.

with   e in store

go c   behind s

ee u   in public

' he   vent to th

cy.   grabbed

d. I

raci   t, so firm

t, ha

h my   bing dicl

ng, I   n cock, b

ound of unzipping filled the small space. I don't know who's hand

t before I knew it, I had his rod in my hand, and mine was in his. '

do?" he asked, his tone challenging. I knew exactly, and sank to

LOOKING FOR

MORE HOT STORIES?

WOULD **YOU** LIKE TO **CONTRIBUTE**
TO AN **UPCOMING ANTHOLOGY?**

VISIT
http://www.STARbooksPress.com

Hot Deals!

Subscribe to Our FREE E-mail Newsletter!

Submission Guidelines for Authors!

Buy Books and E-books Online!

VISIT
http://www.STARbooksPress.com
TODAY!

www.ingramcontent.com/pod-product-compliance
Lightning Source LLC
Chambersburg PA
CBHW031114030726
47496CB00002BA/542